WE ARE TOTEN
(Book 1 of the Toter

C HARRISON

Alien Noise Corporation

Hi Alisha
Thanks for taking the
time to read the book.
Hope you enjoy it.
The theme of the story asks
'if you could live your
life again what would
you do differently?'
A question I think a lot
of readers would be
interested in.

Chris Harrison

We Are Toten Herzen

Published by Alien Noise Corporation
copyright 2013 C Harrison

ALSO BY THE AUTHOR

Toten Herzen Malandanti
Who Among Us...
The One Rule of Magic
There Will Be Blood
The Fine Art of Necromancy
Lords of Misrule
Behind the Wall

We Are Toten Herzen

We Are Toten Herzen

by
C Harrison

We Are Toten Herzen

Discover the truth about Toten Herzen and the Malandanti at

TOTENUNIVERSE.COM

Features, interviews, shorts stories, a collection of articles introducing the characters in more detail, filling the gaps between novels and expanding on events and subjects featured in the books.

TOTEN HERZEN ARE:

Susan Bekker - Lead guitar
Born, Susan Johanna Bekker, Rotterdam, 1951

Dee Vincent - Vocals, rhythm guitar
Born, Denise Leslie Vincent, Lincoln, 1953

Elaine Daley - Bass guitar
Born, Elaine Daley, Lincoln, 1950

Rene V - Drums
Born, Rene van Voors, Rotterdam, 1952

Peter Miles - Rhythm guitar (disputed)
Born, Peter Miles, Ipswich, 1953 - 1973

ALBUMS

Pass on By 1973
We Are Toten Herzen 1974
Nocturn 1975
Black Rose 1976
Dead Hearts Live 1976
Staying Alive (unfinished) 1977

FORMATION, DESTRUCTION AND RETURN

Toten Herzen were formed in 1973 when Suffolk based rock
promoter and scrap metal merchant Micky Redwall put the band
together following a gig at Hooly Goolys in Ipswich. Bekker and

5

van Voors' original band was After Sunset from Holland, whilst Vincent and Daley came from the British band Cat's Cradle.

Between 1973 and 1976 Toten Herzen sold over eight million albums, but their success was cut short on the night of March 21st 1977 when all four members were murdered by Lenny Harper. Harper was never charged and the band disappeared for thirty years until they were found by Rob Wallet, a British music journalist, and persuaded to make a comeback.

This is the first part of the story of their comeback.

PART 1: SALVATION

1 - The builders are in

Three men struggled to carry one body. Weight wasn't the issue, the corpse was, according to Ronnie the Peeler, small enough to fit in his inside pocket. No, it was the narrowness of the steps dropping into a mouldering basement that caused the anxiety and Elmer, doubling at the knees to fit his lanky frame beneath the low door, complained the loudest.

"It's all right for you two, I've got the 'ed."

"What's wrong with that?" said Ronnie.

"It keeps, you know, nudging me groin."

"She was the lead singer, she won't mind."

"What's that got to do with it?"

Cynics would say it wouldn't matter if they dropped the body now and again, but Ronnie was a professional, didn't like to do things by half and when he said he'd dispose of your embarrassing waste you knew it would be in a safe pair of hands. After ten minutes of how's your father, the three manhandlers set foot on the floor of the basement. Elmer blushed one last time and turned ninety degrees to lower the body next to the other three.

"Hang on, that's not right." Johnny Smith took a sheet of paper out of his back pocket and prodded it. "She's supposed to be in the middle, next to the punk."

"Right, get on with it then." Ronnie and Elmer dragged the lead singer next to the wall, pulled the drummer fourteen inches to the left, pulled the guitarist alongside him and finished off the arrangement by lowering the singer into the new gap.

"Don't see what difference it makes. Not exactly a pleasing composition. I mean, look at her, she's nearly half the height of the other one."

Smith sniffed and coughed up some of the cement dust circulating in the stifling atmosphere. Up above, London roared, made its usual din necessary to conceal the hammering and banging, the pneumatic cacophany of subterranean construction work. Excavating basements, extending basements, subdividing basements, bricking up basements. A universe of cyclists and pedestrians, bus passengers, taxi drivers, harrassed, lost, clueless, ditherers, all oblivious to Ronnie the Peeler's waste disposal service, no questions asked.

"I think we're done, gentlemen."

"No, we're not." Smith looked beyond Ronnie's shoulder to the top of the steps where a strange man stood watching them. "Can we help you?"

The man hesitated. "Well," he laughed as if he couldn't think of any other reaction, "I've got a feeling I'm too late."

"Too late for what?" said Ronnie. "You're interrupting."

"Sorry. I was supposed to meet. . . ."

"Yes."

"Sorry, is that Susan Bekker?" His curiosity made Ronnie sweat.

"Which one?"

"The tall one, next to Rene van Voors. What's she doing down there?"

"Late night," said Smith. He rubbed his gloved hands with a bundle of tissue paper. "You know the Dutch. Drink like fish when you put free booze in front of them."

"Coffins arrive tomorrow," said Ronnie. "Always looks better when they're in their coffins." Ronnie didn't need telling his gold tooth never reassured anyone when he tried to pass them off. The man at the top of the steps made no effort to leave.

"You're not the manager, are you?" said Smith.

"No, I was supposed to be interviewing them."

"Journalist." The penny dropped. Ronnie winked at Elmer. "You're that Rob Wallet geezer, aren't you?"

The man held his breath. "Yeah."

"Didn't know you were Irish?"

"Yeah. Dublin. When will they be in a fit state to talk? Or is that a stupid question?"

So far, the conversation had taken place over a height of seven feet. The man, Rob Wallet from Dublin, talking from on high, Ronnie, Smith and Elmer down below, fidgety and eager to return to sunlight and a van full of breeze blocks.

"Let me make a quick phone call," said Ronnie. "Why don't you go through to the kitchen."

Ronnie made the call. Ronnie listened and nodded to the instructions. Wallet wasn't meant to be there. Wallet had vanished, in fact someone, someone with too much knowledge, someone who had been in hiding for thirty years and had chosen now to creep out from their tombstones, had spirited Wallet away to a clandestine location. By the end of the one sided conversation Ronnie had to hold the phone away from his ear.

"Didn't sound too 'appy," said Elmer.

"No, they're not. They are most displeased, to use the vernacular." Ronnie sucked in his cheeks and forced his chin against his chest. "We're going to need the bow saw, gentlemen. Mr Wallet up there is telling porkies."

Like Old King Cole's men they marched up to the top of the steps into a gutted hallway. Ronnie locked the door to the basement and scratched his throat. Without soft furnishings the interior of the house repeated everything that was said. Ronnie leaned towards Smith's ear. "We're to make it gruesome, apparently. Make it look frenetic."

"Frenetic?"

"Not frenetic, frenzied. Like a psycho done it or a monster. We can do it here and then decorate over the mess. Chuck the bits and pieces in the Thames near Millennium Bridge. Once he washes up it'll all make sense." With the delicate details out of the way Ronnie raised his voice. "Another victim of the Toten Herzen curse."

Next to a stack of plasterboard, a lump hammer waited to enter the drama, a solid object and Ronnie's weapon of choice when he needed a quick result. The hammer fitted the front pocket of his coveralls. In the kitchen, the Irish man had helped himself to a brew.

"Make yourself at home," said Ronnie. Smith and Elmer loitered in the hallway. "What's the matter? That wall's not going to brick itself up, is it? Bring the stuff in."

Ronnie waited for the front door to close, but his colleagues were born in barns, left it wide open for the inquisative street noise to intrude. "Mr Wallet," he tapped the boiler unit with the hammer, "remind me, you came here to speak to them?"

"Yeah. Find out what all the fuss is about, what are they doing." The man added the last brown sugar lump to his tea. "Why do four septuagenarians want to make a comeback now?"

"Septuagenarians? They're not in their seventies."

"That lot down there aren't in their seventies, no."

"No, I don't mean that. Toten Herzen are in their sixties. That makes them sexagenarians. No wonder your journalism career went down the toilet."

"Whatever. They don't look in their sixties. Who are they?"

"I don't know, do I? I'm just told to take care of them. And if you were Rob Wallet you'd know all that, wouldn't you, Mr Wallet? The man who allegedly discovered them alive."

The man didn't have time to finish his tea. When Ronnie finished hammering and banging he got to work with the saw. Smith and Elmer whistled in competition with each other until Smith, who was the more tuneful, prevailed, a combination of lung power and perseverence. Leaving Elmer to mix the first batch of cement, Smith stood at the door to the bathroom.

"You should have waited a few hours. Let the bood thicken a bit."

"Yeah, it'll be all right. I thought I could mix it with the mortar for the flooring. Look nice with those terracotta tiles we're using. Bit of contrast, you know."

"There was something bothering me a bit. The gases."

"The what?" Ronnie had to concentrate going through the thigh bone. "Give us a minute, Johnny, lot of arteries in the legs."

When the sawing was done Ronnie turned around. He had blood on his chin. "Gases?"

"Yeah. They've not been embalmed have they?"

"Embalmed? They're not mummies. Anyway, that's someone else's problem."

"Yeah, but, it's like an oven down there and once it's bricked up, no circulation or anything, the gases might, you know, build up. Explode."

Ready to work on the other leg, Ronnie tutted and shook his head. "You don't unerstand the human body, Johnny. You should watch CSI Miami. You might learn something." He pointed the bow saw at Smith. "They're not wales. Yeah, they'll bloat a bit, but you're talking about them like they're twenty kilos of Semtex. They won't blow up. Get the brickwork done and the plasterboard up. For Christ's sake we've got the plumbers coming in tomorrow."

2 - Discussions of death

No one spoke on the fourth floor of Gillard House in south London. Staff at the headquarters of Gillard Publishing were in shock at the news of one of their own, music critic Mike Gannon, being brutally murdered four days earlier. Gannon's editor Chris Sparios from Pucker Up magazine was in a crisis meeting with several members of the board of directors. They wanted to know, just to be clear on things, (investors were asking) if Gannon had brought on the attack by his own conduct.

"You mean shouldn't he have kept his mouth shut?" said Sparios.

"He criticised the band in no uncertain terms and we want your opinion on whether he went beyond what is, let's say, responsible journalism. People are getting more sensitive to these things, Chris."

"Mike was always outspoken," said Sparios. "That's what made him a popular critic. That's why you hired him. His work was syndicated all over Europe. You can't expect to muzzle someone like that. He didn't libel anyone. And you know the rules: if you can't take the stick don't join a rock band. You wanted him and his provocative style so long as none of it poisoned your own reputation."

"Not exactly the sort of people you'd want to upset though." The finance director read from a memo: "Band members suspected of killing their own manager, suspected of killing the head of their own record label, suspected of killing the person suspected of killing them!"

"It's all a load of bollocks," laughed Sparios. "It's publicity. For Christ's sake they were a wild rock band who are now a bunch of sixty year olds wanting to make a comeback. For all we know Mike's probably sitting in the bar of a five star hotel in Hampshire while we sit here fretting about his alleged brutal murder."

The finance director placed his memo carefully on the table. "Mike Gannon is lying in a mortuary in south London. To be more precise, Mike Gannon's dismembered remains are lying in a mortuary in south London. Mike Gannon is dead, Chris, and Toten Herzen's long blood-soaked history has just added another victim. And can I just add," he repositioned himself in his chair, "that Gillard Publishing can consider itself collateral damage in all this."

"Advertisers pulling out?" said Sparios.

"On the contrary, we think revenues might actually increase in the short term, but in the longer term we don't want clients advertising in our magazines who specialise in chainsaws and body bags."

-

A wall mounted screen in the reception area was streaming a live feed from the BBC. The calm of Cromwell Road in Hounslow had been interrupted by a mass of camera wielding bodies fighting for space as a solitary figure was led from his flat to a police van. In the pushing and shoving strobe flashes lit up the evening, but none of them caught the features of the man under arrest. Fifteen minutes later he was in a secure room at an undisclosed police location.

BBC News 24

"Police have arrested a man in connection with the murder of music critic Mike Gannon. The Metropolitan Police refused to name the suspect, but did say a 46 year old man was helping them with their enquiries. The man is believed to be Rob Wallet, publicist of the rock band Toten Herzen who recently announced plans for a comeback. Rob Wallet is also wanted under a European arrest warrant as a suspect in the murder of a British man, Leonard Harper, who was found dead in Germany in March earlier this year."

3 - Helping the police

Back in 1977, not long after Toten Herzen had been murdered, a young boy sat in the office of his school's deputy headmistress. He wasn't expecting the cane, but he wasn't in line for an award either. Having loosened the tops of fifteen vinegar bottles he was in deep shit for ruining over a dozen school meals, including a plate of roast pork and chips about to be eaten by a maths teacher. The boy was summoned, made to wait, admonished by Mrs Baxter and her magnificent bouffant hairstyle and given detention. The tampering of the bottles didn't quite go down in the folklore of the school, but for several days the boy was a hero amongst his closest mates.

Not so now. Rob Wallet looked back on that innocent time and felt a slight feeling of regret that he didn't appreciate it more. For as long as he could remember Wallet had told anyone born after 1979 that the seventies were the lost years of civilisation; the decade was a social and cultural black hole swallowing anything that might one day be considered enlightening. There was no avoiding the smothering sepias and ochres, and when their time was up they were replaced by the even more soul destroying magnolia. It was a time of FA Cup confrontations across windswept mud baths and brainwashed teenagers in tank tops dancing to Living Next Door to Alice on Top of the Pops. After the power cuts the lights would come back on and the carnage of another IRA atrocity made itself apparent. The Sweeney always got their villain, usually because the villains were trying to escape in cars made by British Leyland.

But incarceration changes a man. Slumped on an uncomfortable plastic chair, he sat in a glowing white police interview room alone with his juvenile thoughts. Wallet remembered a time when coming home from school meant holding his own FA Cup fixtures on his Subbuteo pitch, played by two teams with three meticulously painted Adidas stripes down their sleeves. The miniature Tango footballs were the closest he'd ever get to owning one of those spectacular black and white footballs they used in the '74 World Cup finals. He saw British Leyland cars at the first Motor Show at the NEC in 1977 (six months after Toten Herzen had been murdered); they were shiny, rust free and were almost as tempting as the Panther 6 and Saab Turbo. Curly Wurlys and Haunted House, a Revell Space Shuttle on the back of a Jumbo Jet and too many packs of Top Trumps. Maybe he was wrong about the seventies. Van der Valk, Jeux sans Frontiers, Fawlty Towers on a Tuesday night after Pot Black. Wallet started to make a mental list of stuff he was going to find and collect when the police let him go.

The door rattled, stuck in its frame, and then blew open. "Don't you have any better chairs than these?" said Wallet to DI Toker, the arresting officer.

"We don't want you settling down," said Toker. He placed an A4 size photograph on the table and sat down.

"Lovely. What's that got to do with me?"

"Well, I think you should look at it again, Mr Wallet, because I think you know what happened to the man in that photograph."

The man was Mike Gannon. "You knew Mike Gannon, didn't you?"

"Of course I knew him. Before I started working with Toten Herzen we were both music journalists. Well, he was a music critic, so strictly speaking not a proper journalist, a sort of pretend journalist actually, but yeah, I knew him. If there were any parties or celebrations the minute he walked in the place would empty."

"Really," said Toker. "I've heard he was very popular."

Wallet tutted. "Having a girlfriend isn't enough to describe yourself as popular. Gannon was a first class twat. Whoever writes his obituary will be a better writer than me. I suppose you could praise him by saying he wasn't as bad as Adolf Hitler."

"Really?"

"Well, at least Hitler had a go at painting. Gannon had no artistic flair whatsoever. He was born to be a critic. Nearly everyone in the music industry had an excuse to kill him and quite a few outside it too."

"Hated him enough to do this?" Toker held up the grisly photo.

"Have you found my DNA at the scene of this crime? Any evidence at all? If you ask me body piercing's a mug's game."

"Yeah," said Toker. "Lots of people seem to die in ugly ways where you're concerned. Micky Redwall, Lenny Harper, now this." Toker sat back with his hands in his pockets.

"That's three, and I'd be about twelve years old for one of them."

"Granted Redwall's death was too early for you, but Lenny Harper in Germany. There wasn't much left of him either."

"That's not what I heard."

"You were the last person to see Harper alive according to the police in Germany. You show up at a motel near Obergrau and a few days later you're on the ferry home and Lenny Harper's dead in his back garden. You don't have an alibi for last Monday."

"Ask the other members of the band. I was with them."

"And where will I find them?"

"I don't know. They don't tell me everything. It's a bit frustrating at times."

"I know the feeling." Toker sat forward again and took a pen out of his inside pocket. "They weren't at your flat."

"I went back to organise some things. I'm moving out to Europe with them and needed to arrange the shipment of some stuff, storage of some other things. . . ."

"What were they doing in London?"

"There were legal issues over publishing rights, mechanical rights and they came to collect the master tapes of their albums. They were based in England before they moved to Europe. If they're gonna make a comeback they need all the legalities to be in place and they need to get the master tapes before someone else gets them."

Toker was satisfied with the answers, but he wasn't going to go soft just yet. He chewed the end of his pen as he listened to Wallet speak. "If you are innocent why don't they walk into the station and verify your whereabouts for last Monday?"

"That's not how they work. They won't just turn up like that."

"Why not?"

Wallet looked Toker right in the eye. "Because they're vampires."

-

Outside the interview room, seeking comfort in a cig, Toker found himself surprised by his reaction to Wallet's menacing expression.

He was over-familiar with the audacity and cockiness of some of the people he'd met in that room, seasoned criminals, legal experts, others knowing that a deal would soon be on the table, but Wallet? Wallet was a muso, a hack, where was his self-confidence coming from? Toker needed two cigarettes before he was ready to go back in, but only after commandeering DI Evan Silvers for some post-nicotine support.

"Oh, this isn't good cop bad cop, is it?" said Wallet.

"No," said Toker. "This is DI Evan Silvers. I want him here as a witness when you start answering my questions."

"Why no tape recorder?"

"You don't need one."

"Why not?"

"Because you're not like other people." Toker couldn't stop adjusting his coat, crossing his legs, rubbing his nicotine stained fingers. "Don't believe everything you see on those daytime tv programmes."

"Okay. Okay, Susan did it."

"Susan?"

"Susan did it all."

"Susan who?" said Toker.

"Bekker. Susan Bekker."

Toker studied Wallet's body language; he didn't seem that uncomfortable on the chair, slouching at a casual angle towards his questioners. "Go on."

"Well," said Wallet, "based on what she told me it went something like this."

-

Obergrau was smothered by one of its regular cloud invasions.

We Are Toten Herzen

When the mist was blown in by a strong wind the village would appear and disappear, but the locals had become accustomed to losing their orientation and relied on instinct to get about. Then the mist would lift and the world around them would re-emerge, familiar and reassuring, with everything exactly where it was before it had vanished.

Lenny Harper looked through the window of his small kitchen, but the view was only as far as the thickness of the glass. He could just see his own pale hazy reflection like a watermark. His drawn, tired eyes stared back at him with equal weariness and his mouth drooped, pulled down by the aged excess of flesh draped over his jaws.

But he was not alone.

Susan Bekker announced herself. She had travelled under the cover of the cloud, so thick and dense it was blocking out direct sunlight. Lenny was astonished to meet her so early in the day.

"I couldn't sleep," she said.

"Can I do anything for you?" Lenny was worried.

"No. And that's the reason I'm here," said Susan. "You look tired, Lenny. You look like you're past it."

"I have to admit life in these mountains doesn't get any easier." He sat down at his kitchen table and swirled around the dregs of his coffee cup. "Maybe I'll survive one more summer, but next winter is going to be a hard one."

"Are you expecting sympathy?"

"No. I've come to expect anything but. Are you ever going to let me leave here?"

"Oh, someday. In one form or another. Don't forget the reason you're here." Susan joined him at the table. "Truth is, Lenny, I'm as bored as you are living up on this mountain and now this opportunity has come our way."

21

Lenny knew what she was referring to. "Have you turned him?"

"Yeah. He seems to have reacted to it okay. Suppose he had a bit of time to think about it. He wouldn't have come otherwise."

"And he knows the deal? He knows what he's letting himself in for?"

"Maybe." Susan thought a moment. She picked up the sugar bowl, dipped her little finger in it and sucked off the sugar coating. "But it's not really my concern what he knows or thinks he's knows. But we can say your days are done here. We don't need you any more, Lenny."

Lenny put his head in his hands. "Is this going to hurt?"

"Twenty years ago definitely, ten years ago maybe, but, I don't know. I don't think I have the energy any more to make you suffer for what you did."

With enormous effort Lenny lifted himself off the chair. "Give me a moment." He left Susan alone with the sugar bowl. She examined the spartan little kitchen with its wall clock, stopped at six forty, the surface of the cooker stained with baked gravy and food remnants, an upturned mug on the sink, half finished loaf of bread, and what was once a rectangular block of butter was now reduced to a greasy smear of yellow slime on a small saucer. An attempt had been made to decorate, but the painting had been abandoned half way along the wall where the extractor fan had proved too much of an obstacle to persevere. Was death preferable to this? Was Lenny Harper any more alive in this kitchen than he would be in a grave where he would be unaware of the limits of his existence? Everyday he would come downstairs to this mess, this confinement, with its view of the birch trees when the mist allowed and another tasteless meal, another cup of over-sweet coffee.

Shuffling footsteps gave Lenny away as he appeared with a long Samurai sword. "I bought this in Munich eight years ago," he said almost proudly. "It isn't genuine Samurai, but I've always kept it sharp in case I ever needed it."

"For what?"

"For a day like this." Lenny looked at the blade, running his right thumb ever so gently along its edge. Susan took another fingertip of sugar from the bowl. "If you swing it correctly I shouldn't feel a thing." Lenny knelt down as he spoke.

"There isn't room in here to swing a cat, Lenny, let alone a three foot long Samurai sword. Come outside."

Lenny handed the sword to Susan and unlocked the back door. Outside he moved far enough away from the house and knelt down again. The ground was cold against his knees and the cool floating mist stung his face. Susan was barely visible in front of him.

"Hold your head up," she said. Lenny looked to the sky with eyes closed.

"Consider this a favour, Lenny. Your first and your last." And Susan swung the blade.

-

"So don't give me any bullshit about Lenny Harper being a mess, unless the wolves got him," said Wallet as Silvers studied a photo of Lenny's headless body lying face down in a light layer of snow at the back of his small mountain home.

"And can you testify in court that Susan Bekker killed him?"

"Course not."

"Course not, no. So we've just got the murder of Mike Gannon for now. That's still good enough to put you away."

"You can't put me at the scene any more than you can put DI Silvers there. The CPS don't prosecute on a hunch. They don't watch daytime tv programmes either."

Silvers tried to compose himself with a swift flattening of his jacket before asking: "Why did Susan Bekker kill Lenny Harper?"

"She'd finished with him. They all had. I'd come along and they had someone younger to feed on, someone who could get them back into the music business and Susan Bekker was ready to make a comeback. She was crawling the walls up there on that mountainside."

"Hang on, hang on. You're talking about this like it's all perfectly normal," said Toker.

"What do you mean, feed on?" asked Silvers disgusted.

"The four of them," said Toker, "used Harper to bring them blood, now they use Mr Wallet here. Is that a fair summary?"

"Close enough."

"Fuck off! You're not vampires. Just stop the act now, Mr Wallet. I don't know what the fuck you are, but you're not fucking vampires." Toker stood up, his chair went flying. "I'm going for a smoke."

"Bad for you," said Wallet. "You feel safe in here on your own with me, DI Silvers?"

The two men remained in the room for several minutes, separated by an awkward silence. Both of them were alerted by a commotion in the corridor before Toker came back in a state of anger and disbelief.

"Get lost Wallet," he said gathering up all the crime scene photos.

"DI Silvers was looking at them," said Wallet.

"Well he can have a look at some new ones."

"What's wrong?" said Silvers.

"There's been four more. Last ten minutes right across London."
Silvers watched nervously as Toker rolled up the photographs. Rob Wallet stood up and stretched. "Don't leave the country," Silvers said as Wallet stepped past him.

"Or you'll do what?"

Wallet quietly collected his belongings from the desk in reception: money, the keys to his flat and a phone. He stepped outside and said hello to the constellations visible through the gaps in the dark settled clouds. Draco was visible, as always, watching and waiting. Up there, somewhere, the others were travelling this way and that, unseen and with barely a whisper. He wasn't sure yet how they did it and he hadn't been let in on the secret. He wasn't trusted with the power. They could move as they wished through the infinite vacuum, but Wallet, well, he still had to travel by taxi.

4 - All over the papers

Twenty four hours had passed since Wallet had slipped away from the police station without fanfare or publicity thanks to the secrecy and embarrassment of his arrest. The investigation that had been a sure fire result was upside down and Interpol had been put on hold. Now he was at the Cromwell Hotel reading the modest reports of his release and why the police had been forced to let him go.

Perched on an arse-numbing chair and watched over for five hours, left alone for only six or seven minutes, there was no way he could have left the interview room, visit four more music critics spread across London and kill them all in the time it took Toker to smoke a couple of cigarettes. All the papers were now running page after page of lurid details and sickening conjectures of the night's events.

The Times announcement read: *Toten Herzen manager released after multiple murders. Rob Wallet, the man behind the comeback of the 70s rock band Toten Herzen, was last night released by the Metropolitan Police after four more music critics were found murdered across London. A spokesperson said the Met had no option but to release Wallet. The statement did reveal that the murders did not follow the same pattern as that carried out on*

Mike Gannon. The spokesperson went on to say that the charge against Wallet for the murder of Gannon will now be dropped.

The Daily Mail included an article on other music critics 'going underground' to avoid becoming the next victim. The Mail had arranged for its own critics to receive security surveillance until the murderer or murderers were caught.

The Independent had a map of London and a time-line of events with the location of each attack indicated by an explosion symbol!

6.09 pm Police are called to an address in Southwark. Officers find the body of sixty two year old Andreas Buscher on his own doorstep.

6.11 pm Neighbours alert police after a pedestrian is hit by the body of Martha Croft, aged sixty-nine, thrown from the upstairs window of her flat in Tottenham.

6.12 pm Police arrived at an address in Ealing after the body of Johnny Taylor, seventy one, is found by his wife.

6.15 pm The body of Trevor Mercetti, fifty nine, is found in a wheelie bin outside his apartment in Wapping.

The Sun's front page had the cover of the band's blood soaked second album We Are Toten Herzen with the two word headline *'THEY'RE BACK.'*

As Wallet immersed himself in report after report he sensed Elaine Daley at the far side of the room sat with one leg over the arm of her chair. "Does it surprise you how quickly the press can produce so much work in such a short space of time?" she said.

"Suppose they've had years of practice."

"It surprises me. Forty to fifty pages of news and pictures, maps and illustrations, eye witness accounts, police statements. There must have been an army of people running around yesterday to come up with all that. That takes organisation. How do they do it?"

"Editors, sub editors, desk editors, duty editors. I suppose it is a small army. Everything is in place before a story breaks and it all goes into action. Lines of command and responsibilities. I always admired the speed that they got the papers out across the country."

"You were part of it once," said Elaine. "Do you miss it?"

"When I see all this going on, no. But, I don't know. Maybe not. Ask me again in a few month's time."

Whenever Elaine spoke it was always to the space in front of her as if she was talking to herself. She had a distance that still unnerved Wallet; in her calm manner there was an unpredictability that made him anxious. Her physical appearance, her outward display, was as fascinating as any painting or sculpture; it was meticulous and modern, a carefully chosen palette of vivid colours that complemented her engineered hairstyle of spikes and contrasted with the ancient symbol tattooed on the side of her head. Elaine was the only member of the band with a facial tattoo, the others had fantastic animals and names drawn across shoulders, arms, ankles and no doubt other places he would never see. But Elaine's tattoo was married to her facial features and acted like an exclamation mark to her expressions, transforming and confusing them.

Wallet took great care when he was close to Elaine. "Susan was feeling guilty that you got arrested for Gannon's killing," she said. "She wanted to make it up to you."

"But now it looks like a gang of killers are on the loose. Four of you, four murders. They'll put two and two together. . . ."

Elaine laughed. "Yeah and come to four. You've got such a way with words. I'd like to see their forensics teams deal with the science behind all this. They must be a lot better than they were in '77."

"They're probably a lot better than they were in '77. So it was Susan's idea?"

"Yep. Heart of gold, that girl."

"I should thank her."

"Don't bother. You're evens now."

"Wasn't four people a bit of an over reaction?"

Elaine came over to look at the pages spread out before Wallet on the dining table. "Don't ask too many questions, Rob. A few scores were settled last night." Elaine ran a sharpened fingernail across the Times, slicing the paper open at the headline. "So, you're our manager now? Does Susan know that?"

"Their words, not mine."

"Mm. Don't start to believe everything you read in the press. But then I don't need to tell you that, do I?"

5 - A choice of music

After the washing up was done and everything dried and tidied away, the moment came for Patrick Wells to relax. His ritual now, as an evening of homework marking began, was to carefully and fastidiously select the right music to supplement his mood and prepare him mentally for the grammatical battlefield ahead. The study of his house was a small converted bedroom. It had a large desk facing the window and an antique low backed chair with hand carved arms crafted from rosewood. One wall was covered by shelves of reference books, another concealed by his record collection and it was here at approximately seven pm every night that Wells would run an index finger across the spines of his album sleeves looking for the right choice. The perfect choice.

His day had been fraught, yet no more nerve shredding than usual. His evening meal was still settling, but the choice of wine had been good enough to prevent too much interruption. Now his gaze glided across John Coltrane and Robin Trower before arriving at Pat Metheny. Jazz, blues, no, he wasn't free wheeling tonight, he wasn't feeling smooth enough to let his homework soundtrack mollycoddle the text-speak interpretations of Twelfth Night; he needed something edgier to counter the gangsta cap poppin and bitch lickin of Aguecheek and Malvolio.

He continued on past Loreena MacKennitt's Alhambra concert; too much attention needed there. Dan ar Braz was seriously considered, but then the Celtic sounds might start to make him confrontational. He wasn't looking for a fight. He passed Stravinsky and Mussorgsky, even Elgar drifted by, dismissed as too bombastic. James Last, Mantovani, Matt Munro. Not even the toothy charms of Olivia Newton John circa 1972 could stop his roving finger! Wells stood back a moment, hands on hips, his square shoulders topping off a tall mathematically angular body as his head looked right, left, up and down. Maybe he should just continue listening to Radio 4 until his mind was made up. Perhaps Mark Lawson would have the answer.

"HelloPacoGrano's new one man show at the Omnicon in Washington finally arrives at Covent Garden after two years of legal arguments. I'll be asking him what it's like to be caught up in the expensive world of the corporate lawyer. The comeback announcement of seventies band Toten Herzen has once more put the subject of old rockers who can't give up their guitars back into the spotlight. And why an Iraqi film about tortured Sunni insurgents is causing headaches for organisers of the first Liverpool Film Festival."

Wells had frozen. His whole body solidified in a tight, gripping strangulation. The wall of record sleeves was suddenly an unrecognisable puzzle of narrow lines and slivers of meaningless titles. This was a tiny room, he thought. A tiny world. A world in which time wasn't linear, it was all around us, swirling and swooping like a flock of birds. He sat down, swivelling his antique chair to face the radio and waited; waited for the feature on Paco Grano to end, waited for the Sunni insurgents to miss out on a chance to tell their story to the festival-goers in Liverpool. No, he waited to hear how and why Toten Herzen were coming back now, why now and not in a hundred years or a thousand years or any time long enough for Wells to die without hearing it, seeing it, experiencing it and all the sick nastiness that followed them as surely as plague follows infected rats.

An unsteady personal truce that had lasted thirty years was gone in a moment. All the bad feelings that had settled like sediment would now be stirred up again. Outside the study the sun had already set. Wells knew it would return in the morning, but he could feel an inner sunlight fading. The stubby pile of exercise books on his desk was the first victim of anger churning inside him: they were scattered across the room. He pinched his forehead, pushed himself back from the table immediately regretting what he had just done and stepped out around his desk to gently pick them all up. But there, already, the dagger-like logo of Toten Herzen had been carefully drawn on one of the covers. He shook his head. Why is this happening now? Slumping into his chair and faced with the outward symbol of a group of people he detested, he mined his subconscious, dug down and extracted every particle that might provide a response.

After three hours of silence he found the answer.

Terence Pearl: Blog post
Are we at risk from ourselves? Human and antihumans
cannot exist side by side in a relativistic universe.

A question that came up in a recent pub quiz I frequent left me in a confused state for several days. It was a trick question: who devised the thought experiment known as Schrödinger's cat? Now the obvious answer is of course, Erwin Schrödinger (a detail predictably lost on the other quiz contestants), but the reason for leaving its mark on me wasn't the fact that the question came up, but the implications of the original experiment. In short, a cat in a box is either dead or alive; until the box is opened and the cat's condition observed it is both dead and alive.

The idea that a cat can be both dead and alive is called superposition: being in two opposite states at the same time, and the reduction to one state at the moment of observation is described as a collapse. There have been numerous interpretations of the experiment, but what struck me was the possibility that the issue of matter and antimatter had not been taken into account. If everything has a duplicate, it's anti-form, let's call it, then objects can exist in two states. Not necessarily alive and dead, but in some other form of superposition. That would mean somewhere in the universe there is another Terence Pearl!

Associates of mine would probably shriek at the thought of there being two copies of me, but Yves Sunier and Diana May Ronson at the Institute of Quantum Biological Studies in Vienna have considered the possibility and implications of every human being possessing an anti-matter version of themselves. In a recent paper published in the Vienna School's journal they gave a name to this anti-human: the Janome, after the double faced Roman god Janus, and postulate what properties a Janome would have. Where antimatter differs in that it has opposite charge and spin to matter, a Janome would have to portray some outward (anti)human equivalent of this opposition.

So, just as scientists question why matter seems to outweigh antimatter in the observable universe, an asymmetry brought about by baryogenesis, Sunier and Ronson have left open the question: where are the Janomes?

All around us, according to Alexei Berkoff, the Ukrainian philosopher and author of the book Quantum Effect and Supernature (Megelev, 2002). Berkoff argues that all elements of myth and folklore can be explained by looking to quantum mechanics and theoretical physics. In a symposium held in September 2011 at the University of Kiev, Berkoff, Sunier and Ronson shared a stage and discussed the possibility that Janomes could account for the myth of the vampire, werewolf, ghosts and other elemental forms that are found throughout the world's cultures in their folklore.

Accepting for a moment the idea that the vampire is an example of a Janome, separated from its original body it would contain a different physiology on account of the charge and spin of its component antiparticles, it could be prone to annihilation if it came into contact with some bosons and hadrons (the particles responsible for forces), it might well interact differently with light resulting in three dimensional shadows where its four dimensional self blocks out antiphotons (Solidity of Nothing: the effect of anti-light in four dimensional space. Wadjanewski and Soamas, 2009).

What Berkoff refuses to be drawn on is what happens to the real human if the antihuman comes into existence? 'That is a postulation that strays too far into moralistic philosophy, which

We Are Toten Herzen

Erwin Schrödinger may have been prepared to discuss, but not me. The ephemera of morality is a radioactive by-product of factual research.' What is common to many myths and legends is that the human body must first die before its Janome can come into existence.

Is death caused deliberately or accidentally by contact with the Janome? Does it kill us or come into existence after death? Is there a superposition regarding human existence and what causes the collapse that brings about the Janome's life? Sunier and Ronson don't have the answers yet, but as scientists in the field of theoretical and experimental physics continue to unravel one quantum mystery after another we may soon know how these supernatural creatures come to exist and perhaps, if they pose a threat, how to stop them existing in the first place.

6 - Over the garden fence

The flowering of the daffodils and crocus was an event Terence Pearl could relate to. Finally, after the long winter, and the sneaky hide and seek with early spring cold snaps and snow, these delicate characters were able to safely uncurl their heads and look out across a garden exhausted, but alive. The vivid striped green leaves and chaotic mix of colours were the first tentative musical notes of a composition still in its opening bars, but give it another couple of months and the symphony would be in full flow.

The philadelphus would blind with its white brilliance, the messy hebes spreading their gangly stems over everything around them. Teasels and astilbes wooing the bees and butterflies, as the ajuga continued its mission to carpet the flower beds with its green and purple leaves before throwing up spikes of dark violet blossom. Even the interlopers from the buttercup family and the clover clans would be allowed their days in the sun, polka dotting the rich, springy lawn. It didn't look like that yet, but Pearl's memories were as accurate as a photograph; he knew where everything was, what it would look like, how it would make him feel. Green finches and the resident greedy blackbird would provide a choral backing, arguing territory with the blue tits and wobbling wild pigeons blundering in for their scraps of dried bread. The sudden surprise of a leaping frog and the bashful delight of a wandering hedgehog would add the finishing touches to his carefully crafted, meticulously managed Suffolk haven on the edge of the village of Westerfield.

And then there was the tree. Out of the corner of his eye Pearl could see Cedric next door in his kitchen. Washing, brewing up, polishing his cutlery; without sight of his hands it was impossible to know exactly what Cedric was up to, but you could bet any minute now he would be out, standing at the fence to engage in small talk that was merely a pretence to raise the subject of the tree. Here he came. Cedric vanished from the window and his back door opened.

"Hello, Terence."

"Cedric."

"Bit warmer than the weekend."

"Yes. I think there's another cold blast coming though. Maybe one more and then we can relax."

"Aye." Cedric was studying Pearl's garden enviously. Cedric's garden was a cliché. Square lawn, straight path down to the shed. A rag tag of shrubs planted with no awareness of colour combinations or consideration for complimentary forms and textures. He had a potentilla next to a berberis! No height contrast, similar leaf size. It was offensive. But what did Cedric know? He was a retired engineer. His shed was probably bomb proof, but the garden was an affront to aesthetic study.

"It'll be time for a first cut."

"Yes. Be nice to see the stripes in the lawn again, Terence. I still don't know how you do it."

Now that's a bare face lie, thought Pearl. Cedric was told every year to get a mower with a heavy roller, not one of the plastic excuses that doesn't flatten the grass after the blades have passed over it. But no, Cedric doesn't listen and he doesn't listen because he's only after one thing.

"And the tree will be a bit bigger this year. You don't mind if I trim some of the branches again? Keep Wanda from complaining, you know."

"No, not at all." Why doesn't Wanda say this? She gives Cedric the bullets to fire. The tree's branches don't go anywhere near the washing, but Wanda won't have it. It's a territorial thing. Pearl's tree was invading Wanda's space, but Wanda never came out to argue. Instead she sent Cedric forward to start the argument and Cedric wasn't man enough to stand up to her.

"Can I ask you something, Terence," said Cedric leaning on the fence, pushing it forward by several millimetres.

"What?"

"At the quiz last night, Tony's Tractor Boys won the play off, but they were wrong weren't they? The first communications satellite was Telstar not Sputnik."

"It was. I've said for a while now the reason we never win is because we keep coming up with all the right answers." Pearl could hear the phone ringing.

"It's about time we told the question setter. . . ."

"Excuse me Cedric, I need to answer that." Cedric complied. The fence sprang back a few millimetres as Pearl jogged into the house, through the kitchen, down the short corridor and grabbed the phone. "Hello, Terence Pearl."

"Good morning."

"Oh, hello." Pearl repositioned the solitary umbrella in the rack next to the front door.

"How are you, hope you're well?"

"Oh pottering, you know."

"Good, good. Liked the article, by the way. Very informative."

"Oh thank you. Pretty good opening salvo, I thought," Pearl said.

"Yes." The word came out with an uncertain drag about it. "Thing is Terence, it was all true wasn't it?"

"True. I'm not sure what you're implying. Yes, it was researched and checked if that's what you mean."

"Yes. And a fine piece of writing it was, don't get me wrong, but I felt it could have been, how can I put this, more sensational."

"I see."

"Good. The whole point of this exercise is to provoke and I mean get people talking, not in an inspirational sort of way, there's a time and a place for all that, but cause a stir, whip things up a bit, put Schrödinger's cat amongst the pigeons." The voice laughed heartily.

"Oh, very good, very droll. I wish I'd thought of that." Pearl spoke with all his weight on the umbrella, rocking back and forth.

"Maybe the next one, you can make it a bit more... dare I say controversial."

"Controversial?"

"Smoke the bastards out, Terence."

"Ah! Yes." Pearl had owned the umbrella for more years than he could remember. British made, built to last. Not like the ones you buy for a pound, but you get what you pay for.

"I thought you were going to write something about anthropology and the expectations of human behaviour?"

"Yes, waiting for confirmation of some references," said Pearl awkwardly.

"You're not writing for the Royal Academy, Terence. This is the internet. We need to wake up the ignorati, all those antagonistic Janomes that have already collapsed on top of the host body."

Pearl laughed again, but apparently the comment wasn't meant to be funny.

"Are you having second thoughts? I'd rather you were honest with me than make excuses."

"They're not excuses. I always mean what I say," said Pearl. "I was looking for an important reference which eludes me, but I spoke to a friend of mine last night, haven't seen him for months. Apparently he's been ill with an irregular heart beat."

"I'm not interested, Terence."

"No, but I spoke to him and he gave me the nod as to the direction I need to look to find this reference, so, you know, we're good to go."

"You mean you're good to go. I hope you haven't told this friend what you're doing."

"Heavens, no. I've been discreet all along. I keep telling you I haven't mentioned it to a soul."

"I'm sorry. I'm sorry, Terence. I don't mean to put pressure on you. You are doing me an enormous favour and I do appreciate the detail and the level of thought you apply to everything that you do. The education system's loss is my gain and you must remind me of that when I get above myself."

"No, that's all right." The umbrella was not prepared to stay in position. Pearl lifted it and put the point down in a slightly different position . . . It worked.

"I'll look forward to the next article."

"Okay. I'll get onto it right away."

"Thank you. Bye."

Pearl put the phone down and considered the possibility that Cedric was, at that very moment, hacking his tree down to the stump. Or maybe he wasn't. The only way of knowing was to go back outside and observe.

7 - Intrusive phone calls

There weren't many people who could wake Todd Moonaj at 4am without being sacked. Since being promoted to Sony's Acting Chief Commissioning Officer (and he often left off the word Acting, or used a small 'a' in his correspondence) he had set out on a drive to find the saviours of the music industry: the pushers and pullers of debate; the engine rooms of fashion, the drivers of trends; those with the magic ability to make headlines that write themselves. And above all anyone who could make a quick buck. To do this he needed his sleep and only Constance, his hand chosen PA, had the authority to wake him, preferably in extreme circumstances such as assassination attempts, deliberate asteroid attack or the end of the world. She wasn't sure which category this message fell into so she had taken a chance and called him anyway.

"This is either a wrong number or it's you Constance," said Moonaj fumbling for the bedside phone.

"It's me, Constance."

"Is it the Soviets or al-Qa'ida?" said Moonaj.

"The Europeans."

"Fuck. As bad as that!" He sat up.

Moonaj listened to a summary before rolling out of bed, putting on his robe and heading for his home office for a conference call.

His labrador groggily followed to listen in. Coffee cup in hand, he turned on his computer screen and listened patiently to some incomprehensible jibberdy jabbery history lesson about a lunatic journo who had tracked down a dead band (a dead band!), tried to steal a seventy thousand dollar album sleeve, slept in a tomb in a cemetery, killed the band's bodyguard in a former East German ski resort and walked into the offices of EMI in London with a reunion concert deal. Naturally he had been laughed at and thrown out by security. So he tried a smaller label a few blocks away called Sanatorium Treatment.

"And what did they say?" asked Moonaj.

"They wanted him to pay them."

Moonaj paused a moment. He was weighing up whether to have more coffee to keep him awake or give up now and hope he was still drowsy enough to get back to sleep. Nobody spoke. Constance was already sliding off her stool in the kitchen of her apartment and in Europe, Jan Moencker stood in his office in Berlin fully sentient. He was part of the A&R team in Europe with his ears usually stuck in the sub-woofers of industrial metal or the clubs playing Europop, but even he was confused by the noises he was hearing over his Skype connection.

"Can I say something, Todd?" said Constance.

"Go ahead."

"Wasn't there a music critic in London murdered last week after saying bad things about Toten Herzen."

"So what? John Lennon was murdered for having no connection whatsoever to Jodie Foster."

"Sorry, I just thought it might be relevant."

"Well it isn't and I still don't understand why this was worth waking me up at four in the morning. A dead band from East Germany. How we going to hear them?"

"There is potential here, Todd," said Moencker.

"I don't think so. You've been getting more and more desperate over the last twelve months, Jan. That group you convinced my predecessor to sign, the Abba-meets-Laibach bunch, are all back in Denmark taking their welfare cheques. I think Sanatorium Treatment had it about right. And Constance, take some time off. Take as long as you want. I'm going back to bed people."

-

Jan Moencker blinked in disbelief. He was sure he'd found the deal Moonaj was looking for. It ticked all the boxes: backstory, tick; back catalogue no one owned, tick; predominantly female, tick; (good looking females, especially the vocalist, tick;) good press potential, tick; retro angle to appeal to older people, tick. He could go on all day ticking a list of boxes as long as the Danube. What did Moonaj want? Blood? Fuck it, he could even tick that box! If the target was something that appealed to a contemporary audience with monetizing potential there was no reason why a writing team couldn't be put together, line up a group of A-list producers to add a 21st century name to a 20th century legend, photograph them with a fleet of Volkswagens and off we go.

For now there was an appointment to keep so Moencker pulled on his winter jacket and grabbed his car keys and mobile. As he drove away from his office on Marienburger Strasse he noticed a woman waving to him. He forced a smile and wound down his window. "Eva Matheus? What are you doing here?"

Eva stepped forward. "Sorry, I'm not stalking you. I was coming to drop off the disc you asked for." She waved a CD in the air like a tiny flag. "It's the four tracks you asked us to work on."

"Oh, great," said Moencker. "I was going to an appointment, but. . . ." He could see Eva was shivering in a long overcoat, thin flowery dress just long enough to cover her knees, big clunky boots and beeny hat. "Do you need a lift somewhere? Maybe it's on the way."

"Sure." Eva jumped in without saying where she wanted to go. "Do you have a CD player in here?" She pulled the seatbelt on. The car was filled with an aroma of citrus and cigarettes.

"Yeah." Moencker ejected the current disc and watched out for traffic as Eva eagerly inserted her own recording.

"It's good of you to do this, thanks."

"Where are you going?" said Moencker.

"Oh, all the way hopefully."

"No, I mean where do you want me to drop you off?"

"Anywhere." The music started. Oh god, an acoustic guitar!

"My boss," said Moencker, "if you can call him that, doesn't know where he wants to go. He doesn't know what he wants. Well, he does, but it's nothing musical."

"I wrote this section here with an aunt of mine who lives in Hamburg."

"He wants tie-ins and three sixty degree potential, he wants to inherit existing publishing deals. To him these are just acquisitions like buying a soup factory or a travel company." Eva half listened wondering what it all meant. "He has to trust his A&R team or there's no point having one."

Eva nodded. "What do you think so far, are we sounding better?"

"Yeah, much better. Maybe he doesn't like European acts. But David Guetta's European, U2, people are going nuts for Kraftwerk again, Air, Daft Punk, Coldplay, Radiohead,"

Moencker tickled the steering wheel, "you know, lots of successful European acts."

"Sorry, who are you talking about?"

"Todd Moonaj at Sony. Okay, so he likes his stars to be American, but Toten Herzen were big in America."

"Toten Herzen?"

"You heard of them? You might be too young. They were successful in the seventies. Now they want to make a comeback. Their management are fishing for opportunities."

Eva studied the traffic building up. "Are they like the Scorpions?"

Moencker hesitated and pulled faces. "They, well, no, sort of yes, but not all the time. They're early seventies. No, not as explicit as the Scorpions. They were influenced at the start by Deep Purple." The second song on the disc started. Another acoustic guitar! "Did you write this one with your aunt too?"

"No."

"Guitars only get you so far in the digital age, unless you're stadium drum and bass or already big. But Toten Herzen were already big."

"This song is about homecoming, the relief to be home, the sadness that the journey has ended. You know you want to go back, but it's not the same the second time. Can never be the same," said Eva to the windscreen.

Moencker heard half of that. Eva had a very attractive profile. A strong outline. "We should make them big. What are marketing people for? They make small things big."

Half way through the song they arrived at Granzer Studio and Moencker found a space to park. The band he had come to meet were already here and the session with an engineer was under way. Blast did anything but what their name suggested and

We Are Toten Herzen

Moencker couldn't get Moonaj's criticism out of his head. Here he was in a chilly, matt grey Berlin recording studio surrounded by framed prints of musicians unheard of outside the building. In front of him a band of gangly young men covered in tattoos and superfluous sweatbands, posed with their guitars round their knees. Next to him stood a twenty-first century flower child with a disc full of earnest songs recorded beautifully alongside two of her friends from the same squat. He had lied. She sounded better live than on disc, but his centre of attention had been shoved so far out that nothing from the last forty hours sounded tolerable. Everything either annoyed him or bored him rigid. Blast were puny, following a set of instructions; an unfocused tribute band with a derivative sound and a template attitude. They sounded so good in the club where he first heard them, obscured by the feedback and flattered by the attention of an admittedly enthusiastic crowd. But between that night and this afternoon Moencker had been listening to We Are Toten Herzen almost non stop and had made it his new benchmark.

He felt guilty and turned to Eva. "I need time to give your disc proper attention. I've got a head full of rock and it's a little difficult to switch between this kind of noise and your kind of poetry. When are you playing live again?"

"We are due to play at the Goldenkellar a week tomorrow night."

Moencker made a note in his smartphone diary. "Okay. I'll listen to the disc between now and then. I'll come down to see you and let you know if there's some news for you."

"Okay, thank you." She tried to look excited, but it was hard to tell. But then if you jump out at someone in the street you can't expect a rational response. Moencker had been ambushed, but at least his indifference wasn't just about her. He wasn't listening to

Blast either and he'd made a point of coming down here to see them.

"Can I ask you a personal question?" Moencker was easily heard over the tinny roar of the music in the control room.

"Yes."

"How old are you?"

"Twenty-three. Why?"

He led her over to a computer at the back of the studio and found a website. It was Rob Wallet's blog. "Have a look at these pictures and tell me what you think."

Eva studied the first image. It was obviously old, taken way back when; certainly before her time. "Who is that? Toten Herzen?"

"Yes," said Moencker. "This was taken in 1975 at the Astoria in London. There's the singer Dee Vincent," he pointed out each band member, "Susan Bekker, that is Elaine Daley and the guy there is Rene van Voors, the drummer. Okay, now look at this image." Moencker navigated to another part of the blog where Wallet had uploaded a photo of a group of unnamed friends. "This is a hotel somewhere in London and there is Dee Vincent, Susan Bekker, Elaine Daley and Rene van Voors." Eva could see that. "Nothing leap out at you."

"Dressed differently, a little more fashionable."

"This was taken three weeks ago."

Eva's eyebrows raised. She was impressed. Then the eyebrows changed shape. "Three weeks! The first was in 1975 you said?"

"Yes, nearly forty years ago."

"They look good," she said hesitantly.

"Not bad for a load of sixty year olds."

-

Todd Moonaj walked into his office on Madison Avenue and tried not to look too interested in the printouts on his desk. He had to get his coat off, calm himself after the traffic. He had to arrive properly.

"They were emailed through about twenty minutes ago," said his secretary.

"From who?"

"Jan in Berlin."

Moonaj leaned towards them. The first printout was a photo of four people, one holding an old guitar. He looked at each of them closely. A woman, smaller than the others, short black hair, white as a ghost, leather jacket, black jeans. The second had long black or dark greyish hair, shadowy eyes, looked dead on her feet, as pale as the first. The third woman had a hairstyle that Moonaj couldn't easily identify; part mohican part Statue of Liberty, but like her colleagues she was the embodiment of late nights and ill health. The man, only identifiable as a man by heavy stubble, was also black haired and white faced, a sort of musketeer from the other side.

Moonaj shook his head and continued to hang up his coat. "What are they goths, emos, vampires, what?" He picked up the second printout. Again, the same four figures stood together, not looking at the camera, but the image was of a poorer quality, slightly blue and faded. In a corner were the handwritten words 'Toten Herzen c1975.' On the other image 'Toten Herzen 2013. Notice the difference? Me neither.'

"What am I missing here?" asked Moonaj, "I don't know what I'm supposed to be looking at here. Is it a hairstyling mailshot? Why are people even bothering me with all this?"

The secretary took the images and studied them. She could see the discolouration, the ageing of the second image, but apart from the band looking the same in each photo the significance was lost on her too. "Well, I guess they've aged well for a rock band. I mean, look at Ronnie Wood. He doesn't look as good as these guys."

"Ronnie Wood's seventy if he's a day. How old are these people? Twenty, thirty."

"In 1975, twenty something, so that would make them fifty something, almost sixty something. . . ."

"What?" Moonaj looked at the first image again. "They're the same people."

"I didn't think there were plastic surgeons in Europe as good as that," said the secretary.

"Plastic surgery my merry ass. The only doctors these guys have seen is Dr Photoshop. Whoever sent the email, get back to them, tell them to stop wasting my time." Moonaj tore up the pictures, threw the pieces in the bin, loosened his tie, repositioned the photograph of his wife and sat back in his chair. "Who else do I have to endure today?"

His secretary checked the diary. "Dianne Warren has another song she'd like you to hear."

"Oh, for fuck's sake."

Terence Pearl: Blog post
Cathar survivors or the new apocalypse

In my book 'The Hidden Agendum in Art and Musik' by Terence
Pearl I identified numerous examples of occult practice hidden by
the symbolism of the creative arts. I have now identified a bigger
more specific threat.

*Five murders in as many days and they all have one thing in
common: Toten Herzen. If you didn't know about this group of
people before you certainly will now. They present themselves,
when they choose a moment to do so, as a rock and roll band, but
the truth goes far beyond that.*

*Back in 1977 they performed a ritualistic suicide, abetted by a
man from Norfolk who had been brainwashed into doing so.
(Fortunately for him the Metropolitan Police saw through the
escapade and brought no charges against him except one of
wasting police time.) Leonard Harper was only one of many other
such unfortunate people lured into a cult of personality that
involved other forms of animalistic sacrifice including that of a
horse. The group were successful in earning huge sums of money,
all of which was done in the guise of record sales and concert
tickets, but a closer inspection of their output reveals some tell
tale signs of what was really going on.*

*Their first long playing record was called Pass On By, an ironic
title in which the group are calling out to their followers and
anyone else ready to receive their message. They specialised in
attracting those marginalised by society: drug users and anti-
social drop outs. Pass On By was also a poem by the 15th
Century necromancer Thomas Gwynn, a Scottish Catholic who
was accused of heresy. To quote Gwynn (with somewhat*

modernised wording) 'Go not the path of deceitful righteousness, but pass on by all signs that claim to offer salvation.' The group will have been in no doubt as to the provenance of their title, knowing that they alone were aware of its significance.

We Are Toten Herzen was the name given to their second long playing record. We Are Dead Hearts is the translation and whilst Dead Hearts may seem an innocuous albeit melodramatic name for a rock band, Die Toten Herzen were a Germanic branch of the Cathars who rejected the gospels and indulged in various shape shifting practices using herbs and potions. The lead figure of Die Toten Herzen, Augustus Wurlichter, was beheaded during the Albigensian Crusade in 1225, but his colleagues escaped persecution. Their whereabouts remains a mystery to this day. Or does it? Records show that four men close to Wurlichter had the names Beckersteiner, Dalen, Vincentius and Vornemburg. The four members of the group Toten Herzen are named Bekker, Daley, Vincent and van Voors. This is more than coincidental.

Nocturn, the group's third long playing record, is a reference to the night and the various forms of life that exist there when the rest of us are asleep. There are stories throughout history of people subjected to 'night terrors' and there is an obvious allegiance to these creatures, in the same way that various tribes and warriors call on the spirits of animals to help them in their activities. The group call upon the various night creatures to instil them with malevolence, powers, physical strength and the ability to draw energy from innocent people.

The final long playing record released by the group was Black Rose and it is here that the first indications of their ritualistic suicide appear. For many practitioners of the black arts the black rose is a potent symbol of death and life combined: the blackness of death along with the life embodiment of the rose. The songs on the record Black Rose were, in total, fifty eight minutes long. This seemingly arbitrary number takes on a macabre significance when you multiply it by four (one for each member of the group) to make two hundred and thirty two, double it (two being the lowest prime number and very important in ritualistic practices dating back to the third century) and you arrive at four hundred and sixty four. From the group entering a recording studio to work on Black Rose to their ritualistic suicide on March 21st 1977 was precisely four hundred and sixty four days.

Toten Herzen will one day make announcements regarding new concert shows and records and it will be interesting to note the significance of titles and related numerological correlations. Having survived death the group will be ready to elevate to the next level of consciousness as they leave this realm. However, there will be a danger in that they will not go alone. How many people, both willing and unwilling, they take with them should be of great concern to all of us.

THE INDEPENDENT

Toten Herzen Have Not Been Spotted Alive

The Mirror's 'Catch the Vampires' Campaign has produced hundreds of false sightings

The villagers of Sabden in Lancashire's Forest of Bowland have grown used to being associated with witchcraft. The Pendle Witches of the seventeenth century have long been a magnet for tourists to the small upland village in the shadow of Pendle Hill, but vampires have never been part of local folklore until the Daily Mirror was informed of the four members of Toten Herzen buying a book of stamps in the local post office.

"I didn't even know who Toten Herzen were until a reporter from the press rang," said a surprised Emily Connor, the village postmistress and manager of the attached newsagents. "He asked me how old they were and to be honest I had no idea who he was talking about."

The confusion follows a campaign run by the Mirror inviting members of the public to send in evidence of the reclusive rock band following a surprise reunion announcement. Sightings have been reported from the Isles of Scilly to Aberdeen, with one man claiming he had seen them on a bus in Darlington 'looking a bit worse for wear.' The fact that this was at three in the afternoon somewhat undermined the campaign's title Catch the Vampires; a breed not known for its fondness for daylight.

The band's spokesman Rob Wallet has tried to calm the Mirror's fevered initiative by claiming the band are currently located in Rotterdam, which resulted in a number of sightings on a

Rotterdam to Hull ferry. The Mirror is offering ten cases of wine (red obviously) for the first verified sighting of the band, but for now pensioners all over the country are the subject of speculation and smartphone photography. And history repeats itself; just as they were in the seventies, Toten Herzen are again at the centre of press attention with not so much as a curl of the lip. Modern celebrities take note and learn the dark art of minimal effort publicity.

DAILY MAIL
Anger Over Toten Herzen Misidentification
I am not a vampire, says Susan Buckley of Milton Keynes

A retired headmistress from Milton Keynes has expressed outrage after being wrongly identified as a member of the seventies rock band Toten Herzen. Sixty two year old Susan Buckley has seen her home become a campsite for the local press, goths, heavy metal fans and a devil worshipper from Italy.

The confusion began after Mrs Buckley was mistaken for the Toten Herzen guitarist Susan Bekker. A tip off to the Daily Mirror's Catch the Vampires campaign led to her detached home on the outskirts of Milton Keynes being besieged by dozens of people.

"They started turning up last Tuesday. I can only think someone must have tipped them off after I bought a cd in Sainsburys. If I was a vampire would I be shopping in Sainsburys at eleven in the morning?"

Mrs Buckley initially began making cups of tea for the first visitors, but as the numbers swelled she was forced to call the police. A spokesman for Thames Valley Police said they can't do anything because the visitors are all on the public highway and not causing an obstruction.

"I don't play the guitar, I've never been in a rock band and I'm certainly not a vampire." Mrs Buckley also observed the fact that the press contingency was the worst behaved and had made friends with the devil worshipper from Italy. "He's called Mauro and works for Starbucks. He's quite a gentleman, but I don't agree with his beliefs."

The Daily Mirror has asked for the visitors to Mrs Buckley's house to leave her alone, but when a reporter from the Mail arrived yesterday there were still over twenty people camped out on the pavement.

"Of course she's gonna deny who she is," said eighteen year old goth Mary Ann Bloom from Luton. "If I had her history I'd deny it as well."

8 - First contact

The police had blocked the road bringing the traffic out of Rotterdam to a crawl. The blue lights of emergency vehicles were multiplied in the raindrops across the windscreen forming flashing constellations before the wipers flicked them away. But back they came, again and again. There was an accident somewhere and a victim hidden in the confusion of hi-vis clothing. Bad night to have an accident, thought Jan Moencker. Bad timing too. He needed to get going, to get a result, but someone somewhere was conspiring against him.

He was in the passenger seat of Rob Wallet's car being taken to a farmhouse a few kilometres east of the centre of Rotterdam, located in a hideously black countryside, which late at night was made all the more forbidding by the rain. Either side of the road there was nothing, no indication of life or where it might again emerge. Wallet had picked him up from his hotel near Central Station and was now taking him out into the void to meet the band. They had spoken a couple of times by phone and Moencker had insisted Sony might be ready to speak to them, but there was a snag that had to be sorted out first. "Did EMI give you a reason for not signing them?" asked Moencker as the accident scene rolled by. There was some activity behind the ambulance, nothing that could be identified.

"It'll be a motorbike," said Wallet.

"Uh?"

"The accident. I bet it's someone come off their bike."

"Oh, right."

"EMI? No, nothing at all. I don't think I went about it the right way to be honest. I knew a guy there and thought I'd try to get an introduction, but when I met up with him he just said he couldn't get any interest from anyone who mattered. I was a bit too eager, I think. Didn't plan properly, just went at it. Then I knew I wasn't far from the Sanatorium Treatment office so went over there and wished I hadn't, to be honest. Spoke to a twenty year old so-called executive who asked me to put thirty thousand on the table before he'd even invite me in. He could have been the building's caretaker for all I know. It's been a long time since I've felt as old as I did when I was in there."

"You're wasting your time with EMI anyway. They'll be gone in eighteen months. No use if you're planning to last longer than that." Moencker relaxed into his seat as the traffic passed the last ambulance and was waved off by a soaking wet policeman. A hundred metres farther on were three more officers stood around a prone motorbike, buckled and scratched, lying on its side like a dead two wheeled animal.

"You were right," said Moencker. "You see a lot of these accidents do you?"

"Call it insight," said Wallet. He put his foot down and accelerated into a wall of darkness.

"So what do I need to know about these four?" said Moencker.

Wallet gathered himself and drummed his fingers on the steering wheel. "Be honest with them. One thing I've learned is they don't like bullshit, don't like lies and liars. Susan is the decision maker, pretty much everything goes through her, so if you get her approval you're pretty much in. She can read people like a book so don't try to be clever with her. Dee Vincent reads books like a book. Never stops reading and talking, very mercurial, hard to get a straight answer out of her and I think sometimes it's a game she plays until she's ready to trust you. Rene is like a second opinion on everything. Susan has known him since childhood and trusts him more than anyone. I get the impression that he's like a, I don't know, a filter or a valve that keeps her on the straight, if you know what I mean."

"Not really."

"She can be very volatile. He's probably the only person who can make her see sense, but he's not always successful."

"There's always one member with a stronger personality than the rest."

"Don't get me wrong, she's not a tyrant, but she is the engine of the band. It was her decision to make the comeback."

"She say why?"

"Not in any way that I understood." Wallet looked at Moencker as if he had some insight, what the hell, he'd never heard of her a week ago.

"There are four of them?" said Moencker.

"Yeah," Wallet's hands gripped the wheel momentarily. "Elaine. All I can say is you'll have to make up you own mind about Elaine. She's scares the fuck out of me. Quiet. Hardly moves. I wouldn't like to be on the end of her temper. Then again, I don't think she needs an excuse to turn. Just step carefully around her."

"The mad bass player. It's all fitting a pattern."

"You've met bands like this before?"

"Quite a few."

Wallet turned to Moencker and grinned. "No you haven't."

59

Moencker received a text. He read it and put his phone away.
"What exactly do they want from this reunion?"

"It's not a reunion because they never split up. It's a comeback.
And what do they want out of it? I could only speculate. Maybe
they got bored, maybe they need the money."

"That's the usual reason. And why are you here?"

Wallet entered that zone where the driver of a car is so deep in
thought that it almost drives itself. "A sense of achievement. I
want to achieve something in life. When you write about music,
or anything for that matter, for as long as I have you start to get
frustrated and want to be closer to it, part of it. You want to cross
over from spectator to performer or at least part of the production
and make it happen. The chance came my way and I took it. It
was a risk, but I could see my life ahead of me and it looked like
this road."

The car was taking them both along an illuminated strip of
tarmac no more than twenty or thirty metres in length and beyond
that there was nothing. An unbearable unknown gloom. When
they did finally arrive at the farmhouse there was evidence of life,
but it was extraterrestrial. The cloud was breaking up and
glimpses of constellations normally dimmed by the latent light of
the city were hanging like tiny beads of light filled raindrops,
their patterns gradually emerging out of the background. That's
where all the light had gone, up there, to illuminate those stars
and nebulae and gas clouds, leaving this part of the earth as black
as the deepest pit and as quiet as a tomb. Moencker wanted to do
the deal and get away.

-

"But you need to understand that whatever I do I'm only a middle operator. There's a big team of people way above my head, some of whom I will never meet, who make the final decisions." Moencker was presenting his case to the four members of the band who were gathered in a spacious living room in their farmhouse. Moencker had been surprised by the modern furniture and, more than that, the tidiness and order of the place. It wasn't the ransacked hovel that he expected four members of a 'notorious rock band' to inhabit. He didn't need to think hard about it; he'd never met a band like this. They politely shook his hand and when he spoke they quietly listened like a small class of schoolchildren. Susan Bekker sat in a large chair next to a table with an elaborate stainless steel candelabra and four golden flickering smoking candles. On a large l-shaped settee was Dee Vincent, cross legged, almost meditating, next to her was Rene van Voors, arms folded across his chest. And at right angles to them Elaine Daley, just as Wallet had described; her feet up, motionless as a sculpture, her eyes locked onto him all the time he was talking.

The mood, with the reflective light catching the edges and corners of the furniture, was warm, welcoming and tranquil. It could almost have been the perfect place to live, a refuge from the incessant demands of his job, but Moencker couldn't shake off an insistent unease. The feeling of being suspended inside a gently glowing bubble surrounded by the infinity of nothingness outside the walls of the room made him twitch, occasionally shiver even though he wasn't cold. No one in the room joined him to drink. They had offered him slices of meats and cheeses, with mango pickle, fruit and chilli sauces, but they weren't hungry and ate nothing. He was relieved to be in a place of sanity and calm and unnerved by its abnormality. A threatening peace like a lull in some localised conflict. Wallet's words were never far away and Moencker told himself again he hadn't met a band like this before.

He continued to explain the structure of Sony, their aspirations and those of Todd Moonaj with his remit and expectations. "So, any questions?" he asked.

"This remix, you mentioned earlier," said Susan, "what exactly does that involve and what control do we have over that?"

"As I said, having listened to your back catalogue over and over again there are two issues: the quality of the original recordings is technically lower now than most home made demos. What people can do on their computers at home is better than the original sounds of your albums. The people at Sony will simply not listen to those original recordings. They want to hear what you're going to sound like if you walked into a recording studio right now and then they'll compare that to what everyone else sounds like."

"We don't want to sound like everyone else," said Dee.

"I don't mean that in terms of style, I mean the technical sound: the engineering, the mixing, the mastering. Will you sound as loud as other similar bands, does your producer understand what a modern audience expects to hear in the mix of a rock song."

"Think back to when you recorded Nocturn," said Rob, "how many tracks would you have on a song, typically?"

Susan pulled a 'don't know face.' Did anyone know? Could anyone remember?

"A dozen, maybe" said Elaine. "Depended on the song. Two or three on the drums, one on me," Rene nodded, "two or three on vocals if there were harmonies, two, maybe three on lead guitar, maybe one or two on rhythm guitar. The main melody in your solos, Susan, was usually recorded in mono and panned hard left and right. Sometime's Dee's rhythm guitar might fill in on a lead guitar track to fill the sound out, give it a little more dimension."

"Micky Redwall had us in and out of the studio as quick as possible to keep costs down," said Rene. "Lucky we could work as quickly as we did, but it never got complex. And we only played the instruments we had. There were no synthesizers or piano. A few bits of percussion now and again."

"Even so, two or three overdubs on lead guitar, a dozen tracks in total." said Moencker. "Evanescence, doing what you might be doing, used a hundred and fifty tracks on a single of theirs. What You Want. Over twenty tracks on drums, twenty for vocals."

They didn't look impressed. Susan was teasing a flame on one of the candles next to her, waving her index finger through the tiny playful fire. "Evanescence? Is that where you see us?"

"No, I'm not making any comparisons, I'm simply reminding you how far on production has moved, especially, from what you're saying, the production methods you had to work with. You have so much more available to you now and you need to demonstrate what you would do with all that production power." Moencker was mesmerised by Susan's trick of holding her finger in the flame as she listened.

"So what do you want us to do?" asked Rene. "Record something new for 2013?"

"No," said Moencker. "There isn't time for that. Better to take an original track, Rob told me you have the master tapes now, and remix it, bring the sound up to date. Fill it out. Let Sony hear the genuine Toten Herzen song, but with a twenty first century production quality."

"I'd like to think about this," said Susan looking at Wallet.

"It's your music," he replied. "You shouldn't rush things, but at the same time this is a real opportunity."

"True," said Moencker, "but also this isn't double glazing. There's no fourteen day cooling off period. I'd prefer to hear a decision tonight." For the first time in the evening he felt uncomfortable with the way Susan Bekker was now looking at him. He tried to sit back in his chair, but he was already sat back, he crossed his legs, scratched his chin, he should have shaved before coming out here, but there wasn't time.

"And we can trust you?" she finally said.

"Of course you can. It's in everyone's interest that we make the best impression we can to get that introduction to the process that'll bring you back. Once we've got this part out of the way and all the directors and managers and executives have made their financial decisions, we can get on with new material and planning concerts and production design. But we can't do anything until we've got their attention."

"You weren't there in 1973, Jan," said Dee looking at Rene. The drummer nodded.

"What happened in '73, what do you mean?" said Moencker.

Rene explained. "Micky Redwall heard the band we were in and the band Dee and Elaine were in and pulled them both apart to create Toten Herzen. Wim Segers and Marco Jongbloed from After Sunset, our band, were promised their fare to get back to Holland. That was Redwall's deal. They agree to let Susan and me go and he pays for them to get home. He gave them petrol money to get to Felixstowe and when they arrived at the ferry terminal there were no tickets. He said it was a mix up, but they were stuck there for two days going through rubbish bins for food until the police caught up with them and they were deported. They got a bill once they got home and blamed us for it all."

"It took three years to persuade them it wasn't our fault," Susan said to the candle flame.

"We're very wary of promises, Jan," said Elaine. "We've been stung a lot of times. It's not happening any more."

Moencker surrendered to them. "I'm not going to fuck you guys, believe me."

"Damn right you're not," said Susan. "We'll go along with what you're recommending. We'll put our trust in you, but you have to come good on that."

"Let me give you one more piece of advice, please," said Moencker. "If you can't trust me the music industry today is going to eat you alive."

Wallet rolled his eyes.

"You need to develop a thicker skin than what I can see tonight. There's a lot of shit heading your way. I'm saying this because Rob told me you respect honesty. It's not going to be easy. This comeback is going to generate a lot of interest and a lot of comment. You need to be prepared for that. I'd like to say you should have the wisdom of age and all the experience you have, but I have to admit seeing four people who look as young as you do," he threw his hands in the air, "I'm finding it difficult to believe that you were in a band in the mid-nineteen seventies." He waited for an explanation. "Is there something you want to tell me?"

Susan snuffed out a single candle on the chair-side table. "You couldn't handle it, Jan. Let's wait until we know you a little better before we start going into all that."

"I'll need to know sooner or later," said Moencker.

"Don't worry, you will," said Dee smiling innocently. "We'll just have to hope you're ready for it."

-

On his way out of the farmhouse Jan Moencker would have stopped for a quick smoke, except he didn't smoke! Away from the living room - and he really did like that room, it was just a pity it was surrounded by the world's end - a short corridor linked the front hall to the kitchen and he noticed a dotted line of blood drops, maybe a metre in length. He jumped slightly as Rob Wallet caught up with him to take him back to his hotel. "Cut yourself shaving, Rob?" asked Moencker.

Wallet noticed the blood. "They're a clumsy bunch."

"You don't have a cigarette on you by any chance," said Moencker.

"Don't smoke. Never have."

"Me neither, but it's what I want more than anything in the world right now."

"They weren't that bad. Or did you experience something I hadn't warned you about?"

They stepped outside and the late night chill gripped Moencker a little too eagerly. "This whole thing, the vampire image," he said wondering if he should finish his sentence, "do they want to continue with that?"

"Whole vampire image," said Wallet. "What image? They never had an image, Jan. It was the press and Micky Redwall who concocted all that."

"Maybe, but it's been killed by so many TV programmes and novels. They might want to rethink how they market themselves otherwise they're going to find a nice little niche that nobody else knows about or cares about."

A satellite passed overhead. A tiny star, unblinking, travelling slowly in a perfect line, unmoved by the universe around it. "Sky's cleared after all that rain," said Wallet.

"Yeah. Are you not cold?" said Moencker waiting for Wallet to unlock the car.

"No. I'm English. If you can't get used to cold weather you'll be dead by the time you're five years old. See there, Pegasus, the big square of stars." Wallet was looking round for the rest of the cast. "Cassiopeia, still flaunting it. Shameless hussy."

Moencker wasn't listening. "How do they do it?"

"And the dragon's still watching us. How do they do what?"

"Cause so much trouble without actually doing anything? Five murders, all connected to them, but yet they've been in a hotel and a farmhouse, gone nowhere near an awards ceremony or celebrity party. They do nothing and yet all this turmoil is going on around them."

"Jan," Wallet leaned against the car, "stop reading the papers. Believe only what you see with your own eyes." The alarm blipped and the doors unlocked. "Ride the publicity, milk it, use it, exploit it, whatever. That's how it's always been. Just don't fall for any of it. You want to compare them to other bands. The other bands couldn't begin to comprehend what this lot can do."

Moencker was relieved to finally get in the car and get away. Back to latent light, streetlamps and civilisation for all its mess and disorder.

9 - The Jolly Troubadours

No one entering the Ring of Strawberries did so without leaving a damp stain on the doormat. The rain was teeming down and made an uninvited dash for the bar every time the door opened, blown in by a combination of strong wind, high pressure and the shock waves of thunder. One by one the participants of the Monday Night Quiz, hosted by Dave and Donna and attracting eggheads and thickos in equal numbers, settled their sodden backsides in anticipation of a first prize of thirty pounds and free ham sandwiches. The bigger the team the better the chance of success, but the thinner the spoils were spread. Terence Pearl's combatants, the Jolly Troubadours, were already in place. Pearl (chief brain and arbitrator) sat opposite his bearded nephew Clive and his wife Kylie, a former pupil of Pearl and not named after a pop diva whose early hits were written by Stock, Aitken and Waterman following an acting career in which Australian soap opera? Patrick was an English teacher and in spite of working at the same school as Pearl before his retirement, didn't socialise with him except on a Monday night when he attached himself to the team for no particular reason. Cedric from next door was parked up next to his sly, ammunition producing wife Wanda. And finally, Liz. Liz, the school librarian who had contributed a large sum of money to Pearl's early retirement present. Liz, the fellow author who once joined the same postal writers' circle even though she had never written anything and had to leave. Liz, the starstruck admirer who wished Pearl would join her on the local coach tours to Caister and Stretford Mill.

A weekly ritual was carried out in which everyone had their quiz drinks supplied and a handful of pens of mixed provenance were scattered across the table. Clive wrote down the answers, ninety per cent of which were supplied by Pearl, forty per cent of which were usually wrong, but no one dared to complain. Around the oak beamed room, those punters not allied to one of the factions stayed close to the bar while the Creeky Cruisers, Tony's Tractor Boys, Red Letter Day, The Mucky Nuns, the Lemondrops, Laurel and Hardy and The Bad Hair Mob joined the Jolly Troubadours in what was often billed as a battle to the death, but was usually a race to the bottom.

Rounds one and two covered art and the human body. At the end of the questioning, answer sheets were swapped between adjacent teams for marking. As usual the answers supplied by the Creeky Cruisers, sat close to Pearl's table, had a disturbing correlation to the Jolly Troubadours' answers and as the night wore on the two teams fought for position.

"Round three is the music quiz," announced Dave putting his glasses back on. "As our local heroes have been all over the press recently," there were collective groans around the pub, "this round is about Toten Herzen. Five questions and a maximum of seventeen points."

"I've never heard them," said Clive.

"You've never heard of them?" Pearl's biro was blocking up again.

"No, I've heard of them, I've just never heard them."

"I don't know what you mean."

"I've never listened to any of their songs," said Clive. Bubbles from the head of his pint spilled onto the table. He wiped them away with the edge of his beermat.

"No, you don't want to," said Liz. "I saw them one night, about 1974, with an ex-boyfriend and the crowd was just, I don't know, pure evil. That's the best way I can describe them. They were holding up dead rats and mice by the tales. It was horrible." Patrick nodded.

"Question number one. Two members of the band are originally from Rotterdam. The other two are originally from Lincoln. Can you name the two members from Lincoln? Two points for each name."

"No idea," said Liz.

"You went to see them," said Patrick.

"We didn't speak to them though, did we."

"Dee Vincent and Elaine Daley," said Pearl.

Clive wrote the names down. "What does the D stand for?"

"It doesn't stand for anything. D double-e. As in Dee, short for Denise."

"Oh, sorry."

"Denise Leslie Vincent and Elaine Daley. No middle name. Parents probably couldn't afford one," said Pearl confidently.

"Since when have you been an expert on Toten Herzen?" asked Cedric.

"I thought everyone knew that."

"Question number two. Toten Herzen had six chart hits." The quiz master was interrupted by a clap of thunder so severe it blew a window open. Women screamed, pints went over, the lights flickered, but no one died. There were mutterings that the spirit of the band was watching over them. Pearl wasn't amused and felt a hot flush dance all over his skin. Patrick glanced nervously at the ceiling. "Toten Herzen had six chart hits. Can you name two of them for two points each. And there are two bonus points if you can name the albums from which the hits came from."

"Go on Terence, amaze us again," said Kylie.

"Were you in the band?" said Clive.

"I most certainly was not. You could have Facelift, from the second album We Are Toten Herzen. That got to number four in the charts. And After I'm Gone from the Nocturn album. That got to number two."

"You know 'em all don't you," said Clive.

"I'm starting to worry about you, Terence," said Cedric.

"Any self respecting citizen of Ipswich will be familiar with local lore and legend. Even the bad bits."

"And keep your voice down," said Wanda. "The Creeky Cruisers are trying to listen in." Pearl gave a disapproving glare across to the boat owners sitting within eavesdropping distance. "We'll know if they have an identical score."

"Question three. Which famous American rock star invited the band to tour with him in the States, but was turned down. Two points."

"It wasn't Elvis, was it?" said Wanda shaking her head.

"Of course it wasn't Elvis. Alice Cooper," said Pearl quietly, then he raised his voice towards the Creeky Cruisers, "although it might have been Pat Boone."

"So who is it?" said Clive.

"What? Alice Cooper!"

"Question four. The author Jonathan Knight claims to have written a novel based on Toten Herzen. For two points what was the name of the novel? And for another bonus point, can you name the vampire story written by Sheridan lc Fanu?"

Pearl squinted, the title, both titles, eluded him. The rest of the team sat silent to allow his thoughts to arrange themselves. Patrick observed the muttering and conferring going on around the room. The other teams looked equally stumped and their ignorance forced a barely perceptible swelling of pride, and some relief, in Patrick's stomach. Individual punters sat at the bar watched the quiz as if it were a game of chess with multiple players.

"Oh, dah!" Pearl clicked his fingers furiously. The Creeky Cruisers waited patiently.

"The Dead Heart Weeps," whispered Patrick to Clive's pen. "And Carmilla. That's the le Fanu story."

"Got it," said Clive. He grinned at the Cruisers.

"Of course," said Pearl. "Carmilla."

"Question five and you're going to hear a little bit of music. If you're wearing a hearing aid you might want to turn it off a minute." A blast of music competed with the thunder outside. "Hang on a minute, Donna," said Dave. "You're going to hear a clip from the live album, DeadHearts Live, but for two points I want you to name the band who recorded the original version of this song." Panic set in at Pearl's table. No one, including Pearl, had ever heard any of the music, and Pearl knew next to nothing about rock music other than Toten Herzen's raucous contributions. He recalled Susan Bekker and Rene van Voors being influenced by a British rock band, but he couldn't remember if it was Black Sabbath or Deep Purple. The music went by without acknowledgement; a cacophony, a live blur almost drowned out by the sound of the audience; a frenetic display of guitar notes that pierced the ears with all the subtlety of a blunt masonry drill.

Wanda blinked and rubbed her eyes with a handkerchief. "Deep Purple," whispered Pearl. Clive made a note.

We Are Toten Herzen

The round over, answer sheets were exchanged and sure enough, according to the cheating swine at the next table, Toten Herzen had turned down a lucrative offer from that arch-hellraiser himself Pat Boone. The bastards. And the pattern was repeated for the rest of the night. In round four the Cruisers blagged Pearl's audible suggestion that the pre-revolution leader of Iran was Ali Baba. In round five, the picture round, the Cruisers mistook Richard Nixon for Harry Corbett. And in round six, the science and technology round, which Cedric always sat up for, but never answered anything, the Cruisers graciously and surreptitiously accepted the answer, a chemist's shop, to the question: where would you go to look for the Higgs boson?

Competition over and the winners, by a single point, were the Bad Hair Mob, but the usual controversy, played out every week as the ham sandwiches came around, blighted the hairdressers' success. According to Dave, Toten Herzen were influenced in their formative years by Black Sabbath. The quiz master's crime was compounded when he reeled off a list of Black Sabbath's greatest hits which included the apocryphal Smoke on the Water. Pearl wanted to join in, but he didn't know who had written Smoke on the Water, Highway Star or Strange Kind of Woman, but he was certain it wasn't Black Sabbath. His only consolation was that the Bad Hair Mob had also answered Deep Purple - and been marked wrong - so they hadn't won on the strength of an error, but as one punter suggested, with a mouthful of ham sandwich, "It's the same bloody tale every week, Dave. You get the answer wrong. One of these days there'll be a decent sum of money at stake."

With the battle over, normal pub chat was resumed and Kylie showed off her new iPad. "Have you ever googled your own name," she said. "I mean, obviously I know what's going to show up if I google my name, but what about you Cedric. Cedric Fowler? Let's have a look." Pearl, uninterested in Kylie's faddish toy or Cedric's accidental online presence, stood up to go to the bar. "Oh, One Against the World, by Cedric Fowler, didn't know you'd written a book." Wanda looked at her husband; Cedric blushed. He wouldn't know where to start unless his wife told him, thought Pearl.

When Pearl returned to the table he was greeted with silence. Liz fiddled with her glass, Kylie had put the iPad away and Patrick was playing the one armed bandit. Clive offered a smile, a strange kind of facial shape formed by the contortion of his beard. Cedric sat with his arms crossed in a mirror image of his wife. "Something wrong?" asked Pearl. "Has Dave corrected the scores?"

"You were right about Deep Purple," said Clive. "Not sure we agree with you about the Black Death being a form of germ warfare."

"You've got some funny ideas, Terence," said Wanda.

"I'm not with you."

"We found your website," she whispered. Cedric was still blushing. "Bit of a dark horse aren't you."

Pearl didn't answer. Outside, the thunder rolled and the rain battered the windows with long intensive sweeps of anger. The storm raged, it's victims unable to escape a vicious saturating. Pearl decided now was the best and only moment to go. "One likes to provoke debate, Wanda," he said as he put his coat on. "It's such a dull world, don't you think?" He left the Jolly Troubadours with that thought and threw himself to the mercy of the deluge. Patrick was distracted by the one armed bandit and didn't see him leave.

10 - Paying your dues

The band had given Wallet a nickname: Worker B. He wanted to believe it was affectionate, but he knew he wasn't fully part of their world yet; he was still the feeder, the errand boy, going out most nights to gather blood and take it back to the nest. He had the responsibility of guiding the comeback, using those 'contacts' he liked to boast about; most of them had turned out to be nothing more than strangers' phone numbers and part time acquaintances who had forgotten him a long time ago. Let's face it, Jan Moencker had found him and the band were aware of it. Wallet may have been steering the ship, but he wasn't the captain.

Tonight he took the opportunity to call at the band's office to check the post. They had arranged to rent the first floor rooms on Zaagmolenstraat in Rotterdam from a local businessman they knew from years back. There was the usual business junk mail in a sloppy pile behind the door, but amongst the litter lay a large manilla envelope addressed to him care of the Rotterdam address. It must have been intended for his house in London before being redirected by the Post Office. The envelope was marked HM Revenue and Customs. He opened it.

We Are Toten Herzen

Dear Mr Wallet

I am writing to inform you of income tax and National Insurance contributions that are now outstanding. It is my belief that the individual members of the music band Toten Herzen may be owing taxes to HM Revenue and Customs dating back to 1977. As you may currently be their appointed agent I am writing to you to make the necessary arrangements for them to settle their accounts in order to bring their tax situation in the UK up to date.

You will be notified separately of any corporation tax and VAT that may also be outstanding on any companies and/or other organisations representing the band.

You can fill in a self assessment tax return online. I have attached an information sheet that explains how to do this. Owing to the complex nature of the band's financial affairs and the timescales involved I suggest you may wish to consider a specialist tax adviser to respond to this demand.

I have made estimated calculations on the individual accounts based on the most recent financial information available to me dated April 4th 1983. On this basis the following amounts may be due:

Denise Vincent£1 317 240.00
Susan Bekker£1 876 129.00
Elaine Daley£1 109 087.00
Rene van Voors£1 227 376.00

We Are Toten Herzen

Please ensure this matter is dealt with urgently. HM Revenue and Customs will impose fines on any outstanding and late payments. May I remind you that tax evasion is a criminal offence and may be punishable by the seizure of assets and possibly prison sentences.

Pages 2 and 3 of this letter provide a detailed summary of the amounts and dates affected by this claim. If you require any further information please do not hesitate to contact me.

Yours sincerely

Harriet Summerbee

Revenue Investigations Manager

"A million quid. Fucking hell, they'll hit the roof." Wallet wondered why Susan's bill was bigger than the others then remembered she probably had her name on more publishing deals. But this couldn't be right. There was no record company, no deal, maybe some long lost royalties that had built up, but the band had been in Germany for the last thirty odd years. Wallet phoned Susan.

-

She was in a side room at the Mybuurg Grill restaurant in Utrecht feeding on a man who had approached her at a bar, all swagger and aftershave and no idea how offensive his tee-shirt was: 'keep calm and punch her.' Now her phone was ringing. She saw the caller's name. "Excuse me a moment," she said. The victim moaned and threw up again. "Yeah, what do you want, I've got my mouth full here."

"Did you lot pay any tax while you were in Germany?" Wallet asked.

"What?"

"You were still earning money from royalties and sales in all that time, did you keep your tax affairs up to date?"

"I can't believe you're asking me this right now. Harper dealt with all that. I presume so. Will you get off the phone? Why are you asking that anyway?"

"It's just that you've all got a tax bill for over a million pounds each."

"Well, pay it, get someone to pay it or sort it out. Find an expert somewhere." She hung up. "You know," she said to the victim as his final moment floated away from him, "some people just live to bleed you dry. Do you know I've got a tax bill for a million pounds? A million! Are you dead?" The victim was silent and still. "Oh well fuck you then, forgive me for speaking."

Daily Mirror
Taxman Demands Pound of Flesh
Toten Herzen faced with five million pound tax bill

HMRC watches helplessly as the likes of Starbucks, Amazon, Google and a succession of utility companies walk away from paying their tax bill, but the British public can rest assured that another blood sucking load of parasites will not get off so lightly. Seventies shock rock band Toten Herzen have been ordered to pay individual tax bills of over a million pounds each.

A spokeswoman for Revenue and Customs said the bill goes back to the last recorded payments in the 1980s and may even be higher than the initial estimates. Toten Herzen's record label, the appropriately named Crass, folded in 1983, six years after the band made a hasty retreat to the not-so-offshore haven of Germany. With no management representation to handle their financial affairs it's uncertain just how much money the band made from continued royalties. Their worldwide record sales are estimated to be over five million copies. (Their music has never been released digitally.)

The bands spokesman, Rob Wallet, whose own journalistic career was in freefall, expressed his disappointment at the band's tax affairs being made public. "We'll be asking why the band has been singled out in this way, when there are far more serious tax avoiders running around apparently untouchable. We're not trying to avoid the bill, the four members of the band have been living outside the UK for the last thirty five years and will be happy to explain and settle any outstanding debts. Who knows maybe we could set an example for some of the other leeches trying to get out of paying what they owe."

The idea that Toten Herzen, a band renowned for encouraging their supporters to sacrifice animals, should set an example to anyone is astonishing, but when the Mirror contacted Starbucks UK head office to see if they would follow Toten Herzen's example and pay their own Vampires' Tax no one was available for comment.

PART 2: REBIRTH

11 - Reliving the past

Dee noticed Rob Wallet staring intensely at his laptop screen, probably on one of his crazed webshopping runs that filled the Rotterdam office with parcels sent from god knows where. His room was a growing museum to the seventies filled with board games, a football with black and white hexagonal panels he'd always wanted as a boy and children's annuals that even she had been too old to read when they were first published. She crept in and continued a closer look at the poster of Johan Cruyff. Rene had threatened to rip down the image of the ex-Ajax (and Feyenoord) player and replace it with one of Ove Kindvall. Elsewhere Matchbox cars sat alongside old jigsaw puzzles and videos were arranged alongside DVDs of old British TV shows: Van der Valk, The Persuaders, Arthur C Clarke's Mysterious World, recordings of Jeux sans Frontieres and On the Buses. Programmes familiar to Dee, but all of which had passed her by; when she was awake in the seventies television was off the air for the night.

"Van der Valk, Johan Cruyff," she said. "You're an honorary Dutchman aren't you."

"Funny coincidence, isn't it," he said without looking up from the screen.

She came up behind him. "End now you hef yer liddel houshe inderpoldersh. What are you buying now?"

"I've just bought Tournament Golf. A board game I had when I was a kid. Haven't seen that one for decades."

"Lovely. We can throw water over you if you want a real golfing experience when you play it." Dee picked up a packet of Top Trumps. "How many of these have you got now?"

"Ten."

"Anything interesting online?"

"Usual filth, extremity, hyperbole, Serbian racism versus Croat nationalism, trolls, perverts and intolerant weirdos. And that's only the Guardian's Comment is Free section."

"Why do you bother reading it? It doesn't make any difference."

Wallet paused and sat back into Dee's stomach. "Well, actually it does. There's a chance, minuscule, but a chance nevertheless, that something will be said on one of these sites that we do need to be aware of."

"Like what?"

"Well, if I knew that I wouldn't need to visit all these websites. I don't know. Imagine all this in 1976? You might have found out about Lenny Harper and saved yourself a lot of trouble." Wallet was scanning through a Twitter feed, endlessly scrolling down for more and more messages, most of it abbreviations, hash tags, symbols and truncated gibberish. "Look, look at this one... All the shit surrounding TH only makes me want to meet them even more."

"Who's that,"

"RavensWish." Wallet clicked on the name to see the user profile. "B Turkington. Toten Herzen follower. Out on a mission to meet the band who cannot be found."

"That's all we need," said Dee. "Another Rob Wallet. Set up an account. Keep the wolves at the door. We don't want any more surprises like you." Dee strolled over to the window seat with a Beano annual from 1979 and looked out across the flat endless farmland topped off by the perfect horizontal line of the horizon.

"I've got four thousand subscribers to my blog, you know," said Wallet.

"Good for you," said Dee holding the annual in front of her as if it was radioactive. She didn't care; she was wondering if Dennis the Menace's giant snowball was going to flatten Minnie the Minx. "Are they the ones sending you all this shit from the seventies?"

"Shit, what shit? Before I met you lot I had fifty-seven subscribers. They're only interested in me because of who I know."

"And not what you know obviously. And you a professional journalist. Fifty seven subscribers, eh? And you're expected to promote us. You couldn't even promote yourself to your own profession." Biffo the Bear! Still hadn't been shot by trappers.

"I'm a writer not a," he stopped before he talked himself out of a job. "Why did Susan agree to me representing the band? She's not an idiot, she must have known it was a big deal for me."

"You're an interface," said Dee. "You know, like when the shit hits the fan?"

"Yeah."

"You're the fan."

"Great."

"Do you ever read anything worthwhile on there?" she asked wondering what Lord Snooty was up to these days.

"Sometimes, but common sense on the internet these days is hard to find."

"You rely on it too much. Anyone would think the world would stop if the internet disappeared."

"Do you never look at anything on here? What about book buying, all those books of yours, where do they come from?"

"That's about all I use it for. Rene checks the results, Susan emails and chats with people. Elaine, she's more interested in how it works than actually using it. Oh no, I tell a lie," Dee jumped off the window sill and rushed over to Wallet's laptop. "She saw an old video of us performing live on Youtube the other day. Go to Youtube."

Wallet searched for 'Toten Herzen live' and found Newcastle Trocadero 1975, a washed out televised clip of the band performing Blood on the Inside. "Do you remember that?" he said.

"Yeah that's it. Susan broke three strings that night. Wonder where they found this?"

"Someone must have taped it when it was rebroadcast," said Wallet. His attention had been caught by another playlist item, but he kept quiet.

"We only appeared on TV when we did something wrong. I thought the Old Grey Whistle Test performance might be on here." Dee noticed the same playlist item and stopped talking.

"You've seen it too?" Wallet asked. Dee threw the annual onto the bed, ran out of the room and within seconds came back with Susan followed by Rene and Elaine.

"There," said Dee pointing to the thumbnail image of the band's logo and the title Toten Herzen Give Me Your Heart new single.

There was a moment's silence. The temperature in the room started to increase.

"Fucking click on it, Rob," said Rene leaning against the table where the laptop was sitting.

Wallet clicked the thumbnail and the band stood listening for four minutes and eight seconds until the logo, no video just the logo, was replaced by a mosaic of smaller images and titles. The song sounded like Toten Herzen, but it wasn't Toten Herzen. Susan's guitars could be heard playing, but they were distorted, flattened, almost secondary to the layering of autotuned vocals. And the vocals weren't Dee's vocals. The music was Toten Herzen's, but the lyrics and voice belonged to someone else. The drums sounded like Rene, but they were in the background, floating, occasionally making themselves heard, but only as a token rhythmic element like a digital clock. The bass guitar was merely a dim pulse and unrelated to Susan's playing; Toten's signature bass and lead guitar driven arrangements had been pulled apart. The composite was a modern rendition, stripped of its native energy and replaced with machine-made regularity and precision that washed the speakers clean. It was a sterile facsimile, a well dressed fake.

Susan spoke. "Who put that there?"

"Username is Generus." Wallet clicked on the name. Generus had a channel made up of videos and tracks scooped up from all over Youtube. The profile was blank. No indication of who Generus might be, no suggestion of where they could be located or how to track them down for questioning. How had they come by this track? Who had done it? Why had they fucked it up beyond all recognition? Why hadn't an original Toten Herzen song been remixed? Why a discarded backing track from 1976 with someone else's voice pasted all over the top of it? Wallet was encased by the four members of the band trying to click on links, grabbing at the laptop's keypad. Uploaded two days ago and already 11943 views, 3474 likes, 4 dislikes. Wallet scrolled back to the top of the screen to hide the comments. The initial confusion was transforming into a growing rage with one point of focus: Jan Moencker.

"I'm not going to fuck you guys. His very words," said Susan. "He sat on our fucking chair in our fucking house, drinking our fucking beer and eating our fucking food and he said to my face I'm not going to fuck you guys."

"Where is he now," said Elaine looking at Wallet for an answer.

"He'll be back in Berlin," said Wallet. "Can I say something?"

"Uh oh!" said Dee.

"I don't know, Rob," said Susan straightening herself in expectation. "You seem to know him better than us and you know all about this social media shit and Youtube shit and uploading shit. Is there something you want to say?"

"Look, before you tear my head off, I had nothing to do with this. Let me finish. Give him a chance to explain, don't just go flying out the window and killing the first poor sod you come across."

"Was that my intention?" said Susan. "Fly out the window and kill someone. I was thinking much closer to home."

"Hang on," said Rene pushing Susan away from the table towards the door.

Susan softened and breathed out heavily. She picked up a box containing an Airfix kit. On the cover was a painting of a Spitfire and inside the various separate bits and pieces. Until it was all put together this was nothing, not a toy, not a plane, not a Spitfire. Its components were not the finished item until it was all constructed in one way according to a specific set of instructions. She replaced it carefully on the shelf next to a small plastic trophy. She shook her head. "Is all this supposed to be your life?"

"Earliest things I can remember," said Wallet.

"What if someone told you it was worth fuck all? What if someone came in here and replaced it all with what they thought should be in here?"

"I'd take it all back out again and tell them to mind their own fucking business."

"That's the right answer, Rob." She placed the trophy on the table in front of him. "You win a prize."

Susan left the room followed by Rene, still keeping an eye on her. Elaine was the next to go, but couldn't leave without saying something.

"Don't tip him off," she said to Wallet. "He needs to answer to us, not you."

"Mm, not a happy bunch," said Dee massaging Wallet's shoulders. "We opened a can of worms there, didn't we?"

RavensWish - omg new @totenherzen track released #givemeyourheart rocks cant wait to see the vid dee vincent sounds a bit weird what they do to her voice?

12 - The Plan

He wondered when the call would come. Marco Jongbloed knew it would be made only after Toten Herzen's first incarnation, but not this long after. He had almost given up on the idea. In the years since The Plan was drawn up he'd been married, had kids, built and sold a business and grown old. He could deal with the first four events, but growing old, that was the killer. That sucked.

But no use grumbling now, the call had come and he was off, maybe not so quick out of the starting blocks, but quick enough. He left the low open fire to crackle alone in the lounge; the landscaped gardens outside peered in wondering what the fuss was. Into the hall, long and slender, bare wood, white walls, nothing to interfere with the Giacomettis or the line of sketches by Klimt. He bounded up the stairs and along the top of the open well of the geometric stainless steel dining room below. Through a partition door he entered the original part of the house with its crooked timbers that were even more ancient than his sixty-three year old bones, mullioned windows like compound eyes, low ceiling intent on making him crouch before he was ready to crouch. One day he would scuttle through this part of the house like a hermit, but not yet. He was still in his slender steely years, not ready for the crook and beams of his twilight.

The room he eventually found himself in was a box room. A repository of cardboard waste, files, shelves crammed with old books and magazines - cars, bikes, photography, old music periodicals and newspapers - yellowed, some of them on the verge of powdery disintegration. On the floor were bigger boxes full of old telephones, prototype mobile handsets when batteries were almost as big as televisions. He couldn't even remember what some of the other gadgets were. Cables: straight, coiled, caked in dust . . . what the hell were they doing here? What possible purpose could they serve other than to strangle someone? The box he thought he was looking for offered no prize. It was a jumbled pile of scrapbooks with cuttings of Toten Herzen headlines, articles, stories, reports, the whole dreadful story played out in big bold letters and hazy pointillist photographs. Jongbloed allowed himself to search through the pile a little more slowly, but the procession of portraits and images like a ghostly roll call eventually forced him back to the quest.

The Plan. Where is it?

The shelves around him were bending with old business files and, in one corner, a bust of Beethoven. But no Plan. A crate next to a discarded bass guitar contained musical manuscripts, a foot pedal, two old microphones, part of a microphone stand and the handle that should have been on the case to carry the discarded bass guitar. But no Plan. The old cabinet with shoe boxes of music tapes, was actually empty. So, no Plan there either. He took a stack of books off an armchair, put them inside the cabinet and sat down. Jongbloed, surrounded by detritus and junk, exhaled. And the thing was, the annoying fact about all this, there was an absence of memories. Hardly anything he had rummaged through was here for nostalgic reasons. There were no keepsakes, no mementos, no treasures. It was the room of what never became. The room of lost opportunity.

Had events turned out slightly different, Marco Jongbloed would probably have been sat amongst framed platinum discs, gold discs, silver discs, photos of famous people, photos of crowds, of arenas; photos on the road, on the tour bus, on the floor of a hotel. But there was none of that. Instead he had deals, purchases, investment meetings and apart from keeping the receipts they didn't really come with memorabilia. No one ever became misty eyed over that meeting in Groningen in '84; there were no fond memories of the licensing agreement of '89; no need to get out the Macallan and tell stories of the programme of expansion in '95. It didn't work like that. Business was business and show business wasn't real business. Show business, when it worked out, left you with an indelible tidemark and bad skin, a house full of reminders and an autobiography people would read. Business, when it worked out, just made you rich. The only positive side to all this unwanted, unwarranted rubbish was the certainty that The Plan had never been thrown out. One last look around gave no clues, but then he remembered.

The Plan wasn't in here, because it wasn't junk. It had never been discarded, was never rendered obsolete. It was still a live document, a work in progress. It was in his library. Jongbloed upped and left, scurrying back to the extension, to the white walled modernity. The library was at the opposite end of the house facing the woodland that screened the house from the North Sea coast. He could hear the waves when the doors were open. Without any effort he scanned the books and there, at the end of a line of encyclopedias was a comb bound document, A3 in size and folded in half. He took it down and with barely contained excitement flicked through the pages. And it was all still there: the chapters; the section summaries; processes, methodology, protocols, rules and guidelines; ambitions, aspirations, targets, time-lines and diagrams; maps, drawings sketched by hand, drawings produced by computer, plans, elevations, isometric angles, exploded views; specifications, descriptions, details. . . . All of it, all intact, all complete. Perfect in its construction, simple in its ambition. After thirty-five years of dormancy, ready to be revived.

13 - Improving your swing

As late night conference calls go this was one of the more complex and fraught that Jan Moencker had been involved in. At one end of the line in Rotterdam was Rob Wallet struggling to communicate the shitstorm blowing around him and in the malevolent atmosphere illustrate how unhappy the band were with the remix and the not insignificant fact that Moencker had sent it to Sony without their prior approval (and the colossal fact that someone had leaked it online for the whole world to judge). On another phone line, in a small recording studio in Berlin, was Martin Lundqvist who had carried out the remix and was casually justifying the 'muted lead guitars,' and the over-autotuned vocals, and the distant drums, and the excessive reverb, and the absence of any serious bass, in addition to the left right panning of the intro, and the flat mix and out of context vocal fills, and the omission of Dee's voice in favour of some unknown singer. In short, an unholy mess, to paraphrase Wallet.

"It will appeal to a wider demographic," pleaded Lundqvist.

"It sounds like something Lady Gaga would play around with," said Wallet.

"Lady Gaga's big," said Lundqvist.

"Rob, there's no harm in reaching out to that audience if you can catch some of it," said Moencker. "Beg, steal, borrow an existing fan base to get you going."

"We don't want to catch part of that fucking audience, Jan," said Wallet. "We have an audience. They're called rock fans. Not pop fans. Toten Herzen are not a fucking pop group."

"Rob," said Lundqvist, "at the moment Toten Herzen are not anything. They're four memories from a different era. They might not be interested in earning any money, but some of us have bills to pay and that means getting the music out there in a form that sells?"

"Country and western sells, Martin. Why not just mix in a slide guitar and some harmonica?"

"I don't know why you're so upset, Rob," said Moencker who was running out of fingernails to chew. "The suits at Sony were impressed. They liked it after one hearing, straight back on the phone wanting to take it further. They want to meet you and here we are yelling at one another because you don't like the sound of the guitars."

"I'm not getting through to you am I? What did I say to you before you met the band? Be honest with them."

"That's all a bit sentimental," added Lundqvist. "Does that still happen in the real world?"

"You said yourself, Jan, you sat in that chair and you said I will not fuck with you guys. And they trusted you."

Moencker needed to turn down the heating in his office. "And I also said to you and to them they would need to develop a thicker skin. And it sounds like they're throwing their toys out of the pram because they didn't like the sound of the guitars. Rob you have to persuade them to understand how the industry works now. This is not the stage to get picky about details. Wait until you're in the studio with the money in the bank. We're over the first hurdle, for god's sake don't throw it away at this stage."

"It's not just the guitars, Jan," said Wallet.

"What is it?" said Moencker falling into his chair. Eva Matheus's CD was still on his desk. He hadn't listened to it and couldn't find the enthusiasm to endure any more of her observations on loss and regret. Moencker already had that by the tonne.

"Come to the point, Rob," said Lundqvist. "It's getting late."

"We've started everything on the wrong foot, Jan. Sony have heard this demo and now they'll expect more of the same. And that's not us."

"Rob, Rob, you are getting not just a modern sound, but an effective modern sound," said Lundqvist. "Listen to Jan. It got the band through the door and he's sweated blood to get this song heard. Do you even know what you're talking about?"

"What I'm talking about, look, both of you," said Wallet, "if you take a swing at a golf ball and you start it off a few millimetres out it eventually veers off into the rough. . . . " Wallet went quiet.

"Well you're up there with the old rockers now, Rob," said Lundqvist laughing. "You know you guys couldn't be managed worse if Susan Bekker's mother was in charge."

"Martin," said Moencker, taking the silence as a warning, "I think it would be a good idea if you shut up for a moment."

"At last you've said something I agree with." Susan Bekker had taken the phone off Wallet. "I'll say this once. You made a promise to us that you'd let us hear the remix before it went away."

"Susan, it was a question of timing. I had to get the file to Todd Moonaj at Sony before he went on vacation. There was no point sending it to anyone else. They couldn't make a decision. He was going away for two weeks and I don't have two weeks, Susan. I really don't have two weeks, do you understand?" Moencker hurled Eva's disc at the far wall.

"Was this guy stood in line on the tarmac at the airport? The song is six minutes long; you couldn't send us that electronically so that we could hear it first? My belief is you didn't want us to hear it because you knew we'd stop it and you didn't want it stopping. My belief, Jan, is that you just want a result and any old shit will do so long as you get what you want."

"It's not like that, Susan. We're running against time here. It's nothing more sinister than that," said Moencker. He waited for a reply. "My job is always against the clock. What I'm doing for you is no different than anyone else. Trust me."

"And who the fuck is this other prick?" said Susan with a darkening tone of voice.

"Jan," Lundqvist was trying to get a word in.

"Just a moment, Martin. Susan, who do you mean?"

"Jan."

"This little pumped up piece of shit who did the remix? Was it his idea to make it sound like this or yours?"

"Susan, let's just leave things as they are and move on. I will make it up to you, I promise, you'll see how this works out. . . ."

"Jan!" Lundqvist was yelling.

"What?"

"Jan, Susan Bekker is standing right next me!"

"What? Susan, I thought you were in Rotterdam?"

"I don't care where you think I am. Let me tell you again because I hate it when I can't make myself clear to people. You broke your word. Fuck the guitars, it's the trust that's the big deal here. Ten years ago I wouldn't have given you a second chance for that, but I'm a little more tolerant these days. So make things right. Let Sony know that the demo was a mistake. You make it public that the leaked audio file is nothing to do with us, that we had no part in it, is unauthorised and does not have our approval. However you word it I'll leave it up to you, but you put things right, is that understood?"

"Yes," Moencker was listening to Susan, but he knew before she spoke what she wanted. It was almost a relief, whatever happened now, the meeting was on and he could sit back issuing take down notices to websites, whatever. The meeting was on. "Leave it with me. I'll contact Rob when I've spoken to the people at Sony okay?"

"No, it's not okay. You won't be dealing with him any more, you deal directly with me."

"Fine. I'll be in touch."

"Goodnight."

Moencker put the phone down. The broken case of Eva's disc reflected the ceiling lights. Moencker looked around for a spare. He even had time to go to Eva's show, though he wasn't sure what he could tell her. No, he could tell her anything. Another artist spotted. Two in a month, chalk and cheese, the sublime and the ridiculous. Then he remembered Martin Lundqvist and rang his number, but it went straight to voicemail. The options were to stay here and let Lundqvist, a grown man, take care of himself. Or he could go round to his studio and walk in on god knows what! No, Moencker had his meeting. Time to go home.

-

To the east of Rotterdam, in the loneliest farmhouse on earth, Rob Wallet listened as Susan and Moencker hung up. So that was it then. He was out of the equation and without any evident responsibilities. Surplus. Redundant. Dee Vincent was the only person in the room standing; astonished at what she'd been listening to. She started to practice her golf swing.

"You know it's like when you take a five iron, but you mean to play a sand wedge and you hit that ball and it just comes off the heel and spins right and then you're looking around those lateral water hazards hoping that Peter fucking Alison hasn't run off with your ball in his mouth. You stupid fucker!"

She wasn't alone with an opinion. "Are we expected to let you handle the management responsibilities of this band," added Elaine with her eyes closed. "We are so so so fucking angry with all this shit and you start talking about a wayward golf shot?"

"I'm sorry. I talk in metaphors sometimes."

"I talk in metaphors sometimes," Dee mimicked. "Sounded more like a fucking allegory to me. You'd think a public schoolboy would know the difference. Useless bastard. You've been a freeloader since the day you knocked on our door. Susan should have left you in jail. Four critics would still be alive if it wasn't for you."

"Where did Susan go?" said Wallet.

-

Martin Lundqvist sat in the chair of the recording studio control room more carefully than he had ever done anything in his life. Susan Bekker walked in front of him. "Turn everything on, set everything up and then we're going to record the guitar parts until they're just how I want them."

Lundqvist obeyed.

"And if it takes us forever then that's how long it will take."

Lundqvist nodded. "Your guitar."

"What about it?"

"Where is it?"

"Oh, it's right here." She was holding it! A black Gibson Flying V. Susan rested the pointed ends of the body against Lundqvist's chair, pinning him in place. The headstock nuzzled tightly against her stomach. Without the blink of an eye, she grabbed the arms of the chair, impaled herself on the neck of the instrument and pulled her body along it until she was face to face with the petrified producer. She gasped, inhaled a long deep satisfying breath and laughed revealing razor canines licked with the teasing tip of her tongue. Lundqvist started crying.

"It sounds so much better when I tune it this way."

INDEPENDENT COMMENT - Andrew Parnell
A digital stake through the heart

It now seems that when Toten Herzen's comeback single Give Me Your Heart was leaked online the only people in the world who batted an eyelid were the band. The backtracking by Sony's European A&R representative Jan Moencker was so hasty it's easy to assume that before a contract has even been signed a huge rift has opened up between the band and their would be (could be) record label.

'The band in no way endorse, approve or support this track; it's re-engineering, remixing, release and unauthorised uploading to social media sites was done without the band's consent. All four members are disappointed and extremely angry at this unfortunate episode.'

It's the 'extremely angry' bit that should have people worrying. Just ask Micky Redwall, Lenny Harper, Mike Gannon or even Martin Lundqvist, the producer of the single who has already been hospitalised after being subjected to noise levels in his Berlin recording studio, reportedly in excess of 160 decibels. Someone obviously made a mistake and by the sounds of it are now worried sick, but there is a lesson here that Toten Herzen must also learn, no matter how hard it may be to stomach.

In the 1970s, when the band first experienced success, they would have been unaware of the extent of people borrowing and copying their albums and singles. Ignorance is bliss, but with no way of knowing the scale of the copying they could happily carry on without seeing proof of the effect on their incomes. Not so today.

Give Me Your Heart will have been listened to on Youtube and links from Facebook and Twitter. Bit torrents will be heading their way along cable lines as we speak and if they want to, the band will be able to see just how many times the song has been 'viewed', 'liked,' 'favourited' and downloaded. It may make grim reading that quantifies their anguish and puts accurate numbers to their sense of outrage.

And they'll just have to get used to it. They can probably expect to see twenty to thirty per cent of their material disappear through the darker regions of the internet without anyone paying a penny. Back in the 1970s if a bell at Toten Herzen's headquarters had rung every time one of their songs was copied the constant noise would have driven them mad. No doubt this one solitary episode will have set alarm bells ringing long before the first act of this comeback is about to begin.

14 - Astronomical thoughts

The gods were always looking down on people, thought Rob Wallet as he sat back along the windscreen of the car gazing up at the head of Draco. They created humans to make themselves look good. That's confidence for you: impress your peers by surrounding yourself with losers. "You know, you look nothing like a woman sat in a chair," he drawled at Cassiopeia. "Queen of the couch potatoes. You could be anything." All of them for that matter. Hercules, let's cut to the chase, it's a giant swastika, whatever time of year you clock him; a celestial nazi. "Like this bastard here. Draco the Dragon. In the cold light of day you look more like a fucking tadpole." Pegasus looked nothing like any horse he'd ever seen. Oh, the old myths bigged that one up. Untouchable, unobtainable. "Re: a euphemism for stuck-up, arrogant. Or, wait, is it a metaphor . . . or an allegory. You still don't look like a fucking horse."

Wallet fiddled with the car keys. His original plan was to drive, drive anywhere, but whichever direction he chose would take him nowhere he wanted to go. Not even back home to pick up where he left off the previous year. His old career in journalism had been taking in water before finally sinking and his options now were the graveyard shifts of low paid work and a life of nocturnal secrecy, or stay here and be humiliated every waking moment.

Overconfident, unrealistic and deceitful, like a one man myth he had acted out virtually every vice contained in that starry gallery circulating above him.

In the forty eight hours since the conference call with Moencker the offending track had gone, extinguished, taken down from the internet wherever it was found. But like any crime scene the evidence was still there: descriptions of it in blogs and online articles, broken links; digital DNA scattered all over the place. Wallet closed his eyes and spread his arms out across the top of the windscreen. His right hand brushed something fabric, leathery. It was Susan's jacket.

"Susan?"

"It's half past three in the morning," she said quietly.

"Where've you been?"

"Finishing off some work. Getting the guitar levels right. They're much louder now. I've had a few conversations with people, called in some favours." She leaned back against the wing of the car placing her silhouette across the constellations along the horizon. "I hope you still feel pretty shit about what's happened."

"I do. Even saying sorry makes it seem worse."

"Yeah, it does. Spare us the self pity. But you have to make any opportunity you can out of something like this so Moencker's got us a meeting and that will give us an insight into how these people work, how things are done, maybe introduce us to a real manager.

"So you're gonna meet with Sony?"

"Why not? We don't have to say yes. It's become apparent to me that everyone is using us to get what they want. And that includes you. It's always been like that, we can't expect it to be any different, but this time we can play the same game. We're not the enthusiastic kids being taken for a ride like we were the first time. We can use people to get what we want."

"And what do you want? I still don't understand why you agreed to all this."

Susan pushed herself off the car. "Get down off there. Hold my hand," she said. Wallet jumped off the bonnet and felt her fingers instantly wrap tightly around his as the stars began to dim.

-

"This is where I grew up," Susan said as a narrow street of high, dull brick terraced houses appeared around them like prison walls. Several storeys of irregular patterned windows and concealed balconies rolled away in four directions from the junction where they stood. Planted in the street were lines of malnourished trees, not much more than timber stakes, shivering naked as a brutal April wind ripped through their empty grey branches. "It was always so cold here, it never seemed to get any better. That apartment in front of you, on the first floor with the cream curtains, that's where I lived. It's where I grew up. Down there is the old Fish Market where I twisted an ankle. I had a day off school and spent the time in my bedroom listening to the Yardbirds and Jimi Hendrix for the first time. When I went to school the day after my teacher asked me what I'd done and I sang Hey Joe. The teacher wasn't amused. Nobody had a clue what I was talking about except Rene. He loved it. He couldn't believe there was someone else who liked that stuff. The Beatles, Stones, everyone had heard of them. But not this. Can you hear that." Susan pulled Wallet closer to the building and the muffled sound of a guitar was coming from the walls. "Jeff Beck," Susan whispered. "My mother had all the albums and just about

*everything Jimi played on before he made it on his own. The Isley
Brothers, Curtis Knight, Lonnie Youngblood. People bringing
singles back from Britain. My father didn't really take much
notice. He was as square as a tulip field, but Rene thought this
flat was Shangri-la. He listened to Mitch Mitchell and Ginger
Baker, I was all ears for Jimi and Jeff and Jimmy Page, Eric
Clapton. We wanted to be like that."*

Susan and Renes' school was an uptight block watching over a
wide street with unsmiling authority. Built with the same
charmless brick as Susan's terrace, the school epitomised
discipline and conformity. Devoid of decoration, every unit of its
exterior seemed to be designed to contain expression and thought
rather than encourage or celebrate it. "Rene and I used to walk
home together wondering how long it would take to get to that
level of skill. And even if you learned how to play the notes like
that where do you get the emotion without living the way they
did? Look at this place; what sort of emotion comes out of a
place like this? What sort of music does it produce? We talked a
lot of bullshit, but I never thought I'd be talking like that to a boy
at my school. You know the Netherlands has produced more
crimes against music than any other country on earth and even at
that age it felt like I was the walking dead. No one to talk to about
what I was really interested in. And Rene felt the same way."

The lower branches of a street tree framed a small cafe on the
end of a concrete row of shops. An overflowing rubbish bin
spewed its wrappers and newspapers across the pavement. A two
stroke motorbike belched out smoke and an echoing din, whilst
cyclists struggled past on their clanking bikes. "We both got jobs.
Nothing special. This is where we'd meet and talk. Rene was
drinking Coke and I was wiping icing sugar off my lips when he
suggested we form a band and do something more than listen to

other people's music. He had two other guys lined up, Wim and Marco, who played guitar and bass and knew a bit about rock. I had my guitar and a half decent voice. Better than any of those three anyway, but Rene suggested Wim should sing and let me concentrate on playing lead. That's when life finally started to warm up."

Across a wide road lay the shell of the old Ahoy Arena. "November 10th 1967. We all came down here and saw Jimi Hendrix. My mother was with us, about twenty-five years older, but as eager as we were to see him. We left the hall afterwards elated and crushed at the same time. We had to get on and do something, we didn't want to be just any old cover band pretending to be someone else. But we lived dull lives. We had nothing to draw on. Nothing to say. We were no different to our audience, we didn't offer them anything."

A succession of venues came and went. Neon lit doorways down narrow alleys, the reactionary posters of a trade union club stranded in the middle of a capacious car park with its solitary rusting Volkswagen, a youth club attached to a bland Protestant church, the anonymous entrance to a city centre bar and finally, lining up to remind Susan that she and the band were going nowhere, the upright brick walls of the school and its empty hall. Right back where they started. "We played here in front of twenty-six people. I had a bigger audience when I sang Hey Joe."

From the expanse surrounding the Ahoy to the expanse of the river channel feeding Rotterdam's harbours and quays, Susan stopped to watch a container ship float through a dusky landscape dominated by sky. The dark water, flanked by a distant line of trees, flowed towards the toy cranes and model warehouses. A putrid yellow haze hung over the skyline from Rotterdam's latent light. Somewhere to the west, across the void, was a better future. "We had a bit of money from our jobs and what we didn't spend on equipment and printing posters we saved. We thought we could tour Holland, maybe find an audience in Amsterdam or Den Haag, Arnhem. When we felt ambitious we had plans to conquer Belgium. Belgium!

"It was when Marco's father came back from Felixstowe with Deep Purple albums we decided we had to get to England. That's where all the bands we loved came from, so we added up how much money we had and bought a van". The van, an old Commer, had bug eyed lamps and a roof rack. It had been the workhorse of a local Rotterdam builder whose logo was still visible through a layer of whitewash hastily daubed across it with all the finesse of an act of vandalism, which it would have been on any other surface. Standing on a crate, Rene was finishing the artwork by painting an indecisive mix of jagged and scrolling letters: After Sunset.

"Wim and Marco were worried, it was a big leap for them, giving up their jobs and going to another country. We drove round Rotterdam for a few months, gave them some time to think about it, but it was only when we heard Machine Head for the first time that they started to see the possibilities. The sound of that album and Highway Star did it, like something coming alive, heading towards you and it either runs you down or you jump on board. Wim started to think he could match Ian Gillan," Susan chuckled, "but at least he was ready to give it a shot and make the leap." From the back of the ferry Rotterdam gradually faded away behind the oil terminals and power lines before finally disappearing from view like it had never existed.

"The van wasn't just our transport, it was our meeting room, psychiatrist's couch, jail cell, hotel room. Now and then someone would twitch in the middle of the night and catch their foot on a

snare drum and that was your sleep well and truly wiped out."
The Commer was parked alongside a large ornate pub called the
Queen's Head, which stood like a brick and stone tooth on the
corner of a demolition site. Slightly more upmarket, partly due to
the fact that it was surrounded by occupied buildings, was the
Kings Lynn Social Club; a flat roofed building with red window
frames. Black jacketed youths slouched past a couple of Triumph
motorbikes and a blue Vauxhall Viva parked in the Secretary's
space. On the wall next to a yellow ochre door was a glass
fronted display case with various events listed from the bingo
night to Tony Valentino (accompanied as ever by Eric and Joy).
Tonight was rock night and last on the bill 'from Holand AFTER
SUNSET.' "A few people hung around to watch us."

Now the van was parked at the gate of a field on the outskirts of
Ipswich. Traffic was relentless and slow moving. The field was an
arable quagmire surrounded by lifeless hedgerows and the
captured litter of Quavers bags, Black Jack wrappers, cigarette
packets and a soggy collector's football card with the unsmiling
face of Leighton James. "Inside the van we're counting the money
we have left. It doesn't take long to count one pound note and
some silver. We had one gig at Hooly Goolys in Ipswich, which
wasn't paying enough to get all four of us home. I guess England
wasn't really ready for a Dutch band playing Deep Purple
covers."

Hooly Goolys was probably more attractive in the evening
darkness when the gloom combined with the drizzle meant you
couldn't see what it really looked like. A converted theatre, all the
ornate details had long been stripped for architectural salvage
and parts of the roof had corrugated sheets instead of tiles.
Squalid would have been a compliment. But to the rock fans of
Ipswich who didn't have the cash to see the big names at the

Gaumont, Hooly Goolys must have been a goldmine. "By playing in Ipswich we could say we sort of followed in the footsteps of Hendrix. Every Wednesday night was rock night and for two shilling you got three live acts and a rock disco." On the steps outside the front entrance was a pot bellied bald man in oversized black jeans and a denim jacket, collecting the entrance fees off the punters queueing up. "Micky Redwall did it all himself. Manager, promoter, booked the acts, took the money, paid the fees, policed the venue, announced the bands, ran the disco. You couldn't question his enthusiasm for the music. We talked to him a lot that night. He knew everything there was to know about music: how it evolved, where the bands came from, what influenced them. He couldn't play a note on anything, but he thought he sounded like Robert Plant when he sang.

"Top of the bill was a band from Cambridge. The Scavengers. Their bass player fell off the front of the stage and injured his leg so we and the other band, Cat's Cradle, had to cover for them. We took a chance and did Child in Time . . . without a keyboard player. About ten metres from the stage was an upright piano and we persuaded some guy to play Jon Lord's parts. I think the crowd appreciated the effort. Micky was grinning like a Cheshire cat all the way through it. He hadn't seen bands like us fill in like that and he was pretty pleased and impressed. We earned our money that night and he didn't mind paying a bit extra. It was a good night. It should have been a great night, but we were preoccupied with how we were gonna get home."

Susan was no longer holding Wallet's hand. He was round the side of Hooly Goolys where Susan and Rene were up ahead in animated conversation with Micky Redwall before walking away from him. Wallet cautiously stepped closer to listen. Susan looked upset, Rene was walking round in small circles avoiding eye contact.

"I know it's probably the last thing you want to hear," Redwall was saying, "I'm not trying to take advantage of you, but I've heard eight people tonight and four of you have real talent. Problem is, those four are not in the same band." Wim, the second guitarist, was leaning against the van, the back of his hair soaked by the drizzle running down the sides. Marco, the bass player, had his hands stuffed into his pockets. He stared at the windscreen unaware of Wallet's presence over his right shoulder. "I'm sorry lads, but you two bottled it tonight. These two were stars. I could see they wanted it and they rose to the challenge, but you looked uncomfortable. You're gonna hold these two back, you know that?"

"I don't want to see this band split up, Mr Redwall," said Susan. "We've only just started, we don't expect to be big overnight. . . . "

"You'll never be big, Susan. You sound like a million other local bands, competent, devoted, but you're wasting your talent if you don't find a way forward and get yourself a better band. Stop playing the covers, write your own stuff. The two girls from the other lot were almost playing on their own. They're a match for you two. You need to decide what you want. A group of friends making a bit of music now and then or a professional rock band. A real rock band."

The tears she was crying that night dried up as Susan turned away from her friends and Redwall and took Wallet's hand to lead him away from the van and Hooly Goolys and the midnight drizzle. Before them was the terraced street in Rotterdam. The wind had relented and some of the trees were finally in leaf. "I was prepared to come back to this rather than split the band up," said Susan. "Micky gave us ten minutes alone to come to a decision so we made a deal. Rene and I would give it three months and if we were no further on we were coming home and we'd start again. But we never came home."

-

"You know the rest of the story," Susan said as the stars reappeared. "We expected excitement, we were ready for the challenges, we were actually looking forward to figuring out how we'd take them on, but the challenge that night in Ipswich was a real punch, a low punch. Watching the two of them leave. It was their choice to go in the end, but the guilt never went away." Susan hugged herself as she spoke and looked for the constellations with Wim and Marcos' names, but there were no real stories up there: no real people who had suffered real regret. No mortals. Just a load of fakes.

"I don't think you have any idea what all this means to me," Susan said. "How far back it goes, where it all came from. You're not gonna last much longer with us if you don't start thinking like us. My story is the same as Rene's. It's the same as Dee's: she never backed down in a fight, never let a problem get in her way. And Elaine was brought up to believe if you can't do something properly don't even try to do it at all. I don't know how it compares to your story, but you've got something to measure it against now. Think about it and decide what your priorities are."

15 - The past revealed

Rob Wallet had never really stopped to think about the farmhouse. It had been chosen for its proximity to Rotterdam, a spiritual connection rather than anything physically logistical. Wallet wasn't sure how far away from their target the others needed to be before they 'took off' as he described it when they vanished into thin air. Could they visit someone in the small hours on the other side of the Atlantic or did some unseen vampiric generator limit their range to a specific number of kilometres? They still hadn't trained him in this particular dark art and it looked now like they never would. He bought the Audi A8 because it had room for the driver and up to four passengers, another point of embarrassment that he was often reminded of. And the car was starting to earn its keep even if it did look a bit excessive being driven around with only one occupant.

No, the farmhouse had been chosen for its symbolic value and also because it belonged to a friend of the band, one of a number of nameless acquaintances who made up a network of assistance that had furnished and accommodated them over the thirty-five years of their hermetic existence. The main building was timber, single storey with a double height dining room and pitched roof. The bedrooms were along a wing of the building with a corridor leading from the front door and separating them from the main living room. The kitchen was ultra modern, fitted out with hardwood and chrome, its fixtures and fittings moving with silky precision and respectful silence. And none of it ever used. The farmhouse was surrounded by a minimalist landscape, trim and tidy, surrounded by metal mesh fencing and acres of unmanaged fields that were once arable crops, but had now been left to grass.

Wallet's bedroom looked out across one of these informal meadows. It was a large room, as they all were, and a mess. The seventies museum was becoming more like a junk shop as the available shelving and storage proved inadequate for the ragbag of items he was scavenging. Variety was the enemy of order, he thought. Having uniform interests led to interior uniformity. Take Dee's room; her sole interest was books and her room was a library, a cornucopia of book spines as regular as a mathematical equation. Elaine's room was a laboratory embellished with the exoskeletons of functional gadgetry that included a lampstand designed by the Swiss architect Bernard Tschumi and a chrome trimmed record player that would have been retro in the 19th century. Rene's room was dominated by his drum kit, but even in there the remaining space was organised around a vast, meticulously arranged vinyl music collection. And Susan's room. . . It could have been an office, it appeared to be lacking any sentimental touches, but then he had never ventured far enough inside to see what was on the wall that was out of sight from the corridor. Like Susan herself the room gave nothing away, said very little, offered no clues.

But on reflection, as Wallet fell backwards onto his bed, that was the old Susan. The Susan Bekker he had known twelve hours ago before she had taken him, like Virgil leading Dante, through her pre-vampiric past. Whatever her intentions had been the experience had revealed the trace of a human being inside her carnivorous armour. Wallet wanted to understand her more, to experience that rational, enthusiastic human side with its inexhaustible love of music and the almost childlike naivety it created. His bedside table had a small pile of unfamiliar notebooks. They had rich ornate covers, gold edges, embossed surfaces. Opening the first book he read the printed introduction 'This is the diary of' and the name written in the space: Susan Bekker. The date February 1974. "Jesus Christ!" Wallet sat up as he realised what he was holding. The truth direct from the source; no anecdotal evidence from the likes of Lance Beauly and Eric Mortimer, no fabricated headlines and underground gossip. Jonathan Knight's Gothic speculation was about to be put to rest. Susan must have left them here?

February 22nd 1974 - Feel like shit again, hate not being able to keep the entries going, but today is the first time I feel strong enough to lift a pen.

The handwriting was light, scrawled, printed rather than long hand. (A quick flick through the rest of the diary revealed most of Susan's handwriting to be partially printed.)

February 23rd 1974 - had another shot for rabies, fuck me they hurt. I'd rather die than take any more of this. I wish I was dead. I don't believe in god, but if there is one will you please take me away from this.

There were no more entries for another eight days.

March 3rd 1974 - Rene, Dee and El came to see me. So good to see someone I love. It helps. Dee loves the colour of my eyes.

Bloodshot is cool apparently. Doctor thinks I might recover.

The suffering continued, but the band were turning up everyday to help her get through it.

March 10th 1974 - Doctor keeps telling me to eat, I keep telling him I'm not hungry. El says they've all been told off for smuggling food in for me, but she doesn't know what that means. Neither do I. The last thing I remember eating was that guy's face at the Valentine's Day party. Wonder where that bastard is now.

March 11th 1974 - Doctor gave me a long examination today. He seems puzzled that my weight is getting back to normal even though I'm not eating and don't feel hungry. He's decided to turn a blind eye to the so-called 'food smuggling.' Uh?

March 13th 1974 - I asked the doctor today why he thought I was suffering from rabies. He told me all the symptoms along with the bite mark were the key indicators. I don't remember any of it, but apparently I had flu-like symptoms, mania, depression, freaking out at the sight of water, screaming pain, violent paroxysm. It was rare to survive when the disease reaches those stages. I asked where the bite mark was and he told me it was just above my left collar bone. Funny place to be bitten by a dog. But there it is. It's fading now, but there are the mounds of two teeth marks about three centimetres apart. I wonder when it happened? Dee told me it was Valentine's Day! We went to a post-gig party and I met some guy and didn't go back to the hotel that night. The day after the police found me wandering around, bleeding and delirious and took me to a hospital. Then nothing. The doctors started treating me for rabies after I started going mad! (I've always been mad. . . .) Mm?

March 14th 1974 - Apparently the doctors are calling me White Rotterdam, a sort of codeword to imply my pale complexion, sickly pallor and, go on just say it, dead eyes (to go with my dead heart). I told them I've never been the bronzing type, but they say I'm whiter than a lot of corpses. Thanks doc! Dutch girls in mid winter with black hair do look a little paler than their olive skinned sisters. Wish I had Dee's complexion. Maybe now I should adopt a Byronesque lifestyle and move to a house on the shores of Lake Geneva. Yeah, to one who thus for kindred hearts must roam and seek abroad the love denied at home. Fuck me, where did that come from? There's still one problem we need to overcome. This sunlight is killing me.

She left the hospital in Essen on March 17th. Her parents took her home to Rotterdam in a car with the windows covered in layers of newspaper. The walk from the hospital to the car almost put her back in bed.

March 18th 1974 - Rene, Dee and El were waiting for me when I got home. What a nightmare trip. The last couple of hours after the sun had set were so much easier. My skin is itching like fuck now, but I don't want to scratch. The doctors didn't tell me that dermatitis is the after effects of rabies. Now I know why dogs are scratching all the time. And so good to hold my V again. Can't wait to plug it in and make some noise. Gonna wring its neck first chance I get. Micky's booked a studio in England to start recording a new album. What? Thanks for giving me time to get over everything even though I do feel so much better.

Wallet speed read entry after entry. Recovery was rapid, Susan's strength was greater than it was before the illness. The band shared her concern that Micky Redwall was pushing too fast to get a second album recorded, but Susan had written eight songs in three weeks. The others couldn't keep up.

April 14th 1974 - Today's session was the best yet. I haven't played like this since the day I started. Walking along the coast at night helps. Seeing the lights out at see, the silhouettes and sound of the waves out there somewhere. Would love to capture that atmosphere. The others are at the top of their game right now, fired up. Dee sounds great, I've underestimated her in the past, but she can say so much with so little effort. El is on fire. Can't wait to play live alongside her when she's in this form. Rene is like a man possessed. Wish Micky could appreciate it, but his non stop crap about vampires is starting to piss me off. He thinks it would set us apart from everyone else, but I think it's a stupid idea. Rabies wasn't funny, but then he is a scrap metal merchant. You can take the guy out of the scrap yard, but you can't take the scrap yard out of the guy.

So, Susan and Micky Redwall didn't see eye to eye about the vampire image and yet We Are Toten Herzen was only the start of a long line of lurid bloodsoaked promotional material. Wallet flicked through the pages unaware of time passing and the sun rising ever closer to the horizon. Redwall didn't like the way Susan slept all day and often argued with her about her new lifestyle. In one entry he told her she was nowhere near famous enough yet to behave like a superstar. Wallet almost missed the entry for April 22nd.

We Are Toten Herzen

April 22nd 1974 - As if yesterday's photo shoot wasn't embarrassing enough I still haven't got all the red paint off me. The album cover's gonna look shit, total nonsense. When we washed the fake blood off Rene he was still red from the embarrassment! The promoter guy was in the wrong place at the wrong time to come around kicking off like that. I don't think he expected me to follow him back to his club. I didn't expect it either. I didn't like the way he passed Micky and Rene and came onto Dee, El and me. Does he think we're the little girls who can be pushed around? I think four guys being just enough to pull me off him was a strong message. He wasn't the only one surprised by that. My temper seems to be so much shorter these days. But he was still laughing at me as he walked out of the door. Don't like that. He doesn't do that to me. He wasn't laughing when we met up again as he was closing up his club. And you know what, that first bite, deep deep deep into his throat. . . . I don't smoke except for a bit of weed now and again, but nothing lifted me like that. Not even the morphine they put me on in hospital turned my head inside out like that bite. My whole body felt like it was in outer space, every nerve relaxed, every muscle loose, no need to breathe. I'll have to do it again. Must do that again. Just need to find another fucker who doesn't mind dying though.

April 23rd 1974 - Had a chance to think about last night. Hadn't really noticed what sort of teeth I was wandering around with inside my mouth. Had a look in the bathroom mirror tonight and now it all makes sense. The bitemark, never feeling hungry, the white skin, bloodshot eyes, and now last night. I can't see my teeth in the mirror because I can't see anything in the mirror . . . What the fuck happens now?

117

We Are Toten Herzen

April 24th 1974 - I cannot be harmed, I will never be hurt, I can do what I want, I am physically stronger, mentally sharper, I will never grow old. I'm in charge now. My future is whatever I say it will be.

Wallet looked for the day when the others followed suit, but he felt a scorching point of light across his forehead. He dashed for the blinds just as the sun exploded over the distant fields. He would have to continue the following night, but when he woke up ten hours later the diaries were gone. Instead there was a note on the table, written in Susan's familiar choppy semi-printed style. 'It wasn't easy to live through that. Still not sure I'm comfortable with it, but I can't turn back the clock. Your golfing buddy Jan has left a message. We're meeting someone in England who'll shepherd us through some preparatory stuff before we go to New York. Could be interesting. Hopefully, we've regained the initiative. If not heads are gonna roll, Rob. Take care of the house until we're back.'

16 - Great career prospecs

Dexter Collier left a comment on his Facebook time-line
'Just got the call to tell me that I'm going to be shaperoning a band before they leave for New York. Major deal going down. Can't reveal the name of the band yet but everyone who hasn't already heard of them soon will.'

Vikki Tomson replied
'Great news. Pleased for you :-)'

Bernie Caspar replied
'Wow Dex!! great news.'

Mike O'Sullivan replied
'Lucky bastard. Is Nicole Scherzinger involved?'

Dexter Collier replied
'No. Alas! (At least I don't think so.)'

Mike O'Sullivan replied
'Whoever it is give them my regards and if they need a good looking backing singer with absolutcly no ego give them my number.'

Seb Mauser replied
'Are they looking for groupies?'

Dexter Collier replied
'I'll ask them.'

Turner Collier replied
'Don't forget your condoms you got for Christmas.'

Dexter Collier replied
'Used em already bro. And anyways they might be male.'

Bernice Jaxon replied
'Good luck, Dex, you deserve it.'

Ann Cheung replied
'So jealous. Tell us all about it when you can.'

Every room in the the Bellevue Hotel, or the Belle as locals referred to it, had a sumptuous booklet proudly describing the heritage. Dee was bored enough to read it twice, but still couldn't find the reason for Sony's UK management team dumping them here. A former gentleman's residence, it was once owned by the Earl of Oldbury who had made his fortune in the plantations of Central America. He died in World War I after being hit by a shell fired from his own side. After his daughters were married off and moved out the house became a hotel in 1961 and retained its gentility, character, landscaped gardens with nine hole golf course and, most importantly, its mock Gothic turret. Gothic turret, of course. Gothic turret. Clever. Vampires, gothic turrets. Funny bastards.

The Balmoral Suite would be their home for the next two days. "Monarchical, flamboyant, ideal for the foreign guest with a large entourage," said Dee reading from the introduction, "or the traveller in need of real relaxation, or the rock band who are missing the gothic turrets of home."

"It says that?" asked Rene who, along with Susan and Elaine, was reading some of the tourism leaflets.

"Course it doesn't. Typical drummer."

There was a gentle knock on the door. "Is this him?" Dee put the book down, opened the door an inch and peeped out. "Who's that knocking at our . . . chamber door, bleurgh, bleurgh, bleurgh!"

Out in the corridor was a grinning, fidgeting boy too small for his jacket and wearing trousers with flares like boat sails. Stepping in with all the enthusiasm of a man with toothache visiting a Victorian dentist he nervously told them he was a student of Business Management at the LSE and twenty years old and had applied for the intern position after seeing it on the Monster job recruitment website and thought that a few months of unpaid excitement in the giddy world of rock music would look seriously good on his CV and thought the hotel was fantastic and that his cousin had a house in Southampton a bit like it but not as big. . . .

"What's your name?" interrupted Rene.

"Dexter."

"Dexter. Is that your first name or your last?"

"First."

"Never met anyone called Dexter before. Your parents weird?"

"Sorry?"

"Your parents," said Rene "are they like hippies or something."

"No. They're from Loughborough."

"Is that relevant to anything?" said Dee.

"No. Not really." Dexter giggled then tried to sit down without looking embarrassed. A small occasional chair had been placed in the middle of the room specially for him. The curtains were drawn across the bay windows of the suite and the lights were dimmed. "So, they christened my brother Turner. After the painter."

"Lucky for you they weren't fans of Heironymus Bosch," said Susan. She waited for Dexter to sit on his chair before she rose out of her own settee. In her heels she almost brushed the chandelier with the top of her head. "Now Dexter you'll probably notice that you're alone. That was our request. We like to get to know the people who are working closest to us, but with you it's a little different. We get hungry and when we get hungry we can't just send out for a meal, do you understand?"

"No. Yes, I understand. I could order or collect your meals if you want I used to get the vegan specialities for . . . nearly mentioned their name. I'm not supposed to confidentiality clauses and all that you know I've signed one for you guys too did you know the lead singer of one of the UK's leading boy bands is intolerant to salt?"

"Dexter, shut your fucking mouth."

He nodded.

"We don't eat meat. We also don't eat seafood, dairy products or vegetables or fruit. . . ."

"Or nuts," Elaine added.

"No nuts, Dexter," Susan said, wagging her finger. "We don't eat English food or Italian food, no Chinese or Indian or Thai, Mexican, Ethiopian or Lebanese. We don't eat salads, special diets, lo-fat, lo-carb, high fibre. We don't graze, nibble, eat on the move or grab snacks when we can or pop out for a sandwich. No business lunches or breakfast meetings. We don't do any of those things. Do you know why?" The other three stood up and slowly walked towards Dexter who was close to wetting himself.

Susan stood in front of him and leaned into his face. "Because we get all the nourishment we need from our interns." She smiled revealing her white teeth and two long predatory canines. Dexter evidently felt a hot flush in the groin of his trousers. The band burst into hysterics.

"You bastard," shouted Dee.

"I knew I should have said five hundred," said Susan. "Sorry Dexter, just a little bet Dee and I always have with our assistants: will they piss their pants when we suggest we're going to eat them. And you pissed your pants, so she owes me two hundred pounds."

Dexter laughed again. "Does anyone have any spare trousers?"

"No," said Susan. "You wet them so you'll have to sit in them."

The band sat down again like automatons or furniture programmed to come alive on the hour every hour before settling back into the decor. "What's your purpose here?" asked Susan. "What have they sent you to tell us?"

Dexter dragged a small notebook out of his inside pocket. "So, Some instructions, they said. Des Tomlinson, from the UK management company."

"Go on. Instructions?"

"So, they thought you might need to be brought up to date with how the industry works these days. It's changed a bit since the seventies."

"Like what?"

"So, like today there are no more vinyl records. There's still a market, but it's like thousands, not millions."

"No shit. No more records?" Dee looked horrified. Horrified!

"They were replaced by compact discs in the 1980s."

"And what happened to all those old gramophone players," said Dee.

"Those what?" asked Dexter.

"Gramophone players," said Dee, "you know with the fucking big horns and the dogs sitting next to them."

"No, well, compact discs are played in cd players, but even they were superseded by audio files and now everyone listens to their music in what we call mp3 format. . . ."

"Wait, wait," Elaine raised one hand as she typed with the other, "What does mp3 stand for, Dexter?"

"Er, it's a standard industry standard format."

"A standard industry standard. Answer the question, Dexter," said Susan. "What does mpfuckingthree stand for."

"It's a multiplatform format, part of an ecosystem that includes avi, er, acc, wma, a multi-format listening experience. Sorry, but it's what music files are these days and you play them on a. . . ."

"Let me guess, let me guess," said Elaine clicking her fingers. "An mpfuckingthree player."

"Come on Dexter, open up," said Susan.

"Some of it's proprietary like, er, but it's all developed for an enhanced visitor experience. We don't call them mp3 players as such. You play mp3 files on your ipod or smartphone or some other device synced to your computer. Or they can be stored somewhere else and you stream them to your device from the cloud."

Dee looked across at Elaine. "Does that answer your question, dumbfuck?"

"Yeah. I suppose it does." Elaine looked up at Susan. "Do we have any mpfuckingthrees, Susan?"

"I'm sure we could find some."

Dee pulled at her earlobe. "Dexter, I've read all of Umberto Eco's novels, including Baudolino, and even I don't understand a word you're saying."

"Dexter, sweetheart," said Susan, "what other wonders of the modern age should we know about? Do people still drive around in motor cars?"

"Yeah. But a lot of them are hybrid electric these days."

Susan rolled her eyes. "Can you believe they sent this guy down here with this. Dexter, we haven't come out of a coma. We didn't travel here from the stars and we haven't been living underground in North Korea for the last thirty years. We know all about music formats, changing trends in music sales. Tell us about fans. Do bands still have fans these days?"

"Yeah."

"Are they edible?"

Dexter giggled. "There are ecosystems with walled gardens so they might be part of a food chain." Nobody laughed.

"How do they listen?" said Susan. "And if you say with their ears I'll cut yours off."

"So, you build up a consolidated fanbase by maximising social media opportunities. You need a big reach strategy and keep the dialogue continuous."

"How?"

"Activity. Keep the Twittersphere buzzing with your name. You're already part of the blogosphere so you're trending already. Especially after the single was uploaded."

"Don't mention that single," said Susan licking her canines.

"Exactly. That's what everyone says: *that single*."

"I said don't mention it." Susan looked at Elaine. "How many are we doing?"

"Eleven so far," said Elaine.

Dexter tried to continue. "So, the single got people talking. That's what made the label sit up."

"They liked it for some reason. What do they want out of this, Dexter? You're immersed in this world. Salt intolerance, cannibal ecosystems, experiences in walled gardens. Are we about to be eaten alive?"

"Oh, no. It's like. One guy I worked with, well not musically, but you know what I mean. Singer songwriter from Basildon. His three sixty degree deal has a revenue stream that pulls together naming rights, branding royalties, agreements across worldwide territories, the ones that matter, you know, Europe, US, South Korea, other monetizing arrangements. The whole exploitation of his brand and earning potential means income maximisation for him and the label."

Susan checked Elaine again who was busy finishing the typing. "Nineteen."

"Nineteen," Susan considered the number. Dexter chewed his lip.

"If you find other collaborative opportunities," he continued, "you can extend the exposure to other markets, you know, reaching across genres, mixes, mash-ups. The old unplugged performances are still there, but now they can be done in a studio in London and everyone in the world can listen to a live streaming broadcast."

"Twenty-two," Elaine announced.

"That's a good number," said Susan. Dee stared at Rene whose eyebrows and twisted mouth said he also didn't have a clue.

"Things have come a long way," said Dee. "At one time all you needed was a washboard and an overcoat and Hughie Greene would take care of the rest."

"Derrick Guyler," said Elaine without looking up. "Imagine if Derrick Guyler was here today, Dexter. A streaming broadcast across a multi-platform ecosystem, reaching out across a range of territories, including South Korea, with nothing but a washboard and rock hard fingertips."

Dexter nodded, the way people do when they're spoken to in a language they don't understand.

"Do you earn anything, doing this, Dexter?" asked Rene.

"I've got savings."

"And rich parents in Loughborough with a son called Turner," said Elaine.

"Weird rich parents," said Rene.

"We're not here for the money, Dexter," said Susan. "You should go and change those trousers now, please. Nice touch, by the way, wearing big flares like that." The band stood up as Dexter limped towards the door.

"I know a joke about seventies clothing," said Dee.

"Some other time, eh," said Susan.

"A man walked into a clothes shop in Birmingham and said I'd like some seventies style clothes. And the shop assistant said certainly. Flared trousers? Yeah, said the guy. Jacket with big lapels and a shirt with frills down the front? Yeah, yeah, perfect, said the guy. And the shop assistant said what about a kipper tie and the guy said, oh lovely. Milk and two sugars please."

Susan rang down to reception. "Hi, it's Susan from the Balmoral Suite. Can you replace one of our occasional chairs? A strange man has urinated all over this one. Thank you."

DAILY MAIL
Faces From the Past
New software used to identify missing persons helps to track down rock band

Experts at a security agency in Birmingham have issued photographs showing how the members of rock band Toten Herzen might look now, thirty-five years after they disappeared. Bromwich Detection Sciences used the software to 'age' photographs of Dee Vincent, Susan Bekker, Rene van Voors and Elaine Daley who were last seen in their mid twenties.

"It was quite exciting seeing the faces emerge in front of our eyes as we put old photographic images into the software," said Connor Goodmans, Managing Director of BDS. The firm, which employs eighteen people, operates from a small industrial unit in West Bromwich and normally helps police forces from numerous countries in Britain and Europe search for missing people.

"A lot of our work helps to track down people who went missing over ten years ago. Certain facial characteristics tend not to change, whilst other elements such as musculature, skin tone and hair colour can. The software retains those unchanging features and ages the others." BDS's last success was identifying a man in Spain who went missing twelve years ago as a teenager. He was found this year in Portugal.

The four images of the band members show the three women,Vincent, Bekker and Daley looking tired, chubbier, but surprisingly respectable considering the band's notorious past. Male drummer van Voors is shown to be paunchy and almost bald.

"We heard about people being misidentified so thought these images might help the search to be a little more accurate," said Goodmans. Asked if he thought the band would be the same as they were in the seventies Goodman replied, "Doubtful. Old women don't make good rockers. I'm more of an Elton John fan myself."

GUARDIAN COMMENT - Sarah Knowles
This obsession with age demonstrates the media's unashamed
sexism

Old women don't make good rockers, says the managing director
of a firm that helps find missing people. When he isn't wasting his
time redirecting a useful police resource to help a ridiculous
tabloid press campaign, Connor Goodman of Bromwich
Detection Sciences is encapsulating what the media thinks of
women in the arts. From actresses virtually redundant at thirty
seven, television presenters jettisoned as soon as the first laughter
lines appear, to rock guitarists subjected to ageing software that
makes them look, according to the Daily Mail, tired and chubby,
the obsession with Toten Herzen's twenty first century appearance
overlooks more serious issues.

The band has a string of questions to answer relating to its short
and violent history. Why weren't they charged with wasting police
time back in March 1977? Did their former manager Micky
Redwall really die after being savaged by his own dogs? Why
weren't numerous reports of fans disappearing taken seriously
and, most disturbingly, will the family of Peter Miles, a musical
associate of the band in their formative years, ever find out the
truth about their son's disappearance? Why isn't Bromwich
Detection Science's issuing his picture forty years after the event?

Instead of these questions we have women being doorstepped in
Milton Keynes and senior citizens being harassed by teenagers,
claiming them to be geriatric vamps. As soon as Toten Herzen's
reunion was announced this paper predicted the tabloid nonsense
that would ensue, but instead of the focus being on the band's

lawless image the media picked up one of its favourite hobby horses: writing off the older woman.

My colleague at the Guardian, Jemima Tollet, has already pleaded with the band to emerge, axes shining, and show the media that it's the tabloids who are the dinosaurs, not Toten Herzen. The number of prominent older women in rock can almost be counted on one hand; for every Doro Pesch (b1964) there are hundreds of male rockers approaching their fiftieth year. If Ronnie Wood and Keith Richards can strut their Strats at their age, so can Susan Bekker with a Flying V. If Robert Plant and John Paul Jones can still rock way beyond their retirement pensions, Dee Vincent and Elaine Daley will be more than a match.

Connor Goodman probably didn't realise the irony in his closing statement to the Mail. Old women don't make good rockers. Why then, in his own words, is he still a fan of Elton John?

17 - Stonebag

Rob Wallet's hunch about the maximum distance a vampire can fly on one tank of petrol wasn't exactly answered by the band travelling to New York on an aeroplane out of Heathrow airport. Simply 'turning up' on the pavement outside 550 Madison Avenue was preposterous, but no one said it was impossible. It was a question to be answered some other day. Susan's diary had explained one or two puzzles and misunderstandings, but it had raised other dark issues, notably how, when and why she had turned the others. For now Wallet was waiting for the right moment, an appropriate moment (if such a thing existed), to talk to Dee.

Wallet found the singer to be a mercurial person, always quick to change subjects, fly off at tangents, contradict and question whatever was said. But she had a strangely approachable character that Wallet was drawn to. She was brittle and caustic, but could take it as much as she dished it out and enjoyed it. Wallet didn't have any of the wariness he felt he needed around Elaine and Rene. There was, of course, the risk that she'd turn on you purely out of malevolent glee, but where Susan played the role of vampire queen, Dee was the joker. Knowing her taste for the unusual and obscure he now wondered what she could possibly find interesting in an airport bookstore. She was fluttering from one stand to another, hardly settling long enough to read the titles. Everything was a paperback, recently released or a universally known classic. There were none of the enormous back breaking monstrosities that bent and buckled the shelves of the farmhouse, no sign of any grizzled first editions or moth eaten original copies dug out of book piles in lost European shops.

"I can't decide if Susan is happy in her current form," Wallet said.

Dee spoke as she glanced at the books. "Current form. Is she a racehorse now?"

"Vampire. Undead. . . ."

"You have to admit, they're very unflattering terms. Why not just refer to her as guitarist who looks good for her age. Ah, here he is. Dan Brown. Oh, what that guy doesn't know!"

"That sort of sidesteps the issue."

Dee groaned. "What issue? Get to the fucking point."

"Sorry. I'm getting off the point." Before he could make it Dee had vanished, then her head reappeared in a gap in a James Bond promotional display.

She held up a paperback. "Captain Corelli's Early Prototype ESP Signature Michael Wilton."

"I read her diary," said Wallet.

From behind the display Dee's voice said, "Oh, fuck!" She appeared, leaning against Daniel Craig's cardboard effigy. "If you weren't already dead, you'd be dead. Have you not figured out yet that girl is a walking timebomb?"

"No, it's okay. She left a couple of them in my room. I read the entry from 1974 about how she became a vampire."

"Oh. Yeah, well, we all thought she was going to die when that happened. She did too. I don't think any of us had ever seen someone so ill. It was grotesque."

"She appreciated you all being there for her."

Dee walked away. "Of course she did. Doesn't take an Einstein to understand that." She spotted a copy of The Exorcist. "Ooh, scary projectile vomit. Bleurgh!"

Another browser heard the noise, but didn't see the book. Dee's face appeared through another gap in a pile of cut price bestsellers. "Of course we cared for her, you knobend. We were nice people once." Then her face was gone again.

Wallet followed her. "I'll get to the point."

"Hurray!"

"How did you turn? How did Susan persuade you to go the same way?"

"None of your business," Dee replied. "That's a very personal question. Now, this is more like it. Look Rob. Stella Stevens' new proto-feminist bonkbuster for bored housewives not getting enough: The Stableboy Fucked the Middle Class Idle Rich Woman up the Arse Again." She turned it over to look at the blurb on the back cover. "Must be a sequel." Wallet shook his head. "Look Rob, there's even a picture of the stableboy's hand rubbing her minge."

"It doesn't say that."

"Six ninety-nine. You gonna buy it? Ah!"

Now what? Wallet peered over the top of the stand to see Dee reading intensely the blurb of a paperback that was thicker than most of the others in the shop. Distracted by the opening pages, Dee's head bent forward and her jet black bob hairstyle parted to reveal the eye patched skull tattoo on the back of her neck; underneath the grinning face was the name Morty. So that's why she often called Wallet a pain in the Morty! "Salvatore Scallio's Una Montagne di Dolore. Mm. Buy that." Dee caught Wallet watching her. "What? You thought I was gonna buy The Stableboy. . . ."

"No, no. I've taught myself not to be surprised by anything any more." Well at least one mystery had been solved. This was about as far as he was going to get today, he thought, as he watched her stroll around, book in hand, Morty hanging on at the back there. Then she stopped and without looking up, took a book off the shelves and waved the cover back in Wallet's direction.

"Here's one for you," she said, still immersed in Scallio's Mountain of Sorrow, but holding up Tiger Woods' autobiography. "Should tell you how to correct that wayward swing of yours." She tossed it towards him and headed to the payment counter.

-

Once again Wallet was back on his own, sat on a row of chairs of the departure lounge surrounded by bored travellers with their backpacks and long handled suitcases, walking that slow walk so common at airports and stations, every travel bottleneck where plane, train or boat stands between you and where you really want to be. Rene joined him, settling into the low chair and letting out a slight old man's sigh as artificial as it was subtle. "Having a tough time?" he said.

"Sort of." Wallet fiddled with the strap of his hand luggage.

"Yeah. You're still not exactly flavour of the month. We're having to do everything we thought you were going to do."

"Tell me about it. I tried talking to Dee just now, but she's like a clockwork toy."

Rene agreed. "Try her after she's gorged. She gets a bit drowsy, slows down a little and talks with a bit more sense. Or maybe you could ask her about something she's interested in. She's been

135

stuck with us for so long now and doesn't get a chance to talk to other people much. She can get a little lonely just like anyone, you know."

"I suppose she would, yeah. Which subjects interest her the most?"

Rene smiled. "What does she not like? History, science, politics, philosophy. All the books you see everywhere, she's read them all. Pick one up, read it, talk to her about it. Show an interest."

"I do try to take an interest, but you've had forty years to get used to all this. I feel intimidated. I think Susan's trying to help me, but, it sounds strange saying this, there's a generation gap. Or it feels like a generation gap. Whatever you are or how you look, you're still older than me, wiser, more experienced. Do you ever stop and think about everything you've done?"

Rene clasped his hands behind his head exasperated. "Rob, thirty-five years we've had to think about it."

Stupid question. "Point taken. Susan showed me some places from her life. Took me on a tour around where she lived, the school she went to, places where she played her first gigs. I didn't know you two were in the same class at school. I thought you were a year younger."

"No, just a few months. She was intense even then. It's hard to make people appreciate how tough her life was before she turned. That was the deciding factor for her, I think. That's how she sold it to us; a form of protection, invincibility, strength. It was okay at first, we were a little naive about what was going on around us, but we felt insulated from it all. All the pressure may have crushed some people, but we didn't worry so much. It's only when you find yourself with nothing to do that you start to have second thoughts about it."

"That's what I was trying to ask Dee, how she felt about it all, but she as good as told me to get lost."

"Dee was easy to persuade. I think she's always been a risk taker. Someone who'll try anything once. Put yourself in Susan's position; amongst the four of us who are you going to tell first you've turned into a vampire?"

"You. She knew you the longest. Wouldn't she confide in you?"

"She told me last. I guess she always turned to me last to say, you've heard everybody else, now what do you think? No, you ask the risk taker first, then the easy going one. Then me. See if it kills the others first then ask me!" Rene chuckled and folded his arms. "I was there when Micky Redwall broke the band up." So was Wallet, but he kept the thought to himself. "The other guys, Wim and Marco, changed her mind, but she didn't want to do it. She was determined she would never be in that position again. When she came to me and explained what had happened and what she was, I didn't want to do it at first, I didn't want to change. It scared the shit out of me. I only agreed for two reasons: no one would ever exploit the band, push us around, make us do anything we didn't want to do, we could take it or leave it, no need to worry about starving if things didn't work out; and the second reason was because we both came from families who suffered during the war, who pulled together to get through all the shit that was happening in Rotterdam. We'd never be vulnerable like that. No one would try to destroy us to make a point. We'd be indestructible. When After Sunset split Susan and I promised the other guys we'd do the best we could for them, as much for them as for us and now we could do it, give it everything.

"It was great, that feeling, you know, whatever happened we could just take it or leave it. The headlines and the horror stories, none of it was true, but so what, let them write what they want.

Micky was playing the part of the big guy so he was happy. We didn't think he'd take it literally and spread the stories, but he never actually knew the truth."

Micky Redwall must have been as thick as one of his car crushers. "In four years he never found out? He never once saw you near a mirror, never saw you appear and disappear?"

Rene pulled his face. Obviously not. "We took care not to let him know. Maybe he had some thoughts about it. Maybe he just couldn't bring himself to believe it. He was a man who made a living out of solid metal and iron, stuff you could feel in your hand, that broke your bones if it hit you hard enough. He formed his own opinion and turned it into a gimmick."

"Susan hated the cover of We Are Toten Herzen."

"We thought he knew something at that point, but then he never asked the question. He'd laugh about it and then go home. It was money; everything he did, every urge was money. Everything was an opportunity and to give him credit he was good at seeing opportunities."

Wallet puffed and shook his head. "He could see everything except the fucking obvious. He had four vampires in front of him and he thought it was an act!" Mind you look at this: two vampires sat in the departure lounge at Heathrow, three others loitering somewhere and all these people walking their traveller's slow walk: no one suspects, not one taking sneaky pics of the vampires, nobody passing the time with their vampire detection app; all of them more interested in hearing the life saving announcement to board. And later one of them will be sat next to or in front of or behind a real, physical, solid, in the flesh, no different to you or me fuck-off Vampire. Micky Redwall could almost be forgiven for not noticing. Let's face it, you wouldn't believe it even if one came up and bit you on the neck. "So Lenny Harper must have come out of the blue?" said Wallet.

"For us yes, but. . . ." This looked like an issue still waiting for an explanation. Rene's features knotted together. "We still wonder if Micky saw it coming and let it happen. Another money spinner, more publicity. But, yeah, that was lucky. He was only a few inches away from fucking it all up. And he had four goes to get it right. It really brought everything into focus. Knocked us out of our complacency. We didn't take it seriously, to us it was like being Dutch or vegetarian. We had to step back from everything and ask some serious questions."

Wallet suddenly felt self-conscious. A boy, maybe eight or nine years old, visible through a forest of legs, was staring at them both. He could have been fascinated by Rene being in a dayglo orange tee-shirt, or maybe his ghostly juvenile radar was picking up on something that adults were no longer sensitive too. Rene noticed him and stopped talking. Then stuck his tongue out. The boy looked around for his mother and in a second of uncertainty ambled away.

"The big change came in 1985," Rene continued "when Susan's mother was ill. She was visiting and her father was asking all sorts of questions. You look at your daughter and she's like over forty years old and doesn't look a day over twenty five. Your own daughter's catching you up, but moving further away. Susan told him it was the mountain air in Germany, but you could tell he wasn't convinced. He didn't have the answer, but he wasn't convinced. Susan knew he suspected something, he was there when she was ill in '74. She could never tell him. It's strange how you can't tell the people closest to you. None of us told our families."

"Was that hard?" Wallet hadn't reached that stage yet where people start to notice he wasn't changing. No ageing, no middle aged spread, no male menopause and mid-life crisis. No increasingly agitated partner watching a mental car crash take place with all its debris and bleeding heart analysis.

"Yes. It still is. What you don't need is one of your parents dying. Susan was very close to her mother and they buried her during the day. The questions that emerge at a time like that are the most cruel. Do you keep someone alive or watch them die? I think part of Susan died with her mother that day and my worry is she's trying to turn the clock back. And she never will. Her father's in his nineties now. She hasn't seen him since 1986. Imagine what he'd think if he saw her now?"

Wallet could see her now, waiting for them at the door of the departure lounge, tapping her wrist. She turned heads without effort, Wallet could see men glancing at her even if Susan couldn't, or didn't want to. "We have to go," he said. "Do you regret the change?"

"No, not really. Maybe somehow we can enjoy it again, but it's still early days. And you keep fucking things up." They walked towards their waiting guardian. "I think she wants to complete what we started. We split After Sunset to make Toten Herzen work and I think that's what she intends to do, pay back what we owe to people and then, who knows."

"You boys talking football?" said Susan.

"Sexist comment," said Rene. "Not all of us men like football."

"Oh yeah, I'm forgetting."

"All right, all right. Can I just make it clear I don't actually play golf," said Wallet.

"So what's the board game all about?" And there was just the hint, the slightest twist of Susan's lips to suggest a smile.

-

There was one last ritual before the band boarded the plane. As the other passengers gathered Susan asked Elaine if she had the stone bag. Wallet whispered to Rene, "What's the stone bag?"

"Watch and learn."

The band stood at a safe distance as Elaine casually stepped up to a middle aged man dressed in a dark business suit, punching out a text message with the stylus of his smartphone. "Excuse me," she asked politely, leaning a shoulder towards him, "Can you just take my bag while I get my passport?"

"Sure," replied the guy as Elaine slid the bag off her shoulder. He was instantly pulled double and dragged to the floor by the weight of the bag, which almost ripped his arms out of the sockets. The bag hit the floor with a dreadful thud. The band creased with laughter, wiping their watering eyes, spluttering and choking. Elaine, without acknowledgement, but with the straightest face in the room, took her passport and boarding pass out of her inside pocket, thanked the guy and lifted the bag back over her shoulder without a hint of strain. Returning to the band she grinned and winked as the business guy rubbed his hands and stared at her with a mixture of embarrassment, confusion and respect.

"What's in the bag?" whispered Wallet.

"About a hundred and fifty kilos," said Susan. "Gets them every time. Oh, if you didn't laugh you'd cry."

18 - Don't touch

A memo had been sent to all staff in the New York office reminding them of 'sunfree afternoon.' Word was already out about Martin Lundqvist's irreversible hearing loss and Jan Moencker's lucky escape and people were eager to find out more about the Europeans responsible. When senior management heard about the potential for an adoring flash mob forming in the corridors of Sony's headquarters another more urgent memo went out to be picked up by email, text, iphone and ipad (both sizes) or photocopied and pinned, glued and blu-tacked onto kitchen and corridor walls. It contained a list of instructions to be followed on the arrival of Toten Herzen.

staff will not:
speak to any member of the band
make eye contact with any member of the band
approach to shake hands or greet any member of the band
request autographs
take photographs
make any kind of video or audio recording of the band
attempt to retrieve hand or fingerprints from any surface
collect as keepsakes or mementos any object handled by the band
invoke or provoke a response from any member of the band

stand within eight feet of any member of the band

On a wall near a watercooler one of the photocopied memos had an additional entry handwritten at the bottom: 'in other words all staff should fuck off out of here when they arrive.' Todd Moonaj saw it, considered taking it down, but then thought his actions might be seen as heavy-handedness, censorship, just what the band would want. Trouble.

The executive meeting with the band was to be held in a long wood panelled room on a floor with all window blinds closed. No amount of sunlight, however small, was allowed into the building as per the band's request. Moonaj had been happy to go along with the rider, well maybe happy wasn't quite the right word. "Whatever the assholes want, let them have it and get them on a plane back to Europeland," were his exact words. He occasionally stumbled across articles about Mariah Carey or Axl Rose and thanked every Abrahamic god there was he didn't have to deal with people like that. Evidently his luck had run out.

"How long will it be, Todd, before you accept the music industry is like this?" said Mike Tindall, proposed Toten Herzen Finance Director.

"Mike, I accept that traffic congestion in New York is shit, but that doesn't mean I have to like it."

"They're here. . . !" A receptionist burst into the room. Moonaj deliberately hid his reaction by adjusting the angle of the back of his chair. The rest of his 'team,' hastily put together and open to restructuring should events take a certain unforeseen twist, took their positions along one side of the table. An executive silence greeted the visitors as Rob Wallet walked in and said hello. He looked for the most appropriate chair to sit on as the rest of the band appeared one by one behind him. All four of them were smartly dressed, as rock bands go, no outward signs of substance abuse unless painting your face white could be classified as such. One male, three females, possibly two, Moonaj wasn't sure about the one in the white jacket with red spikes in her head like an exotic fruit. Of course they were all surgically attached to their smartphones and tapped them as they sat down. No hellos, no eye contact, no admission of existence. There were no stories about the building being haunted, but then who would be the ghosts in here? Finally, finally one of them looked up. The tall one with the longest matt black hair like she'd been colouring it with the ashes from a crematorium nodded to Wallet.

"Ready? Do we need introductions?" asked Wallet.

"I think that would be the polite thing to do," replied Moonaj, loosening his tie. He spoke to the receptionist who was still waiting for an instruction. "Sharon can you pour some drinks for us please. I'm sorry we don't have any blood, but there is coffee."

"We're fine thanks," said Wallet. Drinks were served, but none were drunk.

Moonaj exhaled and blinked rapidly. "I'll go round the table, shall I? To my left here is Mike Tindall." The large geometric man in the tailored white shirt and silver tie smiled at the band, but quickly withdrew it when the void of four faceless expressions looked up at him. "He will handle your finances, expenses, receipts, recording costs, tour costs and any other expenses you may incur which I'm sure will be substantial. He has the enviable task of monetizing you for all you're worth."

Dee's eyebrows raised and she tapped her phone. Rene looked at her suspiciously and copied her actions.

Moonaj tried to continue. "Next to Mike is Bob Tazares, your tour manager. When we eventually get round to such things and from what I'm told there's already a clamour out in the blogosphere and Twittersphere and social mediasphere." Wallet, Susan and Rene responded with a flurry of taps on their phones. Were these bastards listening? "Bob has twenty-seven years experience working with some of the biggest names in music, so bear it in mind he's seen everything there is to see. Throw it at him, everything you've got." He also had a receding hairline and bags under his eyes like two hammocks.

"I'm unshockable," Bob said. He'd need to be. There was no response from the band.

"Linda Macvie will be your marketing manager," Moonaj continued semi-patiently. "I know Toten Herzen is already a pretty strong brand with exploitation opportunities," tap tap! "and widely recognised, but Linda will guide you through the twenty-first century and what a modern audience expects and demands. She'll explain the big reach strategy later." Macvie was a mirror image of the woman sat opposite her by tapping on her phone and scrolling through her ever expanding list of messages. On second thoughts maybe Susan Bekker was making notes. For the next few minutes Moonaj was prepared to give the band the benefit of the doubt and speak a little slower so that they could get it all down. Or he could fuck off for a late lunch now and leave the others to it. He didn't need to be here. Didn't want to be here. "On my right are probably two of the most important members of the team," he said sarcastically.

"Shock, I don't believe it," said one of the two most important members of the team, holding up his empty Starbucks cup. "Songwriter is given credit by record label executive screams New York Times headline."

"Torque Rez and Mike Flambor will be your songwriting production team. You will work with them on all new material and remastered material. You can continue to write your own songs, but Sony will not release them and you will not release them independently. All work comes through Torque and Mike, so welcome them into the team. Yours will be a collaborative arrangement and you'll be making use of their familiarity with multi-format platforms and proprietary ecosystems." There was a collective gasp and a spike of activity with the phones. Moonaj paused a moment, but the table was too wide to allow him to see what they were up to.

"To their right is Bill Brandt, your legal manager. He'll deal with contracts, deals, all the boring stuff. . . ."

"Naming rights, legal issues affecting territories other than the US and Europe, including Russia." Rene smiled at the little man in the big jacket, who was also given an inexplicable acknowledgement by Wallet.

"And getting you out of jail," said Moonaj finally. "At the end of the table, Tom Scavinio is your manager. He will be your first point of contact on a day to day basis. After this meeting you'll have no more dealings with me. Everything goes through Tom."

Susan transferred her attention from her phone to her new manager. Scavinio was half a man, a remnant of what he'd once been. He wore a suit like a bad thought and was the only one leaning forward at the table with his chin resting on his fist, pushing his mouth upwards until it was almost underneath the tip of his nose. He had a permanent disinterested scowl. His hair was the only part of him that came close to any sense of animation, statically electrified and grey, like an old mobster or a cartoon drawing. He could have been asleep with his eyes open, but Moonaj knew he was fully alert on the inside. Susan may have imperceptibly adjusted her body angle towards Scavinio and they occasionally, briefly exchanged mutual observations.

"You'll see a lot of Torque and Mike and Linda," said Moonaj, "but Tom will pretty much be with you everyday from now on." He sat back, arms outstretched. Job done. "And that's pretty much it. I'm told by people I trust that you have potential and I have a duty to exploit that. But please do me a favour and just now and again drop the masks and behave like rational human beings, which I'm sure you are. It will make life so much easier for everyone."

There was an awkward pause before Wallet felt the need to respond. "We just want to make music. Everything else is outside our control. Whatever you read or hear about, it's all media driven exaggeration and ninety-nine percent of the time not of our making."

"Not of your making? Are you taking the piss?" said Moonaj.

Susan Bekker moved noticeably for the first time. She took a folded sheet of paper out of her back pocket and read from it. "Staff will not speak to any member of the band, make eye contact with any member of the band, approach to shake hands or greet any member of the band, request autographs, take photographs, make any kind of video or audio recording of the band, attempt to retrieve hand or fingerprints from any surface, collect as keepsakes or mementos any object handled by the band, invoke or provoke a response from any member of the band, stand within eight feet of any member of the band." She threw the paper at Moonaj. "Are we fucking infected with something?"

"We wanted to save you the embarrassment. . . ."

"You have the fucking gall to accuse us of excess and you're circulating things like this. Well let me introduce you to our side of the table. To my left is Elaine Daley, she plays bass guitar. Dee Vincent is our vocalist and plays rhythm guitar. Rene van Voors is our drummer and comes from Rotterdam like me, Susan Bekker, lead guitarist. You guys can sit there feeling as self-important as you like, but just remember without people like us, you'd probably be working on Wall Street and you know what people think about bankers. We make you guys look respectable, so don't hate us."

"We don't hate you," said Bill Brandt offering the palms of his small hands. "This is purely a business agreement, Miss Bekker, it's a contract and if you break the terms of that contract we will seek redress. But we don't hate you."

Wallet was signalling to Brandt to calm down. "We've had contracts before, we know the score. All Susan is trying to say is that we have a way of doing things which works, don't disrupt that or else you'll end up with a different band to the one you think you're signing."

"A way of doing things that works?" said Moonaj. "Hasn't worked for the last thirty-five years if you ask me. When did you last release an album? 1976?"

"What's your market position?" asked Macvie. The band simultaneously looked at their phones as if her voice was coming out of them. "Amongst all the hard rock acts who are out there, why should anyone listen to you and not one of the others? Why you and not Metallica or Slipknot, Rammstein, ACDC."

"I thought the job of marketing was to find that out," said Susan. "Earn your money and tell us."

"No, that's your responsibility. Instead of drinking a lot and staying out late you have to speak to people, establish a relationship that creates a consolidated fanbase," tap tap, "what you're known for doesn't impress a generation who didn't bat an eyelid at wars in Iraq and Afghanistan. It's all about respect, making people feel as if you really are there at the other end of that Twitter stream or replying on Facebook. You can't act like gods these days. You have to be part of their circle not giving them permission to access yours." She started fiddling with her own phone to bring up pictures of the band's old record sleeves. She held up an image of the Dead Hearts Live artwork. "Stuff like this is a dime a dozen. You can see real gore on a million websites these days."

Wallet was clicking his fingers. "We had nothing to do with that."

Macvie smirked. "It has your name on it, sweetheart. Look, I'm saying all this for your benefit. You're coming back after thirty-five years. How will you feel when you go out there for the first time and no one stops to look, no one stops to listen, everyone passes on by and tuts, 'yeah seen it done that.' I'm trying to make sure that the Onion doesn't give you the Marilyn Manson treatment."

"So what do you suggest?" Wallet asked. "Do we have to guess are or you going to feed us clues. Why don't we build up a large art collection or relocate to a tax haven. We could get really close to our fans by suing the arses off them for the occasional illegal download. Or maybe just sign over the rights to some licensee who can sue them on our behalf then we don't get shit all over our fingers. Worked for Nuclear Blast and Century Media."

"You're being stupid now," said Bill Brandt.

"No, I'm being honest. We build up a large fan base and then distract them while you lot mug them from behind."

Susan grinned.

"Let's arrange another meeting sometime to discuss this properly," said Macvie. "Drop the old Munsters routine and bring you up to date."

"Munsters?" said Dee. She turned to Elaine. "I told you those Russian plastic surgeons didn't know what they were doing."

"We'll have that meeting, Linda" said Susan. "I think we should make it a priority. It's important for you to get to know who we really are."

"I'll give Tom the details of my diary after the meeting," said Macvie.

"And what about you two? Tweedle Dum and Tweedle Dee." Susan was casually waving her phone like she was waiting for someone to ring her back. Making small talk to pass the time.

"We're ready," said Torque Rez. "We spoke to Jan in Berlin about what not to do. Would have been nice to speak to Martin Lundqvist, but you know."

"All went a bit Beethoven for him, didn't it," said Dee.

"That's one way of describing it, I guess," said Torque sharing Bill Brandt's evident disgust. Moonaj was solidifying with boredom.

"Let's not run before we can walk," said Mike Flambor. "Why don't we just get together, book some space somewhere, crack open a few beers and just play some music. Keep it real, you know, a little bit unplugged," Rene and Susan got a shock off their phones. Flambor waited for them to deal with the cause.

"Sorry, did you say unplugged?" said Susan.

"Yeah, just see how we all get on. Hang out for a while, go places. I know you weren't happy with the song Jan arranged for you."

"On our behalf," Wallet corrected.

"But one friend to another," Flambor continued, "your music is the rock equivalent of Gregorian chant. And you look more like a group of hairdressers than a dangerous rock band. But," he held up his Starbucks cup again, "that's Linda's problem not ours. Trust us and we'll make sure you don't get bottled off when you support Uriah Heap next time they play Carnegie Hall."

"Okay children," Moonaj stood up as Torque Rez walloped Flambor's ankle under the table. "this is where I go back to the real world and leave you babies to throw things at each other. I think everyone wearing a suit and tie is done here."

But Mike Tindall wasn't done here. Moonaj remained on his feet to keep his colleague brief. "Can I just add something," Tindall said examining a document in his leather folder. "Our investment is underwritten and we'll need a medical examination from all of you as part of the insurance conditions. Tom can I leave that for you to arrange?"

"Yeah, sure." Scavinio was making to leave too.

"Medical examination?" said Wallet.

"Yes. If one of you drops dead from a medical condition you already knew about we lose a significant sum of money from lost revenues and we don't want our insurers surprising us with a get out clause."

"We'd be delighted," said Susan. "When would you like us to do that?"

"Leave it with me," said Tom. "I'll fix a date and feed back to you."

As the suits stood up Moonaj couldn't resist one final speech, a farewell gift. "I try to stay out of the more excessive corners of this industry. I am a self confessed rock atheist and pop agnostic so your image and all the terrible historic baggage it comes with is of no interest to me whatsoever. I don't want to see you on the cover of Rolling Stone magazine, I want to see you on the covers of Time and Vogue and Cosmopolitan and GQ and anywhere else there's a market waiting to be razzle dazzled by your particular brand of sound and fury, I want you trending. . . . ."

"Bingo," Rene was the first to make the call and his triumph drew a collective groan from his colleagues.

Moonaj was almost out the door when the call stopped him. "What? Bingo, what is that, a Dutch word?"

"We got some tips and advice off your intern in England," said Susan as Dee and Elaine put their phones back into their pockets. Wallet was inspecting Rene's phone and handed it back to the drummer with disappointed resignation. "Bullshit Bingo," said Susan. "And Rene won."

"Goodbye." Todd Moonaj pulled his jacket on taking several attempts to control an awkward left sleeve. On his way out Bill Brandt attempted to shake hands with the band.

"We don't shake hands, Mr Brandt" said Elaine holding the paper memo in his face. "Haven't you read it? And stop looking at my tits, I'm not Rihanna."

-

Rob Wallet followed Tom Scavinio who was sneakily grinning at Susan as he left the room. The executives' polite retreat to the corridor exploded once outside with a salvo of belches and wall thumping. Bill Brandt described someone as assholes, but as Linda Macvie, Torque Rez and Mike Flambor remained in a huddled whisper at the far end of the table, the target of the little man's bile was unclear. Eventually Wallet came back, still in need of a bathroom now and again obviously, and said quietly to Rene, "I keep thinking his name's Torque Wrench. . . ."

"Sh," said Susan. The band could hear what was being whispered in the other group.

-

"I think there's a huge disparity between the band's music and the image," mumbled Linda Macvie.

"Yeah, I agree," replied Torque Rev.

"They've been sold on the back of all this so called vampire gore and excess, but then you listen to them and it's like psychedelic sixties crap? Where's the energy that matches the image? It's like Lamb of God going on stage and playing the Carpenters. No one gives a shit about their image and the music is straight out of the ark."

"And another problem," whispered Mike Flambor. "The vocalist," The other two agreed. "She's the weak link. Jan knew what he was doing cutting her out of the track. She's just a passenger."

"I was already thinking about that," said Macvie. "Well, how about this. This is just off the top of my head, but I was chewing it over during the meeting. We approach one of the networks with a proposal for the band's next vocalist. X-Factor meets the Human Centipede or something. We have a tv show to pick their new vocalist. It would give us another twelve to eighteen months prime time before the next reinvention."

Torque Rez nodded.

"It wouldn't be impossible to engineer a split. Wouldn't be the first time. Maybe pull the Dutch away from the Brits. The fault line's already there. Two bands pulled together to make one. There's always guilt hanging round in the background when that happens. If we can pick out that guilt and build on that, you can split them up again."

Flambor breathed in deeply. "Strip them down and then rebuild it from the bottom up."

Macvie agreed. "Bekker and Daley, definitely, maybe the drummer, but the vocalist has to go."

-

Back at the dead end of the room the band listened without acknowledgement. The two clusters eventually met and exchanged smiles of varying intent. "Let us know when you're ready for that discussion, Linda. See if we can tease out the essence of Toten Herzen."

"Then we can bottle it and sell it like all the other whores do," said Dee.

"I'll be in touch. Next twenty four hours." And with that Linda Macvie was off, arranging her scarves and juggling all the hand held gadgets. Torque Rez and Mike Flambor made their excuses and followed her. Rob Wallet carefully drew back one of the window blinds.

"Hurry up," he shouted. "Sun's going down."

"And I should be joining them." Tom Scavinio rolled into the room like tumbleweed, overcoat on, small rucksack over his shoulder and studied the band who were now sitting all alone like abandoned children.

"They left us all alone, Mr Tom," said Susan.

"A word of advice." Scavinio sat on the edge of the table alongside them. "Mike is just doing his job and doesn't care about you guys one way or another, but the others. They see you as a lump of modelling clay and they're gonna try to mould you to suit their own needs, not yours. Don't let all the dismissive bullshit fool you. They've all been up all night jerking off at the thought of being in charge of Toten Herzen. Let them ride it for a little while,

let them have their fifteen minutes and then do whatever you do.
Trust me, you'll enjoy it more."

"Thanks for the advice," said Susan. "And what were you doing
all night last night?"

"I was taking care of my wife."

"What's that a euphemism for, Mr Tom?" said Dee.

"She's dying of cancer. I like to be with her as much as I can
these days." The silence left him uncomfortable and he tried to
reverse what he'd said. "Looks like I'm showing you out of the
building."

"Well you are our manager, now," said Rene.

"What prize did you win?" asked Scavinio as he led the way.

"I don't know. What prize have I won?" asked Rene.

"Linda Macvie's head mounted on a silver plate," said Dee.

"Don't let them get to you," said Scavinio. "That's what they
want. There's no other way of controlling you other than
provoking a reaction."

The weary group arrived at the elevator doors. "On a scale of
one to ten," said Susan, "how much influence do we have over
what happens?"

"One to ten?" said Scavinio pressing the button. "This scale
doesn't start at the ground floor. It's ten levels under the basement
and you have to be pretty forceful to get on that scale in the first
place." He turned and leaned back against the wall. "Two things.
You, along with every other artist signing to a major label for the
first time, you don't have any say in anything. And secondly, I
know that you guys are not going to get anywhere near a contract
with Sony."

"What makes you say that?" asked Elaine.

"You haven't come here to sign a contract." Scavinio was
smiling. Fuck, this man was cleverer than he looked. "Call it a

hunch. Now are you flying back to your hotel or do you ride elevators?"

"We'll come down with you," said Susan with a broad smile.

Scavinio stepped inside the elevator. "When we get to the ground floor will I still be alive?"

"You ask a lot of questions there, Mr Tom," said Dee and the elevator doors closed with a rattle and a crunch.

Financial Times
Sony's Deal With Toten Herzen Could Be a Welcome Boost to Dwindling Coffers

Signatures haven't been signed in blood, not yet at least, but when they are Sony's latest addition to its catalogue could be more lucrative than they think. The clamour to see what Toten Herzen look like after thirty five years, along with existing titles ready for remastering and re-release in digital format means that Sony have a lot of work already done for them even before a deal is signed.

Davinia Trench, International Media Analyst at Speakman Venture Fund says the deal could be worth as much as twenty million dollars a year to Sony before they even begin to spend money on new material. "There will be a clamour of sponsorship opportunities with companies lining up to associate their brands with a familiar name. People of one generation, brought up in the seventies, will buy into the 'nostalgia fix,' whilst a younger audience, constantly looking for new material will buy into the granddad horror which they won't have experienced before."

Taking a leaf out of EMI and Apple Corps, the Beatles back catalogue was remastered and released in CD format in 2009, digital format on iTunes in 2010, followed by the whole lot reissued a second time in vinyl, individually and as a sixteen album box set. "Toten Herzen don't have the following or the amount of material that the Beatles had, but the example has already been set. There is a precedent for multiple reissues of an old band's recordings."

But Whilst EMI came good with the Beatles, they will also

remember their less than successful dalliance with another 'notorious' rock band the Sex Pistols. "I'm sure Sony are too sophisticated to make the same mistake. The music industry's core values and business aspirations have moved on from the late seventies. Due diligence as a business concept probably didn't exist when EMI signed the Sex Pistols. Sony will not allow any kind of unauthorised behaviour to take place when so much is at stake."

Sony's share price was unaffected by the announcement, remaining at 1,442.50.

RavensWish@TotenHerzen are signing a deal #yippeeeeeeeeeeeeeeeeeeeeeeeeeeeeeee (is that 140 caracters yet) #yipeeeeeeeeeeeeeeeeeeeeeeeeeeeeeee

19 - Losing one's head

One of the advantages of working with Toten Herzen, according to Mike Flambor, was that you only got to work at night, which left the rest of the day free to do what you wanted and in Flambor's case that meant shopping. One of the disadvantages, according to Torque Rez, was that you only got to work at night, which meant he couldn't go out and get laid. Flambor and Torque continued their disagreement outside Randolph's Sushi on 8th Avenue and strode round onto West 21st heading for Minty Studios. "You don't believe me; check out this shirt, asshole," Flambor said.

"Good camouflage," said Torque comparing the pattern to the tree canopies threatening to burst out of their streetlit urban confinement. "What happened, they sell out of Paisley?"

"Paisley's good," said Flambor. "Not as good as this." He examined his sleeves again. "Felicity Garnier, man. Handmade. So new it still hasn't appeared on the catwalk."

"You know we've been asked to work with an old name."

"Yep. Call it the heritage line. It's like repainting a castle."

"They have castles in Holland?" said Torque, his tongue struggling to extract a fish flake from a rear molar. "I think Randolph's sea bass is a little on the obese side these days."

"Hasn't been the same since he fired his cousin. Mind you, the guy had worse dress sense than you."

"I spoke to Todd's predecessor three months ago and he convinced me that something was gonna happen this summer and I was like hoping we'd be discovering the new Skrillex." Torque stood back as two men came out of a house with a sofa. "You see, that's us," he said as the plump struggling piece of furniture was loaded into a truck. "Carrying weight, man. Carrying weight."

"Nah, build it from the bottom up, like we said. If we can pull this off we'll be treated like gods." Flambor laughed, even he didn't believe what he was saying.

Minty Studio was a red brick wedge, jostled by two stone guardians at each side of it. With a grey fire escape hanging over the double doored entrance it looked more like a dispatch centre than a place of music, of art, of creativity in the constriction of New York's heaving asthmatic streets. "We are going to turn the Brady Bunch's boring older relatives into the new new kids on the block, without the annoying chin rashes of the originals." Flambor allowed his colleague to enter first.

"I hope this isn't gonna go on for too long," said Torque as he yanked the door open. "Remember this was your idea; meet up, hang out, have a few beers," he mocked, straightening his imaginary tie, "maybe we can all be buddies and shit."

Inside, the reception area was clear; the cleaning staff only came in before ten a.m. and the only sign of life was the glow of the telephones' lcd screens. Flambor switched on the lights. A click followed by the buzz of the tubes as they sputtered into life. "What's so good about a Felicity Garnier shirt anyway?" asked Torque.

"Oh, Jesus. I bet you ask that question everywhere." They headed further into the building, automated lights glowing as they moved down the short corridor to Studio Two. "What's so special about this Michaelangelo, what's so special about this Ming vase, what's so special about Naomi Watts."

The control room of Studio Two was a lifeless windowless hole. Nothing more than a broom cupboard until the equipment was switched on, the producers settled into their high backed chairs and the artists cued up their throbbing, premature sense of glory. "What time do you think they'll show?" Flambor's voice drifted in the gloom as he identified the silhouettes and shadows.

"No idea. If they show up at all. I've got mixed feelings about this lot. They obviously don't like us. All that Bullshit Bingo."

"I actually thought that was quite funny," said Flambor suddenly illuminated.

"You think Adam Sandler's funny. You laugh at your own stools," said Torque. On the mixing desk was a sports bag with an A4 sheet of paper on top of it. "What the fuck is this? They let Curtis Painter in here?"

"Maybe I could persuade young Susan to see things the right way," said Flambor.

"You wish. Isn't she supposed to be old enough to be your grandmother?" Torque was unzipping the bag. "Looked pretty slim for a sixty year old. You know what they always say: you can tell you're getting older when the rock dinosaurs start looking younger."

"I'd fuck her anyway. I'm not as fussy as people say I am." Flambor picked up the note to read it. "Make sure you get the levels right. . . ."

"Oh, Jesus. . . ." Torque dropped the bag. A teenage boy's head rolled out of it. Flambor laughed.

"Woh, they caught you with that one, partner." Flambor picked up the head and stared at it. "Wonder where the hell they got it.

Wouldn't surprise me if they stole it." He rolled it around, studying the details of it: the partially closed eyes, gasping mouth, congealed blood around the severed end of the neck. "That's . . . pretty fucking realistic, isn't it? You know you need a sort of warped patience to create something like this." Every hair looked human from the number four head trim to the boyish whiskers.

Flambor was still holding the A4 sheet and fiddling with a remote control to the studio television screen. A further instruction was to watch Channel 599 to see the breaking news. Both men stood and watched as scrolling banners provided lurid details of the murder of fifteen year old Anthony Rawls, a high school dropout from Boston. The boy's picture matched the head that Flambor was still holding. He could feel his sushi coming back up.

"911," said Torque. Flambor vomited. "Call the police. We can't sit here with this."

"You'll have to be quick." A voice from inside the live room echoed through the studio monitors. Torque Rez could see Susan Bekker's form on the other side of the glass. Before he could blink she was stood next to him, the rest of the band behind her.

"You still want to fuck me?" said Susan, stroking a lock of hair off the back of Flambor's ear. But there wasn't time to answer.

-

For the second time in as many months Todd Moonaj was woken up by a phone call concerning Toten Herzen. "They're the vampires," he said to his dozing wife, "but we're all expected to be up all night." He picked up the phone. "Yes, yes, yes."

"I'm sorry to ring you so late, Todd. It's Tom. Er. . . ."

"Get to the point."

"Okay. Mike and Torque are dead. The head of the boy murdered in Boston earlier this evening was in the recording studio next to them."

Tom Scavinio got to the point a little too quickly for Moonaj who was now dumbstruck. "Tell me this is a publicity stunt."

"It's not a publicity stunt, Todd."

"What happened?"

"Police aren't saying much, but they think there's a connection."

"They were supposed to be meeting the band tonight. Where's the band? Are they okay?"

"No sign of the band. It's all a little confusing. Police won't say how Mike and Torque died so we don't know if the killer or killers cut their heads off too."

"No sign of the band. Get in touch with Rob Wallet. He'll know, won't he?"

"I've tried him a couple of times, but keep getting his voice mail. I thought you should know, Todd. I didn't want you waking up in the morning and being greeted with a night of speculation like this."

"Just find the band, Tom. Find the band. Waking up in the morning! You think I'm going back to sleep after this. What are you, nuts?"

-

Tom Scavinio hung up. He was taking one of his evening strolls when he took the call telling him of the murders. His nightly ritual of slipping out of the apartment as his wife slept allowed him to experience a world that didn't care. It was a welcome environment where no one asked how are you keeping, how's Sheila, gee, Tom I feel your pain, which nobody did or could.

Instead, New York's indifference and the unknowing faces on
total strangers was a relief from the well intentioned hand on the
shoulder and awkward nod of sympathy. Here, at night, Scavinio
could wander and wallow, let his mind empty and release all those
dead end questions that would build up during the day.

Along Columbus Avenue his routine took him past the familiar
store where he opened a guitar shop in 1981. He survived for
twelve years before the chains invaded and he was forced to move
on in life. The shop was a sandwich bar now. Everybody eats,
these days, he thought to himself as he studied the diners chewing
and swallowing, unable to talk, unwilling to talk. And his new
life, managing local bands who had come into his shop for advice,
encouragement and occasionally, a guitar, had been consumed by
another invading giant when he was taken on by one record label
that was devoured by a larger label, itself ending up in the belly of
an even bigger predator. Every time the company grew bigger,
Scavinio's status and respect diminished until he was working for
some distant unknowable entity; a corporate metaphysical state.
His final challenge was the cruellest; watching his wife being
consumed, not by some ravenous external force, but by her own
body; her own genetics. A month or so after her diagnosis
Scavinio had half listened to the consultant explaining the role of
certain enzymes. At the time the technicalities were of no help or
comfort, no more than the usual hand on shoulder or awkward
nod, but the words were coming back to him now with increasing
lucidity. This enzyme, not enough of it and you die, too much of it
and you die, but get the amount just right, and nobody has yet,
and you'll live forever.

Scavinio found a bar with a television running the news.
Everyone was now hearing the name Toten Herzen for the first
time, albeit by association. Scavinio hit his second double malt,

rolling the tumbler between his hands and allowing himself the sneaky warmth of respect for the band. They were fighting back. They had walked into the belly of the predator and were now eating their way out from the inside. Rob Wallet's face appeared on the screen, apparently talking from a hotel lobby. "Can you turn this up?" asked Scavinio.

Rob Wallet - Toten Herzen Spokesman
". . . This kind of thing seems to follow us around. And it's like history repeating itself. We're just grateful the band weren't in the studio at the time otherwise this could have been an even bigger tragedy. We only met the guys once, er . . . what can I say? They seemed okay. . . ."
Cheryl Tovey - CNN New York Correspondent
"Where are the band now? How are they reacting to the news?"
RW
"They're in the hotel. They're sort of trying to calm down. You know it's been a long night for them."
CT
"Have the police spoke to them yet?"
RW
"Only to break the news to them."
CT
"Do you know why anyone would want to do this?"
RW
"Is it really a choice thing? Only a monster could do something like this."

As Rob turned to leave his expression to the camera struck a nerve deep in Tom Scavinio's mind as if Wallet had noticed him through the CNN camera, perched on his bar stool. It was the briefest raising of the eyebrow, a knowing look, a momentary slip that told Scavinio there was no sympathy, no empathy, no regret; you might have guessed we'd put up a fight, but not with this level of severity. Flambor, Torque Rez and the kid from Boston were in the wrong place at the wrong time and had become the latest victims of local history. He finished his drink and took a cab over to the band's hotel.

-

"Tom!" Wallet looked surprised to see the band's manager stood in the hallway of the Belle Air Hotel. He stood like a detective; he had a suspicious look on his face.

"I tried to get through to you on the phone. How are the band?"

"The band's fine."

"Are they here?"

"Yes. Do you want to come in?"

"Well, Rob, seeing as I've been given the unenviable task of managing them it might be useful to just check they're all okay."

Scavinio entered the room. The suite was vast, palatial in size as well as decor. He expected to find it a mess with the usual rock detritus of abandoned clothes, empty bottles, suspicious packages and under age girls. Instead there were books . . . just books. And a calm that hung like incense. Dee Vincent appeared.

"I called by," said Scavinio. "I need to know if you're all okay." Dee looked half asleep.

"Fine. Why, what's the problem?"

"The problem? Three people dead, at least one of them decapitated."

"Yeah, so?"

Elaine joined them. The band members were emerging from different rooms off the main sitting area. Scavinio felt surrounded.

"A lot of people would be traumatised to be at the centre of something like this."

"But we're not at the centre," said Susan.

"Your songwriting partners have been murdered tonight; it affects you. You might be next."

"I doubt it," Susan said.

"Yeah, I doubt it too, what am I saying? Can I ask you guys a favour," Scavinio said. His hands were still in his pockets. "Can we meet tomorrow, casually, over coffee. Just to discuss where we all stand. Say mid-day?"

"No," said Susan smiling. "We're vampires. We can't go anywhere during the day."

"Right," said Scavinio. "We're sticking to that line are we? Okay, well I'll see what the company is gonna do to replace the writing team, but don't expect a quick decision. Try to make time for us all to talk."

"What's wrong with now?" said Rene.

"I've been walking around and I'm a little tired. I'd also like to get home now."

"Sure." Susan followed him to the door and out into the hallway. "Is there something you want to say, Tom? Something in particular that's bothering you?"

"No. Not yet. But you might at least try to pretend that you're concerned by what's going on."

Susan shook her head. "We never pretend."

Terence Pearl: Blog post
Glory to the new gods

Extract from my forthcoming book 'In League with Nosferatu: the Record Industry's Secret Vampire Conspiracy' by Terence Pearl

If there is one thing Toten Herzen deserve credit for it's their honesty. They are accused of being vampires and they don't deny it. They got away with their crimes for so long it just seemed like another eccentric display of extreme narcissistic behaviour. How so? Because the industry they are part of is just like them.

It plays on a kind of disinformation known as 'false mimicry.' False mimicry is a term first used by Professor Liam Shoelinsky from the Department of Societal Linguistics at the Caspard Institute in Liege. Professor Shoelinsky has described how any community, social, business, religious, can present a mythological facade which then reinforces people's preconceived expectations of how that community might behave. So, if an industry presents itself as self serving, greedy and dishonest, when it's members behave in such a way, rather than causing outrage and opposition the behaviour instils a reserved acceptance that unwittingly causes the observer to ultimately walk away. There is only opposition and a negative reaction when that community reacts differently to how it presents itself.

In the case of the record industry, the promotion of anti-social behaviour, excessive behaviour, questioning taboos and law breaking is central to its business model, and when individuals carry on this way, the public is satisfied, reassured and rewarded. It's what they have been forced to expect and are only happy when the expectation is fed.

We Are Toten Herzen

Thus, a band openly proclaiming themselves to be vampires and involved in a string of killings and abuse are accepted by the public as if it's the most normal thing in the world. However, we should take note of the observations of Heather Moorehouse, a leading anthropologist who has studied anti-social behaviour for over thirty years. Toten Herzen have so far embodied certain typical messianic features: they have attracted an audience, their messages are accepted without question by their followers, they suffered death early on in their lives, the following continued long after their deaths, they were resurrected.

Toten Herzen far from being vampires are more like gods and it's no coincidence that the word god often goes hand in hand with the word rock. A recent survey suggested that a staggering seventy eight point four per cent of Toten Herzen's followers were prepared to die for the band. Not only are these four individuals gods, they are the figureheads of a suicide cult. I wish I could say that they were merely humans and that their excessive behaviour is simply a product of the record industry's false mimicry, but this is a double false mimicry. It is the band using the industry as a cover, not vice versa. In the next chapter of my ebook I'll examine the mathematical patterns which prove that Toten Herzen's first reunion concert will be the signal for a worldwide suicide pact that could lead to the deaths of millions.

20 - Old flames

"Okay who said this: 'The movies make emotions look so strong and real, whereas when things really do happen to you, it's like watching television - you don't feel anything. Right when I was being shot and ever since, I knew that I was watching television. The channels switch, but it's all television.'" Rene looked up from his laptop as Dee came out of the bathroom towel drying her hair.

"Wyatt Earp!"

"There were no televisions when Wyatt Earp was alive. Andy Warhol. Wikipedia page has everything about him. He had a studio on Madison Avenue. Mind you, Madison Avenue is almost as long as the Netherlands so that doesn't really help."

Susan was all ready to go and was having trouble avoiding Wallet who was moving at a snail's pace. "What's up with you?"

"I can't fly."

"Neither can a tuna fish, so what?"

"Well, you're all going round New York by insta-travel and I'll have to take a taxi."

"You've taken taxis before, haven't you," said Dee flicking her towel at him.

"For fuck's sake. Will someone volunteer to hold Worker B's hand," said Susan gathering phone, purse, jacket.

Elaine stepped out of nowhere with a huge toothy grin and a dreadful look of impending violence. "My pleasure," she said.

"No, not her," said Wallet, but Elaine already had his hand in a crushing grip. "I still feel a slight sense of pain, you know."

The five of them followed an ad hoc itinerary around the city, searching for evidence of Andy Warhol's existence, hoping for glimpses, insights, remnants of his time hanging around Lou Reed and the rest of the Velvet Underground. But every point of the trail led to a furniture store or some repossessed bit of historic real estate. The frustration and disappointment grew until the band and Wallet, released momentarily from Elaine's cruel grip, ambled along Broadway.

Maybe the Beacon Theatre might have treats on offer. The venue chosen by the New York Dolls for their 1975 New Year's Eve concert was now hosting the Ultimate Doo Wop Show, followed by Frampton's Guitar Circus and, for one night only . . . was that right? An Evening With Alice Cooper. Someone inside, some unseen joker with a sense of history, must have seen them coming, must have been tipped off that Toten Herzen would be passing by tonight. The coincidence wasn't lost and the band were forced to step back from real life and consider the meaning of mortality. There he was, Vincent Furnier, in familiar top hat and black eyed make up. 'All Alice, All Night' promised the poster.

"Does that make you feel really old or really young?" asked Rene.

"Let's go somewhere else," suggested Susan checking the time on her phone. "What time did Almer say he was around?"

"Any time after eleven," said Dee. "Half an hour yet!"

They all walked away from under the theatre's canopy with a near backward stepping deference to the man they almost met when they were all at the height of their shocking fame. Furnier-

Cooper had taken up golf whilst Toten Herzen were taking down old enemies. There was no appetite to even discuss the divergence in career paths or even how they had once run parallel before Lenny Harper did for real with a bag of stakes and a thirty pence mallet what Alice Cooper's stagehands would do by sleight of hand, tricks on the eye and thousands of dollars' worth of props.

"Well you came out looking for remnants of the past," Wallet said. "Looks like you found one of them."

And there was another one lined up. Almer. Or Alan Miller to his doctor and immediate family: ex drummer with Cat's Cradle who emigrated to the US in 1975 two years after his musical ambitions had been torn apart by Micky Redwall's grand plan. Almer clung on to the cliff face of rock music, reaching a sort of summit in 1977 when he bought a drink for someone claiming to be a roadie for the Talking Heads. Almer dined out on that experience for another ten years whilst collecting several small bars in and around Brooklyn. "What does he do before eleven?" Wallet asked. No one answered.

"I can hear music," said Elaine trying to pinpoint the source.

The Necronomicon, one untidy block from Broadway, turned out to be the portal of sound she could hear. Wallet was enjoying possession of his own hand again and ready to enter the club when he saw the length of the queue outside and guessed the rest. Elaine took his arm, not quite severing it just above the elbow and they were inside, unnoticed, unseen, unbothered by a crowd already bouncing about like bottle corks on a choppy sea. There was space behind the compacted audience and a better view of the stage, but as soon as she released Wallet's hand, Elaine was attracting the approaches of Cory from the Village. (The village? Branston, Potterhanworth, not Cherry Willingham?)

"Fuckin crazy hair," he shouted. True, Elaine's hair did have the same crimson spikes that Cory was fielding, but the rest of him was uncoloured, unbranded. His vanilla skin was vanilla coloured no matter how much the acrobatic lighting changed hue. Undeterred by her Arctic curiosity of him, the boy from the Village blundered on, beer bottle in hand, stud through lower lip, black tee shirt with Lacuna Coil decoration. "So where you comin from?"

"Lincoln."

"Lincoln, Nebraska?"

"England."

"Right. So, is that Missouri."

"Lincoln, England. Europe. Where your forefathers came from."

"Hey, don't talk about my father. My dad's a jerk."

"I can see the family resemblance," Elaine was starting to warm to Cory.

"He works for JP Morgan." In the absence of any feedback from Elaine or even cognisant awareness, Cory was trying to find some physical response to spur him on: a curl of the lip, a rippling forehead, but instead the only reaction was a kaleidoscopic variation around her pupils. Whenever the light shone whitest he found himself standing face to face with someone almost transparent other than the hair and a pair of eyes like red pool balls. "You drinking?" She shook her head. Cory gave up.

Onstage, at the steaming head of the crowd, a Gothic concoction of melodrama wrapped up in corsetry and heavy leather, navigated the tiny space with a dexterity quite at odds with the metallic chopping and grinding of the music. Behind them hung a stagewide banner (all twenty feet of it) with the roly-poly script declaring Argent Extremus. Wallet wasn't familiar with

173

the name, but then there were probably four and twenty thousand Argent Extremuses playing New York tonight; no music journalist could be expected to follow them all. As he looked on, he wondered how their break would come. How could Argent Extremus grapple their way out of a pack of hopefuls so big no one could be sure where exactly the centre of it was? The numbers game was galactic and stacked against just about everyone trying to play it. Possibly, somewhere in the crowd would be a Jan Moencker or a young Tom Scavinio, but chances were they'd all be at home scouring social media hoping to discover who someone else had discovered. That was the chicken and egg runaround being played these days: get the break by advertising how many 'fans' you have, but by the time you had enough 'fans' why would you need a break from one of the big chequebook holders? You do the work yourself then let someone else convince you that you'll be a star if you hand it all over to them.

Wallet mentally pinched himself as he detected the onset of another rant. To his left, Elaine standing like the club memorial, to his right Susan, ignoring the turning heads and sideways glances that he wasn't sure were on the increase or whether he was becoming more aware of. Rene was criticising the drumming. Must be a bloke thing, thought Wallet. See the faults in everything.

"Wait for it," said Rene as Argent Extremus moved from verse to chorus, "blast drumming any bar now. . . ." On cue the drummer was playing everything on a manic four four beat: kick, snare, crash, kitchen sink. "And now he starts getting tired and slows down and they all lose rhythm." Dee was nodding, in sympathy more than disappointment.

When the next song started and a sense of deja vu raised its head, the five of them decided they'd heard enough and headed for the exit. Cory didn't see Elaine leaving. For one night only he could have had her all to himself. All Elaine, All Night: Elaine Daley of Toten Herzen, from England, Missouri.

Outside the club Susan noticed she had a text message. "It's off Tom," she said separating herself to call him back.

"Well I hope Almer's bar's better than that," said Wallet. "Six months ago I'd be ready for a decent pint by now. Is he. . . .?"

"What?" said Dee, "Gay?"

"No, like us?"

"Bored?"

"Forget it."

"Tom wants to meet up with me?" Susan slipped back into line.

"What now?" said Rene. "It's ten to eleven."

"Not right this minute, but he's out wandering and has some questions that won't go away." They formed a huddle in the open space of a street corner and agreed on Susan meeting Scavinio at the basement beneath Almer's bar. (He'd agreed to let them practice there, maybe even let him join in on drums for old time's sake.) Rene would keep watch whilst the rest of them were on the other side of the ceiling if anything happened.

Almer's bar was called Bonham on 11th and in addition to being a total mouthful - according to Dee - it was also a shrine to the Led Zeppelin drummer. Almer had a long bucket list and meeting his idol was at the top: what he hadn't allowed for was Bonham dying first with no mention of meeting Almer on his own bucket list. The bar was virtually wallpapered with framed prints of every size, live photos, posed studies, monochromatic abstracts in the style of one of Warhol's tin can silk screen jobs. Amazingly, the background music wasn't permanent Led Zep with all the other instruments acoustically removed, but a confusing mixture of dubstep, drum and bass, classic rock and the occasional shriek of punk thrown in to get the last punters to fuck off home at six in the morning.

Susan and Rene headed for the stairs to the basement. Scavinio had his instructions and was only ten minutes away on foot. Dee was the first to spot Almer, leaning against his own busy bar in discussion with a member of staff who wasn't listening. He had a pint of something amber coloured with a head of froth, so couldn't have been American beer, and was wearing a tee-shirt that was oversized even on his already oversized body. Almer's little vocalist friend squeezed into the gap between his stomach and the bar and stayed there for a whole ten seconds before he bucked away in surprise.

"Fuckin ell, thought someone were givin me a blow job then!" Elaine grabbed him round the neck from behind. "I could have done, but you wouldn't have noticed, you fat bastard." Dee straightened up and gave him a hug from the front.

"Wi your fuckin teeth I'd have noticed somethin. Who's this behind me? Is it Smiler?"

Elaine kissed him, quickly, a glancing blow of the lips, but with just enough pressure to avoid falling into air kiss territory. "Susan's downstairs meeting someone, Rene's gone with her so it's just the three of us for now."

Almer was released and he turned to see the third member of the three of them, the unfamiliar face of Rob Wallet. He offered his hand and said "Hi. You're the writer bloke aren't you?"

"Ex-music journalist, sometime writer, full time pain in the arse to these lot now," said Wallet.

"I know what they're like. I tried coming over here to get away from em, but they fuckin track you down in the end. You havin a drink?" Almer knew before Wallet could answer what the situation was. The hesitation, the subconscious search for an explanation. "Fuckin ell, you as well. How did they convince you? Or did they go all Keith Moon on you one night?"

"That's something I wanted to ask you," Dee interrupted, sitting herself up on the bar top and gripping her legs round Almer's midriff. "If you like John Bonham why have you got pictures of Keith Moon all over the place?"

With the breath being squeezed out of him Almer managed to twist around to Wallet. "You'll have found out by now what a fuckin cheeky little shit she is."

"Was she always like this?" said Wallet happy to see someone else being abused.

"Yeah. That's why me and Grant were glad to see the back of em. Every year we sent Micky Redwall a Christmas card as a show of gratitude," the constriction was getting visibly tighter, "and then his dogs ate him." He grabbed her legs and they exchanged cruel eye contact, but it was a genuine show of affection Wallet hadn't seen before even within the band. Almer was old. With his post-eleven pm stipulation Wallet was expecting to find another twenty year old sixty year old, but the old Cradler was both excluded from the hive and in full knowledge of its existence. His spreading weight, marbled skin and grey hair, still quite full but no longer capable of the length necessary for old rocker cliche, was Almer's reward for not joining the club. In front of him was a fresh faced goblin, to his right a steel and stone imp.

"So, you know the score?" asked Wallet.

"Score?"

"What they are, what I am, why we sleep during the day and refuse pints of proper bitter in bars that look like they're owned by Norman Hunter?"

"Oh yeah. But, you know, everyone has their secrets, don't they."

"Rob's secret is playing golf," said Elaine. She dared Wallet to respond.

"I'm playing the long game, Almer," said Wallet. "I wind this lot up until they pay me a wedge to get lost."

"Oh yeah," he said drumming the tops of Dee thighs, "These two don't pay for anything. Tighter than the skins on my drums, short arms and deep pockets. Never bought a round in their lives. I reckon that's the main reason they turned; so they wouldn't have to buy anyone a pint." Dee squeezed again and Almer stopped drumming.

"There was someone in ere askin about you lot a few weeks ago."

Elaine froze and Dee's legs dropped down against the bar. "Who?"

"A bloke, bit younger than me. Local."

"New York accent?" asked Wallet.

"Definitely New York. Asking all sorts of questions about your past, the years you were away from everything." It would have been such an innocuous statement at any other time, but at that moment it landed on the bar like a verbal grenade.

"Did he know who you were?" said Elaine. She and Dee were readying to head downstairs.

"Everyone knows who I am," said Almer. "The guy who used to be in the band with the two who used to be in Toten Herzen. He must have known."

Dee jumped down from her seat and left without speaking. Elaine came round to Wallet. "You wait here. Ask Almer about the plan." She patted her ex-colleague on the back.

"The plan?" said Wallet.

"They haven't told you?"

Elaine was off, pushing through the crowded floor space with a determined and confrontational straightening of her shoulders. "They don't tell me anything, Almer," said Wallet. "I will have a pint after all."

21 - Deep down below

Ian Gillan was ready to go down below, to the inferno. But there were no fires raging underneath Almer's bar. Bare brick walls, a flight of timber steps, a few empty barrels lying around and cables. Long heavy duty cables. Before Scavinio could see her, he could hear her. A gentle aimless strumming on a guitar, a brief flurry of notes, then strumming again. He paused for a moment to recognise a pattern to the doodling; was it a troubled sound, peaceful, searching? He couldn't tell, but as the basement floor opened out before him he saw a range of guitars on stands, a drum kit, Marshalls, and in front of it all, Susan sitting on a simple wooden chair, playing, not the Flying V, but some Fender-type cutaway. From the sound it made he guessed Ibanez and he was right.

He wondered what it would sound like in this closed underground space if she suddenly let go and played it full throttle, full bloodied.

"You found me," she said without looking up. Scavinio grabbed another chair, pulled it close and sat down.

"I could hear you three blocks away."

"Really?" She could see he didn't mean it. "So what's bothering you, Tom? Why the dramatic text and the oh so many questions routine?"

Scavinio pulled his face and let the strumming guitar fill a long long pause. "Curiosity finally got the better of me," he said. Susan nodded. "It isn't that long ago everything made sense, but then Sheila became sick and the questions started."

"So this is about your wife?"

"No, not necessarily. But the first wave of questions started gathering back then. Why her? In a world like this why was she chosen to suffer like that? A beautiful, friendly, loving, caring, sweet natured woman. Why her? You start to question everything and what you took for granted isn't the familiar state of affairs you thought it was."

"And it took you how long to come to this conclusion?" Susan's eyes would look up at Scavinio from underneath her dark, angular eyebrows diving in towards the top of her nose. Her mouth waiting as if another word was on its way and the ever present tips of those canines, two passive reminders of who she was.

"On their own I'd just dismiss them as part of life, part of the great conundrum, but then when you least expect it you get a call and your name is part of the conversation. You'd expect everything to be seen in context, but surprisingly, instead of the unbelievable being shown for what it is, it doesn't seem so unbelievable after all because everything has become unbelievable." Scavinio's weight pushed back into the chair as he laughed. "I mean, your age, your appearance, your teeth. Someone might get the wrong impression and start to believe all this shit." He wasn't sure if he was getting through yet. He'd be at the end of the road when the music stops, but the strumming continued. "When you walked into the room for that meeting did you not ask yourselves why no one talked about your age and how you look?"

"No."

"Okay. It might not be important to you and that's fine if you have your own reasons for being there, but they didn't ask because they don't care. Their minds were already made up. You're a hoax, put together by Rob and to be honest, quite well executed. That's what they were thinking, but when I got the call I was at a place where I was ready to believe anything. If ordinary life doesn't make sense any more what difference do four vampires make?"

The music stopped. Susan searched the space between her and Scavinio and found something. A new riff, a new melody rolling around and around.

"I have other issues to deal with and I'm trying to find a way of trusting you four or at least understanding what you are. In a few days time we might all walk away and never see each other again, but I don't want that."

Susan didn't appear to want that either. The music softened until it was barely audible. Her face was preparing for some display of emotion. She was a beautiful woman with features that couldn't possibly contain the number of stories and experiences she should have accumulated in sixty years. Scavinio whispered, "Did you kill Torque Rez and Mike Flambor?" Now he was straining to hear the music, but it was still there, drifting with the answer that Susan wasn't ready to offer. She turned away and started playing louder.

"Before you came over here," Scavinio continued, "there was Mike Gannon. He was an asshole nobody liked. I can see that one. The other four: they were tipped off by Micky Redwall in 1977 that something was going to happen to you? Is that true?" Susan nodded. "And they didn't tell the police or warn you that you're own manager was up to something."

She shook her head.

"Mike and Torque? They took me aside and mentioned Dee, getting rid of her?"

"And what did you say?"

"I didn't see it myself. No Dee, no band."

"They take one of us, we take three of them."

"Three?" Scavinio waited for the other name, but Susan carried on playing. "I saw your medical reports."

"We're in pretty good shape, don't you think? Considering our age."

"Better shape than me. You know we can all help each other here, but before I can trust you, you have to trust me."

"I can trust you."

"There is one other question that's been bugging me. In 1977, what the fuck were the four of you doing in coffins in a tomb in Highgate Cemetery?" Scavinio casually crossed his legs ready for another obtuse explanation.

"You think it's unusual four vampires sleeping in a tomb?"

Scavinio grinned.

"It's a long story. I promise I'll tell you that one some other time."

Scavinio leaned forward close to the neck of the guitar. Susan's fingers were long, delicate, gentle on the strings as they flowed up and down the notes. "Just give me a sign, a hint, one way or another who you really are and I promise I won't ask any more questions." Susan paused on middle C, holding the note with a slight vibrato whilst she considered his request. Scavinio knew the rest of the band were in the room. He sat up to look around and the three of them were standing and sitting on the steps.

"Give us a moment, Tom," said Susan and handed the guitar to him. He could smell her perfume on it as she walked away.

-

On the roof of the building that contained Almer's bar Toten Herzen gathered for a meeting. Against New York's rooftops they waited for Susan's briefing, but they already knew what she was going to ask.

"Do we tell him?"

"We can't do this without a manager we can trust," said Rene.

"What does he know?" Elaine was the only one pacing around the rooftop.

"He knows pretty much everything. He's done his homework, as you'd expect, but he's trying to make sense of it all. You can almost see him arguing with himself over his conclusions. Unavoidable conclusions."

"Is he ready for the truth?" Rene asked.

"I don't know," said Susan. "His wife's at death's door. She could go any day now. My concern is he's gonna ask us to save her life."

"What? Turn her?" Dee wasn't expecting this scenario. "We're not here to provide some kind of homoeopathy."

"I don't know for sure he'll ask, but it's a possibility."

"It's a possibility," said Elaine, "but it's also his responsibility if he asks. If he asks."

"He might not ask," said Susan. "He might turn himself inside out wondering whether to make that decision, but yeah, you're right. That's his call."

"But we still need a manager," said Rene. Susan agreed.

The decision would be another step along the plan, a big step. There was no further progress to be made until this one significant decision could be made.

"We make this decision now and we can get out of New York," Elaine said. And that was the clincher.

-

Scavinio was still in the basement, sat in the same chair and lost in his own nostalgia as he tried to play the notes from his favourite songs, but all he could manage were a few careful arpeggios. "Not exactly Eruption is it, Tom." Susan's hand pulled the guitar away from him. The four band members came around in front of him and they started to look like they meant business. Without hearing anything other than the original recordings Scavinio felt this was a band who lived and breathed music. They had that desire he had seen in the bands who came into his guitar shop, a disregard for the hoops and puzzles of the industry, the money games and accountancy tricks, the fancy pants deals and convoluted licenses. They didn't give a fuck for the new three sixty degree deals and sponsorship scams, the monetizing fandangos and affiliated corporate mind games that led in one direction: the bottom line of the hedge funds and vulture capitalists. Standing there were four people who could and would spit on Todd Moonaj's business plan, take Linda Macvie's marketing horseshit and feed it back to her one spoonful at a time, and he hoped, in vain, that they had lectured Mike Flambor and Torque Rez on the historic importance of Carnegie Hall before tearing their insignificant heads off.

"Come here." Susan held out her hand. It was freezing; the chill from it ran along Scavinio's arm and engulfed his body. Out of nowhere his guitar shop appeared, the lights still on inside, a few customers visible inspecting the racks of Fenders, Gibsons, Epiphones and BC Rich models new in, still made in America before the production lines halted and shifted out to the far east. Inside the store the smell of wood hit him in the face and the warmth of the electric lights was a relief. There was a hushed background chatter occasionally interrupted by the hysterical squeal of a bum note. It made Scavinio laugh to hear that again. Eventually he saw himself, explaining the settings on a Marshall amp that was way beyond the thirty dollars the kid had to spend. He pointed out more affordable models that would do the same job, or at least make a good fist of doing the same job until the kid was earning Eddie van Halen's salary and he could come back for the real thing. Behind them the door opened and a little bit of the dark street outside peeked in. Scavinio should have closed up for the evening ten minutes ago, but he never threw people out. There was always the risk of another and another desperate young hopeful slipping in when he was wanting to slip out. Tonight was no exception and in walked a young woman. Tall, lean, silver skinned with black hair like liquid jet. The recognition was instant. She gazed around. Scavinio noticed her, but was still preoccupied with the kid and the amp. They acknowledged each other with a brief nod and she continued to look over the Gibsons. She took a price tag in her hand.

"I wanted to see what mine was worth," said Susan softly.

"I knew it was you," said Scavinio. "When you walked into the meeting room. I was ninety-nine per cent sure, but this. This seals it. You look at the Firebirds and Explorers and then leave." And she did. Two more minutes and the girl was gone.

"We came to see Almer. The first time we'd been to New York and we wanted to make sure he was doing okay. I saw the shop and thought, that place looks cool. Scavinio's Guitar Shop. You don't forget a name like that, Tom."

Scavinio rubbed his eye and swallowed heavily. "The other kid bought the amp, but I don't know if he ever got his Marshall."

"We can hope, Tom."

Back in the basement Rene was sat behind his kit, Dee and Elaine were trying to familiarise themselves with the strange bass and guitar Almer had left out for them. Seeing Scavinio back in the real world they started to play the opening bars of New York, New York. Dee stepped forward to the microphone and began a breathy Monroesque version of the lyrics that made Scavinio's knees weaken! "Start spreading the news. . . ."

Rene clattered his cymbals and started a simple two four beat, the band broke into the theme tune to the Munsters. "This is who we are, Mr Tom," shouted Dee. "Ha haah!"

"Can you play something real," Scavinio said.

"We don't do requests, sir, we aint no tribute band," said Dee. And Susan played the final notes of Any Old Iron. "We's a rock n roll band, mister."

"You should know that by now, Mr Tom," said Susan playing an expectant series of notes. "You know who we are. . . ." The volume grew louder. "And now you know what we are. . . ." and louder. "Fuck it, Tom, fuck everything, fuck the world, fuck life, fuck the beginning and the end, Tom. FUCK IT ALL."

-

The volume went through the roof as the band launched into one of their own songs. The sonic boom vibrated every panel in the bar, higher frequencies shaking the glasses and the prints. The floor thudded with the bass notes hammering their way upwards and the kick drum sending a shock wave through every skull that was still in the building. Almer looked at Wallet who looked at

Almer. Both men waited for the missile to come through the floorboards at any minute. Their grins were a mile wide and not the only ones in the bar as the other drinkers started to howl and yell, arms up, fists gripped with the devil's horns out for the first time that evening. And the charge continued, every freight train coming in from Grand Central, every Airbus landing at Kennedy Airport, every vehicle in the city revving its six cylinder engine, every nerve and fibre of New York unleashed in a single cacophony of visceral noise. Almer lost all sense of shame and started playing his air guitar like a demon, accompanied by air drummers, air conductors, shakers, jumpers, headbangers, nutters. The whole place was a blur of stupidity, a dancing wreck, chairs went through the air, tables flipped over. The bar top was lost amongst people clambering to get on top of it, and down below in the inferno the sound continued, relentless, intense, bass heavy, unstoppable; for ten minutes Bonham on 11th was on the verge of collapse, shaken to bits by the aural battery and the combined weight of a bar full of crazed rockers hearing their lives played out with no sense of control or restraint. A joyous ten minutes they thought they'd never hear again this side of Armageddon. The four horsemen could fuck off and take their trumpets with them. The end of the world would sound like this.

22 - Big ears

Tuesday was always a long day for Todd Moonaj. He knew Mondays were terrible because they followed on from the relative relaxation of the weekends. But his Mondays were so bad they tainted and violated his Tuesdays as well, which wasn't supposed to happen. Moonaj's week only really began to settle by Wednesday before the bedlam of Thursday and Friday began when everyone was trying to contact him before the weekend arrived.

So Tuesday was finally over and about to surrender to the evening before grinding to a halt when Moonaj took a call from Mike Tindall asking if they could meet for a quick beer on the way home. Gregg's Loco was usually a quiet bar at seven pm Tuesday so they both rolled up to a table and sighed audibly as they sat down. Tindall couldn't help laughing.

"We sound like old men, Todd."

"We are old men," said Moonaj."Old before our time."

Tindall opened up his smartphone. "If only we could be vampires. We got the medical reports through this afternoon for our delightful friends from Europe."

"Go on, humour me. Are they as clinically dead as they claim to be?"

"Far from it. The staff at Crendale Medical Clinic are wondering now if their test procedures are correct. They're not sure how four people their age can be so healthy. Some of the headline details, and this applies to all four of them: 20/05 vision."

"Is that good?" asked Moonaj.

"Well, let's say a bird of prey would be proud of that. Hearing range 12 hertz to 30 thousand hertz."

"Bird of prey?"

"It's okay. Not exactly in the same range as a vampire bat, but for a human it's going beyond the normal limits. The ability to hear low decibel sound raised a few eyebrows. Then blood sugar, 72 mg/dl, haemoglobin A1c 3%, blood pH 7.4. Here's a strange thing: everyone's blood produced exactly the same results, like they had a fifty gallon drum of the stuff and injected themselves with it. Rene's blood is the same as the girl's, which is just plain wrong."

"Okay so, he's a woman . . . with a beard. . . ."

"And testicles," added Tindall. "What else? At rest oxygen consumption 245 mL/min, on the treadmill oxygen saturation remained at rest levels of 99% which is better than a drug-free Olympic athlete."

"Better than a drugged up Olympic athlete, I think. Do they ride for any cycling teams? Maybe we should get them in the Tour de France this year."

"Your not taking this seriously, Todd," sang Tindall. "BMI range 21, cholesterol 95."

"Fuck me, even I know that's low."

"Could account for them being so aggressive all the time. Like I say the clinic's checking their procedures because they think there are errors in these figures. I mean LDL cholesterol 3 mg. That can't be right, even for a healthy person. Let alone four sixty year olds."

"Oh, not that old bullshit again. Mike, they are not in their sixties."

"Birth certificates say they are."

"We can't say that for certain. The certificates could be faked."

"National Health Service in the UK supplied the data and matched their National Insurance numbers."

"Fraud. It's the easiest thing in the world to steal the identities of four people who died in 1977. There's your explanation why their results are so healthy. They're twentysomethings who take care of themselves. Come on, Mike, you've seen them. We all agreed this has to be a hoax. It hasn't played out yet."

Mike Tindall lowered his voice. "Todd, to pull off the conspiracy you're suggesting, they would have to fake and manipulate a lot of things. The bands history, press reports, their own physiology, other people's witness accounts. How many people are involved? Why hasn't one of them let slip what's going on?"

"And the alternative, Mike? Vampires? Which implausible scenario do you think I'm going with?"

Tindall had to agree. No matter how difficult it was to comprehend the scale of the hoax, the alternative explanation didn't begin to stand up to scrutiny.

"My biggest concern, Mike, and I've spoken to Bill about this. I just hope they're not opening us up to legal proceedings somewhere down the line. There's a whole nation of litigious nuts waiting with a writ for us to fall on our faces. People have been sued for miming, what are people going to do if they find out the whole band is a fake? Maybe Tom can speak to Rob and get some clues on how they're managing to pull this off. I don't mind concocting some kind of confidentiality agreement with them if, and only if, what they're doing is legal."

"Okay. Fine. I understand that. One other thing. Do you know your ears are identical to how they were when you were a kid?"

"Thanks for that, Mike."

"Your ears never change shape as you grow older. I just thought you might like to know, next time you meet the band."

"There isn't going to be a next time," said Moonaj finishing his beer.

"Photographs of the band taken in 1976, off an original album sleeve, Dead Hearts Live. They have the same ears."

"Plastic surgery, Mike," Moonaj was exhausted. "Glue on fakes, I don't know. Were Mr Spock's ears real? Let me spell it out for you. The only thing unnatural about Toten Herzen is that they still have their own livers. Now I'm going home to laugh at another episode of True Blood."

"And there's the teeth."

"Email the report to me, Mike." Moonaj's patience ran dry. He picked up the bill and left Tindall to think about teeth by himself. On the way home he heard his phone ring and go to voicemail. It was Mike Tindall, determined to ruin what was left of Moonaj's Tuesday.

"Hi Todd, it's Mike. I just thought you really should know the dental report was interesting. The fangs, you know their sharpened canines. According to the dental reports the enamel is real, that is they're not veneers or crowns, and the teeth are not dentures, all roots and nerves are still intact. And of course they show no signs of the enamel being shaped or filed. In other words they're pretty damn real. Who would have thought? Have a nice evening, Todd. Oh, and the clinic's x-ray machine is bust. Expect a bill for that."

Moonaj pulled the car over and paused a moment. He pinched the skin between his eyes wishing the voicemail message would suck itself back into the ether unheard. What was he to do? He tried to think of other hoaxes, real or otherwise and how much trouble they had caused their authors. Was Elvis dead? Was Kennedy killed by a stranger on the grassy knoll? When Neil Armstrong landed on the moon was he serenaded by starmen or NASA engineers? Maybe, just maybe, this was a cleverer band than he was giving them credit for. Maybe, just maybe, their deception was something he should go along with after all and milk it, or rather squeeze every last drop of blood out of it. Tuesday was done. Bring on Wednesday. Wednesday's are supposed to be quiet.

23 - Monetising

To: RobWallet
From: admin.LeeHoWang
Subject: **Toten Herzen; monetizing the brand - draft summary ref255622/13**

Hi Rob
Please find below a summary of the meeting to discuss the first ideas for monetizing potential of Toten Hezen. These are possible outcomes. If you have any questons do not hesitate to contact Tom.

Bex

Attendees:
Bill Brandt - Legal Director
Mike Tindall - Chief Financial Director
Linda Macvie - Marketing Strategist
Tom Scavinio - Band Management
Archie Ragg - Creative Director

Outcomes:

BB - Gene Simmons was doing this when TH were still only biting toffee apples at the fair.

AR - Tie in with **Huawei** over two years. Apple considered the arrangement too dark for its 2013 aspirational message, although the product range white colour scheme suited the complexions of the band
  $14.5 million

  AMD happy for a tie in with its quad-core rhinestone chip for portable devices
  $1.2 million

  Microsoft will use Susan Bekker as the face of its Windows Phone 8 campaign on condition she smiles more, albeit with closed lips
  $750 000

  Wal-Mart thinks the TH Express ready meal endorsement has possibilities. Initial strap line centres around 'big enough to feed the hungriest rock gods'
  $174 000

  Cartier impressed with Rene V's mysterious pallor for its nightlight watch face
  $320 000

  Levis promise to make Dee Vincent look two feet taller in its brick washed jeans

We Are Toten Herzen

$240 000

Live Nation teaming up with **Dr Pepper** not ideal, but could put $1 million more on the table, so we'll take the money
$2.4 million

MT doesn't envy LM's job making that one plausible

AR - **Goldman Sachs** need more time to consider sponsorship; concerned about the 'irony' of the relationship
$?

Donna Karan happy to continue with a 'black' range for the fall 2013
$80 000

Victoria's Secret want to be the closest thing to a vampire's skin
$70 000

'If anyone can shoot a vampire **Canon** can'
$630 000

Anything omitted?

TS - the music?

AR - **Ibanez** refuse to share a stage with Gibson. Bring up the subject of sustainable timber imports and ethical forestry, then

196

light a fire. Accidents happen

Surprised **Seat** want in. (Even got me baffled)
$265 000

Toys R Us taking a big risk pushing an exclusive dark Bratz range, but it's their funeral if it all goes tits up
$312 000

Total income over two years$20. 869 million
TH income at 2.9% $605 201

TS given the task of presenting all this to TH

-

Rob Wallet gave the email a moment's thought then decided to follow the footer's request to consider the environment and not print it out. The only reason he could think of for doing that would be to rip it up. But he had a good idea that once the band saw it, they'd be amused at the scramble to associate with them, startled at the amounts being put on the table and enraged at the cut they'd receive. He wondered how all this fitted into the Plan.

24 - Taking flight

A shaky hand held video on YouTube told the story. Police were waiting at Dulles Airport for a small private jet to coast to a halt. Once stationary the plane was bathed in spotlights like a superstar before a cautious SWAT team surrounded it, themselves watched by the world's media and hundreds of airport passengers and staff. The time was a few minutes after eleven pm. The plane stood in its circle of adoration, but the star of tonight's performance was still inside waiting for a grand entrance not of her making. Nervous fingers covered triggers, sharp eyes bulged from under the rim of kevlar helmets, scopes were trained on the door of the jet as it clicked and folded open. The steps unfurled and a woman collapsed in a heap in the open door. The SWAT team moved in: two officers up the steps, dragging the woman by the arms back to ground level - losing a shoe in the process - then pinned face down as they handcuffed her.

The video was copied and duplicated, uploaded again and again until the combined viewing figures were over two and a half million. In New York, Todd Moonaj was keeping himself informed and swallowing tablets like he hadn't been fed in a week. Linda Macvie, Toten Herzen's Marketing Strategist, was the latest victim of the curse.

-

The whole episode was on YouTube before Linda Macvie could be escorted to a high security immigration facility within the airport where she was given a vile cup of coffee and one chance to phone her lawyer. By the time the lawyer arrived, Macvie's name was headline news and on the way to becoming a household name.

"The flight was fifteen minutes out of La Guardia. A routine business flight to Washington for a meeting about a forthcoming tour and sponsorship deal for a major artist. The details were still embargoed; the only clues being she was nearly as old as Toten Herzen, but not nearly as much trouble.

"I must have fallen asleep, although I don't remember falling asleep. I wasn't tired. The day had been relatively quiet up to then. I sat back on the plane, made a few calls after we had taken off then started to read a book. First book I've read in months. Patricia Cornwell's Bone Bed. Police procedural. I should have known better. The blurb says it's about an enemy that's impossible to defeat!

"Then out of nowhere . . . she just appeared. Just standing there watching me. I don't know how long she'd been there, but I felt her presence before I saw her. As I was reading a voice inside me kept saying Susan Bekker wants to talk to you. And I looked up and there she was.

"I screamed out, it was a jolt. You don't expect to just see someone appear like that. I didn't know what she was doing on the flight. I asked her are you all here and she said no. Then Dee Vincent walked by, or appeared, just appeared out of nothing. They didn't say anything, they just stood there watching me, staring at me. I can't believe this, but I said to them have you read

Patricia Cornwell? I didn't know what the hell to say. What do you say when that happens to you?

"Then Dee Vincent started saying something about replacing her in the band, about a TV show in which we'd find a new vocalist and dump her. I didn't know what she meant at first, then I remembered a conversation at an introductory meeting with the band and I was talking to the writing team . . . but we were at the other end of the room. I started to wonder if the room was bugged, if the plane was bugged, my flat, my office, was it Todd, the band, who was bugging me, why? It was all standard procedures. I told her I didn't know what she meant, but she called me a liar.

"Then Susan Bekker asked if I could fly a plane and I said I could, but not one like this. I'd had flying lessons. She knew the pilot had taught me, she knew everything about the pilot and me: we'd had sex in the past, my husband didn't know, Leo, the pilot, his wife didn't know. I thought they were going to blackmail me or something. I waited for what they wanted, but they stayed still. They never spoke. I was freaking out, asking them what did they want, how did they get aboard, why didn't they say they were coming on the flight with me. Even though they had no reason to be on the flight, this wasn't business about them.

"Dee Vincent went up to the cockpit and went inside. Susan said Dee wasn't pleased and was very unpleasant when she was in the wrong mood. I asked her what were they doing and she didn't answer. I asked her how she had got aboard without me seeing her and she said they did a lot of things that no one ever sees. She said it was funny how so much was said about them, but no one ever sees what goes on.

"Then the door to the cockpit opened and Dee Vincent came out, and she was covered in blood; licking her mouth, licking the blood away from her mouth. Susan Bekker licked some of it away too. She was breathing heavily . . . her eyes were bulging out of her head. Susan Bekker asked her if she was satisfied and she just nodded. She couldn't speak, she just nodded.

"Susan Bekker said to me you need to land this plane on your own now. I went up to the cockpit . . . I didn't really want to look inside. I sort of knew what to expect after everything that had happened to Torque Rez and Mike Flambor. And, Christ. . . . The blood, all you could see was the blood. And Leo, sitting there, his throat or his neck, it was hard to tell. She had cut his throat."

-

Linda Macvie had said all she could say and bent forward resting her head on the table. Her lawyer left the room to talk to a waiting FBI officer called Berry.

"What's she saying in there?" asked Agent Berry.

"She's saying a lot, but it's like she's high on something. It's just a babble. She's talking about someone called Susan Bekker and Dee Vincent." They both knew the names.

"She must be representing them up in New York. There's been some activity up there past week or so. Three dead, two of them were colleagues of hers. Is she implicating Bekker and Vincent in the killing?"

"She's saying one of them cut the pilot's throat."

"Right. Amazing."

"Amazing?"

Agent Berry spoke quietly. "Linda Macvie was the only person on the plane when it landed, other than the pilot. There was no one else aboard that flight."

"She did say she was having an affair with the pilot," said Macvie's lawyer. She wondered if the two police officers standing guard outside the interview room could hear this so nudged Agent Berry away from them. "He gave her flying lessons, they had sex, she didn't say how long this had been going on, but it seems far fetched to think that might be a reason for doing this. I don't know, it's too early to tell."

"Okay," said Agent Berry thinking out loud. "Two colleagues in New York, now her pilot. She says two people mysteriously turn up mid flight and then disappear." He raised his eyebrows for a response. The lawyer had to agree with his unspoken conclusion.

"I think she needs to undergo a psychiatric assessment before you go any further with this."

"Oh I will," said Agent Berry. "We might be some way off a motive yet, but our killer is inside that interview room. I'll speak to you again. Thanks for coming down at short notice."

Before they separated Macvie's lawyer hesitantly turned back. "Is it worth maybe finding out where the two band members were tonight?"

Agent Berry was astonished. "You're kidding aren't you? Was she that convincing?"

"No, no. Sorry, stupid question. I try not to get emotionally involved, but to see a train wreck like that. Four deaths. What has to happen to someone to cause that?"

"Four deaths?" Agent Berry wasn't going that far. "Let's keep it simple. Keep it to one."

"You have someone for the other murders?"

"Did I say that?" He spoke closely to her, making doubly sure no one in the world heard him. "Boy in Boston was beheaded. The other two were turned inside out. Go figure." Agent Berry walked away without offering any further clues or explanation, but his mind seemed to be made up; Linda Macvie was not a serial killer.

PART 3: THE FALL

25 - By the lake

The excesses of the trip to New York were over. The band were back in Europe and taking time out at a rented house in Yvoire, overlooking Lake Geneva. Rob Wallet suggested the band lie low for a while and adjust, take stock, reflect on the process. He thought he'd done all right delivering Moencker (in a roundabout way), who had himself delivered Sony (in a less than satisfactory way), who had in their own peculiar and excessive way, delivered a plan. Not The Plan, mind, the mysterious secret arrangement that Almer should have explained, but never did thanks to an impromptu performance that put his bar on the map for a whole seventy-two hours. No, a plan, which may have some influence on The Plan. But anyway, Wallet wasn't sure about either and so spent his time gazing like a piece of classical sculpture across the sunless waters of Lake Geneva. Besides, the public needed time to replenish its capacity to be shocked. There are only so many songwriters who can be devoured before people switch off and start talking about bread and cheese again.

For Elaine, adjusting and taking stock were bywords for boredom and spent her time surfing channels on French television and the internet. One evening, having come down from the mountains to the south of the village, she found Wallet with his feet up, monopolising the television and watching some catch up rubbish: a subtitled interview with an Englishman calling himself Terence Pearl.

"He says we're gods," Wallet said as Elaine wandered in to the lounge.

"Goddesses, surely," she said dropping onto the settee next to him. Wallet could smell the forest on her clothes; the aroma of bark and berries made more pungent and sweet by the moistening of light rain that had been falling all day.

On screen, in a shiny transparent television studio a smartly dressed, slightly balding man was explaining why Toten Herzen were a suicide cult. "That's Susan's favourite word at the moment," Elaine said.

"He's mad as a meringue," said Wallet. "He talks like a Victorian. All thee and thy and thouest. Ex-grammar school teacher, I reckon."

"Sounds local too. That's a Suffolk accent."

Wallet listened more closely as the interview cut to a film of Terence Pearl walking down the quiet high street of a small English town. He jauntily passed the wool shop and a store selling preserves and home made jams, resisting the urge to doff his hat at the local maiden aunts inside, before springing into a bookshop. In the mullioned bay window was a small stack of books: Pearl's books. 'In League with Nosferatu: The Record Industry's Secret Vampire Conspiracy.'

-

Pearl

"There's no shame in admitting that it's difficult trying to find a publisher who is prepared to take my work seriously. These are challenging times for the publishing world. If I wanted to sell my book in an ironic jokey way like Zen and the Art of Motorcycle Maintenance, no problem. But In League with Nosferatu isn't that type of book, I fear."

Voiceover

"Eventually, a local publisher was prepared to print a limited run of Terence Pearl's book. And here in Stow on the Wold, Peerview's is the bookshop utilising the power of technology to spearhead a new printing technique."

Will Peerview

"It's available on our website and we print it on demand when an order is received. These new ways of printing are helping small independent bookshops like this and we're finding we can be both retailer and publisher which is giving us a much needed second income stream."

Voiceover

"The book is also available as an ebook, in a range. . . ."

-

"What the fuck! Look at that guy there." Elaine sat forward to get a closer look at the television. Onscreen, as the camera panned around Peerview's bookshop Terence Pearl was visible in the background talking to a customer. "Get over yourself. That guy is spitting image of Pete. Hey, quick get a load of this." Elaine shouted to the others to come through to the lounge, but by the time they appeared the camera was looking somewhere else and the mysterious customer was gone in a breath. Pearl was shown buying a copy of his own book and leaving the shop.

"What?" Susan recognised the alarm and appeared first.

"You missed it," said Elaine slapping the settee. "This guy here was in a bookshop and he was talking to someone. . . ."

"What's so odd about that?" said Susan.

"Pete!" Elaine repeated. Wallet wasn't in on the secret yet.

"What do you mean?" asked Susan.

"It obviously wasn't him, but there was a guy talking to this Terence Pearl character who was the spitting image of Peter Miles." Dee arrived expecting more information than she was given.

There were no further clues to the mystery shopper. Why he was around Terence Pearl (whose own name meant nothing)? What he was doing in a bookshop in Stow in the Wold (nowhere near Ipswich)? Why he should show up in an article about Nosferatu's biography or whatever hokum this Pearl guy had found under his hat?

"Pete was always a plain looking guy though," said Dee. "Half the world could have passed for his brother."

Elaine grimaced her disapproval. "There's similarity and there's spitting image and then there's uncannily alike," she said.

"The guy being interviewed. Who was he?" asked Susan.

"Terence Pearl," said Wallet. The aroma wafting off Elaine was filling his head as she squirmed on the settee. "He's written a book about vampires in the record industry."

"Right," said Susan. "Another crank." She shook her head and followed Dee out of the house.

Elaine's face had solidified into an intense hypnotic stare as if willing the doppelganger to step out of the television, identify himself and explain what was going on.

"I'll try to find the interview again on the net. See if we can freeze the picture. Get a better look at him."

"It was him," she whispered.

"I'm not arguing with you. If we can get the video we can identify him properly."

Elaine vanished, but the forest left its scent behind with a softly pungent suggestion scattered on the atmosphere like incense. Inspired by it, Wallet took a walk outside and sniffed the late night air around the stony beach of the lake. He was drawn towards Susan's lonely silhouette on the edge of the lake. Her outline was more classical than his, crafted by a much finer sculptor.

"No reflection here either," he said crunching across the gravel. She shook her head and continued looking out at the distant lights of Nyon on the opposite shoreline. With the lake surface so calm, the lights looked close enough to walk to. "Somewhere over there Byron and Shelley, Mary Godwin and Polidori shared a house writing ghost stories and Frankenstein."

"Is that supposed to comfort me?" asked Susan.

"No. I just thought it was a nice coincidence. Polidori over there writing a vampire novel."

Susan gasped. "You're impossible, do you know that?"

"No, I didn't know that. Has that character freaked you out as well? Elaine looks like she's seen a ghost."

"Well maybe she has. Maybe we all did. And the Villa Diodati is that way." Susan jabbed her thumb over her left shoulder before turning back to the house.

If reflections had still been possible Wallet's would have been the only one floating on the weird waters of Lake Geneva where Polidori prematurely wrote his vampire novel. But then, no he didn't write it here, it only came later on. They all gave up except for Shelley's better half who saw a monster and conjured up a tale that floored the rest of them. He found a flat stone and lobbed it, low down, across the surface of the lake, watching it kiss the water five times before sinking. The ripples radiated towards him then silently disappeared into the evening.

The Independent
Sony Deal Collapses
Music industry gives up on Toten Herzen. Final nails in the coffins

Rock band Toten Herzen have been informed by Sony that they will not be offered a lucrative reunion contract following the deaths of their songwriting team and a murder charge against their marketing strategist, Linda Macvie. In a statement issued to the media from their New York headquarters, Sony's Acting Chief Commissioning Officer Todd Moonaj described the band as 'cursed', uncooperative and lacking remorse following the gruesome murders of two of their management team.

"Since day one," Moonaj said in a charged press conference, "Toten Herzen have been a difficult act to manage. They had come to Sony with unrealistic expectations considering they had been away from the music scene for so long, they were still in a nineteen seventies mindset and expected everyone around them to put aside the realities of the day and join them in a fantasy world of their own making."

The deaths of their songwriting partners, Grammy nominated Torque Rez and Mike Flambor, followed by the arrest of Linda Macvie for the alleged murder of Leo Travner, a freelance pilot, persuaded Moonaj to pull the plug on a recording deal and concert tour that was rumoured to be worth around thirty million dollars.

It isn't the first time the band have been surrounded by violent behaviour and strange deaths. In the seventies, they were the victims of their own publicity stunt when an alleged fan killed them all in a vampire styled ritualistic slaying in Highgate Cemetery in north London. In the same year, the band's manager Micky Redwall was killed by his own dogs at his home near Ipswich, but rumours persisted that he may have been murdered by someone acting on behalf of the band. Last month the fan at the centre of Toten Herzen's faked deaths in 1977, Lenny Harper, was found decapitated by police in Germany. (The murder of 14 yr old Anthony Rawls in Boston in a similar style, whose head was left at the scene of the Rez and Flambor slaying, has not yet been linked to the band according to the NYPD.)

A spokesman for the band, ex-music journalist Rob Wallet, confirmed that Toten Herzen were disappointed by the news and that they would still be looking for another deal and continue with their planned comeback. He also quashed rumours that the band were being framed for the murder of the pilot of the plane. "The rumour is coming from the accused. You can draw your own conclusions from that," said Wallet.

RavensWish - gutted at @TotenHerzen deal being canceled #badsony will never get to meet them now def want to kill myself after this

WhiteRotterdam @ravenswish you don't want to kill yourself over this deal there are other opportunities

RavensWish @WhiteRotterdam so let down everything I do is to meet TH feels like the world is against me

WhiteRotterdam @ravenswish put things into perspective and live with hope

RavensWish @WhiteRotterdam all hope went down when the deal blew up

WhiteRotterdam @ravenswish trust me. . . .

26 - The radio speaks

Mark Lawson

"Hellobackin1977 there was a twelve hour gap between the discovery of four bodies in a tomb in Highgate Cemetery and the public hearing the news of the murders of four members of the rock band Toten Herzen. Today, with twenty four hour rolling news and instant reactions on social media, that kind of delay is simply unimaginable. When the band's comeback single Give Me Your Heart was leaked online the public heard the remixed track before the band did. So tonight I'll be asking the question who is in for the greater shock? The public faced once again with the antics of a rock band best known for fans taking a dead horse to one of their concerts, or a band who haven't been involved with the music industry or modern society for over thirty-five years?

"My guests to discuss this are the rock historian Anna Parkinson, former band photographer Lance Beauly, gothic novelist Jonathan Knight, and new age blogger and writer Terence Pearl. If I can start with you first Terence Pearl: is the public shockable anymore or is their reaction more morbid curiosity?"

Terence Pearl

"I don't think they are shocked, I think they are entertained and the shock is more akin to that experienced on a roller coaster ride or a horror film. It's a reaction that is expected. They expect to be shocked and they expect things to happen that will shock them. It is a new virulent form of entertainment."

Mark Lawson
"Anna Parkinson, there's nothing new in this behaviour or the response it provokes, but is the audience's reaction today different in any way?"

Anna Parkinson
"Not really. What it takes to shock a modern audience is obviously greater year by year. If a singer split his trousers on stage people would giggle. . . ."

Mark Lawson
"And call it a wardrobe malfunction. . . ."

Anna Parkinson
"Exactly. But fifty years ago P.J. Proby was virtually deported for that kind of thing and we saw the kind of headlines we see now. So the reaction will always be the same and it comes down to, basically, the same old generation gap, with young people wanting to upset their elders and their elders, who write the headlines, reacting right on cue. It's as if everyone is following a script or stage directions and no one has bothered to update that script."

Mark Lawson

"Although the incident from which we get the phrase wardrobe malfunction did cause a near hysterical reaction when it happened."

Anna Parkinson
"I think that was more to do with the context. A Superbowl final, the display of a female body part and an America that is seeing a revival of protestant conservatism. If that had happened during a regular concert the reaction would have been different. I think it would have been confined to the arts pages, maybe a bit of titillation in some of the tabloids, but happening in the middle of a mainstream family event like that raised the bar."

Mark Lawson
"The reaction to Janet Jackson's wardrobe malfunction was transmitted around the world at the touch of a smartphone button and that may have multiplied the severity of the indignation."

Anna Parkinson
"Yes, but if the technology to do that had existed in the 1970s the reaction then would have been exactly the same as it is now and by the same people. The usual suspects."

Rob Wallet had just woken up. He slept better in the isolation of the farmhouse near Rotterdam. Yvoire was a stunning place to be, but it was busy. A tourist beehive, buzzing all day with the ever present threat of distant voices and accidental trespassers. The band had been back at the farmhouse for a week and were almost entering a state of idleness following the hysteria of New York. Things were happening, but nothing he was being made aware of.

215

Susan kept telling him be patient, we'll explain when there's something to explain and he was starting to feel like a turkey who had been promised better things to come once December arrived.

Now he could hear the television in the lounge as he dozily wandered into the kitchen to make breakfast. Seeing the empty fridge he remembered he hadn't eaten a breakfast since staying in the motel just outside Obergrau. And then he remembered you don't have breakfast at twenty past ten at night. He joined Elaine in front of the television and saw Jonathan Knight sitting next to Lance Beauly.

"What channel's this?"

"BBC2, I think. What did we do before internet streaming?"

"What did we do before BBC2?" asked Wallet. Sat in front of the telly all afternoon waiting for the test films to come on about building Liverpool Cathedral and power boat racing.

"Recognise any of them?" said Elaine.

Wallet studied the line up. "I've met him there, Jonathan Knight, and Lance Beauly and I know Mark Lawson, but never met him. Her face looks familiar."

"And the other guy?"

"Is that Terence, what was it, Terence Pearl?"

"Yep. The guy in the bookshop when Peter Miles's doppelganger appeared in the background."

Wallet remembered the ghostly response from the band the last time Pearl was on the box. Coincidence? What was he up to now?

"How long you been up?" asked Wallet.

"Half hour. Others have gone out, but I'm already full. I saw this advertised on a forum so thought someone should stay in and watch it."

Lance Beauly
"The technology you're talking about expands the level of outrage, but don't forget it can be used to create an expanded outrage in the first place by artists and their management and record labels."

Mark Lawson
"Where you ever asked, I suppose you would have been, to engineer a publicity stunt or collaborate on something knowing there was going to be a strong public reaction?"

Lance Beauly
"With Toten Herzen? Not directly, but then you didn't have to engineer it. No one engineered the dead horse in a horse box when the police stopped it."

Anna Parkinson
"But who tipped them off? Why would the police arbitrarily stop a horse box in Halifax unless they already knew something?"

Lance Beauly
"Probably something to do with the trail of blood following it round the streets of Halifax city centre."

"And we get the blame for it," said Elaine. "You going out later?"

"No," said Wallet. "Got things to do."

"You should get out more. You'll get stiff cooped up in here all day."

"I already am stiff," said Wallet going back to his room. "I'm dead remember."

Elaine watched him go. "So, get over it."

-

Wallet turned on his laptop, activated his anonymising software and surfed to the BBC's site and continued watching the programme on iPlayer. He split the screen to search the net for anything he could find on Terence Pearl. As his ears listened to the debate criss crossing the decades he found numerous pages reproducing Pearl's deranged essays. His personal site was littered with animated gifs, advertisements for his own books, most of them ebooks, and an endless list of subjects ranging from Black Death being a 14th century form of germ warfare to the Hindenburg tragedy being carried out by a prototype CIA with a Bolshevik agenda. Pearl was unconcerned with the usual anti-Semitic conspiracy theories and a lot of his essays were apparently written within a few weeks of each other: between April 19th and June 4th Pearl had penned twenty-six articles, four of them about Toten Herzen and vampires.

Mark Lawson

"Jonathan Knight you were writing about Toten Herzen back in the 1970s. You were suspicious of their behaviour and I believe the first person to suggest there might be something supernatural about them. How did they react to you at the time?"

Jonathan Knight

"I'd be surprised if they even knew I existed. I contributed to several underground magazines at the time such as Macabre, Within the Gothic Arch, Land of Plenty, that sort of thing and had a number of short stories published in anthologies, but I doubt if more than a few thousand people read any of it. There weren't the outlets back then. Terence has probably been read by more people in the last week than I had in several years in the 1970s."

Mark Lawson
"And of course that kind of coverage brings with it a responsibility which is being heavily debated at the moment. It's very easy to use the power of social media to attack somebody, especially if you can do so anonymously. Terence Pearl what has been the reaction to your accusations that the band are a suicide cult?"

"Can you hear this?" said Elaine to Wallet.
"Just reading one of his essays now. Apparently you're the relative of a 13th century German Cathar called Dalen."
"That would be my Uncle Brian. Wonder where he found that."
"Ancestry.com probably."

Terence Pearl
"The usual reactions. That I'm mad, that I'm making it up. That you can see anything anywhere if you want to. But what I think is important is that the band are provoked into coming out into public scrutiny and speaking up for themselves. We're just not getting that."

Jonathan Knight

"I agree. It's what I call the complicity of silence. Back in the seventies there was a whirlwind of gossip, rumour, the wildest stories about what the band did and didn't do and yet they hardly ever came out in public and say that's all rubbish. They knew it was great publicity and the more extreme it became the more records it sold. They allowed a vacuum to develop and people filled it with whatever preconceived notion they had. In the press the silence was evidence of guilt, in the public the lack of denial was admittance, for the fans it was like a knowing look, a nod or a secret handshake."

Anna Parkinson

"A good publicist knows just how much to feed the press and then let them run the story in any direction they want. When it's done well the publicity can be enormous and cost you nothing. Madonna, for example, was the arch exponent of this. Someone like Michael Jackson, on the other hand, was eventually consumed by adverse publicity. It reached a stage where he and the people around him were no longer sowing those initial seeds and they lost control of their own message and stories."

Mark Lawson

"It's a risky tactic played by politicians now, at their peril some might say. Do you think that's what happened in 1977 when Toten Herzen were allegedly murdered? In terms of publicity, was that, to use a phrase, a botched job?"

Anna Parkinson

"Well they obviously didn't recover from it, so something must have gone wrong somewhere. Whoever was responsible doesn't seem to have been identified."

Mark Lawson
"Lance Beauly, Rob Wallet, the band's spokesman now, interviewed you when he was investigating the publicity stunt from 1977. Do you think he was getting close to what really happened back then?"

Lance Beauly
"He must have found something."

Wallet heard Elaine turn up the television volume.

Lance Beauly
"I think he was zoning in on Lenny Harper. The funny thing is, we're all talking about information on the internet nowadays, but Rob Wallet found very little information on the net apart from headlines from newspaper archives. I think finding Lenny Harper in Germany revealed something because the next thing there's an announcement and the band are making a comeback."

Jonathan Knight
"Except, Lenny Harper is now dead and the band have only been seen by executives at Sony. Allegedly. We don't even know if it's the same band."

Terence Pearl

221

"So there are still answers to be addressed even now. Why haven't they shown their face in public. What happens if they appear in public?"

Mark Lawson
"There were reports of an impromptu performance in a bar in New York owned by the former Cat's Cradle drummer Alan Miller."

Lance Beauly
"People heard it. No one saw it. There's a difference. Something like that would have been all over YouTube, but there's nothing other than anecdotes. Give it time and you can bet forty thousand people will claim to have been there that night. The reality is probably closer to twenty or thirty."

Wallet studied Terence Pearl's body language, baffled as to why Mark Lawson was offering him any kind of respect. Had he not read Pearl's theory about Scientology secretly buying the Vatican? An A4 sheet of paper glided out of the printer.

Terence Pearl
"What I find incredible is that we have a number of murders, five is it? Five critics in Britain, Lenny Harper in Germany, three people in America. . . ."

Mark Lawson
"Well four people in America if you include Anthony Rawls, the fifteen year old from Boston."

222

Terence Pearl
"Well, even more yes. And yet nobody is questioning the band. The manager Rob Wallet was arrested, but released and there's no suggestion that they're still under suspicion or being watched, monitored. How many connections do these people have? Germany, Britain, America."

Jonathan Knight
"There is a worrying correlation here. You can look at every person who has died and they all have one thing in common. They've done something that upset the band in one way or another."

Mark Lawson
"A fifteen year old boy in Boston?"

Jonathan Knight
"Apparently he had created a pretty disgusting Facebook page about the band and I don't really want to repeat its name, but it had a lot of faked images on it. It was only taken down by Facebook the day after he was killed."

Wallet heard Knight's words and shouted through to the lounge. "Didn't you like being described as a MILF?"

"Children need to learn to respect their elders. He knows now some lessons in life are tougher than others."

"Here, take a look at this." Wallet walked in and handed Elaine the printout. It was a screen grab. "I thought Terence Pearl might have a video of his appearance on that news item and I was right. There's your man. The Peter Miles lookalike."

Elaine sat up. Wallet had casually presented the past, a lifetime's memories, on a single sheet of paper. He would have given anything now for Susan's ability to get inside someone's head just to find out what unanswerable questions were bubbling up from the depths of Elaine's subconscious. Her eyes gave nothing away, but they darted around the image looking for any clues secretly stored in it.

"So who is he?" asked Wallet. "Is that Peter Miles? Is he like us? I don't know what he looked like, but you do."

"It's not him," said Elaine. "He looks just like him, his face, his build, the way he stands, but it's not Pete."

Pete? An overly familiar term for a man last seen in 1973. Wallet was afraid to probe any further. He knew the limits of Susan's patience and how far you could push before Dee finally snapped, but Elaine was a quiet volcano and didn't need an excuse to blow up in your face. Never one to give too much away she was permanently steaming and gave no indication of how long you had left before the boiling magma emerged. Wallet tip toed around her.

"What about Terence Pearl, who's he?" she asked, still studying the print out.

"Not too sure. All I can find is a PDF of a school governors' meeting in Ipswich. I think he was a teacher, might still be."

"When?"

"Recently. PDF was dated 2011. All the stuff on his website was written this year. Links to his books are broken. Maybe they don't exist."

"What do you mean by that?"

"Call me paranoid," said Wallet, "but you announce your return and he starts writing about you. Maybe he's got a different agenda. Especially with this guy literally in the background." Wallet tapped the A4 sheet. "Someone needs to talk to Terence Pearl."

"You think he's drawing us into something? Can you dig a little more, find out what you can about him?"

"Yeah. I'll try."

Lance Beauly
"Whatever the reason for their secrecy now it was always the same back then. I had very limited time with the band, you know. You'd do a photoshoot and that was it. In, out, no time to set things up, talk to the band, discuss things with them."

Mark Lawson
"And who was behind that? Who was controlling access to them?"

Lance Beauly
"The band were. Initially it was Micky Redwall, he did everything, but he was slowly squeezed out of decision making and left to deal with the administration. He managed the affairs of the band, but by the end of 1976 I think the public face, the publicity and what have you, all came down to the band and in particular Susan Bekker."

Anna Parkinson
"I think you can see why the Sony deal may have gone bad. If the band still had that attitude, that desire to control things, I

think they would have found it very difficult to deal with the highly detailed intricate management systems that labels have in place for major artists. No label like Sony is going to give a band carte blanche in the way that Toten Herzen enjoyed in the 1970s. Nobody has that these days. Whatever happened to sour that relationship was either unexpected or calculated."

Mark Lawson
"You mean the band deliberately engineered the fall out?"

Anna Parkinson
"I don't know for sure, but it's not impossible. They're not the only major label and the others might be looking on now and thinking we can handle them. I think what they do next will give us a big clue. If they disappear again it didn't work, someone pulled the plug, but if they walk into a bigger deal then it was a clever piece of gamesmanship. Quite remarkable actually."

Mark Lawson
"Lance Beauly, are the band capable of that? Are they clever enough, or should I say, are they informed enough to string out a major label like Sony?"

Lance Beauly
"Susan Bekker certainly is. It wouldn't surprise me. If you knew her you'd realise straight away what she's capable of."

"Fucking amen to that, Lance," said Wallet to the television.

27 - What to say

Wallet listened to all the activity in the farmhouse: the whispers, the tapping of laptop keyboards, the ticks and clicks of gadgets, the plastic soundtrack of modern preoccupation. What does a publicist do when there's no publicity to talk about? He had considered turning proactive, but that becomes information invention and, historically, Micky Redwall was the arch-master of that technique and look where it got him. All chewed up and spat out. A dog's dinner of a man.

A publicist starved of information becomes a fidgety, nail biting husk confined to long midnight walks around the perimeters of the farm and in a country as flat and squared off as Holland Wallet was starting to wish he was human again. All this because of a golfing analogy. There was information, but the rest of the band weren't sharing it. He occasionally heard talk of partners, investment, production quality, itineraries. The vocabulary of action; the vocabulary of touring. And what bugged him the most was that this was his idea. Fuck it, he wandered up to their front door like a tinker, put the plan to them, not The Plan, His Plan, and they went with it. The fact that he was jettisoned after one error was evidence of their determination and, he selected a curious word, professionalism. They were serious. Too serious for him. He thought Sony was big, but Sony were like a beached whale, everything out of the water, blubber and all, visible and obvious. This lot were an iceberg; Ninety-nine percent hidden.

Susan came out of Elaine's room with the A4 sheet Wallet had printed off. She waved it at him. Was that gratitude? She wouldn't say if it was. Her personality was a maze, but it had a key and the key was her collection of diaries. Susan Bekker's instruction manual. Every action, mood, statement, emotion, wish, opinion, the whole system, was forged in the furnace of her diaries. She had given him just enough material to get to the core of her existence: the creation of her love for music, the genesis of the band, the revelation of the life changing Valentines Day in 1974. All the fundamentals were in one book, but for Wallet the smaller details could be the most significant, particularly the contempt she had revealed for the album cover photo shoot awash with blood, revelling in the vampire image with all its gory awkwardness. He didn't know if that was the conclusion she was hoping he'd come to, but those formative years helped him to understand her behaviour now.

He stared at his laptop, returned to DuckDuckGo and waited for inspiration to create another list of purchases, another inventory of nostalgia. The webcam on his laptop pointed its beady eye at him and without words suggested an idea that floored him with its brilliance. He rushed out of his room. "I'll be back in an hour," he called to anyone who could be bothered to listen. No one responded.

-

The time was almost five am when Wallet knocked on Susan's door. She sat cross legged on the bed with her laptop balanced on a pillow, lost to an online discussion with someone, typing then pausing, typing then pausing. Occasionally she'd smile or laugh gently, shake her head, open her eyes wide; expressions Wallet had never received. "I've got a present for you," he said.

"Thank you," said Susan without looking up.

"Something you've wanted for a long time."

"That could be one of a number of things."

"Mm. I think you'll like this. It's probably quite high on your list." Wallet waited for her attention. Her body language hardened as if to suggest a pause and she typed some unknowable conclusion, closed the lid of the laptop and followed Wallet as he walked to the bathroom.

An expectant light was glowing. On the shelf above the sink the toiletries had been moved to one side to make way for a screen, a small flat rectangular gadget about thirty centimetres high. It was a tablet pc propped up like a small mirror.

A mirror!

Susan's steps were uncertain, wary of the gadget and what it was doing or where it had come from. She wasn't sure if she wanted to get any closer to it. What had Wallet done? The top of her hair slowly appeared as she crept forward, then her forehead, her curious eyebrows and lines pinching between them. Her eyes were scared, nervous, darkly made up like two heavy shadows. A narrow, aquiline nose above her mouth, lips slightly parted, unsmiling. Her chin completed the picture of her face and finally there she was, blinking, breathing, living. Her pupils were tiny black dots surrounded by brownish red circles; she had laughter lines etched ever so gently across her skin, mixed with the faintest blue capillaries that meandered across her temples. She had seen them before, but in pictures they were always still, lifeless, just a record of the moment. A possible fake. She had never seen them alive, but now she knew they were real, they were moving with her. She reached to touch the screen and her own hand reached back towards her. She didn't know her eyelashes were so long, or that the cleft above her top lip was so narrow. The gentle bulge of her mouth where it covered her canines was now obvious; she could see her tongue rolling over them. She stroked her cheekbone, and the bridge of her nose, the near straight line of her chin. When her face tightened she could see it responding, her mouth was starting to curl upwards and as she watched and waited a solitary tear escaped down her face and paused before dropping from her soft round jaw. This was the same woman she remembered from the last time they met. She hadn't changed, hadn't changed a bit.

"You need to remember to invert the image horizontally," said Wallet hesitantly.

"What? What do you mean?" Susan sniffed and leaned on the sink. Wallet brushed her shoulder as he pinched the base of the tablet's screen to reveal a line of icons, one of which was a double triangle.

"The video camera is for web conferences so it films you the right way round. To make the image look like a reflection you need to press the triangle icons and it flips horizontally. You'll see yourself as if you were looking in a mirror."

Susan nodded. "Thanks."

"I'll let you have a play with it. Battery lasts about eight or nine hours so it should be just long enough to get yourself ready." He glanced at her digital reflection before walking away.

"Thanks, Rob," she said.

Wallet smiled and quietly closed the door as Susan dropped her head and sobbed.

28 - Who has the bigger engine?

The coming of summer was making normal life complicated as the needs of vampires and humans diverged. Problematic business meetings were held late into the night to avoid the vampires from being fried like bacon, but the midnight hour meant the humans were half asleep. In Rotterdam the band gathered close to Crooswijk cemetery to meet someone who didn't mind working the graveyard shift. Wallet's nostalgia trips were rubbing off on the others and Susan had offered to drive to bring back old memories of being behind the wheel of a car. Squashed in the back, Dee, Elaine and Rene argued about Top Trumps strategies and how to beat the person with the Boeing 747 card. Susan ignored them and parked the Audi close to the perimeter of the cemetery. Everyone piled out except Susan and Wallet.

"The mirror means a lot to me," she said. "Look, you still have work to do to keep up with us, but I'm feeling a little more confident you might be coming through. What's happening now, all the whispering and the messages, it's something we've been meaning to do for a long time and I mean a long time."

"The Plan?"

"Call it the plan if you want. We should have done this a long time ago, but for one reason or another it never felt right and for all your annoying habits and lack of ability it was you who persuaded us that now was the time."

"I think there's a compliment in there somewhere."

"Not really," Susan said. "More of an acknowledgement."

"So why now?" Wallet felt closer than he'd ever been to an explanation.

"Seeing you compared to Lenny Harper made me realise that our friends are getting older. We could wait forever, it means nothing to us, but, well you've met Almer, you'll meet another one tonight, two actually, sort of." She frowned and studied her nails. She didn't need a mirror for those. They reminded her every time what she was. "So, let's say from here on the plan will become apparent, what it is, what it means, but in spite of the mirror, if you mess up on this a lot of people will lose out who can't afford to lose out, so that's the weight you'll be carrying. I still need convincing you're here for the right reasons."

He needed to convince himself. He had been sure at the start, but that reason would get him killed now. Exploit the comeback, make a mint, write about it, live on it for thirty years like Lance Beauly and Jonathan Knight. But insight changes things and Susan's diaries were enough to tell him about all four of them and they were human, whatever crazy nocturnal world they lived in, they were still four twenty year olds with the world in front of them and a chance to take it again and again until they got it right, got it how they wanted. He thought he could help, but that now seemed astonishingly arrogant; admit it, this lot actually had twenty years experience on him, they knew more than he did, more than they revealed, they new more than anyone who dared sit in the same room. They were helping him. "I'm beginning to realise I'm out of my depth," he said, "I just need some steering to what you want me to do. What's best for you."

"We all have to share the same ambition and you haven't convinced me yet what you hope to get out of all this."

"If I had diaries I could let you draw your own conclusions. Look, I led a dull life. Then this happened and it all became interesting. I wasn't born to be anything, Susan. I didn't have that gene in me, I always had to think hard about what I wanted. I'm not like you, I didn't have a light bulb moment during a day off from school. I just drift. I drift around because I don't know where I really want to go. You know I've interviewed so many people and they often get asked what would you be if you weren't a singer, songwriter, drummer, pianist, and they say I don't know. That's why they get to where they are, because they can't or won't consider anything else. I never had that single minded outlook, and without that unless you're loaded you won't get anywhere. I need to become like that."

"You're not here for money?"

"No."

"Fame, ambition, achievement?"

"Achievement probably comes closest. There's not much achievement in writing articles. They don't have a long shelf life, they tend to be forgotten within a week and you have to start all over again, but seeing a band come back to something. Being part of that is an achievement."

"If it works," said Susan, gripping the gearstick. She ran it through the gears. "Like I said there's still a lot for you to learn." She took the ignition key and opened the door. "Remember, I'm a lot older than you. I know what I'm talking about."

-

"If anyone asks we're going to a funeral," said Dee as everyone headed for the entrance.

"You should have said. I would have dressed for the occasion," said Elaine. Her red leather jacket matched the colour of her hair and both glowed under the intense streetlights.

Inside the cemetery the footpaths led the righteous and the damned through a variety of dark forms and figures, some more solid than others. They arrived at a crossing of paths and waited quietly. So many observers, so few eyes. After several minutes another figure appeared and slowly came towards them.

"Is he like us?" said Wallet to Rene.

"Ooh, no. Not a bit. Same age, but smarter, richer, maybe not better looking, but I'll leave that to the ladies."

"Yes he is," said Dee.

"Okay, he's better looking too, but he's a shit bass player."

The figure approached closer. "A bit melodramatic isn't it, meeting in a cemetery?" he called.

"I thought you might like the irony," said Susan.

Rene shook the guy's hand and walloped his shoulder. Susan was more gentle, tender. Hugging him without speaking. The guy stroked her hair back from her face to try to see her in the darkness. "It's a little dark, but I think you look okay," he said.

"Well I got a mirror now."

"What?" He stepped back.

"Marco this is Rob Wallet," said Susan. "Rob, this is Marco Jongbloed, bass player with After Sunset."

"Nice to meet you," said Wallet.

"Yeah, you too. How are you adjusting?"

"Adjusting?"

"Sorry, I'm assuming you're a corpse like these guys now or didn't you know?"

"Didn't know I'm a corpse or they're all corpses." This must be Dutch humour, thought Wallet. "They're all weirdos, but then who isn't these days." He shook Marco's hand. It was warm.

There was a moment allowed for Marco to give Dee a bear hug followed by a more sophisticated kiss on both cheeks for Elaine. "Colour of the jacket's visible even in this light."

"Nothing ironic about it," said Elaine smiling. Smiling!

"Marco, Rob doesn't have a clue what's going on," Susan said.

"Been like that since day one," said Dee.

"But I think maybe we can start to let him in on things," Susan continued. "Not too much because he has a habit of putting his foot in his mouth, but, you know."

"People management," said Marco rocking on his heels like someone who knew what people management was. Someone who was well versed in people management. A people manager. "I told you to give clear sets of responsibilities and parameters. I suppose you didn't listen."

"No she didn't," Wallet jumped in before Susan could answer. "They leave me to do what I want then get upset when I fuck up." They all waited for him to stop. "I'm not part of the Plan, what do I know."

"How old are you, Rob?" asked Marco.

"Forty-six. Give or take."

"You were still at school when this plan was created."

"Okay, so this is where we split up," said Susan. "We can meet back here in a hour." Everyone agreed and Susan and Marco wandered off arm in arm. Wallet hesitated for a fraction of a second.

"Okay. Come on," said Dee tugging his arm. "Let the lovers have their time together."

"Lovers? He's three times her age."

"You're as old as you feel, Wallet. They teach you nothing in the asylum?"

-

A wide path ran alongside a canal that curved its way around the cemetery and out of sight. It was lined and decorated with houseboats, all merry in their accessories and trinkets, the painted watering cans and planting boxes, discarded bicycles and satellite dishes. "So what's the story with those two?" asked Wallet. The four of them were sat next to the water, feet dangling just above the surface. Top Trumps in hand (Motor Cycles, so no need to worry about the Boeing 747 card) they passed an hour or so and enjoyed the still of the summer night-time.

"We've stayed in touch ever since the split in '73," said Rene.

"Really," said Wallet. "Revs, 7200."

Rene shook his head. "We made a deal. When Micky formed Toten we said we'd give it three months and if didn't work out we were going back to Rotterdam, reforming and trying again. We'd be a little bit wiser, better players, know the industry better. 6500."

"7250." Dee waived her card: BMW R 100 RS.

"Feed me," said Elaine. "8000."

"What? What's that," said Wallet handing his card to her. "Hercules K50 RL."

"But it worked out," Rene continued. "We did okay, no need to go back, but we still had that covered too"

"200 kmh," said Elaine.

"Ah, fuck it you've got the Munch, haven't you," said Wallet. No one could beat the Munch 1200 TTS so the other cards were handed over. Elaine was on a roll.

"Susan and I said we'd use our money to help them out if they needed anything," said Rene rearranging his cards.

"And how did that go, he looks fairly well off," said Wallet. He was holding another losing hand.

"182 kmh," said Elaine.

"Ha!" Dee had the winner. "210."

"210?" said Wallet. "I thought the Munch was the fastest?"

"Laverda 1000," said Dee. "Come on, hand them over." She gathered the other cards then looked at her own. "Got a right dog here. 7000 revs."

Rene was still giving the low down on Marco. "He lives just to the west here, Bergweg. Big apartment."

"City apartment," said Dee. "And he has another house near the coast. Come on, what you got?"

"8500," said Elaine.

"8600," said Rene.

"7600." Wallet handed Rene the Laverda 125. "And was his wealth down to you guys in some way?"

Rene stopped to think. His Honda GL 1000 had a big engine capacity. "Sort of. But it nearly didn't work. 999cc." He wiped out the others with that and took the cards off them.

-

About a month after meeting with Lenny Harper we were staying with Wim, here in Rotterdam, Wim Segers, and we were talking about what we could do for him. It was four years after our agreement, but the fact was we had just enough money to look

*after ourselves. We did some calculating and Wim suggested
Micky Redwall wasn't passing on everything we'd earned,
everything we were owed. So we went back to England to see him.*

*Micky Redwall was at home one evening when he got a phone
call. "Hello, Micky Redwall."*

"Micky, it's Susan Bekker."

"Susan! Fuck, Susan, where are you, where's the rest of you?"

*"We're outside the Blue Elephant Curry House. We need to talk,
Micky."*

*"Fucking right we need to talk. Are you coming here or do you
want me to meet you there?"*

"Meet us here. Fifteen minutes."

*Micky turned up and we went inside the restaurant. He booked
a table for five and received a few funny looks, but you could tell
he was on a mission. And so were we. The waiter found a quiet
table for us and Micky said we'd choose something later.*

*"So, where'd you go. Where d'you go without telling me?"
Micky said.*

*"Back to Rotterdam. We have friends there who can help us out
until all this blows over." Susan was in a belligerent mood that
night and as we talked everyone's breathing rate was starting to
go through the roof.*

"I can help you out until it all blows over."

*"Can you? I don't think you can." Susan took a small notebook
out of a purse. "We've been doing some figures and we think
we've sold about eight million albums. And all the concert tickets
we've sold and t-shirts, patches, posters. Would you say maybe
eighteen million pounds over four years is a conservative
estimate?"*

*"No." Micky sounded pretty sure. But maybe he wasn't; he still
hadn't taken his coat off. "No, not that much."*

"Eight million records alone, Micky, and you've paid us about twelve thousand pounds each, per year. Out of eighteen million." Susan added up the figures again. *"Do you want me to tell you how many concert tickets we sold?"*

"No, no, Susan you don't have to add it all up. Look the label takes a cut, promoters take a cut, venue owners take a cut, then there's the distributors, record shops, pressing the vinyl, printing the sleeves, transportation, hotels for all the crew. It all adds up. It all adds up and it doesn't leave much. When you split it five ways, because I need to earn a living as well, you're getting a good whack."

I don't think any of us were convinced. We knew who was taking a cut, we knew the percentages. Susan knew the percentages. She referred to her figures and came back to answer every one of Micky's arguments. Then the waiter came back.

"Ready to order sir?"

"Er, yeah. I'll have a lamb balti," he was at sixes and sevens, probably wasn't hungry. You could have served him a raw potato and he wouldn't have noticed.

"Your friends not joining you yet, sir?"

"Friends?"

"A table for five. I can move you to a smaller table if you wish?"

Micky caught us smirking, grinning, laughing. I think the penny dropped almost instantly. *"They're held up. They'll be here, you're all right."* He completed his order, but I think his appetite was pretty much shot to pieces by then. *"Can he not fucking see you?"* he whispered. Susan shook her head. *"How long you been able to do this?"*

"Took a while, but it's quite easy now," Elaine told him.

"Why are you recorded as the publisher of my songs?" said Susan as the waiter reappeared with a glass of beer.

Micky waited for him to go. "It's normal, that's the normal thing. . . ."

"No it isn't. I'm the songwriter," said Susan, "but I'm getting nothing because my name's not on any publishing deal. You haven't written anything. Look, it's like this Micky. We want what you owe us. Nothing more. We know some of it is due to you, but we should have more than forty-eight thousand pounds each out of all this."

We eventually persuaded Micky to set up another account for us and pay money into it. The account was with a German bank and he wasn't a signatory to it. Money was transferred and then a new publishing deal, or rather the first publishing deal was set up that gave Susan one hundred per cent of royalties. Cut Micky right out of it.

-

The story was familiar. It still went on, but today it was even more voracious. A young band with a sharp manager and little understanding of what's happening outside the studio, sealed away from the offices where the contracts are signed and the money is divvied out amongst the important players, the ones who matter. Except the band also matters, but their lofty ideals and devotion to the craft locks them out of the nitty gritty and shit of the contractual labyrinth. Susan was idealistic, she would have been easy to trick back then, but Micky Redwall wouldn't have known how quickly she could learn. And she soon caught up with him.

"8000 revs," said Rene.

"I done it again. Lovely Hercules," said Dee.

"How many?" said Elaine.

"8600. Suck that, four stringer."

They all forfeited their cards and moved on.

"We went back to his house a few days later, towards the end of April," Rene continued, "and he was waiting for us with another deal. He quits as our manager, but keeps all mechanical rights. In effect the music is ours, but we can't make money from music sales. He has the rights to the recordings."

-

"So you can fuck off back to Rotterdam, or Germany or wherever your fucking tombstones are located and you can start all over again and see how far you get."

"And that's your last offer," said Susan. I could see Dee was starting to get a bit twitchy. She hadn't fed for a couple of days and Micky was a big guy. I remember thinking there's a lot of blood inside you, man, and she can drain you dry when she's hungry.

"You've got your money, you've got your publishing deal. What do you want now, blood?" He thought he was being funny.

"Blood?" Susan considered the offer. "Why don't we give you a minute's start and let's see how far you get?"

Micky was uncertain what to do. This wasn't a contractual offer. There would be no more signatures. Dee was the first to go for him. Maybe Susan should have given some kind of signal, but it was too late, Dee was hanging off him. He was throwing his arms around trying to dislodge her, but she was so far gone it was only a matter of time. The rest of us followed them out of the house. He was screaming, pirouetting, writhing like he was on fire. Dee was like an angry pit bull and you could hear the flesh tearing off him. Then, as if a space had opened up Elaine joined her at the table. There were dogs outside, chained up, and they were going demented.

"You must have known who Lenny Harper was?" Susan asked the question, but I think it was probably rhetorical. She was always suspicious that Micky let the attack happen, or at least knew it was possible. She stepped towards him. "You even tipped people off, you cunt." He was on the ground by now, still alive, but he wasn't struggling anymore. Dee and Elaine were ravenous, but they eventually sat back as Susan stood over the body. She slammed her fist into his chest and ripped his heart out. She wanted to see for herself if he had one.

On the way out we unchained the dogs and they had a late night snack of their own.

-

Wallet wondered where that entry was in Susan's diary and how she remembered it. "So that was late April, 1977. Everyone thought he was killed by his own dogs."

"I think he was a little bit anaemic," said Elaine. "Do you remember he tasted a little bit. . . ."

"Peppery," said Dee. "Oh, cobblers to it. One cylinder."

"One!" said Rene. "One for me too. Harley Davidson SS 250. One cylinder."

"Peppery?" Elaine grimaced. "Red peppers maybe. Four. One for each string, babydoll."

"Wallet?" Dee shouted.

"Just the two," he said.

242

"I was beginning to wonder," said Dee as Elaine snatched the losing cards off everyone.

"You know what we need now," said Wallet taking out his phone. The others checked their cards and waited. Wallet offered his phone to the night so that everyone could hear, enjoy and appreciate Eye Level, the theme tune to Van der Valk. "Now we're in fucking Holland!"

-

To the west, Susan and Marco looked across Bergweg at a bakery next door to a small restaurant. The two businesses shared a name: Seger. The bakery was closed, but the restaurant was still open to late night stragglers so hand in hand, they ran across the road, dodging the slow moving traffic. Marco was out of breath by the time they entered the restaurant. They found a table towards the back, out of sight of most people, and waited for service.

"I like this table," said Susan. "It's cosy."

"Cosy," said Marco surprised. "A word I can't associate with vampires."

"Yeah, yeah. I've told you before, we get a bad press. We're not all monsters." Susan's dark eyes enlarged with menace and followed up with a beaming smile.

"When you smile like that, oof, your teeth. I still think they're incredible." Marco slipped his overcoat off.

Susan ran the tip of her tongue over a sharp canine. "They're pretty lethal you know. Not something to joke about."

"No, I know. But they still look incredible. You never tell me what your dentist thinks?"

"So you're happy everything's in place? Did Almer come through with his investment?"

"Yeah. He's happy with fifteen per cent return, but we'll top that up if everything goes okay."

Susan took her phone out and showed Marco a new trick. "It's an app Rob found for a tablet. It flips the webcam video so it's like a mirror." She held it in Marco's face and he checked the closeness of his shave, the grey highlights in his hair.

"He has his uses."

"Yeah." Susan didn't sound too sure. "Tom Scavinio took some convincing to take over from Rob, but it means we have an expert managing us and we can leave Rob to deal with publicity and one or two other things."

"What things?"

Susan had other thoughts outside of the plan. "If he's good at one thing it's turning things up. Fuck, if he found us he can find anything. Some guy is writing a lot of crap about us and we're not sure what he's up to, whether there's anything more to it than just eccentricity."

"Susan, there are millions of crazies on the internet, don't go chasing them all."

"I know, I know."

A waitress arrived to take orders and Susan was faced with the usual dilemma when she came here with Marco. Order food, pretend to eat it, transfer most of it to Marco's plate, watch him fatten. . . .

"Just the avocado salad," he said.

"I'll have a barbecue chicken," said Susan, keeping her head down as she spoke. "Not too big a portion." She ordered water, Marco had his usual double beer.

"You saw the beers Almer named after you all?"

Susan laughed. "I don't think his customers get the joke. I didn't know what pale ale was until he showed us. The Drummer's Mild - which he isn't - Dee's Golden Sweet, which is a joke if ever there was one because she's neither. English sense of humour."

"Daley Toxin was a good name for his stout."

"She doesn't see the funny side of that."

"Bekker's Bitter?" Marco raised an eyebrow.

"Which I'm not. Not any more." Susan sipped her water. "Anyway, if the Americans like it they buy it so we won't say no to that income stream."

"And what would you call a beer named after Rob?" Marco was grinning.

"God, I don't know. Wayward Swing."

When the food arrived it tasted alien. As usual. Susan picked and pecked at it, nibbled a bit off her fork, took ages to chew a mouthful. It was all an act, but she was here to experience normal life. She envied the other diners who didn't think twice about being bored by an evening of small talk and making the effort to look interested in nothing. Sometimes mundanity had its attractions. Mundanity was seriously underrated.

"How is it?" said Marco grinning.

"Delicious," Susan lied.

"The odd tour venues you asked about," said Marco, "they're short notice cancellations, so we took the slots we could get."

"That's fine. Ahoy and the UK were important. Geneva and Berlin are pretty good. Budapest. . . ." she giggled. "We'll make the most of it. They'll no doubt wonder why we dropped on them, so we'll answer that. It's a pity the Ahoy wasn't available on the tenth."

Marco agreed. "Forty-eight years to the day. Fancy that. Pity you weren't coming back in 2017. Make it a round fifty."

245

"I wonder if he's looking down on us," said Susan. "Do you think Jimi's up there with all the others?"

Marco paused a moment, teasing a piece of avocado. "What if he's like you? What if they're all like you?"

"Being ridiculous now, Marco. You use Rob in the promotion of all this?"

"Yeah. We can brief him and Tom. You sure he's in the right frame of mind."

Susan took a moment to swallow. "Tom? Yeah. His sons have told him to get out of New York. Change of scenery. Take his mind off everything. He told me that he didn't grieve when she died. She died so long ago, he'd already gone through it. Now he wants to think of something else."

"Distraction guaranteed," said Marco. "And you're sure about the vinyl only release?"

"Aren't you?"

"No, I personally think it's genius, but I wanted to hear your reasoning."

"Throws everything up in the air. No trends, no bandwagons, no middlemen taking their cut for doing fuck all. I mean think about it. You take five minutes to upload a digital file to your server then charge the artist a commission for every download. Fuck off. And they're not getting the benefit of all the publicity that we generate. We generated that, Marco. They have no physical presence, pay no fucking taxes, it's easy money for them."

Marco threw up his hands in surrender. "Point made."

"And if we do a deal with a company who make record players. . . ." she winked and took another mouthful of chicken. Then choked on it.

Marco tried not to laugh, but this happened every time. Susan talks, ends up on a subject that gets her going, forgets what she is and literally bites off more than she can chew. "You had enough now?"

"I think I've reached my limit."

"So what was it about Rob that persuaded you to change?" Marco was asking a lot of questions about Wallet. "What magic touch did he have?"

"He came along with his head full of research and having your own past put in front of you like that, seeing the names of all those people we knew and who aren't here any more like Wim, I think we felt there was unfinished business. We wanted to give it another go and, fuck it, try get it right. Not everyone is given that opportunity."

Marco had ordered a glass of red wine for himself. It looked tempting. "I saw the headlines over the Sony deal." Marco looked at Susan through the glass as he swirled it around. "Were you tempted to take the deal with them?"

Susan grinned. "You know me too well. We got our manager. Now that everything's coming together I can't wait to see this stage?" Marco was holding back on the details. No amount of pressure made him crack, but then Susan wasn't really trying. She knew he had the vision in his head. He was one of the few people who had seen it in the flesh, stored in a warehouse down at Europoort. The sleeping monster.

Outside on Bergweg, wide and leafy and waiting to be strolled, Susan and Marco headed back to Oosterwijk. She tried not to think how they looked together. Marco, a well groomed, smartly dressed, sixty year old with no signs of fat or thinning hair, out with a twenty something, black haired thing of exotic beauty in her high heels and tailored jacket. She was businesslike, she could speak Marco's boardroom language when she wanted to and she knew the first appearance on Madison Avenue, when the band walked through the door of the meeting room, had thrown the Sony executives and directors and managers. Expecting four washed out, messed up, feral old timers, they got what? Youngsters. Beautiful youngsters. More than they could handle. It had felt good. It had felt . . . yeah, Rob nailed it: liberating.

"What did you learn from them?" Marco asked.

"How the opposition thinks. Their reliance on borrowed names and associating with someone else's success. The need to tie in one product with another. How to sell an artist to a totally unrelated outside agency. What social media does well and what it does badly. How live venues are controlled by a few operators. How the message is more important than the product and what fans actually experience and expect."

"And your conclusions from all that?"

Susan smiled and bowed her head. "Nothing's changed in thirty-five years. And let's beat them at their own game."

"You ready for that?"

"I'm ready for anything. Are you? You know everytime I meet you it makes me think about who's had the better life." Susan refused to let go of Marco's hand and swung it lightly as he answered.

He took a deep breath. "Lot of hard work, which was fine so long as there was an outcome. Lot of worry when a new product is launched. The increasing hassle and headache around patents and copyrights, licensing and litigation. Defending your back all the time from competitors. Personal issues and people who want to take everything off you. And then you sell out."

Susan nodded. "There I was thinking you quit the music business."

"And then you die." Marco laughed. He cupped Susan's face in his hand. "Losing people is just as hard for me as it is for you."

"Yeah I know. Strange world we live in," Susan said. She could feel Marco's subtle pull towards him and awarded herself the passionate kiss that followed.

-

"So where does Marco come into all this?" Wallet checked his watch. The other two were late. After Elaine won the Top Trumps they decided to return to the graves and the agreed meeting point around one in particular. A nondescript plot with a square granite headstone and the understated detail: Wim Seger 1950-2002.

"Money," said Dee.

"He looks rich."

"Rich, successful, bright. Good businessman."

In contrast, Wim Segers was none of those things. "Fifty two," said Wallet.

"Too young for anyone," said Rene.

"So, you helped them in some way when you got the money off Micky?"

Rene and Elaine had propped themselves against two sides of a large cross, waiting quietly; one consoling himself in defeat, the other secretly revelling an unexpected success. Dee was close to Wallet next to Wim's grave. "It took a while, but we helped Wim set up a bakery and Marco went into telecommunications."

"Bread and phones?"

"Bread and phones. Wim didn't really go back to being a musician. He got a job working in a bakery then decided he wanted to work for himself. I think it was about 1979 or 1980 when we gave him something to start his own place. Then just after expanding to open a restaurant he died. Had a heart attack. Susan and Marco have gone to his restaurant tonight."

"Funny isn't it, if they were like you they wouldn't have to worry about building something up and then having it kill them."

"I don't think the pressure killed him," said Dee, "he drank like a bastard. Triple beer killed him, not work."

"And what's Marco's story?"

"He carried on with music, but being a bass player it's not something you can busk with in a shopping street. Not without annoying the fuck out of everyone. He got a job as an apprentice I think, in engineering. He worked for a phone company here in Rotterdam, but when he heard about mobile phones being the next big thing he got ideas. He bought the first one he came across and used it like a display model, meeting business people when he was out fixing their old crummy systems, took orders, started importing a few and selling them on. He was in right at the start and built up a sort of early mobile phone company. With our money to get him going."

"So he must be worth a bit now?"

"Oh yeah. He's worth more than we are. He sold out a few years ago and was properly wealthy. He's astute too. He got married, had kids, but he set up a fund; a separate company, offshore I think, nobody knew what it was for. Then when he divorced and had to pay alimony and maintenance the fund covered it all."

"And his wife didn't get half of it in a divorce settlement?"

"No," said Dee. "Technically it wasn't his, so she couldn't claim it, but it was set up exactly for that purpose, like insurance, so it wasn't seen as misappropriation. He's a clever bastard. Him and Susan. They're like two peas in a pod, you know."

"And he's retired?"

Dee's impish face looked up at Wallet. "You're very interested in him, Rob. Are you absolutely sure you're not jealous? You know a jealous vampire is a dangerous thing." Her weight pushed against Wallet every time she turned to him. Occasionally she'd tap his foot with the outside of her boot to emphasise the point she was making. "I hope you're not becoming the enemy within."

Wallet reassured her with a withering expression. "I can't get to the other side of a busy road without looking both ways, how am I supposed to take on the four of you? In fact, I can't even beat you at Top Trumps either. How did it come to this?"

"Lenny Harper took us on. The right time, the right place, a few sharpened bits of wood and goodnight sweetheart. You're not that much thicker than Lenny Harper."

"Thanks."

Dee became alert to two figures approaching. "Heads up," she said. "Come on stop fucking about, this isn't the place."

Susan and Marco rejoined the assembly. "We're all set," she announced. "Money, dates, album, stage."

"Stage?" asked Wallet.

"Can't have a tour without a stage, Rob," Susan said. She was still gripping Marco's hand.

"When do we get to see it?"

Dee led him back to the car. The others followed. "You are so pushy. Pushy pushy pushy Wallet. Good things come to those who wait."

Wallet breathed out and put his arm round Dee's neck. "Haven't travelled on First Great Western, have you?"

The Independent
Toten Herzen Sign New Deal
Unknown label puts up fifteen million Euros

The name Toten Herzen is no longer a dark memory from the decade that brought us the three day week, oil crisis, power cuts and mainland IRA atrocities. Following several months of convoluted negotiations with Sony that eventually fell through after a series of murders, the four piece rock band with over six million record sales have signed a deal with Alien Noise Corporation.

Who? A press release issued to news agencies at midnight last night gave no clues or indications as to the identity of the label. The most likely explanation is that the band itself has formed its own company to maximise lucrative financial opportunities and keep all profits in house. Alessandra Marni of the media investment company All Night Ventures thinks the fifteen million Euro figure is on the low side. "When you hear a label announce how much a deal is worth that's sometimes the figure that will be earned by the band, it doesn't include the gross amount that will be shared by label, publishers, distributors and any other parties to the deal."

What sets the ANC deal apart is the announcement that Toten Herzen will not be following the usual channels or music business practices. 'Toten Herzen have learned from past and more recent experience that if you want something done, do it yourself.' One wonders if the spate of murders in Europe and America are included in that sentence!

The exposure to Sony was not without its benefits to Toten Herzen. New York based manager Tom Scavinio will relocate to Europe following an offer to manage the band. Scavinio, whose wife died of cancer last month, responded to the call from Toten Herzen. "It's a fresh start, an opportunity to move on, and I'm looking forward to working with a band who are much misunderstood by the media and public alike."

In spite of all the activity since the first stirrings of the band in March of this year, they still haven't been positively identified in public and questions are still being asked about how they will look and perform after thirty five years. Alien Noise Corporation hinted the band may start to make public appearances now that a deal has been secured.

Daily Mirror
Vampires Offered Lifeline By Aliens
Fifteen million Euros to maintain Toten Herzen's blood filled comeback

A mysterious company has offered to pay for shock rock band Toten Herzen's comeback. After the four rockers were given the boot by Sony earlier this year a shadowy group of benefactors using the name Alien Noise Corporation has stepped in to finance the geriatric comeback. The press statement announcing the deal was, fittingly, released at midnight last night.

A music industry insider suggested the money may be from the middle east, possibly a consortium looking to explore the financial possibilities of sponsoring a music artist. Whilst there is little money to be made from music sales, other opportunities can be lucrative if the artist is noteworthy and rarely out of the public eye.

Toten Herzen qualify on both those counts. Their exploits have made headlines the world over, and whilst the band's public appearances may be rarer than those of aliens, the gory results of their actions are well documented. Award winning songwriters Torque Rez and Mike Flambor, who were due to work with Toten Herzen in New York, were found tortured and murdered in their recording studio hours after meeting the band.

Reaction to the news was mixed. Lyle Kraznor of Metal Gods magazine described the news as fantastic. "Since their comeback was announced we've been waiting for details. Now we're a step closer to that and we get to see what they look like." Charlie

We Are Toten Herzen

Coombs of New Rock described the deal as a 'poisoned chalice.' "No wonder aliens are the only ones prepared to deal with them. No human would go there." A spokeswoman for Simon Cowell's management company Syco denied any involvement in the deal. "We don't do heavy rock bands."

Timeline of Toten Herzen's atrocities:

1973 - Toten Herzen formed in Ipswich by local scrap metal dealer Micky Redwall

1974 - fans on their way to a concert are stopped by police and found with a headless horse in a horsebox.

March 1977 - the four band members are found murdered by a mad fan in Highgate Cemetery. The murders turn out to be a hoax.

April 1977 - manager Micky Redwall is killed by his own dogs, but rumours of his murder are not denied by the band

March 2013 - Lenny Harper, the fan accused of killing the band, is beheaded in Germany

April 2013 - music critic Mike Gannon is murdered and dismembered in London. The band's publicist Rob Wallet is arrested for his murder. Four music critics are murdered in one night. Rob Wallet is released by police

June 2013 - Torque Rez and Mike Flambor, award winning songwriters, are murdered in New York. Anthony Rawls, aged

255

fifteen, is murdered in Boston. Linda Macvie, a marketing strategist with Sony, is accused of the murder of pilot Leo Travner

Terence Pearl: Blog post
The alien connection, numerology and the cult of mass
suicides

Extract from my forthcoming book 'In League with Nosferatu:
the Record Industry's Secret Vampire Conspiracy' by Terence
Pearl

It was only a matter of time before Toten Herzen completed their
progress from rock band veneer to suicide cult reality. They have
now announced a new partnership with the aptly titled Alien
Noise Corporation. As is the usual practice with this musical
group the full details have not yet been disclosed, but closer
scrutiny of what information there is results in some surprising
conclusions and clues to the group's true intentions.

The key to the puzzle, like so many secret societies before them,
is in the numbers. The modern music industry is more about
numbers than music and Toten Herzen are no exception. But
where other music groups and recording labels look to
numerology to fatten their bank accounts and use accounting
magic tricks to avoid paying taxes, this group uses numerology
for purposes of encrypted messages and mind control.

The most significant date to turn to is the ritual murder of the
band in 1977. Or March 21st 1977. March 21st is critical here
because it is the day after March 20th, the Spring Equinox. In
some pagan circles this celestial event is known as Oestre or
Ostara (in the Christian Calendar Easter). Whichever belief
system you choose, they all share the same theme of rebirth.
Choosing to die on the day after the celebration of rebirth is
Toten Herzen's way of asserting their statement of a new

beginning: the first day of life is their first day of death. And thus the cycle begins.

May 1st is another important date and the most terrifying in cultural and historic terms. Known variously as Beltane or Mayday it's most well known manifestation is Walpurgisnacht. A range of celebrations take place to mark the point halfway between the Spring Equinox and Summer Solstice and to the musical group their celebrations were of ritual sacrifice and blood letting. In the weeks leading up to Walpurgisnacht, five people were murdered in mid-April of this year and at the end of April in 1977 when the group's manager Michael Redwall was killed in an animalistic sacrifice. Then, the group adopted the spirits of wolves to combine both the qualities of the vampire and those of the werewolf. In Germany and parts of Eastern Europe, the stronghold of the vampire myth, Walpurgisnacht is seen as a time to execute witches by burning. (Interestingly, two members of Toten Herzen are Dutch and Walpurgisnacht is not celebrated in the Netherlands because Queen's Day was made a public holiday instead to celebrate Queen Beatrix's birthday. However, Beatrix was born on January 31st 1938, and it is interesting to consider the possibility that a greater conspiracy is at work to mask the true celebrations hidden from and ignored by the general public.)

The Summer Solstice was celebrated with more sacrifices in America, this time involving four victims. By comparing the dates of Toten Herzen's activities with those of other suicide cults an interesting parallel emerges:

*1 - **People's Temple**, Jonestown, Guyana - November 18th 1978 (909 victims)*

*2 - **Order of the Solar Temple**, Switzerland - October 1994 and March 23rd 1997 (74 victims)*
*3 - **Heaven's Gate**, California - March 26th and 30th, May 1997 and February 1998 (42 victims)*
*4 - **Movement for the Restoration of the Ten Commandments of God**, Uganda - March 17th 2000 (718 victims)*

You will notice how all these suicide cults chose Spring and Autumn to carry out their ritualistic acts. By using numerological convention to analyse the dates we reach the following:

1 - 10/18/1978
1+0+1+8+1+9+7+8 = 35
*3+5 = **8***
2 - 10/1994 and 3/23/1997
1+0+1+9+9+4+3+2+3+1+9+9+7 = 58
5+8 = 13
*1+3 = **4***
3 -3/26/1997 and 3/30/1997 and 5/1997 and 2/1998
3+2+6+1+9+9+7+3+3+0+1+9+9+7+5+1+9+9+7+2+1+9
+9+8 = 129
1+2+9 = 12
*1+2 = **3***
4 -3/17/2000
3+1+7+2+0+0+0 = 13
*1+3 = **4***

That leaves us the number 8434, which doesn't immediately mean anything until you add the figures and arrive at 1 (8+4+3+4 = 19, 1+9 = 10, 1+0 = 1), and when the musical group's own sacrifices are added to the data:

Ritual murder - March 21st 1977, Manager's sacrifice April 1977, Walpurgisnacht sacrifices April 15th 2013 and April 19th 2013, Summer sacrifices, July and August 2013 you get the following:

1 - 3/21/1977
3+2+1+1+9+7+7 = 30
3+0 = 3
2 -4/1977
4+1+9+7+7 = 28
2+8 = 10
1+0 = 1
3 - 4/15/2013
4+1+5+2+0+1+3 = 16
1+6 = 7
4 - 4/19/2013
4+1+9+2+0+1+3 = 20
2+0 = 2
5 - 6/8/2013
6+8+2+0+1+3 = 20
2+0 = 2
6 - 6/14/2013
6+1+4+2+0+1+3 = 17
1+7 = 8

That leaves the number 317228, which equals 23, which continues to equal 5 (3+1+7+2+2+8 = 23, 2+3 = 5)

Together we arrive at 1 and 5. Could that be the 1st May? Walpurgisnacht?

With those numbers in mind it is easy to see now why the killings have stopped and the new announcement has been released. Toten Herzen have fulfilled some unwritten preparation begun back in March 1977 and continued by other groups to reach today's apocalyptic conclusion. Next year, May 1st 2014, Walpurgisnacht, could be the date on which Toten Herzen release their message and attempt to leave in a spaceship, just as numerous suicide cults before them have believed.

Research carried out by Professor Yzumi Kanotawa at the University of Yokohama, has shown that the simple use of certain musical chords and key changes, whose resonating frequencies are known to affect alpha brain waves, can initiate a form of induced hypnosis and trance at certain levels of volume. With this technique the musical group will be able to take control of the minds of their followers quite easily.

Keep a note of that date: May 1st 2014. If Toten Herzen announce their reunion concert for that night, we will see the apocalypse.

The Daily Mail
Cult leader says Toten Herzen will escape by spaceship
Rock band crank says thousands will die when shock rockers leave planet earth

An online blogger with a string of unpublished books has predicted that the seventies rock band Toten Herzen will leave by spaceship after inspiring their fans to commit suicide during a reunion concert. Terence Pearl, a retired schoolteacher from Suffolk, has become a well known figure on the fringes of Toten Herzen's following. His writings on the band have brought ridicule and support in equal measure. In a typical gesture by the BBC Pearl's mad rantings were given airtime in a late night programme hosted by the Beeb's art correspondent Mark Lawson.

Pearl has already subjected the band to bogus anthropological studies and said they are related to a Germanic sect of Cathars who were executed in the Middle Ages. His latest wacky offering is that the band's first concert will be performed on Walpurgisnacht (a popular festival for witches in some parts of Europe) using a mixture of mind controlling chords and key changes designed to cause mass suicide. They themselves will then escape by spaceship in order to avoid arrest.

A spokesman for the Metropolitan Police told the Mail: "We have not received any complaints about the online article and we have no evidence of the band's activities described in it. We don't even know if the concert in question will be performed in Britain, in which case it's not part of our jurisdiction." When asked about the investigations into the murders of Mike Gannon and four other music critics, mentioned in Pearl's article, the spokesman declined to comment other than to say the investigation was still ongoing and leads were being followed.

The article reminds people that suicide cults, far from being a mad fantasy are a reality. In November 1978, 909 people committed suicide after being instructed by Jim Jones, the leader of the Guyana based People's Temple. Up to 75 people associated with the Order of the Solar Temple killed themselves in the late 1990s. 39 followers of Heaven's Gate committed suicide in 1997. Both they and the Solar Temple members believed that they would be transported away in spaceships.

Terence Pearl told the Mail "My writings are based on careful study, accurate analysis and reasoned conclusions. Of course everyone is entitled to interpret what I publish any way they see fit, but I'm confident events will speak for themselves. There's no doubt the Toten Herzen reunion concert will make headlines."

The band's publicist, Rob Wallet, refused to be drawn on the subject of Pearl's articles, but did issue a statement saying 'the forthcoming concert is not a reunion because the band has never split up. It's a comeback.'

We Are Toten Herzen

GUARDIAN COMMENT - Alistair Macillroy
Cult leaders are only as extreme as their followers

It may be stretching credibility to compare Susan Bekker, Dee
Vincent, Elaine Daley and Rene van Voors to Adolf Hitler, Joseph
Stalin, Pol Pot and Mao Zedong, but that is what Terence Pearl
would like you to believe. Up there with the maddest mass
murderers in history, the four piece rock band from Rotterdam
and Lincoln by way of Suffolk, have been planning an
apocalyptic publicity stunt since 1977. A stunt so far out that it
will dwarf anything previously seen in the annals of rock music.

The stunt, that has so far involved such dangerous lieutenants as
milkman Lenny Harper, scrap metal dealer Micky Redwall and
music journalist Rob Wallet, has only touched the surface, but
will apparently explode in an orgy of mind controlled musical
mayhem on Walpurgisnacht 2014. The band, satisfied that it has
fulfilled its destiny, will then leave in a spaceship along with any
number of its fans willing or otherwise who have made the
appropriate sacrifice.

If the modern music industry is anything to go by many of these
fans will have already made a huge sacrifice in order to buy an
extortionately priced ticket and then bled dry by further
merchandising extravagance. Over the moon with the commercial
free for all, if anyone will be leaving in a spaceship it'll be the
hordes of parasitic hangers-on who feed off the enthusiasm and
desperation of fans wanting to see their heroes.

To describe Toten Herzen as extremists is to condemn their
followers with the same epithet. That is the usual pattern. Without

their legions of like-minded psychopaths no one is able to carry out alone the kind of atrocities achieved by the likes of Hitler, Stalin, Pot and Zedong. Instead they were able to pass on their warped and twisted dogma to any number of willing accomplices who were prepared to put to one side morality and decency. Had he wanted to, Hitler may well have been able to kill a significant number of European Jews on his own, but with thousands of willing maniacs at his disposal he was able to multiply his crimes beyond all imagination. Likewise for Stalin in the Soviet Union, Pol Pot in the Killing Fields of Cambodia and Mao in Communist China, the figureheads had enough sympathetic labour to carry out murder on an industrial scale.

No one in the music industry has yet to achieve the controlled barbarity of Hitler et al, but in their own environment, pop and rock stars have a responsibility to instruct their fans to behave. This may be very un-rock and roll and no one wants to see music sanitised to the level of children's television or Radio 4 mid-morning comedy. In the case of Toten Herzen it's not known how much of their fan base from the 1970s is still around and still willing to fork out on an over-sixties reunion tour, but with all the recent publicity, (of which some of it raises serious questions about the band's behaviour) there should be enough to fill arenas across Europe.

Without fans Toten Herzen are nothing more than an echo, a background noise. With fans they become a potent force. How they use their influence to manipulate their fans' behaviour and whether their fans are prepared to become accomplices, will determine whether they are good or bad, not fatalistic calculations determined by the position of the sun. Crank numerology (and

Pearl's conclusions are pure manipulated hogwash) diminishes a serious issue and is utterly disrespectful of victims of extremism everywhere.

We Are Toten Herzen

THE INDEPENDENT COMMENT - Sarah Lee
The media's outrage is outrageous

I'm angry. In fact, I'm bloody furious. Hopping mad, incandescent with rage. I feel like writing to my MP, as if that would do any good and that makes me angry too. And I don't want to write, it takes too long for a letter to arrive and by the time it does my anger has subsided a little bit. I don't want it to subside, I want it to endure. And that makes me howl with uncontrolled frothing rabid fury.

Well, actually, if I admit it, just between you and me, dear reader, the real reason why I'm angry is because I get paid a lot of money to be angry. The higher I hop when I'm hopping mad, the bigger the fee. The more foam that comes out of my mouth when I'm incandescent, the more cash slides into my HSBC bank account. (The special high interest easy access saver's account initially set up for drug dealers where you had to pay in a minimum $250 000 a day to get all the benefits like travel insurance and free legal advice.) Banks make me angry.

I'm not alone in the world of the professional mouth frother. I join a long list of illustrious angry men and women: Richard Littlejohn, Jeremy Clarkson, Melanie Phillips, Peter Hitchin to name four. All could have represented Britain at the Angry Olympics; all do very nicely out of being in a permanent state of rage, lashing out at whatever injustice is driving the UK onto the rocks. How do they cope with the stress? You can tell who is professional and who is just a bit upset. Where most people have a personal bete noir - letters arriving in the afternoon, blackfly, the ever rising price of fish - the professional can get worked up

267

about anything - urban foxes, Barrack Obama, the moon, wholesale gas prices, Eurovision, cyclists, the Hungarian Prime Minister, triage nurses, pop up ads and bell ringing - at the drop of a hat, to a deadline and under so many thousand words.

A wander through the British press, telly and radio on any day of the week and there they are. The thunderbolts of indignation in the Times, the pneumatic exclamations of one Sun correspondent after another, and rantings of such extremity in the Guardian there simply isn't time to spell check anything. Even the quiet ones succumb in the end. John Major, Sir Richard Attenborough, Bill Oddie, Leo Sayer. They can't just let it go, have to mouth off about something; the decline of blue tits, too much sea water, nazis on the backbenches.

You'd think by now that everything that could have been said about poor confused Toten Herzen has been said. But no. The BBC had to have a late night gawp at the band to see if they're behind all the horsemeat in our beefburgers, or the acute shortage of music critics. They used to be more dangerous than the IRA (Toten Herzen, not the BBC, although Norman Tebbitt might quibble over the detail), but now that the IRA makes up a large part of the Irish Assembly we need to find another terrorist group to compare them with. Al-Qa'ida have gone off the boil a bit lately, so it's all those weirdo suicide cults that stand around waiting for spaceships like stranded passengers on one of Ryanair's flights.

You see, I did it again. Did you notice that? A subtle dig at a crummy flight operator. That's why I get paid thousands for doing a few hours work a week and you don't. If that doesn't make you angry, why not? Is there something you're not telling me? Don't make me angry. You wouldn't like me when I'm angry.

29 - Onstage

"Are you sure you know Rotterdam, Rob?" Tom Scavinio gripped the dashboard as Wallet turned the same corner for the third time.

"I won't use satnav, Tom. I saw a picture once of an articulated lorry stuck up Hard Knott Pass in the Lake District."

"Hard Knott Pass," said Scavinio, "sounds like a football move."

"It's a one in four road with severe hairpin bends in the north of England."

"Hardly the satnav's fault if the driver is so stupid he thinks he can get his truck up a road like that. What was it, foggy?"

"Hang on, what's this . . . oh, bollocks, pull over." Wallet parked the car on the kerb and looked again at a hand drawn map of the route.

"That's just an analogue satnav, Rob, admit it."

"Elaine's nuts about Chris Squire," Wallet said cross referencing his drawing with a Rotterdam road atlas. "Toten Herzen's mad bass player influenced by a prog rock guitarist."

"He's one of the best in the business. You can talk about John Paul Jones and John Entwistle all day, Chris Squire's a very underrated bassist."

"A15, that's the one I want." Wallet set off again along the road to Europort and the warehouse with the big surprise. "Still prog rock though."

Scavinio had to allow himself another chuckle. "Still can't believe they never told you about any of this."

"Did they tell you about any of this?" Touché. "In fact, did you even know they only went to the US on a pretext of finding and poaching a manager?"

"To replace you." Touché. Again.

"So we've both been cooked. I just hope this is the last surprise they've got for us." The road Wallet was on was a direct route to the west, to the coast, the open pounding heart of Rotterdam's port where all the trade in the world appeared to enter Europe. Every commodity on earth squeezing through one narrow doorway and everyone concerned and preoccupied with loading, unloading, checking and inspecting, monitoring and examining the tiniest computer components to the largest aerospace parts. And all the time, in one warehouse, lay a secret world; a secret world of light and sound waiting to be woken by magic words and supernatural orders. A secret world of music and theatre. The secret world of Toten Herzen.

"Didn't you ever suspect something was wrong?" said Scavinio.

"No. The only thing I've ever been certain of is that they can run rings round me. I mean, they're nearly twenty years older than me," (Scavinio raised both eyebrows), "they know this business inside out. Know it better than me."

"How can you be a music journalist and know so little about how it all works?"

Wallet wanted to find an excuse, but all he had was justification, or an acknowledgement of his shortcomings. "I suppose I've only ever written about what's already been written. I wrote about press releases, press statements; you know, you keep your ear to the ground and then write about what you pick up."

"You never did reviews of albums, concerts?"

"Did once. Slated an album by the Stereophonics; record label never sent me anything else by any of their artists. If you say the wrong thing, Tom you get cut out of the publicity rounds. You're left to opinion pieces and managing your own time." So many oil terminals. The smell of hydrocarbons was getting stronger. The smell of energy was increasing. "It was getting harder and harder. Things to write about were becoming more abstract and esoteric. Another two years and I would have been appearing on Graham Norton claiming to be the son of god."

"Sounds like we did a good job then," said Scavinio. "You journalists are a pain in the ass."

"Thanks."

"Just kidding. You still know where you're going?"

"Shouldn't be long now. Railway line narrows, big junction, right turn, right turn, left turn."

"What will probably happen is you'll end up on this Graham Norton guy's show claiming to be a vampire like the rest of the band."

The car drifted to the outside lane of the road before Wallet corrected it. He was going to react to the comment, but thought again. Maybe not. Not sure what he means by that. Scavinio had this habit of saying vague indirect sentences that sounded like one thing, but probably meant something entirely different. Always fishing for answers without appearing to ask a question. "Have you come to terms with them being a bit different?"

"Oh, I guess so. Stranger things in heaven and earth," he said. "Really?"

"Oh yes." Scavinio looked convinced.

"Fucked if I know what they are." Wallet found his junction and followed his own directions. The warehouse was the last one before the hinterland of oil storage tanks and silos. The evening light made the drama all the more urgent; a vast theatre set of some modernist production with flares and beacons breathing fire and fumes. The area around the warehouse was deserted, in contrast to the frenetic neverending coming and going of cars and trucks of every size and shape, coloured up in their international liveries, busying to and fro along the roads and railway tracks. Both men stood nervously one last time before daring to enter the warehouse.

Part one was a single door, dwarfed by the scale of the building. Wallet pressed an intercom button and was soon talking to Elaine. "It's us."

"Who?"

"Tom and Rob."

The door buzzed and opened. Part two was a small reception room, unadorned, undecorated, in possession of nothing more than white walls, a single strip light and a window covered by blinds. At the other side of the room was another door with another intercom. Wallet pressed the button again. Elaine answered.

"Yes?"

"What do you mean yes, it's us again. Are we gonna get frisked at some point?"

"You'll be lucky." The door buzzed and clicked open. This time the room on the other side was a cavernous space, a chilly rectangular cave with some kind of structure filling the opposite end of it. A few weak lights hung from distant roof supports and were utterly unable to reveal any information other than where the misty darkness met the definite blackness of the warehouse walls.

Elaine was stood a few metres away at a large console; the sound and lighting desk of the stage which was still dormant. Small figures, maybe three or four, stood together in a small cluster, talking, conspiring, plotting. The stage appeared to have two long ramps extending left and right down each side of the warehouse. Wallet's eyesight was keen, sharp enough to spot individual specks of dust on a pavement, but he was still adapting to the low light level of the cave when Elaine's voice thundered through the sound system.

"We have guests."

The warehouse lights extinguished and Wallet and Scavinio were pitched into a momentary deprivation of all awareness. The silence was unnerving, Scavinio was gently clearing his throat, the quiet rustle of his shirt giving him away in the darkness. "Good evening ladies and gentlemen," Susan Bekker's voice filled the warehouse, a slight reverb accentuating the scale of the invisible surroundings; she sounded like a goddess, a voice from on high, a visitation. "Welcome to our world."

The lights exploded, the stage awoke and the warehouse was no longer a vast cavern of empty space but an internal kaleidoscope of dazzling stalactites, a brilliant lattice of red, blue, yellow, subtle pale green, then white, then blue then . . . name a colour, it appeared, slowly, gently. Wallet felt like his head was inside out, his vision so attuned to colour, colour that glowed with an intensity he still had trouble comprehending. He stepped away from Scavinio, leaving him to make sense of his own environment. Wallet walked towards the vision. Blue vertical lines either side of a central crown of shifting luminosity. But the big statement was still to come. As the searchlights swept the floor of the warehouse, looking for the crowd, for the audience to come, the back of the stage erupted. Falling at an angle was the

We Are Toten Herzen

Toten Herzen crest, the daggerlike logo of the T through the H, missiles of red and gold beams of light writhing outwards until their energy grew too high and the whole construct burst into flames. The roof trusses of the warehouse suddenly appeared in terror, the heat blasted Wallet's face, then the furnace settled and the flames were replaced by a glow from hidden lamps positioned somewhere around the crest. The lower tip of the T was swollen to form the main centre stage area, glowing like an alien landing site, whilst the lower limbs of the H levelled and surged outwards, runway lights along the length of them, firing upwards and rotating, first vertically, then horizontally.

Wallet stood for a moment washed in the pyrotechnics and the dancing colours. "You clever bastards," he whispered to himself. "Oh, you fucking clever bastards."

The light reached out to embrace every corner of the building, the structure of the stage silhouetted by brilliant gossamer and veils of sensitive pastel hues floating and drifting. The PA system hung down from the roof like giant fangs then without warning spoke out, screamed out, shuddered with low end feedback before roaring the powerchords of Susan's Flying V. She was picked out by a pulsating network of lights, a shadow, standing upright, nothing more than a black form with the distinguished pose of human playing guitar. Wallet's spine bristled as the music, the noise, the bellow of an electric guitar unstoppable through one hundred thousand watts of amplification simultaneously pinned him to the ground and lifted him off his feet, stretching his body in every direction. He wanted this moment to go on forever, just him, the lights, Susan's sound and fury, this experience, this sensation. But it didn't last forever, she played a wrong note, cursed and stopped playing. Then her giggling burst through the PA and the stage turned white.

"What do you think, mere mortals?" said Dee walking down one of the runways. Neither Scavinio nor Wallet had an immediate answer apart from silence, the best anyone was going to get for a few minutes at least. "I hope we're getting this on film," she continued, "Rob Wallet speechless."

Stage left, Marco and Rene were still talking, then joined by Susan all three of them came forward eager for a reaction from the outsiders. Scavinio was finally able to speak. "So, this is it? The stage? The Plan?"

"This is part of it," said Dee.

"Part of it?" Scavinio looked around to see if there was another hidden bit lurking in a dark cranny somewhere.

Dee sat on the edge of the runway, legs hanging over the side. She had a battered pile of paper, scraggy pages bound along one side. Scavinio and Wallet took a closer look. It was old paper, dog eared paper, faded and worn, like an old report released from some secret vault. Dee thumbed her way through it; page after page of drawings, technical drawings, engineering drawings, lighting plans, electrical wiring diagrams, cross sections, thumbnail sketches, colour renderings. Wallet recognised low resolution, low quality, early computer images created in software packages that were long obsolete. He was peering backwards in time to some early ambition and he wondered what its origins were, when was this plan devised? How long had it been mouldering in the background?

"How did all this come together?" Scavinio may have had a few hunches, but no details.

"Stage has been here a couple of months," said Marco. "Design was created," he scanned the roof of the warehouse, "1994."

"What?" Scavinio was astonished. "You mean to tell me you were in New York and this thing was being built?"

There was another one of those innocent silences that the band were so good at. Hard to imagine the sixty year old minds inside the twenty year old bodies. Wallet struggled to figure out if this was the swagger of youth or the mischief of age. Either way they had Scavinio on the ropes. Wallet took the document off Dee and flicked to the front. There was introductory text. "It's like some kind of manifesto," he said. "Stage one: Putting together the team. Stage two: The music. Stage three: Public relations; Stage four: The business plan. Stage five. . . . Fucking hell!"

"What?" Scavinio checked it for himself. "Stage five: The enemy!" He had five determined expressions answering him "The enemy?" He took the document and read the section summary. "Whoever you are, whatever you are, we will find you and we will stop you. And no one will ever know. Jesus Christ, what does that mean?"

"Figure it out, Tom," said Susan. "When you've put up with all the shit that we've been given you draw a line. Anyone who steps over that line will find themselves on a slab."

Scavinio wanted an explanation from Wallet, but all this was news to him too. "I think we all know what that looks like. Is this one of those moments in the film where you say if you want to get out leave now?"

"Possibly," said Susan. "But I know Rob's going nowhere. What about it, Tom?"

"Sorry if it all sounds a bit blunt," said Dee, "but try to imagine the freedom you're gonna have working with us." She was convincing. "No one telling you what to do, no one bothering you about the bottom line, no shit from the accountants, no crap from the legal team, no fallout from the sponsors. Just you, us and music. How it should be. On our terms."

Scavinio was upset. He turned away from the group and took a few steps towards some comforting thought. The band waited for him, allowed him some time. Finally he turned back.

"It just seems so aggressive, so upfront."

"Come on, Tom," said Marco. "You must have dealt with corporate contracts. There's no difference other than the language. The band are stating their position."

Scavinio reread the summaries of the other sections.

Stage One - The Team

We'll gather a team of people who know their job inside out. There will be no gurus, no svengalis, no megalomaniacs, no jacks-of-all-trades. No weirdos, eccentrics, madmen, parasites, freeloaders or liars. Above all is trust.

Stage Two - The Music

We'll play the music we like, not what people want or expect. We'll play it the way we want to play it (and if that means opera, we'll play opera).

Stage Three - Public Relations

Publicity can take care of itself. If you criticise, be prepared to stand by your words. There'll be no artificial image, no focus groups, or market surveys. We are what we are, not what you think you see.

Stage Four - The Business Plan

There'll be no modern industry tactics. No tie ins, no sponsorship deals. Everything will be done in house, with no middle men or third parties. All sales, music, concerts, merchandise goes through us, our company, our world.

Stage Five - The Enemy

Whoever you are, whatever you are, we will find you and we will stop you. And no one will ever know.

"You should be pleased we chose you," said Elaine. "Rob was unavoidable, but you were special."

Wallet nodded. "Takes a while to get used to them, but once you've got through their cold hard exteriors they're just a bunch of pussycats really. Even Rene."

Scavinio wasn't quite ready to smile, but how could he walk away from this. This control, this level of commitment, this desire to do the right thing. No ego, no greed, no posturing. It should be the easiest job he ever had, but still there was that one not so insignificant detail he couldn't pass by. He gazed across the floor of the warehouse at the enormity of the situation; the enormity of the space, the enormity of this ridiculous stage. Fifteen minutes ago he wouldn't have been sure just how big this band was, how serious they were about the comeback. Now he knew. The answer though wasn't the lights and the sound system, it wasn't even the document, it was the forty years of pain and disappointment encapsulated in that one short paragraph. Wallet understood where it came from; it came from the street where Susan lived, the school she went to, the crappy bars and slums they gigged in, the falling apart Commer van and the lay-by in Suffolk. It came from the photoshoot and the rabies jabs and the financial hoodwinking and stealing of publishing rights. And it came from the trickery, the conspiracy that almost had them murdered. Kill or be killed, that was the rule now. Take it or leave it, but ignore it if you dare. That's where Stage Five came from.

Scavinio took a deep breath. "Well, I guess I'd rather be on the inside than the outside. Sounds a little safer."

Susan smiled, one of her big beamers that left you in no doubt what she was. Wallet had felt those teeth in his shoulder, had experienced that mouth sinking deeper and deeper into his flesh, the touch and smell of her hair as her head burrowed into him. And no matter how agonising it was, no matter how exquisite that pain had been searing through his body like a scalding hot blade, he always promised himself he'd one day feel it again. But for now she belonged to someone else. Someone who wasn't going to live forever. Wallet could wait.

30 - Meeting the brief

Another brown envelope sat on the mat behind the front door of Terence Pearl's mid terrace cottage. It stood out amongst the junk mail, pizza leaflets and a plastic charity bag. The neighbour selling Avon had left yet another catalogue and wasn't picking up the message that Pearl bought his soap and shampoo from Tesco. He scooped up the pile, checked the brown envelope's return address (HM Revenue and Customs) - they're after me now, he thought - and went into the kitchen. He was moments away from a repeat of Nigel Slater's suggestions for cheap and tasty suppers and the table was laid out with raw ingredients like a medieval media luvvie's banquet. An old block of parmesan which cost a fortune when he bought it four months ago sat rancid next to a plate of chorizo; plum tomatoes and radish added an edgy touch of crimson as they waited for Slater's subtle magic touch. And on he came, bespectacled and swirly of handwriting, he launched into an impassioned insistence that suppers don't have to be intricate. He then went on to name so many ingredients Pearl had lost count and the plot within seconds. And then the phone rang. "Oh, for heaven's sake!" He threw a half chopped red pepper back into a bowl and headed into the hallway still carrying his fish knife.

"Hello, Terence Pearl."

"Pretty far out article this time, Terence."

"Did you like it? Surprising what the numbers come to if you keep at it hard enough."

"What's the reaction been?"

"The usual mix," said Pearl carrying the phone back into the kitchen. "Half the readers think I've really lost it this time, some have corrected the figures, others couldn't believe I'd managed to arrive at May 1st. One or two nervous jitters already."

"Well that's all well and good, but have they reacted?"

Pearl noticed Slater was weighing a bag of wholemeal flour. "Afraid not," he said. "I don't know what's going to provoke a response."

"Well don't stop trying. I keep telling you to make contact directly with them. Have you done that yet?"

"No. No, sorry. . . . ."

"Well why not? I could say they don't bite, but they obviously do."

"I don't know their contact details. You can't just pick up the phone book. There isn't a vampire section in the Yellow Pages, you know." Slater was coating his steak with a spice mix so thick it looked like a flintstone wall.

"They're on Twitter!"

"Are they?" said Pearl.

"You mean you've never looked?"

"I suppose not, no. I'll do it today. I'll have a good search through all the social media sites and get something to them." He looked around for sesame oil. (Seasoning the pan with lard would be a last resort!)

"Next forty eight hours, Terence. This has gone on long enough. There could be announcements any day now and if we're not part of those plans then all of this will have been for nothing."

"I know, I know," said Pearl. "I'll step it up now. They may not have been in touch, but there have been newspaper reactions to the essay. They're bound to be aware of those. Call me again tomorrow and I promise I'll have news for you."

"I hope so. This has got to work, I'm relying on you. I'm sorry if I sound harsh, I don't mean to be. You know as well as I do I can't do this myself and I am grateful, but if at any point you feel you can't do what I'm asking you must tell me so that I can find someone else."

"I understand. I'll try my best. Oh, for heaven's sake."

"Sorry?"

"Can someone ask Nigel Slater why anyone would just happen to have leftover saffron? And why the hell doesn't he sit down when he eats?"

"I'll leave you to it, Terence. Bye."

"Okay, bye."

Twitter? Toten Herzen on Twitter. Pearl was unsure how that would look, but he made a mental note to head there straight after Slater had finished caramelising a rack of lamb ribs.

TerencePearl2013 - @TotenHerzen what did you think of my latest article?

RavensWish - @terencepearl2013 youre bonkers why arent you locked up?

TerencePearl2013 - Who are you? I was talking to @TotenHerzen

RavensWish - Im the voice of sanity you troubled

#headbanger why do you think @totenherzen would talk to you

TerencePearl2013 - Why not? And I thought people who listen to rock music are headbangers, so presumably that's you.

RavensWish - youre going the right way to get your throat cut

Terencepearl2013 - Why am I not surprised that a fan of @TotenHerzen would talk like that. They've obviously got you trained.

Ravenswish - I havent started yet

TotenBrain - retweeted @RavensWish (youre going the right way to get your throat cut)

TotenHerzen - nice to meet you Mr Pearl. You know your name adds up to #666

Terencepearl2013 - No it doesn't. We need to talk.

TotenHerzen - go ahead

RavensWish - @terencepearl2013 you talk shit you do

TerencePearl2013 - @RavensWish At least it's grammatically correct shit. I take it you failed your English exams.

RavensWish - @terencepearl2013 fuck you knobster

TerencePearl2013 - Nice to see you included the silent k.

TotenHerzen - @TerencePearl2013 Please show our fans some respect. You have a grudge against us not them.

RavensWish - @totenherzen thank you @terencepearl2013 suck that kkkkkkkknobster

Bekkermania - retweeted @TotenHerzen (@TerencePearl2013 Please show our fans some respect. You have a grudge against us not them.)

MarcoJongbloed - retweeted @RavensWish (@totenherzen thank you @terencepearl2013 suck that kkkkkkkknobster)

DeadHeartLover - why u compare us to hitler @terencepearl2013 were not fans of hitler

TerencePearl2013 - @DeadHeartLover I didn't compare you to Hitler. The Guardian did.

TotenHerzen - But it was implicit in what you were saying. We are extremists therefore our fans must be too

TerencePearl2013 - I implied no such thing. I suggest we meet and talk about this.

RavensWish - @terencepearl2013 your walking into the lions den hope they cut you to shreds

DM to RavensWish - calm down: Sent by WhiteRotterdam

DM to TerencePearl2013 - I'll get back to you on that: Sent by TotenHerzen

Success! Possibly. The exchanges were Pearl's first experience of Twitter and his heart was fluttering from the rapidity of it. Who was RavensWish? Whoever it was, he, she or it, was obviously trained at the Toten Herzen school of etiquette. Typical of today's moronic instantaneous textspeak vulgarity. The silent k an errant coincidence. The task now was to sit and wait for another private message and hopefully further details about a meeting. He wondered who it was behind the TotenHerzen name replying to him. Possibly Susan Bekker, or maybe Rob Wallet. Hopefully not an intern or low paid lackey with no authority to set up meetings. And Slater was still standing, still on his feet, nibbling his ribs as sticky hoi sin sauce dripped off his chin.

31 - Meet the press

They all had tablets now. All four of them. Susan, Dee, Elaine even Rene, sat around and paced about regularly glancing at their seven inch tablets (ten inch models were too cumbersome to double as a vanity mirror), checking their hair, mascara, lipstick, as much for novelty as function. They had thirty-five years of vanity to catch up with. Thirty-five years of making do with trust, guesswork and out of date photos.

Not anymore. The vampire mirrors were a Walletsend and never more so than now as they waited to go out in front of the press, gathering in the Koningin Beatrix Hotel on the southern outskirts of Rotterdam. Their first encounter with 'food.' On the menu tonight were journalists, bloggers, photographers, cameramen, presenters, reporters, writers, commentators and the curious. Don't forget the curious. It was on both sides: curiousity about what the band would look like, what they had to say, what they were going to announce; curiousity about how they'd react, what the mood would be, what questions they would ask.

The press pack were on the other side of the double doors separating them from the band sat in a side room with Scavinio. He wanted to go through the press brief one more time.

"Back catalogue reissue: midnight October 31st. Special box set of five vinyl LPs - Pass on By, We Are Toten Herzen, Nocturn,

Black Rose and DeadHeartsLive. With a booklet of previously unreleased photographs by Lance Beauly. Also included, a bonus disc of interactive collaborations with online vocalists adding music and lyrics to unreleased backing instrumentation."

"We need something a bit shorter to describe that disc," said Susan.

"And new cover for We Are Toten," confirmed Dee.

"Photoshoot is in your diaries," said Scavinio. They all waved their tablets in unison.

"Okay." Scavinio continued. "Tour dates. Six in total for this year. November 14th, Ahoy Arena, Rotterdam; November 20th, Midlands International Arena, England; November 24th, Allianz Halle, Berlin; November 27th, WienerHalle, Vienna; November 30th, Laszlo Papp Sports Arena, Budapest; December 3rd, SEG Geneva Arena, Switzerland."

"Pity we couldn't get the tenth for the Ahoy," said Susan.

"Yeah. Try again in 2017."

And that was the brief. The kind of brief the band preferred: brief. And off they went again in a mixed state of agitation, expectation and confrontation. Susan stayed close to Scavinio to focus his attention on backing up the band if things got rough in the next hour or so. She wasn't expecting trouble, but she wouldn't rule it out either.

"If only we were a normal band, Tom, we'd have buckets of coke to keep you awake."

"Normal. Yeah, I'll stick to coffee thanks. I think there's another hour in me yet."

He wasn't going to miss this for the world. Toten Herzen, mid twenties if they were a day, walking out in public thirty-five years after they walked away. Over sixty years since they were born. Wallet was also looking forward to it. He wanted to see what the cameras would capture, what the microphones would hear, what the reporters would say. No, he wouldn't miss this for a pot of gold the size of Holland. Scavinio had said he wanted a distraction and this was it. The only one in town. The only one worth travelling half way round the world to witness. Wallet's distraction hatched so long ago he'd forgotten how it all started.

Wallet heard a momentary leakage of noise through the double doors. The sound of trouble, the din of a fight. "They've kicked off again," he said.

"Are you surprised?" Scavinio replied staying solidly in his chair. "Seventy-five people in a room with no windows and as big as a pick up truck."

Susan didn't look too happy.

"Stops them from getting complacent and cocky. They've turned on each other instead of turning on you. Trust me, I actually know what I'm doing."

"So what do you mean they've kicked off again?" said Susan. "What's been going on?"

Wallet brought her up to date.

-

The last stragglers from the inaugural World Angry Birds contest had left earlier that day. By the time the first members of the media were arriving the late timing was showing. I had a wander around as they were gathering in the bar and one or two were up for it, excited, mystified, others seemed a bit, I don't know, somewhere else.

"It's Rob Wallet," said Alex Roundtree, a fellow freelance music journalist and blogger. She was there on behalf of the Huffington Post. "Looking very pale and withered."

"It's all this working at night with the band," I said. "Reduces all the vitamin c you get from sunlight."

"So how's life on the other side?"

I had to think before answering. Other side? Did she know how many other sides there were these days. "Other side?"

"Publicist. Dishing out the propaganda instead of having to cut through it?"

"Oh that. It's good. Yeah. Liberating. Gets a bit boring at times because they're very private. Quite old fashioned really. They don't believe in trying to be everywhere all the time."

I was spotted by another journalist who knew me from my freelance days before I moved down to London. Charlie Craig was a sub-editor for Csharp, an online music magazine based in Paris. "So who are they really?" he asked standing alongside Alex and me.

"Wait and see."

But he continued a subtle probing exercise. Are they in it for the money (no), do they need the money (no), are they the original four (yes), have they calmed down (not a bit), what did you do to persuade them to come back (turned on my usual charm), what happened with the Sony deal (Sony bottled out).

It was at approximately that moment that someone, possibly the guy from Bild, came in and spoke to everyone in the bar.

"Have you seen the size of the press room? We won't all get in there."

I followed Alex to the room to see what some of the others were saying and there was a consensus.

"It's like a phone booth," said one.

"Twenty four chairs! There must be sixty of us here already," said another. And the photographers who were setting up were

growing tetchy. There was a lot of babble, but two guys,
somewhere in the middle, had started arguing over a chair."
  "It's the last one."
  "And I sat on it. It's not my fault if you didn't see me."
  "You weren't sitting on it, you could see me putting my phone
on it."
  "That doesn't make it yours, now get the fuck out."
  "Or what? Or you'll do what?"
  "I'll do this."
  They must have been grappling; there wasn't enough room to
throw a punch, but others were shouting 'come on, fellas, get a
grip'. Then I heard a chair going over, someone must have been
sat on it. Other voices were shouting 'watch it,' 'what are you
doing,' 'fuck me, this was bound to happen.' There were choking
sounds, people yelling, you could hear the chairs being thrown
around, banging on the walls, bodies banging against the wall,
shrieks. I think it went on for about ten minutes. I heard someone
shouting because his tea cup had been kicked away, one woman
lost her phone, then a crunch - I think that's when she found it
again - then I heard 'for fuck's sake get a doctor.'
  That was the guy from ETV Rotterdam. He was hit by a saucer.
Oh, the irony. 'Flying saucer spotted at Toten Herzen press
conference.' You could see the headlines writing themselves and a
picture taken on a mobile phone of Bert Klaussens with blood
pouring down his face.
  So they eventually settled themselves down when all the bigger
guys had claimed the chairs. Nothing democratic about it. Didn't
matter whether you were broadsheet or tabloid, hard copy or
digital, television or radio. In the end it came down to body mass
index. And then the photographers kicked off. A camera went over
and that was the start of the second round when someone was

291

nudged forwards into the back of the cameraman from ETV Rotterdam who tried to stop his tripod from falling over. The assembled photographers had already been tangling for position like a badly organised rugby scrum. As the cameraman tried to catch his camera he fell forward scattering several bodies knelt and squatting at the front.

Like any scrum that collapses blame was passed around with no one prepared to admit responsibility and within seconds punches were thrown at any face that came within range. Colleagues from the same organisation soon joined in to help their photographer and the whole melee began again and scores settled from the previous round of fighting.

It only stopped when they were all so physically knotted together they couldn't move. It was like a human bottleneck; no one could move up, down, forwards, backwards, sideways. So I stepped in.

-

"I don't want to know this," said Susan.

"I pulled three of them apart and, yeah, I got some funny looks." Wallet's strong arm tactics convinced everyone to settle down and shut up. "I think Alex Roundtree wants to have my babies now."

Scavinio cleared his throat. "Well I'd like to see how that turns out. So, are we ready now?"

The others gathered round. Four hungry looking, uncompromising individuals who were not only ready for round three, were probably looking forward to it. But tonight, Scavinio reminded them, there are no antagonists, no enemies, no threats. Treat them as a partnership; treat them with respect. They have a job to do, bills to pay, some of them will have bosses they'd love to strangle, so make it easy for them - disapproving sideways glance at Wallet - and get them on your side.

Wallet watched them go and felt something for the first time: respect. He realised that he'd never been this close to a real rock band before. Yes, he'd been with them for seven months, but they were off duty for most of the time. Now they were clocking on and going to work. They looked a foot taller, a stone heavier, the expressions meant business, the mood was diamond tipped. With Scavinio leading them out they were the real deal, not the Keystone Cops that Wallet had been organising or what passed for organisation if it included bad planning, lack of preparation and plain old incompetence. He was pleased for them. Pleased for Susan. He knew what it meant to her. Then they disappeared into the strobing brilliance of the camera flashes.

-

Once the band, Scavinio and Wallet were sat behind a long low table the press were formally welcomed. Scavinio apologised for the room and claimed it was out of his control. Questions would come later, but first details of the tour dates and the back catalogue box set. When the cameras stopped and all notes had been scribbled he opened the floor to questions. The reaction was an unexpected heavy silence. Then the first question was lobbed in like a flying boulder.

Q
"Who the fuck are you?"
Susan Bekker
"I'm Susan Bekker and we are Toten Herzen."

293

Q

"You're supposed to be in your sixties. Where is the real band?"

SB

"We are the real band."

Q

"How can you be the real band?"

Dee Vincent

"Because we are. If you don't like it reception will ring for a taxi for you."

Q

"Wait, wait. The real band formed in 1973. You are not Toten Herzen."

Q

"Come on Rob, what's going on?"

Rob Wallet

"You wanted to meet the band and here they are."

Q

"Is this a hoax?"

RW

"No."

Q

"Can you explain your appearance"

SB

"In what way?"

Q

"Why four sixty year olds look as young as you do?"

SB

"We can't say. If Micky Redwall was here he might know, but he isn't."

Q

"Are you a tribute band? Are you lookalikes? What?"

SB
"We are who we say we are. We're not imposters. This isn't a trick."
Q
"But you can't be the real band."
SB
"We're not robots if that's what you're suggesting."
Q
"Susan Bekker, how old are you?"
SB
"That's a very impolite question. You're not supposed to ask a woman her age."
Q
"Rene van Voors, how old are you?"
Rene van Voors
"You're being sexist now. Just because I'm a man doesn't mean you can ask me my age."

Wallet could see chins being scratched and hands paused above notebooks. The camera flashes and motor winds were still interrupting, but at a decreasing frequency as the mental fog began to drop on the crowd.

Q
"Tom Scavinio, can you explain any of this?
Tom Scavinio
"Nope. I gave up asking questions like that months ago."
Q
"Tom Scavinio, is it true Sony rejected the deal after getting the band's medical reports?"
TS

295

"No. That is not true. It was the bad publicity following the murders in New York."

Q

"And none of that worries you?"

TS

"No. I know the band better than most people. There are things that are still a mystery to me, but there are some things we're not meant to understand."

"Q

"What do you mean some things we're not meant to understand?"

TS

"Some people are different. Some people age better than others. I don't know how they do it, but they do. It's beyond me."

DV

"The tour bus won't be a spaceship either."

Wallet detected three different facial expressions within the pack. Those looking at him, wondering what half baked scam he'd created and how he expected to get away with it; those aimed at Scavinio, wondering why a respected artist manager had defected across to join in with all this hocus pocus; and those warily scanning the band like they were the result of a particularly baffling magic trick with four people sawn in half and put back together again forty years younger. He wanted to smile, but figured maybe now wasn't the right time.

Q

"Can you tell us anything about Alien Noise Corporation?"

TS

"It's a company made up of investors and will include the band's label, publisher, tour management, legal representation and so on."

Q

"Does the band own Alien Noise Corporation?"

SB

"Yes and no. It's a complicated arrangement. You don't really need to know the details."

Q

"Where's the money coming from?"

SB

"The band and private investment."

Q

"Why are you only releasing the back catalogue on vinyl?"

RvV

"Because we're an old fashioned band. And you have to listen to a vinyl record. You can't go jogging with a record player strapped to you."

Q

"You could make a tape."

RvV

"Good for you. We like people who show initiative."

SB

"It also means we have better control over the sale of our music. With downloads there are too many retail companies we don't like. They're taking a cut for essentially doing nothing. CDs are all very well, but they're like the sickly siblings of vinyl with their tiny little booklets and fragile cases. We were told CDs are better sounding, indestructible and we were lied to on both counts. With download files territorial restrictions and copyright restrictions are used as an excuse to get more money out of fans

for nothing in return. It's disrespectful. I'm not saying we'll never issue music digitally, but it will never be a replacement."

Q

"Aren't you making this difficult for your fans?"

SB

"No. If they really care about the music they'll understand why we're doing this. It's a totally better package. I know it's convenient having everything made smaller, but we're not interior designers, we couldn't give a fuck how much storage space you haven't got. The music comes first."

TS

"The thing to consider here is that the band are making decisions here instead of a corporate boardroom who place the music fans last in a long list of interested parties. The band are trying to reverse that pattern. Trust them. They know what they're doing."

Q

"Who do you think your fans will be? What age do you think they'll be?"

SB

"A wide range, we think. People listening to us for the first time. People, if they're still alive, who remember us from the first time round."

One or two were shaking their heads. Realisation, when it came, whatever form it took, would spread like a contagious disease especially in such a small room, but Wallet saw no sign of it yet. There was a reluctance to ask all the normal questions when such a fundamental one went unanswered. Couldn't be answered. What was the explanation? Detox, aggressive skin peeling, radical plastic surgery, cloning, black magic, a time machine parked round the back.

Hoax. Had to be a hoax. A bloody good one too!

Q
"Will you repeat the behaviour of the band in the seventies?"
TS
"There'll be nothing like that. No. A lot of it was fabricated, publicity stunts beyond the band's control. That won't happen again. We have no control over what the fans might do though. Especially the equestrian community!"
Q
"What do your families think of all this?"

That made them sit up. Wallet only heard the question, he didn't see where it came from. The camera flashes and squashed together heads made it impossible to find the source of some of the questions. The band paused awkwardly. Scavinio wouldn't, couldn't, answer for them.

DV
"If they were here I'm sure they'd be proud, excited, maybe a bit apprehensive how it might all work out."

A murmuring sound spread around the room and seconds started to pass as an appropriate follow up question was sought, but no one could think of one. The mechanised throat clearing of the camera motor winds filled the gaps between the swish and crumple of the uneasy pack. Wallet's perceived joke was turning awkward. It was turning outward, back on the press pack as if this was the culmination of an eight month plan of revenge for some unknown sleight, some unrecorded grudge. The joke was not the band anymore, it wasn't the mental image of three glamorous grans living it up with their geriatric mate on the drums. The joke looked like it was on them for following a trail of sugary media treats leading to this spectacle of ingenuity, this display of stage managed tomfoolery. A colossal gotcha that no one saw coming. An identikit band, a facsimile more accurate than the original.

And yet, and yet it wasn't a joke. The mirror hadn't been turned around to cast its mockery. The reality was there in all its unreal perfection. And no one could see it. No one believed it. No one could believe it if they stayed up all night trying. Wallet couldn't believe it when the band walked in on him at seven o'clock in the evening, March 21st 2013, in a house in a forest in southern Germany. He had to become like them before he could believe it. Without that contract, without those conditions written in blood, there was no way to join in with the pact, no way of obtaining the knowledge. No way of receiving the truth.

The murmuring grew to a babble and the babble to a cacophony and soon the questions stopped and individuals headed for the door and the uneasy fresh air of the bar. Wallet leaned forward to the others. "Stage two. Go out and speak to them. Mingle. Let them meet you one on one, no bullshit, no rehearsed lines."

Scavinio nodded and the four of them followed the pack as it spread out in a daze to fill the space in the hotel bar. "You look tired," Wallet said to Scavinio.

"If this goes on for another couple of hours I might need that bucket of coke."

-

For the next hour Wallet floated around, casually bouncing off questions and juggling small talk. He was always just over the shoulder of Elaine telling her interrogators, unconvincingly, that she was excited to be starting up again, ready to get onstage. Within earshot of Rene Wallet heard a convoluted explanation about making up for lost opportunities. It was heartfelt and personal. To Wallet it was genuine, it was Rene's soul speaking, but to those observers it must have sounded like a script written for the occasion and played to the camera. Dee was looking forward to using better equipment, not the battered old shit that carried her from town to town, city to city, not performing on sticky floored stages in rank venues and near derelict concert halls. Susan wasn't so forthcoming. Vague and opaque, she had a wait and see attitude to it all; wouldn't be happy until the box set was out and selling and the first concerts over. Then the real business of starting again would kick in. This was just the preamble, a dress rehearsal.

By four o'clock Tom Scavinio had long since given in to fatigue and his hotel bed. The press may or may not have been satisfied, it was hard to tell. Maybe the big question had been too big for them in the end and without a necromancer at hand to answer the pseudo-scientific questions their brains had reluctantly given in to the circumstances and played along. Wallet allowed himself one final satisfied glance at those still left in the bar sending off their copy, their opinions, their comments and conclusions and followed Susan up the stairs to the first floor.

"Elaine won the sweepstake," she said.

"I was wondering who would."

Susan took a scrap of paper out of her pocket. On it were the predictions of what the first question would be. Dee suggested 'Did you kill Lenny Harper?' Susan thought they might ask about New York: 'do you know anything about the murders of Torque

Rez and Mike Flambor?' Rene took a less serious approach with 'have you arrived here tonight by spaceship?' Wallet thought someone might be serious and almost won with 'why did you choose vinyl?' Scavinio's own guess was 'how has the music industry changed since you came back?' But Elaine's five word prediction turned out to be right on the nail: 'who the fuck are you?'

-

The hotel corridor had a settee with a small brass lamp on a table next to it. Its invite was too relaxing to resist. Wallet sat down hoping Susan would settle next to him for a moment.

"So what did Pearl say?" she said standing over him.

Wallet inhaled deeply, a second to recall the telephone conversation. "He has this mad idea that he can help the band. Join you onstage during the first concert and kill you all again in a scene that celebrates Lenny Harper's failed attempt. Then you all rise from the dead, to delirious applause, his words not mine, you get on with the show and the press hails you for your audacity and self-mocking humility."

"Right."

"He asked if there were such things as blood bombs. Bags of blood that you explode over the audience's heads and shower them with it."

"Lovely."

"He then suggested we kill him on stage, and all the pantomime gets written about blah blah blah. It's good for him, good for us, good publicity all around. What was that word he used: Osmodic! And the best part is he doesn't want paying."

Susan finally settled into the corner of the settee with both arms spread like wings and her perfume creating a gently euphoric air around Wallet's head, tranquillising him, pacifying him. She had a lot of Marco's businesslike confidence the way she occupied a space; she became the space, became the illumination and the ambience, unmistakable, unavoidable. "Tell me what he's up to," she said.

"It's a ridiculous scenario, every cliche in the book. It would make Alice Cooper look like Bertold Brecht. It's a cover to get close to us."

"Yeah."

"But what I don't get is why he thinks we're going to agree to something that is so obviously, what's the word?"

"You already said it. Pantomime."

"Well, yes. Why does he think we'd agree to to do all that. He doesn't know we're suspicious, that we're onto him."

"Yeah he does," Susan interrupted. "I think that's it. Strange behaviour, totally over the top ideas that force us to have the very conversation we're having now. There's the option of carrying on talking to him, but he wants to meet us, doesn't he."

"Yeah. And that meeting is probably when the other guy makes his uninvited appearance."

Susan knew who he meant. Everyone in the band wanted to know who the doppelganger was, the Peter Miles lookalike. Wallet felt and understood the urgent need to meet Terence Pearl, but he was held up by a growing sense of animosity inside him. Not with Pearl, but with everyone and everything, the whole fucking world. It was a slow burning fury being prepared and stoked, ready to use as some cruel incentive to get his own way. Wallet could physically feel himself evolving into a creature out of the man he once recognised: the ex-journalist who had a habit of annoying the other members of the band with his facetiousness and flippancy. Far from using golfing analogies to make a point he felt he was becoming more likely to plant the heavy end of a one iron between someone's eyes and this urge to violence bothered him. He had never been a violent man, but as his time with Toten Herzen increased his initial disgust at their easy ability to reduce someone to a pile of mince was turning to an empathy and a casual disregard. Even a mild admiration. He wondered how long he would go before he too was making effortless demands for blood. Blood from total strangers. He could make Pearl talk, but did Pearl deserve it? Did he want to make him talk, force him to open up, bully him into surrender.

"If this guy is somehow connected to Peter Miles, and I'm talking about the doppelganger, what's his agenda? Why might he be after you?"

Susan was reluctant to answer. She folded forward, sitting on the edge of the settee. Wallet wasn't going to make it easy for her. He felt it was time for an answer. Did they kill Peter Miles?

"No. He probably killed himself. And his family knew it, but they always blamed us."

"What happened?"

"He had the chance to join the band. Second guitarist, but he wanted to play lead. He was a good guitarist, but Micky thought I was the better player. I thought I was the better player. And we got together regularly, rehearsed, practised. We sort of got along, the band were happy to have him, but he wouldn't let it go. He was determined to be lead guitarist. It seems trivial now. Such a big fucking deal over nothing. He played on a couple of tracks on Pass on By, but after a few days he was demanding this and demanding that, every dud note I played he was jumping on it. Everyone started to get a bit pissed off by it. So he quit. Said he'd start his own band and we'd see who gets to the top first. We found him that night almost unconscious, he'd drunk so much. And he started going on about how his father beat him and his mother would watch and he was the best at everything he did, but his father wouldn't give him credit. We'd never heard him talk like that before so we assumed it was the drink talking. Micky said he'd get him back to his flat, but apparently, according to Micky, he went off on his own. He could hardly walk. He never got home. No one ever saw him again."

"And with all the rubbish spoken and written about the band you were blamed."

"Micky didn't help. Putting a gravestone on the album sleeve and saying it was Peter's. Can you imagine what his family thought when they saw that?"

"Have you never tried to contact them, tell them what you just told me?"

"We should have done when they took us to court, but Micky wanted it. . . ." Susan turned away, rigid with frustration. "Now you know why we sorted him out. That scrap bastard fucking; we were too young to argue with him." Susan was pleading with Wallet now. "He had us where he could do anything, anything he said, anything he suggested, we thought he was right. We thought it was what managers do. He's not even here and people still talk about the things he created. He created us. The monsters that we are, the monsters the public sees, he created that. And I'm not a monster. Rob, I am not a monster."

Several weeks ago Wallet would have left Susan alone on the settee too nervous to hang around for what might come next. But this was the second time he'd seen her upset and he wasn't afraid of her anymore. He sat closer and put his arms around her shoulders. He wanted her to know he cared. He needed her to know. It would be a reminder that there was still a human being inside him. "You're not a monster," he said quietly. "You're not a monster."

We Are Toten Herzen

Montreal Star
I witnessed the impossible last night

At around nine thirty pm, last night, in a conference room in an
unknown hotel on the edge of Rotterdam in Holland, I saw four
sixty year old musicians who looked like they hadn't aged a day
since they were last seen in 1977.

The band's guitarist introduced herself as Susan Bekker and the
band as Toten Herzen. Now I don't know about you, but when I
wait months to see what this band look like after all these years I
don't expect to see four twenty year olds. I've been asking myself
all night how could this be?

Firstly, the obvious answer is they are lookalikes who, with the
blessing of the original band and a truck load of money from a
Singaporean gambling syndicate, have come back in their place to
restart the Toten Herzen phenomenon. And they certainly lived up
to the hype last night; a thirty second appearance came at the end
of two hours of waiting and a brawl the Canadiens would have
been proud of. I was unlucky enough to be at the front where
most of the fighting happened and I have to say they were
uncannily like the original members, with the exception of Elaine
Daley's shrieking red mohican hairstyle. Everything else about
them was, it has to be said, identical to the real thing circa 1977.

Alternatively the band have used their time away from the
spotlight to indulge themselves in a number of visits to the
world's finest cosmetic surgeons. Yeah, right. Do cosmetic
surgeons alter the skeleton these days. Not one of them groaned
when they sat down, walked with a limp, crouched, slouched or

307

had ears like trash can lids on the sides of their heads. I don't think any of them had voluntarily been under the knife.

I know what you're thinking: hey Lucas, maybe they're real vampires after all. You think that's funny? I don't. I'm not going to subscribe to Terence Pearl's wackowebsite any day soon, but when you see what I saw in a small hate filled room on the edge of Rotterdam last night, you start to think anything's possible. Maybe when all this is over a bunch of tech guys from Lockheed-Martin are gonna come out with huge grins all over their faces and pull a switch out of Susan Bekker's robot ass and turn her off.

RavensWish - OMG Theyre coming!!!! 20th Will get a ticket will get to meet them will become just like them second happiest day of my life @TotenHerzen #tourdates

Darrengroom - @ravenswish whats the first happiest day of your life?

RavensWish - the day I meet #susanbekker

WhiteRotterdam - @ravenswish careful what you wish for

The Independent
Toten Herzen Finalise Concert Dates and Album Reissues
New releases will only be available on vinyl

Forever devoted to being different and after earlier press releases stating the band wouldn't do things the normal way, Toten Herzen have announced that their back catalogue will be remastered and reissued as a box set on vinyl only.

Rob Wallet, the band's publicist explained, "We want fans to experience Toten Herzen as they would have done in the 1970s. On vinyl with a record player, listening to the music." The band feels that digital format allows people to be distracted by other things, making the music nothing more than background noise. "If people want to listen to Beyonce while they're ironing then that's up to them, but you can't carry a record player around with you. You have to make the effort."

The five original albums - four studio recordings and the live album DeadHeartsLive - will be accompanied by a bonus disc containing tracks made up of original Toten Herzen instrumental overdubs with remixed vocals recorded by fans on the internet. The bonus disc will be titled Janus Head, with royalties from sales going to the fans chosen to appear.

Regarding the six concert dates, tickets will only be available from the band's website. Fans will have to collect their tickets on the night with ID to stop them being bought by touts and then sold on at a mark up. Refunds will be available if fans can't make it to the show.

We Are Toten Herzen

Toten Herzen first announced a comeback in March of this year, but the process to reach this point has been fraught, with one major label deal falling through and a series of murders connected to the band's visit to New York in September. When the Independent spoke to Rob Wallet he insisted the band would be arriving at the concerts by coach, not a spaceship. However, there are still no plans for the band to appear in public before the first concert at the New Ahoy Arena in Rotterdam on November 14th.

Barry Steeles, a business advisor to several independent record labels described Toten Herzen's vinyl exclusivity as both an acknowledgement of illegal downloading and the resurgence in the popularity of vinyl. "More people are rediscovering the appeal of vinyl. Whilst it is not going to reverse digital sales, people are finding that vinyl offers a wider dynamic range, which means better sound quality, better value for money in that sleeve artwork is more substantial, and the listening experience is, as Rob Wallet points out, more immediate. You are less inclined to do something else. Of course people will have to go out and start buying record players again, but I suspect a lot of people will buy the box set first and worry about how they're going to play it later."

But some things never change: the box set will be released at midnight on Halloween. "Purely coincidental," insisted Rob Wallet.

Daily Mirror
The Toten Herzen Advent Calendar
Countdown to mayhem begins

Free in next week's Daily Mirror. Every day next week we'll be giving away free your own Toten Herzen Black Advent Calendar counting down to Armageddon, the Halloween release date of their unplayable remastered back catalogue.

To demonstrate their understanding of the modern music industry Toten Herzen have decided to re-release all their albums on vinyl, a format available to less than one percent of the population. Your Daily Mirror Black Advent Calendar will count the days before the fiasco begins. Fourteen days later Toten Herzen will play the first date of the comeback tour where, no doubt, frustrated fans will demand why the band haven't reissued the music digitally.

If you have a record player let us know so that we can tell Toten Herzen who to sell their overpriced white elephant to. Maybe they'll throw in a few unsold tickets while they're at it.

32 - So much detail

Stella Artois was on offer, four bottles for five pounds. Rob Wallet stood facing the windows of the Tesco Metro trying to remember the last time he had swallowed beer. The supermarket was living inside what used to be The Emporor inn; alive inside the dead shell of a former pub. But Wallet wasn't here to do a bit of evening shopping, he had agreed to meet Terence Pearl. The location was significant because the Emperor, in Ipswich, back in 1973, had been the last pub that Peter Miles had drunk in and from here, accompanied and then abandoned by Micky Redwall, had walked off into the night and vanished.

Across the street was the guest house that Wallet had originally planned to stay in, but Susan had convinced him he could travel here on his own. Here and back to Rotterdam in the blink of an eye. He had his doubts. How would he arrive without finding himself on the roof of someone's conservatory or in the path of a lorry. (Not that a speeding truck would make much difference, but suddenly crashing through someone's extension would need explaining.) He tried a few dry runs first: along the corridor of the farmhouse, one side of the meadow to the other, all without accident. In the end it was easy. One minute he was in his room and with a moment's thought he was underneath a lamp post in a suburban street in England. There were no side effects, he didn't fall over from the momentum of being supernaturally catapulted across the North Sea, and he didn't materialise in front of a local resident out walking the dog.

The evening was warm in spite of a day of heavy rain. There was a strange, heightened ordinariness to the environment, a super-ordinariness, the mundanity and familiarity raised to such a level that the houses and shops and streets and cars, all perfectly ordinary, displayed a new glow about them, a reinvention as if a switch had been turned on boosting the radiance levels. An enhanced sharpness to edges, a greater colour contrast, a wider visual dynamic range. He could hear every leaf twitching in the heavy breath of the breeze. Isolated sounds extruded themselves from the latent noise of traffic: a door opening, rubbish emptied into a wheelie bin, a burst of dry laughter, the crunch of gravel, a squeaking gate hinge, the gentle crackling of soil drying out. The traffic lights at the junction ahead pierced through the evening darkness like fairy lights. Remnants of the rain clouds from earlier in the day displayed every drop of moisture; Wallet could still feel damp molecules on his forehead and cheeks. There was a feint odour of spices and barbecued food and from the front of the Tesco Metro he could see the takeaways further down the street. And a chemical, a slightly pungent smell; Wallet sniffed the air and wondered if it was coming from the funeral parlour next door to the Tesco. This didn't feel like a real city street, but this is how the others had come to live, how they experienced the world around them; heightened senses, a keen awareness of the environment and a tightened sense of response to whatever might move out in front of them next. Where Wallet had once walked through his world wondering who and what was a threat and who and what was safe, he was now the threat and welcomed anyone who might think otherwise.

Terence Pearl's solitary figure appeared from a side street. He must have parked his car after driving down from Westerfield. He walked with his head down, avoiding attention, avoiding trouble. He was smaller in real life than he looked on television. Under his left arm he had a thick book wrapped tightly in a plastic bag. Wallet could hear him breathing quickly, awkwardly, but Pearl wasn't hurried, he was nervous. He had nothing to be nervous about, not this evening, not with Wallet. Not yet. The difference in demeanour was too stark, ill matched and unfair. Wallet reminded himself to go easy on the man and concentrate on absorbing his newly discovered ultraperception. Pearl was unsure who he was approaching, but Wallet was alone outside the Tesco. It was Pearl who had pointed out in their emails that the Emperor inn had only recently closed after a long fight to keep it safe from redevelopment.

"Mr Wallet?" he called out.

"Yep." Wallet offered his left hand forcing Pearl to shake it only after shifting the package under his arm and revealing the book inside to be a bible.

"Nice evening after all the rain," said Pearl.

"How heavy was it?"

"Very," said Pearl. "You obviously didn't get caught out in it."

Obviously not, thought Wallet realising he was in Rotterdam an hour ago. He needed to be more discreet if only for a little while longer. "Nice evening to take a stroll though," he suggested. "And you can fill me in on this daft idea of yours."

Pearl laughed as Wallet started to head towards the city centre. "What do the others think? I know you've been having a lot of publicity recently."

"And who's fault's that? Cathars, spaceships, numerology."

"Oh, no one takes any notice of me. At least not until the BBC invited me on to their programme. That was a surprise."

"Mm. Your site's statistics went through the roof after that, didn't they?" Peter Miles could have headed north along this road on the night he disappeared, but according to Elaine he lived in a small house close to All Saints church, south of where he was now. Micky Redwall would have tried to get Miles home and there was nowhere else to take him at that time of night. The smell of food was filling Wallet's lungs as he approached a Chinese take-away. He enjoyed chow mein. He enjoyed food.

"Do you work in Ipswich, Terence?"

"I was a teacher. Took early retirement." He talked eagerly about subjects in which he featured. He enjoyed gardening, had a modest patch at home, and had a tree, but not a large one, and there were the pub quizzes, which he never won.

"Live local?"

"Here and there. I live out of town now. First proper garden I've had in thirty years. Backs onto fields."

"Right. Interesting. The last time you had a garden Toten Herzen would be just up the road doing their best to poison it."

"Yes, no doubt they were."

"What do you know about them?" Wallet stopped, allowing Pearl to think about the answer. "And I don't mean the esoteric nonsense. The day to day events when they were last in the public eye. You must remember those days? Local band making it big around the world for all sorts of reasons."

Pearl's fingers massaged the bible inside the bag. "I wasn't a fan of their music, but I suppose you didn't have to be to know all about them."

"What's down there?" Wallet nodded towards the end of the street facing them, just as a car stopped. Another customer for the take-away behind them.

"A lido would you believe."

"Outdoor swimming pool?" Moonlight swim? Whatever Miles did his body would have been found and identified. Mugged and murdered, knocked down by a bus, heart attack at a tragically young age; there would be a corpse and an inquest. "So I take it you don't approve of what they got up to?"

"What makes you think that?" Pearl followed obediently. He stopped when Wallet stopped, walked when he walked, stop, walk, stop, walk, like a child's game.

"Religious man, all that debauchery."

"It's rock and roll, I suppose," said Pearl shrugging his shoulders. "What they were paid for."

"But do you endorse their behaviour? What would you tell your pupils? If they were still around and you were still teaching?"

"Like I say, Mr Wallet, it's all part of the music. They play a role like actors. Learn their lines, follow the directions. Isn't that what they're still doing?"

"What makes you say that?" Wallet followed the road right at a large junction. He could feel the air temperature warming as the light levels dropped.

"This whole reunion. . . ."

"Comeback."

"Comeback. It's all stage managed, isn't it. What do they say: carefully choreographed? I thought that's normal for the music industry these days. Careful control about every minute detail of the band in order to maximise their earning potential? Building on their fan base, making sure they cover every platform and media opportunity."

"You sound like the one following the script, Terence. Who told you all that?"

"I read the press. I've seen X-Factor and The Voice and all the other talent shows. Everyone neatly packaged and parcelled like little musical commodities."

Wallet's peripheral vision was wider and sharper than it had ever been and he could watch Pearl out of the corner of his eye. This didn't sound like a retired schoolteacher talking unless he was a frustrated reject from Fame Academy. Now Wallet realised why the temperature was rising: All Saints church was standing guard half way down the road; it's red brick walls radiating God's warmth, attracting the local residents, offering strength to the likes of Terence Pearl and his biblical baggage held close to his body like a hot water bottle, holding it tighter the longer they walked. Wallet stopped again to look at the entrance to the church. He felt very hot, but Pearl was the one sweating. "I still don't see what's in it for you, Terence. Run the plan by me again: you kill the band on stage, then they rise again and kill you."

"Yes. It bookends their story. Lenny Harper killed them in 1977 from which they recovered, then to announce their official comeback we do it again. Publicity for the show and the band, and publicity for me."

"Why you though? Do you need the money from booksales? Is your pension running out? Gardening costs getting too high to keep up?" Wallet sat a moment on the church wall undecided whether to play it hard or soft. Turn the temperature up a bit. "Terence, with all due respect, you are an eccentric presence on the internet, should we say. Toten Herzen are not children, they're not some fancy whim thrown together by a group of chancers with a few bob saved up. This is a multi-million Euro concern. All the rumour and gossip might make the band look stupid to some people, but you can bet your bible there's a lot of money swirling around that insulates these guys from everything out there. A lot of investment, a lot of planning. There's a large corporate machine in action now. It's taken all year to organise this comeback, a lot of effort, a lot of resources. We're not playing a game."

"I'm sure you're not, Mr Wallet." Pearl gazed up at the church spire and spoke directly to it. "So, with all due respect why did you agree to meet me like this? Taking time out from your very busy schedule."

Wallet stood up and placed his arm around Pearl with a tight grip on his shoulder to guide him further along the road and away from the church, away from the source of some embryonic self-confidence. Peter Miles lived in a house just off this road. Did he get this far? Or maybe, maybe. . . . Wallet could smell water, river water, dirty river water with stagnant mud and residues, red campion and nettles. Somewhere ahead was the river.

"The reason I agreed to meet you, Terence," he whispered, "was to find out what the fuck you're really up to."

Pearl was shocked to hear such language so close to God's house. Across the street a young woman was walking in the same direction. Wallet admired her figure; tall and slender, with long black hair flowing like a cape behind her. "I don't know what you mean, Mr Wallet, but I'm sure after reading my work it would be pretty obvious. I'm an attention seeker, I have extreme views that I like to write about and provoke a reaction. It's the teacher in me. You've never been a teacher, Mr Wallet. You get an instant reaction in the classroom and I miss it. I used to belong to a writers' circle, but they're so polite and wishy washy and don't say what they mean and don't give the reaction they want to give because they're frightened they'll provoke criticism of their own work, but I want that reaction. I enjoy exchanging ideas and the more absurd the better."

"Your wittering on a bit, Terence." The young woman had crossed the road and was twenty, thirty metres ahead of them. Wallet had never dared to stare in admiration at Susan before, but he could see her now and what a shapely backside she had, rolling and twisting seductively when she walked. (Was his libido also heading skywards now?) He pulled Pearl's shoulder closer: "Who are you working with Terence? Who's pulling your strings?"

Pearl was holding the bagged bible in front of him with both hands. "Nobody. There's nobody else," he insisted.

"I don't believe you, Mr Pearl."

Susan had stopped alongside a barrier and was looking across the grass towards the river flowing alongside the road. Wallet came around the outside of Pearl so that he could stand next to her and breathe in a delicious headful of perfume.

"So your theory ends here," she said to him. As Susan spoke Pearl did a double take when he recognised his second adversary.

"My guess," said Wallet, "and it's only a guess, is that Micky walked with Peter to the end of his street and left him. But Peter carried on and came here to the river. Maybe he had a think about things, as well as he could with a skinful of ale, and then went down there for a swim. They never found his body so maybe it's still in the mud."

"What do you think, Terence?" asked Susan.

"Are you talking about Peter Miles?"

"Yes." Susan leaned on the railings to get a better view of Pearl. "It's interesting how you jump to that conclusion so quickly, unless you've been talking about him on the way here." Wallet and Pearl exchanged a look of realisation, subterfuge, trickery. There was more to this than a stroll to discuss stage management.

"Why would he throw himself in the river? I don't understand. Is this why you met me?"

"Killing two birds with one stone, Terence," said Wallet releasing Pearl's shoulder and releasing himself from the need for intimidation. "Peter Miles wasn't killed, not as far as we know at least, but he did disappear and we thought you might have some answers."

Pearl was still nervously manhandling his bible, the last form of protection he had against this world. "Everyone thought he was killed by the members of the band."

"Do you actually believe all the crap you write about Toten Herzen or is it just for money?" Susan asked.

"He does it to provoke a reaction," Wallet said. "He doesn't get any satisfaction from his regular writers' circle."

"You know what we think?" said Susan. "We think you know something about him."

Pearl was beyond talking now. All his faith, all his defences, were in the bag and he wasn't going to let go of it until he was safely home. The river eased by ignoring his fear and the nearest streetlight abandoned him plunging them all into darkness. But it was no failure. The streetlight was in on the conspiracy. Pearl tried to look around, but he was standing in a void of pitch blackness. The road was visible where he had been a few seconds earlier, but now he was on the opposite bank of the river detached from the safety of the street. Susan and Wallet were still with him, waiting patiently, waiting for him to co-operate.

"I'll leave you two to have a think about all this," Susan said. "We're all after the same thing, Terence. The truth. Whatever you're doing I just hope it's for the right reasons, but think about what you're dealing with. Which side would you rather be on? I think it's a simple choice." And she vanished.

We Are Toten Herzen

"Where . . . where did she go?" Pearl spun on the spot almost dropping his bag.

"Clever girl, our Susan," said Wallet. "Very theatrical. A born entertainer if you ask me. I, on the other hand, am not so eloquent. So, are you going to work with us or not?"

RavensWish - got my ticket for @totenherzen in fact got two, one for midlands arena one for ahoy, first night, so happy :-))))))) don't know how to get there but can swim if i have to

DM to RavensWish - will send you details for getting to the Ahoy. Do you still want to meet the band? Sent by WhiteRotterdam

DM to WhiteRotterdam - do I still want to meet the band? Do I still want to meet Toten Herzen and change my life? In a word yesyesyesyesyesyes: Sent by RavensWish

DM to RavensWish - I'll tell you who to speak to when you get there and then we can have a talk. Keep this to yourself: Sent by WhiteRotterdam

DM to WhiteRotterdam - cool. Who are you? do you work for them? Sent by RavensWish

DM to RavensWish - you'll find out: Sent by WhiteRotterdam

33 - Origins

Selling out or cashing in, he wasn't sure which, was supposed to have lifted some of the pressure off Marco Jongbloed's ageing shoulders, but his freedom had soon regressed into boredom and aimlessness and he joined the idol rich. Something he thought he'd never be. Now everything he owned was a trivial embellishment, a whimsy. He couldn't speed in his sports cars, his large house was a rattling empty box echoing with tedium. His only entertainment came from reading the solicitor's letters during his divorce. And his children. God, he wished he could forget the grabbing little fuckers' names.

But things changed. In retrospect it was inevitable that they would, only the circumstances surprised him. Now his careful step had developed a spring, his oats were being resown, the autumn of his years were alive with colour and noise. He was reborn. Rewired, renovated, redecorated. The old dog was biting again, not quite in the same way as others bit, but well, some days he wondered what might have been, how he would have looked after all this time. Same as Rene, he supposed. No, the time for regret was over, age had taught him that. The pros and cons sort of balanced each other out. He was reconciled to his mortality. He understood.

Unlike Tom Scavinio. The manager had moved out of New York, out of his hotel and was playing yin to Marco's yang by taking up room in his coastal house. Sea breezes and the smell of the brine did little to take his mind off this crazy new life he had fallen into and he bombarded Marco with questions about the past and the lost years, as Scavinio called the period between 1977 and 2013. Marco had been patient, but believed the American was dancing round the subject, afraid to tackle it head on. For what reason he didn't know. Maybe he was a fundamental atheist or secular extremist, but all his questions, his conversations, small talk and asides failed to mention, failed to acknowledge the V word. They couldn't even joke about it.

As a late summer storm blew in from the North Sea Scavinio's alarm swelled like the rising tide as if the band were circling on some terrible ghostly thermal, swooping around the roof of the house, clattering the tiles and kicking the windows. Outside all sorts of paraphernalia were blowing about, a bin, a bucket, garden tools, bits of wood, flapping and rattling, groaning and spitting. The rain lashed the glass and roared at the trees. "It could be worse," said Marco standing at the large patio windows with a glass of Armagnac, "there'll be men at sea in all this."

"Well, that's their choice and good luck to them," replied Scavinio.

Then a shattering sound announced itself and Marco knew it was more than a flower pot going over. "That sounds like the garage." He finished his drink. Both men grabbed their coats and went outside to see what the damage was.

Barely able to stand Marco forced himself towards the garage where the door had blown open, almost torn off its hinges, shattering the small window panes. The door was forced close and the two men found themselves inside the brick and timber shelter next to a gleaming Jaguar E-Type.

"You wouldn't want to drive that on a night like this," said Scavinio.

"No. It's a delicate thing at the best of times."

"You'd have to go a long way to find a modern car as beautiful as one of these." Scavinio delicately touched the curves and bulges of the Jag.

"It was what I always wanted," said Marco standing on the other side of it. "Cost me fifteen thousand Euros and I've driven it once. I saw all sorts of things come and go. You'll have seen them too, I guess, but I always liked these cars. Sports cars these days look designed to scare you. This is like an oil painting. A work of art."

"Were things better in the old days?" Scavinio's question was rhetorical and Marco refused to answer. He wasn't talking about the car. Marco clicked the door open and sat inside. After a moment Scavinio joined him. He was behind the wheel, in control, but Marco wanted to change the subject.

"You're still struggling with all this, aren't you?"

Scavinio gripped the wheel and steered himself along an imaginary journey. "How long does it take to accept what is really going on, Marco? How long did it take you?"

"Doesn't matter how long it took me, we're all different. Look at Rob. He came to terms with it in a few days. For me, several years, but after so long you see they're the same people they always were."

"Were they?" Scavinio considered it.

"Yeah. How long have you known them? A few months. The impact lasts longer than that. If anyone is struggling to come to terms with it, it's them." Marco spat the words out and jabbed his finger on the dashboard. "You don't believe me? Let me tell you a little story about something that happened to Dee a few years ago."

-

The four of them weren't stuck in the house in Obergrau all the time. They travelled; sometimes together, sometimes alone. Dee would hear about some curiosity, an event or an object and she'd go and find out more about it.

One autumn she visited Salzburg, looking for books about the musical heritage of the city. Not the usual names like Mozart, but anything that was a little more obscure. She found a bookshop in the old town and was browsing when she noticed a man walk in with a parcel.

He went to one side with the owner of the shop and unwrapped the parcel. It was covered in linen, folded over and over, and tied with cord. Inside was a book, something big and old, leather bound. The owner of the shop examined it and eventually approved it and the man who brought it in was paid.

Dee's curiosity was too much to control and she asked what the book was. It was a seventeenth century collection of botanical lists, quite rare and very expensive. Not quite what Dee was looking for, but what really caught her attention was what the shop owner said next: the man who brought it in was the last man in Salzburg who could repair and restore books of this age.

Well, she found an excuse to leave and being much younger than the book restorer caught up with him and followed him back to where he worked close to Nonnberg Abbey. It was a tiny place set within a narrow terraced street that followed the steps up the abbey hill. She stood outside for several hours waiting for the book restorer to leave, but he lived here so Dee had to wait until all the lights went out.

Inside, the ground floor was his workshop and it was like a laboratory. There were smells of cleaning fluids and glues; bench mounted tools, racks of card, drawers of parchment. There were inks, quills, brushes, a wooden rickety old printing press. The place looked like a revolutionary's publishing house ready for another batch of pamphlets. But on shelf after shelf Dee found stacks of manuscripts in varying states of disrepair.

Then he found her. The book restorer turned on a light and confronted Dee, but he was obviously not afraid of her. Even though she had got in without a key or smashing a window her presence didn't scare him a bit.

He said his name was Gottlieb. "You must be a collector. No other reason for being in here at this time."

"I'm always looking for something unusual. Never been in a restorer's workshop before."

Gottlieb was very old. It was hard to tell how he still had the eyesight and the steady hand to work, but he managed. He showed Dee all the different manuscripts and what needed to be done to repair them.

There were pages with the tiniest of holes waiting for the finest of threads to bind them together. A book about gloves commissioned by a Bourbon princess; a treatise on ailments associated with hunting for a 15th Century trader from Padua; maps of the Paris swamps and routes through them.

Dee saw the completed spines, glued and hardened, ready for the hardback covers to protect the edges of the paper and the stitching. There were title pages of colourful creatures and unpronounceable introductions in Catalan and Finnish. Around the workshop the manuscripts were brought back to life until they were healthy enough to be returned to their owners.

Except one.

"This, I finished twenty years ago," Gottlieb explained. "The gentleman who paid for its repair never came back."

The book, abandoned like an unwanted child, was only small, maybe fifteen by ten centimetres. It had a vivid blue pigskin cover with an embossed sun and fiery rays in gold. Inside, the text was small and filled every page to the edge.

"And what's it about?" asked Dee.

Gottlieb sat and summarised. It was a small journal, he explained, commissioned by a nobleman in 1210. The book is a report into the events that took place in a small village two years earlier.

'In 1208 five villagers had been accused of heresy and were to be burned at the stake. The wood piles were prepared, the victims shackled and coated with pitch. Then the fires were lit and the villagers stood back from the heat as the five heretics roasted. But the fire was not punishment enough and the bishop who had travelled from Brandenburg wanted their agonies to be even worse. He approached the fires, mouthed his incantations of fury and threw a red powder into the flames. As a consequence, the mixture of fire and the mysterious red powder was an explosion so violent it destroyed the heretics, the bishop, the onlookers, the village and the surrounding fields and woodlands in every direction. From the epicentre of the blast the ground was blackened and at the edges of the destruction, many kilometres away, mature trees were flattened in a fan shape radiating away from the blast. The explosion was heard in adjacent valleys and when people saw the clouds rising ever upwards they took it as a sign of God's anger. They came to see what had happened, but

found nothing except the blackened landscape looking like a vision of hell. Slowly, life in the surrounding areas went back to normal, but then one night a villager who was at the burning showed up in a nearby town. People were astonished that anyone could have survived, but over the following weeks more and more of them reappeared as if returning from the dead.'

"Which is, of course, what they are," said Gottlieb. Dee understood why he had chosen that particular book. "The powder," he explained, "thrown into the fire is believed to have been red sulphur, which some say is used to create the Philosopher's Stone."

"For alchemy," Dee said.

"Yes. But not just for alchemy. The Philosopher's Stone can also be used to heal and to achieve immortality. When the bishop threw the powder on the flames he obviously had no idea what he was doing, but the victims didn't die."

"So what happened?"

They became opposite. Instead of death their existence became opposite to life. An anti-life, an opposite state of existence."

Dee wasn't sure what Gottlieb meant, but he was more interested in making a different point. "There were fifty to sixty villagers and most of them survived. You are what you are because of what they became. Now there may be as many as ten thousand of you."

"Vampires?"

"That's just one of the names to describe you. Your kind continue because you carry some essence of those original villagers who died and yet didn't die. If they kill first before feeding their condition is not passed on, but if they feed first their victim will become like them. They contain the Philosopher's Stone within them and now it's within you."

As the book had been abandoned so long ago he let Dee keep it. Over the years she tried to find the village described, but she never found it and doubts whether the story is even true, but she thinks it's the best explanation for the origins of what she is. She still has the book. It's probably worth millions, but she'll never sell it.

-

"It's a difficult word to use," Scavinio muttered to himself.

"What?"

"Vampire. It means too much. It's a loaded word. Is there not an alternative, something more plausible?"

"They'll still be the same people, whatever word you use."

"Do you ever wonder what would have happened if Lenny Harper's stakes had been several inches to the right?" said Scavinio.

Jongbloed had thought about it many times. He thought about it most at Wim Seger's funeral when the band turned up long after everyone else had left. And again when he met a solitary figure mourning the death of her mother hours after the burial had taken place on a warm, sunny Rotterdam day. If Lenny Harper had known what he was doing he would have spared Susan Bekker the heartbreak later in life that she still talked about in her darkest moments.

"Penny for them?" Scavinio asked.

"What if? Everything has a what if attached to it. You can waste too much time wondering what if: what if Micky Redwall hadn't split up our band; what if," he stopped himself before he mentioned the Valentine's Day Kiss; Susan's fatal meeting in 1974. "So, what are they doing at the moment? Still rehearsing?"

"They've gone into one of their mysterious moods, which I don't get. They're cosying up to this Terence Pearl guy. Nuts doesn't begin to describe it, but they're interested in him for some reason. Any clues, Marco? You know 'em better than me."

Jongbloed sighed. "Maybe they want to keep an eye on him. No more Lenny Harper surprises coming out of nowhere."

"Yeah, yeah. They might not be so lucky a second time. So when do we get to see this thing on the road?"

"I might take her out tomorrow." Jongbloed laughed. "Get another old girl out on the road, eh Tom?"

34 - Onjective criticism

Listening to Toten Herzen rehearsing, Rob Wallet hoped the acoustics of the Ahoy and all the other arenas would be better than this enormous tin shed. The warehouse might well have been the ideal European location for storing ninety thousand tins of peaches, but it buzzed and crackled like the afterburners of a jet engine. It was always the same with guitars and steel trussed rooves; a high frequency distortion that left human ears feeling like they'd been filled with limestone. Watching Toten Herzen rehearsing, Wallet hoped they'd get their act together and move around a bit more. As they finished another song he spoke over the PA.

"Can I make a small suggestion?" They stood, hands on hips and waited. "Can't you move around a bit more. You're sort of huddled in the middle of the stage like you're comparing one anothers' strings." No response. (Could they hear him?) "It's a big stage, use it. From back here you look like one big fat guitarist."

Dee stepped up to a microphone. "It's only a rehearsal. It's not like we're on stage tomorrow night."

"Just suggesting, that's all. Put on a show, give 'em their money's worth."

"Maybe we can get the white tie and tails out, put on a bit of vaudeville."

"I'm not suggesting you go that far, but what are these ramps for here. Come down them. Shove your guitars down my throat."

"We'd love to, Rob" Dee said, "but we don't want to damage them. They're all we've got."

"Promise me you'll move a bit more on the night."

"Rob," Susan stepped up to another microphone, "just shut up worrying."

"I'm not worrying. Look, you're better than this. You want to be in a rock band then why don't you look like one!" He could see them looking at each other. Could he push them far enough without getting eaten.

"Rob," Susan again, "if you want to conduct the English National Opera go and ring them up. We'll move when we decide to move."

"Not sure I can wait that long. That Flying V's wasted on you if no one can see it being played." That was it, he'd lit the blue touch paper and now all he had to do was wait for the spark. Susan finally marched down one of the ramps. Rene stood behind his drums to see this. She jumped down from the end of the ramp and strode over to the sound desk. Once in range she launched a right hook that sent Wallet flying over the equipment into a heap on the hard floor. She stood over him, looking down through a black waterfall of hair. "If you want a show then go out and arrange for the magic ingredient."

"What? What magic ingredient? That hurt, that did." Her legs looked a lot longer from his angle. He was growing to like Susan when she was mad.

"Go and find your mad friend with the Cathar spaceship and find out if he's still willing to join us onstage."

"That's, er, that's a bad idea, Susan. Are you serious?"

332

"Make yourself useful. I got here before Elaine did and I know you wouldn't want that."

Wallet stood up rubbing his jaw. It didn't really hurt. "Tell her to move a bit, as well. She makes John Entwistle look like Freddie Mercury." She suppressed a grin. Wallet saw it: Susan Bekker definitely suppressed a grin.

-

During the day cows would hang their heads over the hedgerow whenever anyone walked along the lane. Terence Pearl would wonder what they were after. Food, probably. That's the usual reason why an animal bonds with a human being. It wants a free meal: it wants nourishment. Pearl didn't have any pets. Not because he was too tight to feed them, but because of the commitment; emotional, temporal and physical. He didn't have children. His wife left him three years after they got married and he swore he wouldn't make that mistake again. So Pearl wandered the lanes around Westerfield alone, but call him lonely and you'd get a short answer.

His evening stroll always concluded along Church Lane coming back into the village. (He wondered what he'd do in summer when his agonising aversion to sunlight forced him to take his evening strolls later into the night: the sun only disappeared at half ten in July!) But on this particular evening he noticed a shadow on the corner of the roof of the Church House. Pearl slowed his walk to a curious stroll. The Church House was a small building with a pitched roof, but Pearl couldn't remember there ever being a chimney or large gargoyle up there. As he reached the gate he could see that the shadow was in fact Rob

Wallet, sat on his haunches peering down at Pearl like a large cat watching a bird.

"Mr Wallet?" Pearl couldn't think of anything more appropriate.

"Off home, Terence?" said Wallet.

"Yes. How did you know?"

"Well, you live thataway," Wallet gestured towards the other side of the village where Pearl's house marked the start of open countryside, "and you're walking in that direction, so I figured, well, call it an intelligent guess."

"I suppose so."

"I thought you of all people would appreciate a bit of intelligence. In fact, have you noticed how intelligence loosely rhymes with Terence?"

"Mr Wallet," Pearl was conscious of other villagers seeing him talking to a figure on a roof, "are you drunk?"

Wallet looked over the edge of the roof. "No. I'm high!"

Pearl couldn't really argue with that. A car was heading towards him, headlights blinding. He stepped aside and as the light passed he wondered if Wallet would still be on the roof. Did the driver see him? Was he really there? Pearl turned back to the church and sure enough Wallet was still anchored to the roof, watching.

"You don't move very quickly, do you, Terence?"

"I don't know what you mean, Mr Wallet." Pearl stepped through the gate and stood on the church side of the hedge. He thought he might be less conspicuous if only the top half of his body could be seen talking to the Church House roof.

"We spoke to you a couple of weeks ago, but you still haven't told us who your mystery colleague is."

"I've been meaning to."

"What's wrong with you, Terence? You're an intelligent man, cleverer than me, and yet you side with someone who's no friend of yours. Haven't you grasped the benefits of working with me? All the things I can do for you? What's he giving you for all this?"

"A sense of right, a sense of righting a terrible wrong."

"Oh Terence. All your efforts, all the time you're devoting to this; how much do you think that time is worth? Don't you have any sense of self-worth? You're a teacher."

"Retired, actually."

"It still makes you a teacher whether you're retired or not. It's a calling, isn't it? A vocation? You can't just stop being a teacher. And besides, I thought teachers were all about spreading the truth. The inviolability of facts. The fundamental truths?"

"Yes, yes, I suppose so, but you can't use facts for evil purposes." Pearl suddenly looked up at Wallet with a fearful expression. He pushed himself against the hedge and felt for the crucifix hanging somewhere around his neck.

"I can show you the truth, Terence. I tried the other week, but it doesn't seem to have fired you up. Maybe I need to try harder to inspire you. What does it take, Terence? What can I offer you to make you see sense and come with me?"

"Please Mr Wallet, you're making me feel very scared."

"You don't have to be scared of me, Terence. I'm just trying to do the right thing for you. You love knowledge, don't you?"

"Yes."

"Come with us and we'll show you the world. We're a rock band. Not your kind of music, I know, but we travel the world. All those cultures, new people to meet, places to wonder at." Wallet hadn't moved an inch all the time he'd been talking. Crouching on his haunches, fingers together, sometimes talking directly to Pearl, other times to the darkness up the road towards the open fields. "Come on, Terence. You've written a lot of toe-curling bollocks about us. Don't you want to know the truth? Don't you owe it to yourself, a man of learning?"

"I would need time to think about it."

Wallet sighed. "Good job you don't play for Ipswich Town, Terence. You get the ball in the box and then need time to think about where you're gonna stick it." Wallet turned to the ridge of the roof behind him. "In fact, forget I just said that."

"I'm going home, Mr Wallet."

"Oh, didn't take long to make that decision, did it?"

Pearl made for the entrance of the church, but his mind was reeling, he couldn't remember where the door was so he went back to the lane and scurried off towards his house. He was well and truly wedged between two immovable surfaces. Earthly and, what was Rob Wallet? Unearthly at the best of times, but squatting like a medieval effigy on a roof with his crimson jacket and short black hair. Eyes ablaze like two tiny lamps. Oh to get home, to the safety of his dining room and a large cup of Greene and Blacks chocolate, which he admitted became less palatable by the day. His world was beginning to make no sense as the things he treasured moved out of reach: his garden was becoming untidy as he struggled with allergic reactions to the pollen and grass seed, pesticides and tomato fertilisers, each turning his skin to raw sandpaper. He woke up later, went to bed later, preferring the peace of the early hours with the chattering birds . . . which, come to think of it, was more of a cacophony these days. And now the dread of cataracts every time he looked at his hazy reflection, reminding him that the loss of his sight would end his passion for books. There was so much he wanted to do, so little time to do it, a raging desire to knock down the wall separating his kitchen from the dining room. Maybe Wallet was right, maybe he did have a better offer.

-

Back on the roof of the Church House Rob Wallet noticed Dee reading a small book. "It's 14th Century this church," she said pointing up at the tower. "Apparently, St Mary Magdalene is a rare name for a church. There's only three others in Suffolk."

"Really. Are these roof tiles not digging into your arse?"

Dee closed the book. "You just couldn't resist a sporting analogy, could you?"

"I tried to stop myself."

"You're fucking impossible. And you were doing so well. You were starting to scare the crap out of me for a minute."

"You've read Paradise Lost, haven't you?"

"Yeah." Dee leaned on her elbow and asked Wallet to quote something from it.

"Since first this subject for heroic song pleas'd me long choosing, and beginning late;

"Not sedulous by nature to indite warrs,

"Hitheto the onle argument heroic deem'd, chief maistrie to dissect with long and tedious havoc fabled knights in battels fcign'd;

"The better fortitude of patience and heroic martyrdom unsung. . . ."

Dee closed her eyes and speaking quietly joined in with Wallet's soothing recital.

"Or to describe races and games, or tilting furniture, emblazon'd shields,

"Impreses quaint, caparisons and steeds. . . ."

And on it went until they both realised they were quoting at each other, eyes blissfully closed, accompanied only by the sounds of a countryside evening and the poetry of their own voices. They ran out of words and Wallet asked Dee a question: "Why were you all sleeping in a tomb when Lenny Harper staked you?"

Dee smirked and took the little local history book out of her jacket pocket. She flicked the pages. "It was all a lie, Rob," she said. "Ask Barry Bush."

"Barry Bush? PC Barry Bush?"

"Yeah, with his daft mate who played for Queens Park Rangers. Someone sent the police up to Highgate on a wild goose chase while Lenny Harper was breaking into a flat we were living in somewhere near Swiss Cottage. And then after all the publicity and everything he started perpetuating this tale that we were all in Highgate Cemetery. He's stuck with it all these years, dined out on it for as long as he's been able to keep a straight face."

"The bastard!"

"Hooked you as well. The great investigative journalist, Rob Wallet." She leaned on her elbow again, but this time her expression was full of mischievous life. "And good luck to him. Didn't do us any harm." Wallet was dumbstruck.

"And who else knew?"

"How many coppers are in the Metropolitan Police? That's why Lenny Harper got done for wasting police time. We weren't up there, we were somewhere else getting our breath back and making plans to get out of London. Get out of the UK."

"So, Lenny did get to you, but in a house, not Highgate?"

Dee nodded. Her thoughts were placing her back at the scene and there was a moment's silence before she scanned the pages of the book. "Could have ended everything that night."

-

The following day Wallet found Barry Bush's phone number and had a brief, terse phone conversation. "You knew all along they weren't staked at Highgate Cemetery?"

"Course they weren't," said Bush, his voice fading in and out of a poor phone signal.

"You spun me a right load of old cobblers. I wrote all that down."

"No, you recorded it on your mobile phone."

"Same thing."

"Look," said Bush, "every time people have spoken or written about Toten Herzen and Lenny Harper they always come to me, they go away with the same old tale and they never, never check the facts. They never follow up on it and you're no different. You believed all that vampire bollocks just like the rest of them."

All that vampire bollocks! Wallet's scorn broke apart, shattered, fragmented and he found himself with a wry grin, a half smile and a sneaky regard for old Barry Bush. A bored copper sent on an excursion up to Highgate Cemetery, why shouldn't he make hay out of it? Stuck in front of the telly all day, what else did he have going for him? Gotcha!

"Barry," said Wallet, "no hard feelings, mate. Makes a good story, I suppose."

"Yeah."

"I suppose Stan Bowles took the secret to the grave with him?"

"Laughing all the way, he was. Laughing all the way."

RavensWish - totenherzen box set out and i cant afford it :-(pisses me off havin noooo money dont have a record player anyways

DM *to RavensWish - don't worry, I'll get one sorted for you (and a record player!): sent by WhiteRotterdam*

The Sun

Box Set Con Trick Catches the Spivs

Toten Herzen's 'limited edition' back catalogue leaves speculators hundreds of pounds out of pocket

For thousands of Toten Herzen fans the back catalogue box sets started to arrive today, after a wait of thirty five years! (The albums were actually released at midnight on Hallowe'en.) With five vinyl albums plus new artwork costing thirty quid not many were complaining, apart from the twenty early birds who pre-ordered the new release.

They were unaware that only twenty customers would be allowed to place an order before the official release date. After paying £350 three weeks ago they thought they were quids in when their so-called special editions started to appear on Ebay, with Buy it Now prices starting from five thousand pounds. One box set being sold by Charlie Clarken in Nantwich was listed for ten grand. "I feel sick as a parrot," said Clarken, a property developer. "I thought I'd make a bit of money out of this, but I've been ripped off. We all have."

But as soon as the items appeared a press release on the band's website clarified the issue saying the box set would go on sale to the general public for thirty pounds, leaving the greedy spivs hundreds of pounds out of pocket. The fourteen who listed their pre-order on Ebay were named and shamed on the website, but spokesman for the band Rob Wallet told the Sun the other six would be refunded.

As for the fourteen who tried to cash in at the expense of genuine

Toten Herzen fans: "They can have their money back too, but they need to ask the band in person." So far none of them have taken up the offer. Charlie Clarken was prepared to swallow the loss. "I won't be asking them for my money back. I don't even like Toten Herzen."

35 - Let the fun begin

RavensWish - just arrived at Ahoy subway station absolutely starving but cant stomach anything so nervous

Raven managed to propel herself away from the metro line and into the Zuidplein shopping centre to find food. This was a problem vampires didn't have, apart from maybe the need to find blood which they wouldn't find in a place like this unless they attacked someone, which would be a bit stupid, drawing attention to themselves in broad daylight, but then if it was broad daylight they wouldn't be out looking for blood. The runaway train of thoughts was in contrast to the muscle tightening excitement at what was ahead of her. All the way from the central station she had spotted people in black - some wearing face masks - who she presumed were going to the concert. But they weren't going where she was going. Not a bit of it. She stopped and took in the familiar sight of a shining, buffed up, spotless array of indoor shops selling the same expensive, unobtainable goods, but with different names above the windows. She thought she might stand out, with her black clothes and blue hair, but she wasn't alone this afternoon. Evidence of Toten Herzen was wandering around, mingling lazily with the regular shoppers, attracting sideways glances and whispered observations from groups of onlookers standing around in twos and threes.

This is what happens, thought Raven, when you are someone, when you have that influence and power to alter the surroundings. For one day this shopping centre's equilibrium was off centre, its familiarity disturbed by an influx of outsiders. When she found a MacDonald's it was half full of Toten Herzen fans being observed by silent children and their worried parents.

RavensWish - hunger begone found a macdonalds

She bought a box of chicken nuggets and a Coke and continued through the mall. Her head was still full of cloud; her thoughts erratic and confused. Her limbs felt heavy and swallowing was an effort with a mouth drying up after every sip of her Coke. She found a seat and sat down. Studying her chicken nuggets she wondered if this could be her last meal? The time on her phone was a little after four. The band would still be hidden somewhere avoiding the last hours of sunlight before evening moved in and the mischief began. For now the black clad figures were following social norms and drifting quietly in anticipation of the coming storm. Raven moved on, outside to the cold afternoon. The grey light of day was already beginning to turn red.

Traffic along the main road ringing the Ahoy was already at a standstill; bumper to bumper, inching along with each change of the traffic lights. People were sat in groups under the trees and across the way, the first indication of the event were the lines of lights launching from the roof of the arena. Banners stood in proud lines with the Toten Herzen crest and at right angles the exclamation WeAreTotenHerzen. Raven wanted a shot of the arena approach, but the traffic was a crawling wall obstructing her view, so she looked for access to the bridge that crossed the main road to the arena car park on the far side.

Elevated above the road and the cars she now had a greater sense of arrival and joined others up here for the panorama. And what a panorama it was as she came to a point midway above the traffic jam and saw the full extent of the invasion.

The arena lights were growing more vivid, swinging in a great arc across a mottled red sky. The banners flapped, arranged around a huge square filled with people. The doors weren't open yet, no queues had formed. Instead gangs were gathering around fires and flares belching great plumes of red smoke which hung in the air like evaporated blood. The smell of the fires and the car fumes added to the Danteian atmosphere. Flags bearing the daggered lettering of the band's crest marked the territories of individual camps: TH Utrecht, TH Arnhem, TH Harlem, TH den Haag, they were from everywhere, disgorged from coaches, trains and cars. They had come from all over Holland and Britain: Lincoln, Ipswich, Birmingham, Hull, Leeds. There were banners from Brussels and Paris, from Stuttgart, Essen, Gdansk, Bratislava. Proclamations from all over Europe were displayed on the flags, sprouting above the heads of the crowds; claiming their territory, announcing their occupation. There was music, unidentifiable, tinny, not the bass heavy thud that would soon come rumbling out of the hall as soundchecks began and the concert start grew ever closer. Raven took photo after photo from all directions. From one side of her field of vision to the other, a mass gathering, a congregation.

The oblivious smoke from the flares wandered towards the metro station, consuming then aggravating the traffic. Raven moved on, down the steps of the footbridge and into the red mist and its ghostly multilingual chatter. Face masks appeared and turned to her as she passed. They were flamboyant and colourful; detailed with lace and jewellery. Some had the beaks and feathers of birds, others the taught skin of bats. The fashion spectrum included everything from the dry black of tour tee-shirt to gothic corsetry and steam punk paraphernalia. Raven thought her blue hair might be the exception, but she counted five girls with similar colours, in addition to purple, turquoise, orange, maroon and red. There were men and women alike with scarlet coloured hair, hanging straight or with poker stiff spikes like Elaine Daley's crimson mohican. For others it was Dee Vincent's jet black bob or Susan Bekker's long, wild, charcoal style with flame tinted flashes around the face.

Raven paused to upload some of the photos and tweet the link, then realised she was still holding the empty MacDonald's nugget box. No litter bins anywhere! A group of fans materialised and saw her phone and the images.

"Sorry, I don't speak Dutch," she said, face to face with a group of girls and their matching purple and black lace masks. One of them pointed at her phone and stood alongside her.

"You're taking pictures?"

"Yeah, from on the bridge." Raven scrolled through the set and the masked girls were impressed. "Can I photograph you? I love your masks."

"Sure." And the four of them obediently lined up for the pose. Then one of them spoke and the others set off in the direction of the bridge to get their own view of the gathering. "Okay, thanks," said one of them as they disappeared.

RavensWish - its like a medievil pagent with red smoke everywhere and people in masks I want a mask check these out pic.ly/66344

She may have been alone in the gathering, but she was different in one vital aspect: they had tickets, she had an invite. They were visitors, she was a guest. One of the few. For the first time in her life she was one of the few. And it was time to follow the instructions. She checked her messages and found the DM from WhiteRotterdam. Don't go to the concert hall entrance, go to the arena entrance at the central plaza. She looked around above the heads of the crowd. The concert hall was to her left. It had a wide entrance facade with an imposing giant illuminated picture of the band's faces. To her right was a smaller entrance with Ahoy over the doors. She headed for it.

Did she need to be invited in, she wondered as she approached the steel and glass doors. Not yet, not for a few more hours at least. Her breathing was shortening and her muscles now were as tight as the bat skin masks. The arena entrance was less chaotic, but no less colourful. Head through the entrance hall, the message continued, to a large kiosk at the far end and to your right. She could see it, beyond the programme sellers and the merchandising stands. They were selling masks. She looked at one with crimson feathers and black costume stones around the eye holes. "Do I really want to look like everyone else though," she whispered to herself as she stepped up to a huge security guard standing outside the kiosk.

"Hello," he boomed.

"Hi. I've got an invite to go backstage." Raven fiddled with her phone.

"Okay, one moment." He entered the kiosk and came back with a tablet. "Your name?"

"Raven. It should just say Raven."

"Raven, okay. Who invited you?"

"I don't know. They just called themselves WhiteRotterdam."

"Yeah. Did they give you a message?"

She checked her phone. At the end of the directions were the words 'come for the right reasons.' "All I've got is come for the right reasons."

The security guy looked at her. He was nearly twice her height, dressed all in black with his security tabard around his neck. "Okay, put this on." He handed her a tabard similar to his. "Keep it on at all times, it gives you access to all areas, okay. And now follow me." And off they went. Without speaking he led her through the entrance to a connecting door to the concert hall and along the concourse to the far end where the stage was set.

"Excuse me," Raven said, "can I take a photo here?" She wanted a shot of the empty arena with the stage down below still bare and naked. Technicians were finalising set ups: amps and monitors being positioned, cables taped, last minute adjustments made to Rene's drums, inspections of the stage edges and runway. The sound desk, at the opposite end of the arena floor, had a knot of people opening up laptops and other complicated looking arrays and desks. This was the business end of things, before the hordes arrived and charged the arena with atmosphere, this was the time when the machinery was tested and weeks and months of organisation came together at the fine point of performance. Hundreds were involved, but the success or otherwise ultimately came down to just four people. Rather them than me, she thought.

The surroundings changed as she followed the security guy through a warren of grey walls, grey doors and finally white brick walls with dressing room notices printed and photocopied on A4 bits of paper. They emerged into another world of pre-concert preparation, less technical, but no less essential. Flower carriers, food carriers, clothing carriers, carriers of comfort and ambience.

Someone rushed past with what looked like Elaine Daley's Gibson Firebird, battered and scratched, held at arm's length like a lethal weapon. The spacious backstage area had a large table with a buffet spread for the staff and guests (wherever they were, no one was eating, the food was untouched). Coats, scarfs and bags lay abandoned across a scattering of plastic chairs. The security guy paused and then, pointing to a far corner, he said: "There."

Raven looked. On her own, in the farthest corner of the space, Susan Bekker was sitting on a settee strumming a guitar. "That's Susan Bekker," she said.

"WhiteRotterdam," said the security guy. "Okay. Have fun and be careful." He winked and left her on her own to complete the final few metres of her journey.

-

There was a sense of relief when Rob Wallet stepped outside the arena. He couldn't feel pain, couldn't feel the cold November breeze, but he could feel pressure; that emotional neurological psychological basket case of a feeling that sat like a fucking monkey on every human being between the age of one month and one hundred years. Finally, the comeback was a reality. He knew it was real because if it didn't happen now there were seventeen thousand multicoloured savages waiting just around the corner ready to drive stakes through his chest. Equipment was set up, the band were good to go. The concert was a sell out. No controversies (which is what Susan wanted), no ticket touts hiking the prices (which is what Tom Scavinio wanted) and so far Terence Pearl's friend hadn't shown up (which is what everyone wanted).

The evening sky was losing its strength and the glow from the arena was filling the air with a hint of red. Even upwind the smoke from the flares was visible and the occasional firecracker generated a distant round of applause. Stragglers and smokers mingled outside, chatting and laughing in Dutch. Toten's coach was parked nearby, the lightproof canopy linking it to the arena entrance folded away. It was quite an impressive coach, Wallet thought, examining its glossy blackness and its enormous wing mirrors like insect antennae.

So this was it; this lull, the empty thoughtless moment as everyone else got on with something that Wallet couldn't do, which was just about everything, was the product of eight months hassle. But it was worth it. A year ago he would have been somewhere round the front, arguing about his press pass, fighting for a space to watch, making notes and finally submitting copy to an increasingly bothered editor who was more concerned with getting that month's/week's issue out on time and within budget. Pressure, you see. It falls heavier on some than it does on others. Now he was in control of the press passes and was in a position to repay favours. So far he owed nothing, so no one got in the strength of blagging. Apparently one local Dutch celebrity had tried and failed to get in free on the strength of his Twitter following, but was told to go and steal a ticket off a Toten Herzen fan if he wanted to get in without paying. It would be easier to steal an antelope leg off a starving lion and in spite of having a choice of seventeen thousand potential victims he skulked away, probably tweeting to his flock how shit life was when you're rich and still have to pay.

Next up was Elaine and Dee's homecoming and England, with its health and safety, noise curfews, non-existant integrated transport system and EU employment laws. The only good thing

Wallet could think of, was the intensity of support. British fans were the ones with the real dead animals. Outside the Ahoy tonight someone had an inflatable horse, but even that wouldn't be allowed in. The band were quietly prepared for any outrage once the tour cavalcade arrived at Felixstowe. Then Germany, the sensible nation with its sensible hooligans and onto Vienna, where the headbangers knew Bach note for note. Budapest was the unknown and whilst the band were adamant Hungary had to be on the list, Wallet couldn't think why. He knew the aggression there would be wrapped in a veneer of nationalism. And what the fuck the Swiss had to be angry about was anyone's guess. Maybe Geneva had been included so that everyone could relax and count the money.

No, Wallet was being unfair on Toten Herzen fans. His first glimpses of tonight's audience reminded him of a baroque army waiting for the signal to charge, but would they charge, would they rise to the call and become the out of control mob that followed the band in the seventies. He headed back inside. Terence Pearl was waiting for him. He looked fucking awful. "Your friend not here yet, Terence," said Wallet.

"No. He will be let in, won't he?"

"I've told you time and time again, if you gave him the message he'll be let in. The problem will be if he uses a different name."

Pearl had arranged with his mystery friend to use the name John Waters. The message to quote was 'come alone.' "He's gonna have to be quick if he wants to murder the band during the concert. They're on in two hours."

"Yes, I know. He'll be here. Maybe I should go and look for him. He's coming in at the arena entrance, isn't he?"

"Near the central plaza. I don't know Terence, you might run off."

"I'm a man of my word, Rob. I promised to help you and I will. You were right all along, about Peter."

"Yeah, well thank me later. We stuff him in a suitcase and sort out the whats and whyfores tomorrow. Just go and find him and keep him somewhere out of sight."

Pearl was wearing the black clothes of security and was inconspicuous. Only the band and Wallet knew who he was, but his red tabard - access all areas - made him unquestionable to anyone else. He left, but Wallet asked another security guy to follow him. "It's his first concert. Don't let him get into any trouble."

-

Susan's fingers stretched along the neck of the guitar. It wasn't her Flying V, but something else. "Ibanez," she said when Raven asked. "It's a back up in case, well, whatever might happen happens."

"You warming up?"

"Yeah. You need to get all flexible, get these old muscles and tendons working again." Susan looked up at Raven. "Are you sitting down?"

"Sorry, yeah."

"It must have been a long journey."

"It was, but I've travelled to Europe before by coach, so it wasn't too bad."

Susan kept her head down as she strummed the Ibanez gently. Without its connection to an amp it made hardly a sound. "I did think of sending some transport to pick you up, but the logistics were a bit complicated. I trusted you'd get here. But I'll help you afterwards to go home." Raven's face dropped. Susan was having none of it. "What's your real name?"

"My real name's crap, I'd rather be called Raven." But Susan insisted. "It's Barbara."

"What?" Susan coughed. "I don't mean to be rude, but that is a strange name for a girl of your age."

"Yeah. Mum and dad where big trade unionists and called me after Barbara Castle."

"Right. Well, look on the bright side, they could have named you after Arthur Scargill."

"My brother's name's Arthur."

"Get lost!"

"No, I'm only joking. He's called Roy."

"Aha. After Roy Castle then?"

They managed to share a smile, but Raven was still not happy about her ticket home. "Why do you call yourself WhiteRotterdam?"

Susan offered her a bowl of fruit. Raven took a banana. "The doctors called me that when I was in hospital."

"When you were bitten?"

"When I was bitten, yes. They knew I came from Rotterdam and I was quite pale, as you are when you're ill, and it became a nickname. They were trying to make me feel better, but by that time I was already feeling better."

"Did you know what had happened?"

"No." She stopped strumming the guitar and held onto it like a child. "They said rabies, I believed them. But you don't wake up with fangs and a black cape. It was weeks before I figured out what was going on. First sign was the appetite; you don't have one. You never feel hungry, never feel like eating, you don't feel thirsty. It's like your hypothalamus just shuts down. But your physical strength is building all the time. I used to carry equipment around with me, Marshall cabinets, and they were as light as feathers. The road crew thought they were empty, until they came to pick them up. After that, over a period of weeks, your senses start to sharpen, you can hear the slightest whisper of sound, your vision is as keen as a bird's, and colour. Colour is intense as if everything is backlit. Your hair, for example, it's as if your head is a lampshade. I can smell that you've been eating chicken nuggets and drinking Coca Cola."

Raven was impressed. "You can smell it on me?"

"I can. Don't worry, no one else will. I can smell the fires burning outside and the gunpowder that's fuelling the flares they're lighting."

"And what about blood? How did it feel to drink blood?"

"It starts like a mild craving, like the inside of your muscles are starting to get itchy. I started by cutting myself, with my fingernails, and sucking the wound. But you don't last long with your own blood, so you go out at night and you find birds or cats. It's surprising how easy it is to catch them, especially cats, they just come right up to you and all it takes is your hand round their throat." Raven was eating her banana more slowly. "You still want to be a vampire or is that banana good enough for you?"

"I'd get used to it. You did."

"Can you handle the aggression?"

"I don't know."

"Think about the last time you were angry, so angry you were shaking, sweating, furious, and then multiply that by a hundred. That's how I feel right now and I consider myself calm. Look around at all these people."

"What's wrong with them?" said Raven watching the quiet coming and going of staff and assistants.

"Nothing. Nothing at all, but I could walk over to one of them now and take their head off with one blow and I wouldn't feel a thing. When I get angry I'd go outside where there's more of a challenge. Do you want to live like that? Our publicist, Rob, when we first met him he was an idiot. He drove us mad with his attitude, but he was harmless. Now he scares himself. He is waiting for the next explosion, the next little problem that will tip him over the edge. And he's only been like us for eight months. His problems haven't even started."

"Are you angry with me?" Raven threw the banana skin back into the bowl.

"I'm not angry with you, just puzzled why you want to be like this. I know you have no idea what it's really like. I guess you've seen the films and the tv programmes and think all vampires are spoiled American brats living in huge detached houses and driving fifty thousand dollar SUVs, whining because they can't get a girlfriend boyfriend and life sucks blah blah blah."

"I've never thought it would be like that. I just thought it would be better than what I am now."

"You can't socialise because everyone around you is a potential victim. Nocturnal behaviour is fine if you do what we do. For everyone else it's a career killer. You're constantly trying to hide your teeth and you have no fucking reflection and you don't want people to know about it because then they look at you and say 'how come you have no reflection, are you a vampire or something?' You're constantly hiding what you are, covering up what you've done. You can't talk to people so no one trusts you."

Raven sat cross legged. "They sound like flaky problems to me. Do you have any real ones like having no money, no job. A career killer! I don't have a career to kill. People like me, my age, we've been abandoned before we even had a chance. I haven't got a future because everything's against me, I'm just a puppet that everyone else controls. I live like an animal: I wake up, eat, breathe then go back to sleep. There's nothing else in my life. I feel angry all the time, but what can I do about it without getting into trouble? Live with it? Endure it? Put up with it? Why the fuck should I? If you have a problem you can just go and solve it. That's the difference between what you are and what I am. I can't solve my problems, I have to wait for someone else to do it."

The card game of life being played across a bowl of uneaten fruit was intensifying as they both tried to trump the other's hardships. But Susan didn't have the answer, only the knowledge that what Raven wanted, what Susan could give her, wasn't a solution. "I'm here by accident. I started out with very little and we all worked hard and it nearly failed. But what happened in 1974, that was never part of the plan. We would probably be here now anyway, the whole vampire thing had nothing to do with it. We would have been a struggling band who did the circuit, got the record deal, did more concerts, sold more records. Dying didn't help, and by the way did I add that you have to die first to be like this?"

"I know that."

"You live while everyone around you dies. And you live with the knowledge that eventually everyone you've ever known will be gone. Your friends, your parents. And when they die you won't be there at their funeral unless they bury them at night and then you spend the rest of eternity knowing you couldn't say goodbye and you go insane trying to make up for it and you end up trying to relive your life over and over except the bit you want to relive is always missing so you end up in stupid comebacks, doing stupid press conferences before stupid concerts in front of thousands of stupid people who are only here because they like watching car crashes and think it's cool to have a fascination with death."

"People die around me too. My friends and relatives are not immune just because I'm human. But if everything goes pear shaped for me I don't get a second chance to have another go at it." Raven sat forward. "All the people you know who died would still be here if they were vampires. If you made them vampires."

Susan bristled and put the guitar to one side. "That's not the answer and it's not my choice to make."

"No, it's mine. And I'm giving you permission."

Susan slumped backwards into the chair and groaned. Was that checkmate or did she still have a way out. Raven would be swapping one set of problems for another, but it sounded like a quick fix, an easy way out. Susan wanted to lecture her on working hard and earning rewards, the same old horseshit she'll have heard a thousand times. She knew the score and so did Raven. Raven was Susan's opposite: alive but not living.

-

Why do people want to live like this, thought Terence Pearl as he mixed with the fans wandering in and out of the arena foyer. The doors were open and the crowds outside were organising into thick snaking queues heading off to the concert hall entrance, their fires and flares extinguished, their flags furled, horses deflated. He stood by the VIP kiosk and was distracted by a conversation taking place at a cafe table on the other side of the foyer. He almost missed the exchange close by when he heard someone say 'come alone.'

Pearl stepped across. "John Waters?"

"Yes."

"Good. Please, follow me."

The two men stepped away from the kiosk and security and the risk of detection. They both knew each other; they sat on the same pub quiz team every week, shared the same disappointment every time they lost for knowing the right answers, left the Ring of Strawberries together weighed down with the conviction that society grew dumber by the day. Tonight though, they weren't part of the Jolly Troubadors, they weren't here to take a beating. They were themselves: Terence Pearl, retired schoolteacher, writer, commentator; and Patrick Wells, trickster, antagonist, and nephew of Peter Miles.

"Where are they?" Wells asked.

"Several places at the moment." Pearl was confident the crowds would only hear bits of this conversation as the two men passed through them. "The drummer is practising in a room on his own, the singer is with the technical crew, Susan the guitarist is with a fan and I'm not sure where the bass guitarist is." Pearl turned to his accomplice. "She's the most aloof, the most elusive one. Be careful with her."

"You've been extremely brave, Terence. I know I've said it so many times, but I really can't thank you enough for this. Trust me, by the time it's over you'll understand just how important this is."

"If you don't mind me saying, what you're doing is wrong. It is wrong in the eyes of the Lord and I hope he shows understanding when you face him."

"Let me worry about that, Terence, when the time comes."

"But I'm an accessory."

"Look," Wells stopped. They were in the concourse beneath one of the heavy concrete roof supports, the only two people not fixed on the gathering crowd and the expectant stage with its promise of visceral treats and wild surprises. "You can walk away from this, even now at this late stage and I wouldn't blame you. I want you to have a clear conscience, Terence."

"It's rather too late for that. I'm a man of my word, but I think you should know that your uncle wasn't murdered. He committed suicide."

Wells closed his eyes and shook his head. "No, Terence, he was murdered. My uncle was murdered and they put his grave on their album sleeve to mock his memory. As if killing him wasn't enough they had to desecrate his memory. They have destroyed his family. My family." He lowered his voice. "How do they know it was suicide if they never found his body? Don't you see, without a body to bury you cannot grieve. You cannot say goodbye. For all we know he might actually be here tonight, unaware of who he is."

Pearl looked at the crowd, the seats disappearing beneath an expanding surface of blackness. Peter Miles here?

"But that's what I'm trying to tell you. The band have looked for him. They have tried to find him."

"They told you that?"

"Yes."

"And you believed them?"

"Yes. There was no evidence to suggest they killed him, none to suggest they didn't. In law that would be called an open verdict."

"And the grave, on the album sleeve, was that an open verdict or were they laughing at his corpse? And what about a statement of regret. An apology. There's been nothing. Once I've done what I came here for you can consider your role in all this finished. I won't ask you to do anything else for me."

Pearl turned to continue and barged into a woman with green hair and blood trickling down her chin. "Terribly sorry," he said. He turned again to Wells, but he was gone.

-

Tom Scavinio stood towards the back of the concourse watching
the hall filling up. He tried not to worry, but he had a feeling. It
came from years of experiencing this moment as the final hour
counted down. There was no support act, so the audience would
have nothing to vent their aggression at (let's face it, that's what
the support acts are there for. You know the old line: the act
before me was so bad the audience was still booing them when I
went onstage.) He'd seen it all from deluded to deranged, hip to
square, suspiciously young to ridiculously old, drunk, high,
crushed, unconscious, excited, disappointed. But this lot . . . on
the surface they looked like any heavy metal crowd, but checking
out those seats closest to him, people looked agitated and
suspicious. He couldn't put his finger on it, why they didn't look
right. Who were they?

   Or maybe he had become the stranger. As he returned to the
backstage area he considered the possibility that he wasn't cut out
for this business anymore. His months with the band had done the
job of taking his mind off things, hell it had stripped his mind of
everything. His disillusionment with the music industry was
already festering when Toten Herzen first arrived in New York.
The ever present suspicion that the band were always one step
ahead of everyone gnawed at his determination not to ask
questions, but the questions were always there, rearing up
involuntarily: why work at night, why are they so young, what are
they up to now, what's Rob Wallet's agenda, and just don't
mention those fucking teeth!

He saw Susan Bekker leaning against a wall, grabbing a moment to herself. He'd seen that before too. "You ready for this?" He asked.

She took a moment before answering. "I can't say no, so I must be. It's all got a little complicated, people back here who shouldn't be here."

"I can get them out if you want."

"No, they were invited. It wouldn't be fair."

"I still don't understand why Terence Pearl is here," said Scavinio.

"He's up to something, so he's better where we can see him."

"And can you see him. Is anybody watching him?"

"Rob's onto it. And don't look like that. Rob's brought him in, Pearl believes our side of the story. Nothing's gonna go wrong now."

"Touch wood." Scavinio tapped Susan on the head.

"I suppose I should find the others."

Scavinio watched her go. She was weary, didn't show any of the nervous enthusiasm he was used to seeing. There came a moment where the band just wanted to get onstage, stop all the prowling about and small talk and just get the job started. Susan looked like she wanted to go to bed.

-

Raven hadn't moved off the settee where she had been speaking, or was it arguing with Susan. Now she was regretting it. You travel all that way to meet a hero and end up giving them cheek like you were talking back to your history teacher. Talking of which, here was one now. Terence Pearl dropped like a stone onto a nearby chair.

"No one talking to you either," he said.

"No." She noticed his security jacket and pass. "Shouldn't you be out there with the crowd?"

"No. I've been ordered to stay back here out of trouble."

"Out of trouble? What, you like to start fights or something?"

"Far from it. Although I have to say I do feel a tad worked up. I've felt like this for weeks. I must have high blood pressure."

"You should see a doctor. Might be something serious."

"Don't like to bother doctors." And they generally don't open at night, except for the A&E departments and he couldn't go wandering in there complaining of feeling a bit worked up, or that his eyes glazed over every time he tried shaving himself, or that the birds were deliberately trying to annoy him, or that all his lavenders had died on purpose. "Did you win a competition to meet the band?" he asked nervously.

"No, I got an invite. And then she clears off."

"Who's she?"

"Susan Bekker. Queen Bee. Don't know where she's gone. Went off in a huff." Raven was nibbling the browning remains of an apple.

"They're not interested in the likes of us. The little people. Look around here; there's a person for every task. Bring me some food, clean my clothes, comb my hair, peel me a grape. And everyone laps it up. They all want to be part of that circle, but don't have the status to be at the centre of it, so they're content to run around like dogs feeding under the table."

"Christ, so hot it burns. What's bothering you?"

"Oh, ignore me. Like I said I'm always worked up these days. Everything gets on my wick."

"Sounds like it. They can't do everything themselves can they?"

"I suppose not. I just wish people would stir things up a bit now and then. Makes life so much more interesting."

"I don't think anyone stirs things like this lot though, do they." She waited for a response, but noticed his name badge. 'Terence.' "Can I ask you something?" Pearl looked up. "You're not Terence Pearl are you?"

"Yes, I am why?"

"Oh shit." She bit a chunk out of the apple.

"Who are you?" He lifted his glasses off his nose to look at her pass. "Raven! Oh, please."

"Yeah. We were having a nice conversation then, weren't we?"

He turned away from her and took his glasses off to rub his eyes.

"You still think they're going home in a spaceship?"

He shook his head. "No, no, no. They're using a coach."

"Sorry I called you a knobster."

"Oh, it's all right. I've had worse things said to me." He saw Rob Wallet. "I need to go." He stood up and looked down at the blue haired girl sitting alone. "Be careful tonight, won't you?"

She nodded.

-

"Excuse me a moment," Wallet said as Pearl approached him. He grabbed his elbow. "Where is he?"

"Who?"

"Who? What do you mean who? Who do you think?"

"He disappeared."

"Disappeared? What do you mean disappeared? Wandered off? Puff of smoke? What?"

Pearl blustered. "He was stood next to me, we were coming backstage and when I turned round he was gone."

Wallet groaned. "He came here to be with you. You were his pass to getting backstage. Where the fuck has he gone?"

"I don't know."

Wallet could feel his authority draining away. He reset himself and started again. "Okay. He hasn't got a ticket, so he can't get a seat. He must be wandering around the concourse somewhere."

"What's going on?" Susan had suddenly appeared. "I can hear you two whispering from the other side of Rotterdam. I thought you had all this under control."

Wallet recognised those angry eyes. He hadn't seen them for a while, but they were back and blazing as furiously as ever.

"It is under control. Wells has gone missing. Mr Pearl here let him slip away. Does he know we know who he is?"

Pearl looked a bit confused, then: "No, he doesn't know we're expecting him."

"You haven't got a fucking clue have you?" said Susan.

"As a matter of fact," Wallet stepped towards her.

"Don't get in my face like this?"

"I'm convincing you that your put downs don't mean shit to me anymore?" he said.

"Put downs? I could put you down right now if that's what you want. Do you want me to do that because I'd really like to." She was stiffening, almost growing in height in front of him. "This might just be the time to clear out all the deadwood." Her skin was starting to glisten. Pearl backed away. Raven could see the confrontation and was standing nervously. Wallet wasn't going to back down. Whatever happened now he was going to stand and take it. And he knew what was happening. Susan's mouth was hanging open, her spine arching, she breathed in, rolled her head back and stretched her arms out just as Dee appeared.

The howl made everyone within earshot jump off the floor and drop whatever they were carrying. They scurried for cover, hands clasped to their ears. Glass shattered, doors vibrated, walls hummed. The noise surged away through the backstage area, knocking Dee off her feet as Tom Scavinio knelt in a corner and covered his head. Through the concourse people ducked, others cowered behind the heavy concrete pillars. The hall filled with the enormity of the cry reflecting off the steel roof supports. Feedback blew off headphones, the intensity made the lights flicker. And still the howling continued breathlessly. The stunned audience stopped their rummaging and seat searching for a few seconds. . . .

Susan heard it, the sound of seventeen thousand people howling back at her, a colossal roar like every animal in the world had been unleashed. She was still standing face to face with Wallet, his ears bleeding, eyes watering, but anchored to where he was, unflinching and impressed by the echo returning backstage multiplied a thousand times. He grabbed her hard around her jaw and kissed her lips. "Let me get on with my job," he said quietly.

He picked Pearl off the ground with one hand and carried him like a suitcase away from the backstage area, along the winding corridors and out to the edge of the arena concourse. The place was full. "Get out there and find him," snarled Wallet. Pearl saw a glimpse of his canines, two terrible glistening points. "If you don't come back with him I'll find him and I'll kill you both myself."

-

Susan's gaze was blank. Raven waited to see if it was a good moment to step past and go find her seat, but the gorgon noticed her. Before anyone could say anything a security guy with a buzzing walkie talkie rushed in looking for Scavinio. "Something's kicking off," he said.

Scavinio and Susan went to look. Out in the hall, down on the floor midway back from the stage a fight had started. A flare had been thrown and someone was on fire. The figure was wrestled to the floor and beaten with coats. A pall of grey and red smoke drifted upwards, but the trouble continued as a large group waded into the arena seating up the side of the hall. More flares were thrown, flags were being unfurled and waved around as if to celebrate the melee. Arena security poured through the upper entrances to separate two sides indistinguishable from each other. Firecrackers filled the air with eager bristling laughter as other members of the audience fled in the opposite direction to the fighting. Chair seats started to fly. One of the flags was set alight and TH Utrecht lost its standard as the trouble threatened to escalate.

Scavinio came away from the hall to find the rest of the band who were gathering backstage. "I had a gut feeling something wasn't right with this crowd," he said.

"Can security control it?" asked Wallet. Scavinio was shaking his head. "There are factions down there, god knows what's going to happen. Let the police deal with it. They're on their way. Keep everyone back here, there's a security cordon between them and us," Scavinio paused. "You don't look too concerned," he said.

Susan had seen enough. "Why would we?" she said.

Scavinio rubbed the back of his head. "I don't like to bring this up, but you were like this in New York on the night three people died."

"Like what?" said Susan. Raven was behind her.

"Like you didn't care."

"We don't," said Elaine. "Did we tell them to start this? Are they going to come up here and start with us? No and no."

"There's a riot down there and several thousand people getting caught up in it."

"The arena has contingencies for this," said Susan. "That's what you told us, Tom. When I asked you what happens if there's trouble you said, and I quote, you don't need to worry about trouble the arena management will have a contingency plan for anything that might happen."

Wallet was the first to hear sirens. But the agreement was to stay backstage, keep the staff close by and be prepared to get into the coach and head back to the hotel. Out in the hall police were pouring in like a black liquid, some in riot gear, but the heavy tactics weren't needed. The main lights stayed on as more people evacuated the area to gather outside. There were whispers that skirmishes had broken out in the car parks and traffic was slowing down as drivers tried to figure out why there were police vans everywhere.

-

At ten o'clock, with several hundred dozy stragglers still in their seats, the concert was cancelled. A few thousand still outside the arena surrendered to the inevitable and wandered away. At the back of the tour coach, the band and several staff members waited for Tom Scavinio to finish talking to arena management and watched a monitor feeding the latest news live as it happened. They were already showing camera phone footage of the flare that started it all off, the groups within the crowd coming together, the scattering of fans as the fists flew, the security members and arena stewards virtually powerless to stop the fighting and trying instead to protect anyone close by from being blown up.

Susan sat with her head in her hands. Dee was incandescent, but so far speechless. Rene was on his back, still holding his drumsticks. Elaine was unmoved. Wallet now had a slight admiration for her inability to be touched by any of this. He was trying to rationalise it all and generate some concern for the others: the sound engineers and lighting crew who were metres away from the trouble; the caterers and hospitality staff backstage who had been deafened one minute and then faced with the possibility of being overwhelmed by rioting thugs. Crowd violence was such an ugly spectacle, unless you were causing it.

At last, as Scavinio came aboard, the door closed and the coach pulled away. The windows were blackened, so no one could see the ordered pandemonium outside. The police vans, the media trucks and satellite dishes, unrepentant factions still waving their flags of allegiance. But the aroma of gunpowder was still so thick in the air even the humans could smell it.

"It might still be possible to come back tomorrow night," said Scavinio.

Wallet was astonished. "What?" He laughed.

"You must be joking," said Dee.

"What's so odd about that," said Susan.

"Because it'll kick off again, won't it?" said Dee angrily. "You'll have another fucking howling fit and another ten rows of seats'll go up in smoke."

"What, are you blaming me for that?" Susan was outraged.

"Excuse me, but it was like the gun at the start of the one hundred metres final. What else started it?"

"That's a big conclusion to jump to," said Rene without looking up.

"Yeah, yeah. Here we are in Rotterdam. You would say that, wouldn't you?"

"What does that mean," said Susan.

"You're forgetting that this band is half Dutch, half British. Why was this concert in Rotterdam?" Dee was on a roll now.

"What are you talking about?" Susan was on her feet and unconcerned the rest of the coach was listening to every word.

"I'm talking about the imbalance. We never get a say, do we? It's always you two, Rotterdam this, Rotterdam that. We are not a Dutch band, but that doesn't matter does it."

"Fuck you."

"Yeah," yelled Dee, "fuck me. I'm just the singer, so fuck me and get another one. Have a TV show and fuck me off."

Scavinio, on the verge of stepping in, saw Wallet suggesting he should back off. The advise was good.

Dee stepped up to Susan. "We'd be on stage now if it wasn't for your hysterics."

"Back off," Susan growled.

"Or what? You'll stamp your feet and have another howl. Go on then and I'll ram my fucking fist down your throat." She grabbed Susan round the neck and within the blink of an eye Rene was pulling her away, Elaine was pulling Rene away and all four of them were a rampaging, snarling knot of thrashing arms.

Wallet hesitated. He was the only person on the coach with the strength to intervene, but Scavinio beat him too it and tried to prize Dee and Susan apart. Their grip was too tight, their bodies too close. Scavinio was about to grab one of them when Dee locked her jaws onto Susan's throat; he was in the direct line of a plume of blood that travelled several metres down the inside of the coach. Susan had her hand across Dee's face and was digging in as far as the first knuckle on each finger. Scavinio was almost gagging, but tried to get a hold of one of them. Dee lashed out and swiped her fingernails across Scavinio's head tearing him open. Wallet was already trying to force himself between Elaine and Rene and saw Scavinio peel away in shock and pain. Pearl, cowering in his seat and still upset at not finding Wells, wanted to help, but Dee and Susan were on the move, locked together, wrestling violently, stumbling against the seats as each tried to get the finishing hold.

"Terence," shouted Wallet, "help Tom, leave those two." Pearl was confused. It would be like trying to come between two tigers. Elaine was on the floor of the coach, face up with Rene on top of her face down, together rolling left and right in a gnashing fury of fists and teeth. Wallet was desperately trying to get a knee between them to get some leverage. He was already scratched to ribbons with a gash running down the side of his head, through his shirt as far as his collar bone.

The coach careered left and right as the weight shifted this way and that. Scavinio was as far up the front as he could get along with everybody else. He was being treated by the tour manager nervously looking over his shoulder as Dee and Susan struggled, inching ever closer to them. The inside of the coach was like an abattoir. Pearl wept as he tried to grab a shoulder, an arm, anything he thought might be a limb, but eventually he could only watch as the ferocity of the battle projected the two women at the side of the coach and in an instant they crashed through the windows onto the road outside.

Oblivious, Elaine and Rene remained locked together. Wallet was crimson from head to foot. He had blood in his eyes, but he could see what had happened. The coach braked hard, more bodies were thrown forward and Wallet found himself wedged between Elaine, panting like a savage and Rene still trying to crawl over him to get at her. He put everything between them and felt Elaine's weight crushing his chest as she locked on to Rene's throat. Then the weight diminished and he saw a clutch of men pulling Elaine and Rene apart. Scavinio, the tour manager and the coach driver were just succeeding as a human barrier, but only because Elaine and Rene had paused for a moment. "Get them off the coach, for fucks sake." He wiped the blood off his face and tried to breath. Several seats were covered in crumbs of broken glass and through the shattered window he could see Susan and Dee back up the road on their hands and knees still eyeing one another as if they were about to start again. Behind them the traffic was backing up out of sight. Then he found Pearl, crouched into a ball between the seats.

"I think you should stay there, Terence," said Wallet. Then he stepped back a moment. "Didn't you predict something like this would happen?"

Outside singer and guitarist were sat down and as Wallet drew closer he could see Dee grinning at her colleague. "You taste funny," she said and spat a mouthful of blood onto the tarmac. "You taste of that stupid perfume you're always wearing.

"You know what just happened," Susan said correcting several dislocated fingers, "some stupid with a flare gun burned the place to the ground!"

Wallet looked on as the two of them rolled around laughing and trying to sing the words to Smoke on the Water like drunken sailors. Dislocated fingers were enough and he turned around and climbed back onto the coach. He checked Scavinio's injuries and suggested the coach driver should get him to a hospital.

RavensWish - concert cancelled fighting everywhere heart

broken nothing left to live for

JarniHeijnkes - sounds bad. can see the pictures on the news. place looks like a battleground #totenherzenriot

Antonlagarde - WTF how did it come down to this?

Carlwallace15 - travelled from Nottingham. Still choking from all the smoke. never seen anything like it! #totenherzenriot bitsy.fr/cw15/2667

Dekuip2010 - they still got their shit, proud of our Rotterdam girl #susanbekker @totenherzen never die

RavensWish - theres nothing to be proud of

Dekuip2010 - fuck u @totenherzen rule the world, people get reminder of that 2nite

RavensWish - how old r u? You probably werent born when they were around. #FAKE

Dekuip2010 - old enough to know the truth @totenherzen take shit of no1 #susanbekker for queen of nederland

36 - Liberation

Raven turned off her phone for the first time since buying it a year ago. In the confusion of the riot she and several others had been bundled out of the building and no amount of pleading saw her bundled anywhere near her 'host' for the evening. Treated like any other hanger on, she was left powerless as the coach pulled away from the Ahoy. Any hope of turning her life around drove away with it. The point of her journey was gone and she was left to wander aimlessly, trying to find a patch of clean air in the sulphurous hate of the Rotterdam night. Around her was the blue light blinking and siren wailing evidence of a large police presence, and armoured men and women rounding up any groups who looked like they might have some fight still in them.

She could see the footbridge over the road and the route back to the city centre. There might still be trains to the central station, but how safe would they be after everything, at this time of night. A deep, heavy unbearable sense of sadness and loneliness pulled her to the ground and she wept uncontrollably.

Then a hand on her shoulder made her jump. "I'm sorry," said a tall man leaning over her. "I saw you earlier, backstage. I wondered if you were all right." He didn't look like a regular Toten Herzen fan, but then what would that look like: flare in hand, troubled expression, blue hair, runny mascara.

"Yeah, I was. And I'm not all right. I'm fucking horrible."

The man knelt down beside her. According to her pass she was called Raven! "It's probably not safe for you to be here on your own now."

What was he saying? What was he up to? Where was this heading? One question after another swept the innocuous concern aside and replaced it with every terror imaginable. "No, I'm okay," she said springing to her feet. "You know what I'm gonna do?" The man shook his head. "I'm going over to their hotel and I'm gonna tell em what a bunch of fuckers they all are."

"You know where they're staying?"

"As a matter of fact I do, yeah. And she probably forgot she told me." Raven set off with a new plan. The guy was left alone to watch her go, mumbling and muttering. "You're not leaving me here like this, you fucking witch. You got me over here, you're gonna sort me out. Yeah, that's what you're gonna do. Sort me out." She turned her phone back on and as she walked through what was left of the event, suspicious police officers, a stray fire engine, several ambulances and shell shocked fans watching nothing particularly interesting, she found the hotel's website. The Rotterdam Crown Hotel. "Five stars, you rich bastards." It was on the other side of the city according to the map. "You better still be there when I get there."

-

By the time Raven arrived at reception she was limping heavily. The time was coming up to four o'clock in the morning and only anger and adrenaline were keeping her awake. The night manager, alone in his spacious empty world, wondered who, or what, was wandering into his hotel at this time. Raven was a left over from the evening's 'events' at the Ahoy. Fodder for hotel security, the trouble was crossing their threshold now.

"I want to speak to Susan Bekker, please."

"Is she expecting you?" said the night manager positioning himself firmly against the reception desk away from the telephone.

"Yeah she is. She invited me backstage at the Ahoy and then left me there when they all came back here and I want an explanation why she would do that." She started filling up. "After everything we talked about why did she fucking leave me there?"

The night manager must have been softened by loneliness. "Who shall I say is asking for her?"

Raven wiped her eyes dry. "Tell her . . . Barbara!"

He made the call. Raven waited. "Hello, sorry to trouble you at this time. There is a young lady in reception called Barbara asking to see Susan." He covered the mouthpiece and turned. "Are you also called Raven?" Raven nodded. "Yes." He looked at her again. "Blue hair, yes. Okay, thank you." He put the receiver down. "Someone will come down to see you in a moment. You can take a seat here if you like."

"Thank you." She turned down an offer of tea even though she had a raging thirst. Before she had time to wince at the pain in her feet, the lift door opened and Susan was standing there beckoning Raven to join her. Forgetting the pain, she limped over and as soon as the doors closed grabbed Susan and poured her heart out.

"You bitch, you left me there in all that. . . ."

"I'm sorry. I'm sorry. It was chaotic, we were pushed around and on the coach and then a fight broke out and everything was, I don't know, all over the place."

Raven saw for the first time heavy bruising all over Susan's throat and shoulders. She had four red lines running down the left side of her face. "What happened?"

"I looked worse a few hours ago. Everything's healing. Dee and I had a bit of a disagreement, but we're all cool now." Susan led Raven out of the elevator and along a rich golden atrium flanked by vivid orange doors. "I'm gonna make it up to you." She put a cold arm around Raven's shoulders and led her into a room. Now at last Raven felt safe.

Susan's room was quiet. Modern. A million miles from vampiric. None of the gothic flourishes she was expecting, but she should have known that from the start. Susan Bekker, in her own words, was no whining teenager. She wasn't the stuff of fiction or films. She was real, and real vampires stayed in real hotel rooms and lived in real houses, slept in real beds . . . Susan's hadn't been slept in, but a suitcase was open with clothes spilling out of it. That looked familiar, that looked almost homely. A tablet was lying on a coffee table. Susan picked it up and looked at her digital reflection. "These marks should be gone in an hour."

"Is that a mirror?" asked Raven.

"Yeah, clever isn't it. It's the webcam, then I flip the image and voilà."

Raven processed part of the explanation, but her feet were hurting so much she only wanted to get her boots off and sit in a bowl of hot water. Susan opened the mini fridge and took out a bottle of cola. "You can gulp this down first and then you can have something stronger if you want."

"What are you going to do?"

Susan sat next to her on the edge of the bed. "I'm not sure. I'm still not sure you're ready to change, so the deal is you spend some time with us until your mind's made up. We've still got a lot to do, you can be part of the team. We'll work out what you can do; personal assistant, I don't know. I can't think of anything right now. We'll see how it goes. I'm making no promises, but if you still want to change and I think you can handle it, then we'll see what happens."

"When you say change. . . ." She couldn't bring herself to say the word. The V word. Sitting so close to Susan she could smell the coldness of her skin, see the veins in her eyes and delicate bulge over her canine teeth, the chill was radiant, cooling the air between them. In the tranquillity of the room, so distant now from the night's chaos, the promise of change was not the casual desire it had once been; it wasn't the adventure she was expecting. It was a long, one way journey, an agreement that could never be cancelled.

"It's what you still want isn't it?"

"Yeah. Yeah it is."

"Okay. Look, you must be exhausted. I don't need the bed tonight so get comfortable here. Take a shower. Take as long as you want. There's a slight chance the concert might be on again tomorrow night, but don't hold your breath. I'm not giving up on this though." Raven didn't remember undressing, or taking a shower, but at five thirty in the morning she woke up in the bed. There was conversation in the corridor that sounded like Susan, Rob Wallet and another woman, possibly Dee Vincent or Elaine Daley. The conversation moved away and Raven was too exhausted to care.

-

Wallet was at the entrance to the hotel when a tall bloke pushed past him. The quality of guest must diminish as sunrise approaches. He watched him pace towards the night manager, head down, square shouldered. Fucking hell . . . it was Patrick Wells! He must have followed Raven across the city. Wallet was about to play hero and grab him from behind, he had the strength these days to take down the big ones, but then an inner voice told him to hang back, wait to see how Wells was going to play this.

"Hello, I'm sorry to trouble you, but I believe my daughter is here. She's running after this rock band and her name is Raven." Wells hadn't recognised Wallet. He turned to look back just as Wallet was about to go up to Susan.

"Can you describe her, sir?" said the night manager.

"Five feet five, dressed in black, black leather jacket, black jeans, black lace up boots, blue hair. She told me she was coming here to meet the band. Has she been here?"

"Yes. A young woman of that description arrived earlier. May I ask who's calling?"

He paused. "John Waters," he said firmly.

The night manager glanced over to Wallet just as he vanished. God knows what he must have seen at that moment!

Wallet appeared in Susan's room, making her jump. Raven was asleep in the bed. There was no time to ask. "Two things: Patrick Wells is downstairs."

"You're fucking joking."

"I never joke, Susan, you should know that by now."

"And?"

"And I think the night manager might have seen me vanishing when I came up here."

She sighed. "Go back to your room, I'll deal with it. Just like I deal with everything else you mess up."

Wallet's phone was ringing in his room. It was the night manager.

"Hello again, Rob."

"Hi. How are you?"

"Fine thank you, never been so busy. There is a Mr Waters in reception to collect his daughter. Raven Waters?"

"Right. I think Susan Bekker might be going down to meet him."

"Okay, I'll tell him. Thanks Rob."

"No problem. Must be quite a weird night. Bet you see all sorts of things on this rota." Wallet laughed.

"I've seen everything, Rob. Or I thought I had." He put the phone down.

"Bollocks."

Susan was outside, marching down the corridor with Terence Pearl. Wallet had to join them. This was as much his cock up as anyone's. In fact, it was exclusively his cock up. One of his better examples. Susan didn't object to him joining her and Pearl in the lift. "Why we going down in the lift?" Wallet asked.

Susan glared at him. "Why do you think?"

The lift doors opened and they saw Wells sitting in a deep chair studying the night manager who turned away as the three oddballs from the second floor stepped out into reception. Wells gathered himself and nervously stood up. "Is there somewhere quiet we can sit?" Wallet asked the night manager who looked confused. Everywhere was quiet at this time in the morning.

"The restaurant, please feel free. It isn't open, but you can talk there. Would you like a taxi or will you find your own way there?"

"We'll walk." Wallet blushed. Susan and Pearl headed towards the restaurant with Wells several paces behind them.

"Right, this is it. The moment of truth," said Susan, "What's the game?"

"Game?" Wells was growing in confidence: the confidence of a man who was finally facing his target, the confidence of a man who was going all the way. "What game? I'm not playing a game. Where's the rest of you?"

"They'll be here in a minute," said Susan. "Who are you?"

"Look at me. Look at me and you'll soon figure out who I am."

"You look like Pete, but I know it can't be him."

"Pete, oh it's Pete. Pete! The same Pete who you murdered in 1973, the same Pete you hid from his relatives, the same Pete who you mocked on your album cover in 1974, the same Pete whose family you destroyed."

"It isn't like that, Patrick," said Pearl.

"Patrick," said Susan. "So which side of the family are you from?"

"Peter was my uncle. His sister is my mother and she has been bereft for forty years because of you."

"We didn't kill Pete. We don't know what happened to him, but we didn't kill him."

"I don't believe you."

"It's pretty obvious you don't believe us."

"You're lying now like you've lied for the past forty years."

"Patrick," Susan took one step forward, "we saw him alive and he was drunk, Micky Redwall took him home and we never saw him again. We don't know what happened. We've tried to find out, but after all this time it's next to impossible."

Wells would have to wait. Without the band here he'd only get half the job done. There might be time to pacify him and salvage some miserable conclusion to this whole desperate episode. No one would emerge from this with any valour, but there was a chance if Wells didn't try anything stupid that some kind of closure, no matter how minuscule, might be possible. But he was already hyped up from confrontation and lack of sleep. He wasn't acting like a man ready to back down.

"I'm not prepared to listen to any more of this. You've had forty years to apologise, forty years to offer an explanation, forty years," he was raising his voice now, "to show some kind of regret, offer some mark of respect. Offer to meet his parents, offer to put yourselves at their mercy, but you've never done that and why? Because you don't care."

"We didn't care," said Susan. "Back then we didn't care, we didn't care about anything, but now we do and we are trying to find out what happened, and we will meet Pete's family, but Patrick I'm not lying anymore."

"Yes, you are."

The night manager appeared. "Is everything okay?" Wallet reassured him, but he probably wasn't the best person to put the night manager at ease. Not after, well. . . .

"I'm not lying Patrick," said Susan, "Terence, can you explain to him?"

Pearl offered to speak, but Wells shut him up. "I'm not listening to him. He's a bloody idiot."

"What?"

"I'm sorry Terence," Wells continued, "but I told you to call it a day. You got me this far. I'm grateful, but I'm not going to listen to someone who is here, in a hotel, with this lot. How much are they paying you?"

"They're not paying me, I listened to them. I listened to Rob, he was convincing and you should listen to him to."

"Wells turned to Wallet. "Who the hell are you anyway? This has nothing to do with you."

"Susan asked me to find out what happened to Peter. I've spent months trying to get to the bottom of this and Terence here has been helping me."

"Months!" Wells turned to Pearl. "You were supposed to be helping me. You were helping me!"

"And I did. You're here now, Patrick. If you let them, they can help you."

Wells was drying up, running out of options, running out of time. "Where are the others?" he demanded. He didn't want help, didn't want a resolution; a hug and a handshake and we'll get back to you. He wasn't being brushed off like one of their fans.

"They're not here," said Susan.

Wells put his hand in his inside pocket and took out a pistol. "Where are the others?" he said slowly taking the safety catch off.

Wallet could see Wells knew his way around a gun, but beyond that the world still had a few mysteries. Who, or rather what, was standing in front of him? Susan glanced at the gun. "Go ahead, get yourself into trouble for all this. Create another tragedy for your family."

"Susan," Wallet warned.

"No, you want to shoot me, if that makes you feel better, if that's your solution, shoot me."

And he did. The gun fired startling everyone and a small red bullet hole appeared in Susan's forehead. There was a deathly pause and months of assurance, months of certainty and confirmation in the supernatural hung on the say so of a single bullet. Wallet knew there was no such thing as a racing certainty, but even though. . . . Everything he'd witnessed, everything he'd experienced, everything he'd learned was about to be tested by that one solitary gun shot. He and Pearl waited for Susan to drop.

But she didn't. Wells looked at his gun and at Susan. He tried again and missed! He was shaking violently now, but she gave him enough time to take a third shot, which hit her in the shoulder. And still she didn't move. Susan simply stood and smiled as one bullet hole after another appeared, effortlessly, ineffectively, until Wells had almost emptied the gun's magazine. Gasping for breath, he readied himself one last time hoping this would be the killer shot and that her refusal to drop was some kind of stiffened euphoric pause, one final beatific smile before death, but before he could fire Pearl launched himself forward.

The two men went over a table backwards as Pearl sank his teeth into Wells' exposed neck. The night manager had already come running and, frozen with shock at the sight of Susan taking one bullet after another with no effect, he now had one man on his back being bitten by a second. Wallet and Susan pulled Pearl away as he tried to apologise to his victim. "You're wrong, Patrick, you are wrong." He pulled himself free and ran towards a staffroom door.

"What the fuck has he just done?" said Wallet as he checked Wells' pulse. It was weak and he was losing too much blood. "He's gonna be dead any minute," he said to Susan whose bullet wounds were already congealing and fading.

"Where's Pearl gone?" She ran to the door of the staffroom, but it was locked. "Terence," she banged on it.

Wallet rushed to reception, but the night manager had beaten him to it, propelled by a state of high alarm. The police had been called and he was now demanding an ambulance. "A man with a single throat wound," he waited for Wallet's description, but he was shaking his head. "It may be fatal."

Back in the restaurant Wells' fate was beyond doubt. He lay across the table with his eyes bulging open. The blood, still eager to take advantage of its premature release, was spreading out over the floor. "Pearl still locked away?"

Susan nodded. "I don't want to kick the door in. He's had enough shocks already." The night manager came back, almost stepping in the blood. "You need to cover this up," Susan said, "and make sure no one comes down and sees it." The night manager paused. "Please." Off he went.

Wallet thought about ripping down a curtain, but he could see the intensity of the darkness was giving way to morning. They only had one or two hours to sort this out and get back to their rooms. Susan knew what he was thinking.

"This is a mess," she said.

Wallet disagreed. "Typical day in the life of Toten Herzen, Susan. One riot, one manager mauled, a stray fan, a murder victim and a vampire locked in a staffroom. It's like a Whitehall farce."

"Trust you not to take it seriously."

"I don't take anything seriously anymore," said Wallet. "Life's too fucking short for that."

-

The first police officers to arrive did Wallet and Susan a favour by ordering them back up to their rooms until the drama was over, but the drama was only just beginning. Wallet wasn't aware of the niceties of Dutch policing, but Susan, standing in the atrium corridor listening to the increasing chaos down below knew the situation was turning critical. Turning red. Wallet listened carefully as she explained the Regional Constabulary had been replaced by the National Constabulary and that even they, with all their gung ho responsibilities, had now been turfed out by the Royal Military Police.

"Military Police?"

"They're not treating this like a normal killing. Not if that lot have turned up."

"What's so special about them?" Wallet hadn't seen this kind of concern on Susan's face. So often she was the calm in the storm. She was usually the calm and the storm, but her senses now were at the razor's edge. This didn't feel right.

"International crime, terrorism, riot, national security shit. Not localised murders. Not timid killers like Terence Pearl."

-

By seven thirty and with sunlight pouring into the hotel, Terence Pearl was still locked in a staff room refusing to emerge. The officer given the task of enticing him out didn't want anymore victims and was hoping for a negotiated end to the crisis. The night manager was gone, taken away as a witness with an account he wasn't sure he believed himself.

The sound of a lock turning alerted the waiting officer. A message went to the armed unit sitting around outside the hotel entrance. Pearl crawled out of the staff room. "Mr Pearl," the officer checked to see if Pearl was armed. He wasn't, but he was distressed, shaking and looking for help.

"Vengeance is a gift from the Lord Jesus Christ. We are his followers, we are duty bound to uphold his ministry and strike forth the demons that crawl upon the earth and prey upon God's children."

"Okay, Mr Pearl." The officer was calm, kept his hands in front of him and did nothing as Pearl slowly crawled towards him. No one moved, the other officers entering the reception area slowed to a halt. An expectant chill enveloped everyone standing there as Pearl inched past an enormous puddle of blood covering an area ringed by police security tape. He squinted as the light level in reception increased. "I want you to come with us, Mr Pearl," said the officer carefully. "Please stand up and put your hands where I can see them."

Pearl followed the instruction and rose awkwardly, hands hanging by his side, head bowed. His body was a walking dead weight, moving on autopilot, but still capable of a sudden and violent reaction.

"Vengeance is a gift from the Lord Jesus Christ. We are his followers, we are duty bound to uphold his ministry and strike forth the demons that crawl upon the earth and prey upon God's children."

"You just told us that, Mr Pearl," said the officer patiently.

Without pause for breath Terence Pearl was led away from the bar and through the reception area of the Rotterdam Crown Hotel. Two more officers gently held on to both arms as Pearl offered little resistance.

Once outside, the commanding officer became aware of his audience. Every hotel window had a face, or two faces, all transfixed by the fleet of police vehicles and the small army of armed officers filling the grounds of the hotel all the way to the entrance where a second fleet of vehicles contained the eyes and ears of the world's media. All he wanted, all he needed, was to get Pearl into a van and get him away.

-

"What's happening now," said Susan staying a safe distance from the sunlit glass. She had decided to keep the television turned off following the unremitting coverage of the concert and the obligatory blame game and who did what and why. Everyone was an expert in crowd control; everyone was an expert in concert management; everyone was an expert on Toten Herzen. Raven was peeking through a tiny gap in the curtains.

"It looks like they're getting ready for something. They've brought him out and they're opening the back door of that police van."

"Wonder what'll happen to him. You can't call him a criminal for what he's done." Susan played with the security tabard from the Ahoy. "Oh fuck, what a mess."

"Can't you help him?" said Raven. "Pay for his lawyers or something?"

"Maybe. We'll have to do something. We can't abandon another one. Or we could bury him next to Peter Miles. We could build our own graveyard just for our victims. Peter Miles, Patrick Wells. Fucking hell, it would go on forever."

Raven looked back at Susan. "It's not that bad, is it? Oh hang on, there's something happening."

-

The officers had formed a protective bunch around their suspect, carefully guiding him through the revolving doors of the hotel, but Pearl was agitating as he walked towards the police van. He started squirming in the keen morning sunlight that hit his face like the slap of a hand. He started crying out, pleading for the officers to get him out of the sun. They reassured him, but continued to walk at the same pace. Pearl struggled to breathe as his initial screams distorted and lowered to a tormented grumble.

His clothes began to steam. One of the officers twisted uncomfortably as a sudden intense heat reflected onto him. He was forced to let go of Pearl's arm, which had become as hot as the hob of a cooker; his colleague on the other side backed away when a small flame suddenly crawled up the sleeve of his jacket.

Panic had seized the commanding officer as Pearl writhed in unapproachable pain. The walkie talkies were overcome with static interference. Car alarms awoke in a deafening chorus of noise and mobile phone signals disappeared everywhere. In the middle of a growing panic and cacophony Pearl was now beyond help, such was the oven-like heat radiating off him; no one could get near. Officers scattered as the volcanic atmosphere pulsed towards them, singeing faces, beards, eyebrows. The commanding officer made a desperate attempt to grab Pearl and pull him towards the van, but the heat was eating into its victim and Pearl was doubling at the knees, buckling under the immensity of an invisible inferno consuming him. Few wanted to look, but no one could take their eyes off the spectacle of this unassuming man disappearing in front of them, blackening, carbonising; flakes of ash separating and drifting around his body that was becoming a formless lump, disintegrating, steaming multicoloured vapours and flashing sparks of intense light. His body popped and bubbled before finally collapsing into a dry desiccated pile of cinders that left a spreading black smear and a thin veil of dark mist.

-

Raven jumped back from the window with her hands over her eyes. "Fuck."

"Speak to me," said Susan. "I can smell burning, human flesh burning. What's just happened?"

Raven couldn't answer. "That nearly burned my fucking eyeballs out." She turned away from the window and let her astonished expression tell the rest of the story. She ran to the bathroom and was violently sick.

What had Wallet done? What plan had he followed to win Pearl's co-operation? Turning a man to get him to talk, turning a man for a brief period of inside knowledge and then leaving him to his fate without warning anyone. Why didn't he say, why didn't he involve the others so that they knew, so that they could deal with the risks? Another victim, another death to explain, another name in the Toten Herzen book of remembrance. The graveyard was growing again.

The hotel was bustling with activity as guests emerged from their rooms. The noise was hysterical; hotel staff could be heard running around trying to deal with an emergency that wasn't in any training manual. Outside police vehicles were moving, but where could they go other than back to base? They no longer had a suspect to escort, no killer to apprehend, the laws of a higher nature had dealt with the case; judge and jury, a sentence of death with no appeal.

Susan looked in on Raven who was slumped next to the toilet, spitting and gasping for air. "I need to go and talk to the others. I'll be back as soon as I can okay?" Raven nodded. "Do not leave this room." She nodded again.

Out on the atrium landing there were suspicious glances, the noise dropped to a whisper, people hid away, slipped back into their room, staff turned to their emergency rotas and printed instructions. Inside Wallet's room the band sat silently. They had the aroma of tragedy in their nostrils and the sounds of disbelief ringing in their ears.

Susan squatted in front of Wallet. "Do you know what you've done?"

"I started having suspicions this morning."

"What does that mean? I haven't been able to look, but I think we're all aware of what just happened. Why did you turn him? Why didn't you tell us?" Her voice was rising to an alarming pitch. "You just killed an innocent man?"

"Me? What do you mean I just killed him?" Wallet could see the same accusation on the faces of Dee, Elaine and Rene.

"You turned Terence Pearl and you didn't say anything."

Wallet paused to make sure he heard her right. "I turned him?" He looked at Dee and then back at Susan. "I always thought one of you did it."

"One of us?" The confusion passed to Susan.

"It wasn't me," said Dee.

Elaine and Rene assured Susan it was neither of them.

"Susan, you can call me anything you like, call me an idiot, a bullshitter, incompetent, useless, but I didn't turn Terence Pearl."

An explanation wasn't in this room, or this hotel, or Rotterdam, or the Netherlands, or anywhere Susan could think of. Her mind raced back in time to 1973 and every point of interest between then and now, but nothing, no clues, no insight, no tell tale sign or coincidental name, no familiar face, or suspicious happenings. Just a blur, a void, an opaque wall. She met Pearl in Ipswich, scared the life out of him, questioned him, reassured him that they didn't kill Peter Miles. Then he was left with Wallet and Wallet did the rest. Charmed him, plagued him, followed him, tempted him, finally won his trust and then . . . turned him? No, he didn't turn him, didn't touch him, never laid a finger on the man and

Susan believed him. Wells didn't know: about Pearl, about her, about any one of them, otherwise he would have showed up with something more effective than an automatic pistol. How could he not know? How could Patrick Wells be so consumed with a fury and yet be so ignorant of who was tormenting him?

"He was so slow in coming forward and telling me what I wanted to know," said Wallet, "I wasn't sure until the concert he was on our side. I still wasn't a hundred per cent certain until this morning which way he was gonna go. So what do we do now?"

"I need to go back to Raven, she's not feeling so good."

"Did she see what happened?" Rene asked.

"Yeah. Everything. The whole disgusting business."

Wallet plugged his eyes with his fists.

"Well," said Elaine, slouching back into her chair, "that was quite a comeback. And we haven't played a note yet."

Dee turned to Wallet. "You still think all this is liberating?"

Daily Mail

Calls For Toten Herzen To Be Banned

Conservative MP demands the band's second concert planned for the UK be halted

The Conservative MP for Bromsgrove and Kidderminster, Dianne Varly, 51, has urged the government to ban the rock band Toten Herzen from going ahead with their second comeback concert, planned for the East Midlands Arena in six days time.

The concert which has already sold out could see a repeat of the rioting following the band's opening show at the Ahoy Arena in Rotterdam last night. Fighting broke out amongst the seventeen thousand concert goers even before the band had taken to the stage. Riot police eventually restored order after at least ninety fans had been taken to hospital suffering a range of injuries from serious burns to cuts and bruises.

Traffic on the S103, a major road through Rotterdam, was later held up by further fighting which broke out on a coach carrying band members back to their hotel. Band Manager, Tom Scavinio, was later treated in hospital for serious injuries sustained in the scuffle.

Mrs Varly, who managed to hold onto her seat after this year's boundary changes to local constituencies, believes the band don't do enough to discourage their fans from this kind of trouble. "Their reputation has followed them all the way from the 1970s and we're seeing it again. No doubt the fans at the British leg of the tour will want to outdo their Dutch counterparts and we can't allow that to happen."

A spokesman for the East Midlands Arena, which has a capacity of eighteen thousand, told the Mail that extra security precautions had been arranged following the events at the Ahoy, and the concert was still planned to go ahead as scheduled. Doubts about further dates in Germany, Austria and Hungary before finishing in Geneva, Switzerland, later this month, have been raised.

The Times
Twelve Hours of Mayhem
Internet blogger Terence Pearl victim of 'spontaneous human combustion' outside Rotterdam hotel

The signs were not good as soon as fans began to arrive at the Ahoy Arena in Rotterdam for Toten Herzen's comeback concert. Eye witnesses reported a fractious atmosphere as groups from all over Holland and as far afield as Turkey and Iceland gathered around campfires outside the seventeen thousand capacity concert hall.

Inside, one hour before the band were due to go on stage, a fan from Belgium was hit by a flare thrown from a section of the crowd and momentarily set alight. The resulting confrontation left eighty six injured, two of them seriously. Police, some in riot gear, took thirty minutes to restore order, but by then the arena had emptied and the show's organisers had no option but to cancel the concert.

A British fan, Brian Hewson, who had travelled from Brighton described the atmosphere as the most aggressive he had ever encountered at a rock concert. "I think the band's reputation had everyone on pins. They were like coiled springs waiting to go. There was none of the good natured banter I've come across at other concerts." Hewson, who had travelled with his girlfriend and paid a total of seventy pounds for two tickets, was still hoping the concert would be rescheduled. "We still want to see them. We're just old enough to remember them the first time round, but we were too young back then to be allowed to go to any of the gigs."

But not everyone was blaming the band. A spokesman for the Ahoy Arena, Adrian Lokeren, told The Times the band were concerned about potential trouble and were hoping to break away from the problems that had plagued them in the 1970s. "We had a lot of meetings with the band's management, label and tour organisers and time and time again they were concerned about preventing trouble. On the night security confiscated a lot of stuff, but obviously some people still managed to smuggle flares into the hall." Lokeren denied that in spite of the concerns security levels were inadequate. "There has never been trouble on this scale before at Ahoy. You can never count it out, but we're satisfied that we were prepared."

As if the events at the arena weren't bad enough, traffic on one of Rotterdam's busiest roads, the S103, was held up for fifteen minutes when a coach taking the band back to their hotel was forced to stop after fighting broke out amongst band members. Unconfirmed reports said that one or more passengers fell through the open door of the coach onto the carriageway, but this was denied by the band's publicist. The coach did make an unscheduled detour to Rotterdam's Erasmus medical centre to allow the band's manager, Tom Scavinio, to receive treatment for serious lacerations to the face. He left the hospital several hours later without making a statement to the waiting press.

However, the most harrowing episode of an already event filled night was the death of Terence Pearl, the internet blogger and writer who had been following the band for several months, and the murder of Patrick Wells, a forty year old relative of Peter Miles, the musician associated with the band in their early days, who went missing in 1973. Wells was attacked by Pearl in the restaurant of the Rotterdam Crown Hotel where the band were staying. Officers called in from the specialist Royal Military Police arrested Pearl, but he died as he was being led away as a result of what one eyewitness described as spontaneous human combustion.

Callum Morgenstein, a businessman from Tampa, Florida, who was in the hotel at the time of the incident said he still cannot believe what happened. "The police were escorting this guy away then suddenly let go of him. There were no flames, but the heat must have been intense because you could see the police trying to shield themselves from it. I could feel it through the window and I was two storeys up. The guy just blackened and broke up and within a minute there was nothing left of him." Guests of the hotel appear to have posted harrowing smartphone videos onto Youtube, some of which show Pearl appearing to disintegrate in front of shocked police officers.

The Crown Hotel later confirmed that Pearl had been arrested for the murder of Patrick Wells, but refused to give any further details. It is understood the band are no longer staying there and their whereabouts is unknown.

Daily Mirror
Did Your Advent Calendar Go Up In Smoke?

Whilst we predicted, successfully, that Toten Herzen's reunion tour wouldn't pass off without incident even we were taken by surprise by the events at the band's hotel in Rotterdam following the riot-torn no show at the Ahoy Arena the previous evening. So, if you can provide evidence, preferably video, of your Toten Herzen Black Advent Calendar spontaneously combusting, we will offer you a month's free subscription to the Daily Mirror.

Upload your video to Youtube and we'll get back to anyone who we believe has witnessed yet another appalling Toten Herzen hoax.

Guardian Comment - Andrew Rice
Was Terence Pearl Right all along?

Forget the riot. Forget the coach fight and the injuries to Tom
Scavinio. Forget the murder of Patrick Wells, a relative of proto-
band member Peter Miles. Terrible as they are, the real story is
not to be found there. Forget the predictable told-you-so press
reaction and knee jerk responses from publicity starved MPs.
There is absolutely no story there.

Consider, instead, some of the writings of the internet blogger
Terence Pearl, whose immolation outside the Rotterdam Crown
Hotel, was described by one eye witness account as spontaneous
human combustion. Whilst many of his ideas were fanciful Pearl
was probably the last person on earth to take them seriously.
Described by residents of Westerfield, the small village outside
Ipswich where Pearl lived, as a vain attention seeking man, Pearl
was adept at doing what many internet bloggers crave: provoking
thought and reaction.

His wild ideas became part of a culture of conspiracy theory that
has plagued Toten Herzen since their formation in 1973. The
band's image, concocted and exploited by their scrap dealing
manager Micky Redwall, was centred around the band's rumoured
reputation for vampiric behaviour and exacerbated by The Dead
Heart Weeps, a novel written in 1977 by Gothic author Jonathan
Knight. For many this way of life was all part of the big rock and
roll cliche that extreme behaviour sells records and concert
tickets, along with newspapers and magazines.

But in the cold light of day let us spend a moment to reassure ourselves that this 'veneer of decay,' as Clarke Delorean of Rolling Stone magazine attributed to Toten Herzen way back in 1977, has no substance in reality.

Apart from the stupidity, why would four apparently healthy young people sleep in a tomb in Highgate Cemetery? Did their manager Micky Redwall really die after being savaged by his own guard dogs? How would the band's alleged killer Lenny Harper die at the hands of a sword wielding murderer in southern Germany earlier this year? And the ever present question of the disappearance of Peter Miles is an all too real tragedy. The stories so far all have one common link: the victims are potential players in a series of publicity stunts, none of whom are here to own up.

However, none of that explains the fates of Sony and Terence Pearl, neither of whom can remotely be considered willing participants in Toten Herzen's grand plan. Much has been said of the tragedies that occurred in Boston, New York and Washington, but little attention has been given to a medical report commissioned by Sony for insurance purposes prior to the band signing a deal. (A deal which ultimately never materialised.) A copy of the report seen by this newspaper, and I should add the Guardian is not a willing accomplice either, contained evidence of unusual physical properties relating to eyesight, hearing, cardio-vascular abnormalities and cholesterol levels never seen before by the laboratory conducting the medical checks. A later genetic report, commissioned in secret by the band's manager, Tom Scavinio, suggested that the four members of the band had higher than average levels of telemerase, an enzyme that controls the stability of chromosome 'caps,' or telemeres, which are necessary for continuous cell reproduction.

We can entertain ourselves with the notion that the reports would produce these results if the tests were carried out on a vampire, but we live in a rational world and such things don't exist. But in the confused conspiratorial world of Terence Pearl such things do exist and his fate followed the traditional myth of a vampire being exposed to sunlight. The villagers of Westerfield are no more accomplices of Toten Herzen than are the police officers and unsuspecting hotel guests in Rotterdam who witnessed Pearl's bizarre death. Dutch police have confirmed that the event was not a hoax and that a criminal investigation is still ongoing.

If Pearl's death has taught us anything it is that we can never be one hundred percent certain that science has found all the answers. Folklore has often muddied the waters around scientific explanations for natural phenomena, so maybe we should put aside our readings of Bram Stoker, Sheridan le Fanu, Byron and Montague Summers, forget our memories of Hammer Horror's portrayals of Dracula, the teenage adventures of Buffy and Twilight and the myriad interpretations of the vampire legend and ask, one more time, just to be absolutely clear: who are Toten Herzen?

We Are Toten Herzen

WE ARE TOTEN HERZEN

AND FINALLY...

Thank you for reading We Are Toten Herzen. That's not just a platitude, it's a genuine thank you for investing the time and a bit of cash. I probably don't have to tell you it's not easy being an author in the 21st century and having my novel picked from the millions that are out there is gratifying.

Thank you.

Can I ask you for one more tiny favour (or two)? Leaving a quick review on a site of your choice would go a long way towards spreading the word, either for this book or for me. If you can find a few more minutes to leave an honest review I would be doubly grateful.

If you enjoyed my storytelling and can't get enough of it (I'll pause here until you stop laughing) you can explore more of the TotenUniverse here.

TotenUniverse.com

This is my ambition to create a new mythology around the rock band Toten Herzen and the Malandanti network of covens. You'll find articles, features, interviews and short stories to fill the gaps between the novels and expand on the issues and episodes contained in the stories.

The other available novels in the TotenUniverse are described in the following pages. I hope they inspire you to continue your journey.

We Are Toten Herzen

TOTEN HERZEN MALANDANTI

After the disastrous events in the previous novel 'We Are Toten Herzen,' the band are forced to count the costs and the repercussions of their comeback tour. The focus turns to the safety of the recording studio and their first album in forty years. Things can't get any worse.

But this is Toten Herzen, the dead rock band: murdered in 1977, discovered alive in 2013. Guitarist Susan Bekker wants to sing, antagonising lead singer Dee Vincent whose catastrophic interview in Hullaballoo magazine leads to a multi-million dollar lawsuit. Rob Wallet, the band's publicist, flirts with insanity when he isn't flirting with Lena, the seductive former terrorist and leader of a network of covens known as the Malandanti.

The story sets down amongst the isolated mountains of the English Lake District, with excursions to post-communist St. Petersburg and Bamberg in Germany, scene of the 17th Century witch trials. Along the way the band are assaulted by an ever growing list of mysteries. Why has a Russian voice coach arrived uninvited at three in the morning? Why are the Malandanti searching for a book owned by Dee Vincent? What is Susan Bekker's Big Lie? And is the valley pictured in a 14th Century painting the source and home of the first European vampires?

Blue hair, black magic, talking sheep, murderous bushes, necromancy, alchemy and leather-clad litigation. All captured on film by a deafening Dutch director in Toten Herzen Malandanti. Book two in the authorised account of the band's astonishing and some would say unbelievable comeback.

We Are Toten Herzen

WHO AMONG US...

Disowned by her family and deranged by anger, Jennifer Enzo views the world as a demonic garden, a film script and a list of names to be assassinated. But when she finds her own name on the list she is forced out of her insular world to counter a sinister threat to her life.

Professor Virginia Bruck's world is divided between her research in artificial intelligence and posing for her husband, the eccentric German artist Earnst Bruck. Suspected of being the source of a destructive rumour she decides to do what her semi-aristocratic family have never done throughout centuries of rumour, and fight back.

Frieda Schoenhofer, a self-made millionaire, is determined to explain the death of a local witch. Police are equally determined to explain a baffling double murder and Frieda becomes their first suspect after the body of a man is found hung above the north door of Bamberg Cathedral.

All three women share a common association: the Malandanti, a four hundred year old network of covens on the brink of collapse following rumours of a plot to kill the leading members. As the conflict intensifies and the familiar world disappears, they will be forced to reassess their own ambitions, confront the nature of guilt and innocence, and question how their beliefs explain the supernatural forces they each control.

We Are Toten Herzen

THE ONE RULE OF MAGIC

Frieda Schoenhofer is dead, murdered in Rotterdam. For her grief-stricken parents the true story of their daughter's life is about to begin.

Her father, slowly demolishing the world around him, tries to eradicate painful memories by throwing out his lifelong collection of film memorabilia. Her mother is convinced Frieda has been reincarnated as a new born foal.

But Frieda isn't dead. She is travelling Europe hoping to rescue her father's discarded collection. A journey of redemption that takes her to Nice, Prague, Turin and Vienna, where she meets a crooked dealer in antique silverware, joins a funeral party full of mourners who can't stop laughing, falls in love with a beautiful marionette, and discovers a plan to destroy the legacy of Mozart.

The One Rule of Magic explores Frieda's attempts to make amends for the crimes of her old life, come to terms with what she has become, and prepare her parents for the bizarre truth surrounding their daughter's disappearance.

THERE WILL BE BLOOD

Having completed their comeback album Malandanti and butchered their Belarussian rivals backstage at the 2016 Gwando Awards, Toten Herzen prepare to tour the world. Taking time out between concerts Rene secretly explores the Lost Valley and the possibility of creating a permanent home there.

But rival band There Will Be Blood refuses to die and a new line-up is created fuelled by Toten Herzen's notoriety and funded by arms dealers. Ambitious plans to sabotage the tour collide with events chronicled in Who Among Us... and The One Rule of Magic. (TotenUniverse books 3 and 4.)

When Interpol's Bernadette Maldini extends her investigation into Malandanti crime and the murder of Frieda Schoenhofer in Rotterdam she begins to unpeel the layers of the Toten Herzen myth. She discovers Susan Bekker's 'Big Lie,' the tragic truth behind the death of Lorraine Daley's father, and a key book in Dee Vincent's private collection.

The man behind the myth, Rob Wallet, sacked but secure on his Monaco yacht, the Agnetha, exorcises his past in the company of ghost hunters, but his past and several other surprises are about to catch up with him.

The world burns in the wake of Toten Herzen's disastrous tour. Goblin sellers, pig hunters, Armageddon Bells and a man called Alf join a cast of thousands and one crocodile to ensure there will be blood in the fifth book of the TotenUniverse.

We Are Toten Herzen

THE FINE ART OF NECROMANCY

Frieda searches for the knowledge that will ensure her own vampiric immortality and enable her to wreak revenge on Susan Bekker at the same time.

Her father slowly comes to terms with his daughter's condition and an encounter with a demon forces him to insist Frieda detaches herself from her old life within the Malandanti. Her mother continues to struggle with the so-called loss of Frieda and insists she seeks psychiatric help, but Frieda is more concerned with her physical condition. Her mental state can wait.

She begins a second odyssey that takes her to the Cornish coast, a circus in Luxembourg and a reenactment camp in Avignon before returning home to Bamberg. Along the way she discovers the secret of brewing beer, encounters a hopeless human canonball, leads a feminist rebellion and becomes mixed up in a convoluted genealogical feud.

The Fine Art of Necromancy explores Frieda's desire to understand herself, a search complicated by the arrival of a woman claiming to be Frieda in a previous life; a twist of events that will have far reaching consequences.

Included in this novel is a short story The Miller's Daughter, which expands the themes of personality, reincarnation and the source of life.

LORDS OF MISRULE

The plan is chaos and the plan begins in the Vatican where a demon ransacks the Sala Ducale. The demon is Eneliziel, inadvertently conjured up by Virginia Bruck and revelling in the conflicts spreading across Europe.

Desperate times demand desperate measures. Interpol abandons its investigations into the Malandanti leaving Leonard Thwaite to establish a new undercover unit instructed to take the fight to the enemy with gruesome force.

The unit is headed by Pierre Dremba after Bernadette Maldini chooses to return to the Carabinieri. Before taking up her old post, she travels to the hotspots of the 17th Century witch trials hunting for occult inspiration and answers to her own personal conflict.

After raising Lena Siebert-Neved from her woodland grave, Frieda steps up her own plans to spread chaos whilst maintaining her distance from a network on the verge of discovering a way in to hidden dimensions including the Lost Valley.

With the intelligence services crippled, Davos disappears in the fog and a long-overdue settling of old scores takes place in front of a watching world. History comes full circle and the end times approach in Lords of Misrule, the seventh novel of the TotenUniverse.

We Are Toten Herzen

BEHIND THE WALL

The discovery of four corpses in a London basement releases a trail of suspicion and expectation. Are the three women and one man the remains of Toten Herzen? The four members of Toten Herzen disagree.

Rob Wallet, still searching for answers to the disappearance of Peter Miles, is drawn to Sigmaringen and a series of local killings which may or may not be the work of a werewolf. His investigation is distracted by Toten Herzen's unauthorised biographer, Raven's gaggle of hapless friends, and a local couple's insistence they own a car that once belonged to Adolf Hitler.

Elaine rejoins Wallet, but her motives remain unclear when details of her father's murder become entangled with the disappearance of Peter Miles and a feud within a 1970s terrorist organisation.

Susan Bekker finalises the soundtrack of Quarter Moon by teaming up with an accident prone conductor, a tight fisted folk musician and an overpowering cellist. Surrounded by sponsorship deals and lucrative endorsements she begins to calculate her own worth and how to exploit it.

But the wall of a London basement is not the only barrier to unsolved mysteries as Frieda's circus in Luxembourg conceals a deadly secret of its own and Wallet's old house becomes the centre of attention and throws the most telling suspicion yet on his motives for bringing Toten Herzen back from the dead.

-

We Are Toten Herzen

Thanks for your support and I hope you can continue on this bizarre literary journey with me.

C Harrison

Printed in Great Britain
by Amazon